Great ambition requires great sacrifice.
And those who attain their dreams must be . . .
ABOVE REPROACH

LAURA DEVLIN

Washington's most respected and devoted new
congresswoman, she struggles to balance her career,
her marriage, and her family . . . and the yearnings of
her own hungry heart.

DOUGLAS RHODES

The charismatic senator from Arizona, he battles
personal tragedy as he falls passionately in love with a
woman he cannot have . . . but for whom he will
make the ultimate sacrifice.

DAWN VAN DOREN

The beautiful blond reporter has come a long way
from her poverty-stricken youth. Power has become
an aphrodisiac no man can equal—and she will do
anything to get it.

LENORE DEERING-KIRK

Washington's hostess extraordinaire, she has built—
and destroyed—many political careers by the wave of
her own imperious hand.

Also by Janis Flores:

LOVING TIES
RUNNING IN PLACE
DIVIDED LOYALTIES*

*Published by Fawcett Books

ABOVE REPROACH

Janis Flores

FAWCETT GOLD MEDAL • NEW YORK

Library of Congress Catalog Card Number: 89-92445

ISBN 0-449-13420-2

Manufactured in the United States of America

First Edition: May 1990

In memory of my grandmother, another Laura, who wasn't a lawyer, or a candidate for high office, but a Renaissance woman in her own time. . . .

The author wishes to acknowledge the help of two very special members of the Los Angeles district attorney's office, who were so generous with their time, but too shy to allow me to mention them by name. Their information and advice about the legal aspects and the criminal court system in Los Angeles was clear, knowledgeable, and precise. If, despite careful note taking and settings of crimes and scenes, mistakes have occurred, or misinterpretations have crept in, I hasten to assure that any such errors are certainly not theirs, but mine.

Thanks, you guys. And to Brigitte, another dear friend who put up with me during this process, thanks to you, too. . . .

CHAPTER ONE

"Remain seated, come to order, court is now in session," the clerk announced in a rush. It was ten o'clock on a smoggy September morning in Los Angeles, and the Honorable Judge Macklin Pierce, who presided over this particular courtroom, expected punctuality. Everyone's but his.

This morning he was on time. Right on cue, the door to his chambers opened, and Judge Pierce strode in. Enveloped in black judicial robes, he went directly to the proscenium, nodded at the room in general, and sat down. Superior Court in Los Angeles County was now in session.

At the defense table, Laura Devlin gave her client a confident smile designed to disguise her true feelings. Tall, slender, with dark hair and deep green eyes, she had been with the public defender's office two years now, and she knew how these things went. So much depended on the jury: were they convinced or weren't they? Sometimes it was hard to tell, especially on a case that had become a minor cause célèbre.

Her client was a petite black woman by the name of Olivia Brown, who had been accused of—among other things— kidnapping her landlord and using a shotgun to hold him at bay until he promised to clean up her tenement. What had really happened—according to Olivia, at least—was that after repeatedly pleading with the man to do something about the rats infesting the apartment, she had finally refused to pay her rent until her requests were met.

The situation might have been handled by an underling if Olivia hadn't managed to sway everyone else in the building to her side; faced with all those mutinous tenants, the landlord had been forced to come down to deal with Olivia himself. His solution had been to push his way into her apartment and demand the rent money before he kicked her out into the street. Olivia's response had been to lock him inside so he could ex-

1

perience the conditions firsthand. Gleeful neighbors had come running at the sounds of his hysterical screams, and some helpful soul had handed her a shotgun to make sure he stayed inside until he learned his lesson.

The whole thing might have faded away as just another poor black woman versus rich white landlord story if some enterprising young reporter hadn't picked it up on the police band and turned it into a human interest item. When Laura was assigned, she had managed to get the DA's office to drop the kidnapping charges in favor of false imprisonment, but because of the publicity, they wouldn't deal on the gun. Now, if convicted, Olivia could face a 16–2–3 sentence—sixteen months, two to three years—with a year tacked on because of the weapon. Since this was also a first offense, it was possible she'd get probation, but as they waited this morning for the jurors to file in, Laura prayed for acquittal. She'd seen the condition of that apartment, and the evidence of the rat bites on Olivia's three children, and couldn't help feeling that they'd brought the wrong person to trial.

Olivia plucked at Laura's sleeve. "I guess . . . I guess this is it, isn't it?" she said. Her teeth were chattering.

Laura gave her hand a sympathetic squeeze. "It's going to be all right."

"I hope so," Olivia said shakily, and glanced over her shoulder at her three young children, who were sitting anxiously behind her in the care of a neighbor.

Laura followed her glance and hoped so, too. But if she'd learned one thing the past two years, it was never to second-guess a jury. Sometimes it was a good sign when they returned a verdict this quickly; sometimes it wasn't. There was just no way to tell, and she knew from experience that the hardest part was waiting to find out.

"Do you . . . do you think they believed me?" Olivia asked. "About the gun, I mean."

Laura hesitated. Use of the weapon had been a sticky wicket in this trial, but when she remembered how Olivia had handled herself through that particular minefield, she was confident they'd stayed the jury on that score. Olivia had been so innocent, so intense, during questioning by the deputy district attorney, Dale Davidson, that no one could doubt she was sincere, even Dale himself.

"And how did you acquire the gun, Mrs. Brown?" Dale had asked. He was tall, blond, and blue-eyed, with a devastating smile that had fluttered many a feminine heart, until the owners discovered he was married to his career. A bachelor, he was steadily working his way up the ladder, and after sitting across from him at various times during these past two years, Laura didn't doubt that one day, he'd reach the top.

But not during the Brown trial, she thought, with a faint twitch of her lips, and thought about the corner Dale had painted himself into with this innocent-looking, earnest little woman sitting beside her.

"How did you acquire the gun, Mrs. Brown?" he asked.

"I tol' you," Olivia had said. "When the neighbors came runnin' that night, one of them jus' shoved it into my hand. As added insurance, he said. Jus' in case."

Dale had pounced. "In case of what?"

"In case Mr. Goldberg broke the door down," Olivia said, her eyes wide.

Dale had been a little too sure of himself. "Come now, Mrs. Brown. That's only in the movies, isn't it?"

Never ask a question unless you're sure of the answer. Like everyone else, Laura had stifled her laughter when Olivia had looked at the big, blond, handsome deputy, and shook her head earnestly. "Oh, no, sir. Why, jus' the other day, the door fell in when one a the neighbors came knockin'. Jus' fell right off its hinges. They all do. We tried to tell Mr. Goldberg, but he wouldn't—"

"No further questions," Dale had said hastily, and retired red-faced to his own side of the courtroom.

Laura had mentioned the gun in her summary. But she had focused on the conditions in the apartment house itself, on Olivia's ignored pleas about the rats, on the bites her children had suffered. She had pointed out that Olivia worked hard as a maid for Travelodge; that she was a single mother trying to do the best she could with the resources at hand. She directed their attention to the poignant testimony she had elicited from Olivia herself, and through her, the jurors heard a mother agonizing over the safety of her children:

"I din' mean nothin', honest," Olivia had sobbed. "I was goin' t'pay the rent, but I jus' wanted him to do somethin' 'bout those rats. My children have been bit four times this pas' year, and I tol' him and tol' him. What could I do? I can't watch my kids every minute. I have to work. . . ."

"Has the jury reached a verdict?" Judge Pierce asked.

Beside Laura, Olivia tensed, and reached for her hand. With what she hoped was a confident smile, Laura gripped the work-worn fingers tightly and wished she could offer more reassurance. It was too late now; she'd done everything she could. The rest was up to the jury.

"We have, Your Honor."

The foreman, a pencil salesman from Duarte, rose slowly. The clerk took the official verdict from him, crossed to the judge, and then turned to face him again. Dressed in a checked polyester sport coat and a J. C. Penney shirt that was so new, it still had creases, the salesman obviously knew this was going to be the only time in his entire life when he would command the attention of an entire room. He looked proud and excited and a little flushed.

"How do you find?" the judge asked.

"We find—" The foreman hesitated importantly, glanced at the taut Olivia, and then said in a rush, "We find the defendant . . . not guilty!"

Exhaling in relief, Laura turned to her stunned client. The little woman looked transfixed, and she shook her arm gently. "Did you hear that, Olivia? You won. You're free to leave."

Looking as though she still hardly dared to believe it, Olivia blinked. "There's . . . there's nothing more? I can really go?"

Laura laughed. This was always one of the best times. "You can walk right out."

"Thank you," Olivia whispered. "Oh . . . thank you!"

Her three little girls were crowding the rail. "I think someone wants to see you," Laura said, and watched her former client rush over to enfold her children. As the little group happily left the courtroom, she turned back to her briefcase with a smile.

"Sort of brings a tear to the eye, doesn't it?"

Laura had seen Dale standing there out of the corner of her eye. Feeling pretty pleased with herself, she gave him a jaunty look as she reached for one of her files. "Do I detect a note of pique?"

Grinning, he reached over and handed her the folder. "No, just grudging admiration. That was a good job—especially about the shotgun. By the time you finished, even *I* believed your client had never even seen the thing before, much less held one in her innocent little hands."

She waved her own hand airily at him. "Then I proved my point, didn't I?"

4

"You certainly did. At least to the jury."

"That's what counts, isn't it?"

"You're right about that," he said easily, and then set his own heavy briefcase on the table. "Have you ever thought about joining the opposition?"

The question truly surprised her. "You've got to be kidding."

"Why?"

"Why?" She knew he was teasing, so her mind wasn't really on the question, but on the fact that she was due in court down the hall in a few minutes on another case, and she only had that much time to bone up on the reasons for the extension she wanted. Slapping the file together, she stuffed that into her briefcase and looked at him as she snapped the catches. "In case you haven't noticed, Dale, we're not on the same side of the table—legally *or* ideologically. You prosecute; I defend."

He gave a mock wince. "I'm aware of that. You just trounced me, remember? But still," he persisted, as they started out, "haven't you ever thought you might do more good if you prosecuted these creeps instead of trying to clean up after them? Everyone knows about your—" he coughed delicately "—somewhat adamant stand on victims' rights."

She glanced up at him. She wouldn't deny it; she had been vocal about that in the past, and would continue to be. "Dale, is there a point to all this?" she asked. "Or are you just making conversation?"

When he looked down at her, there was no doubt he was serious. "Think about it, will you?" he asked, and then gave her a salute before he walked away.

She stood there, her glance following him until he disappeared through a doorway. Someone bumped into her, muttered an "Excuse me," and brought her back to the present with a start. Shaking her head, she turned and walked quickly the other way. But her mind was still on that curious conversation after she'd gotten her extension and was on the way back to her office, and she couldn't seem to rid herself of the doubts Dale had raised. *Would* she do more good in the DA's office than she was doing with the public defender? Annoyed, she answered her own question. The idea was ridiculous. She was perfectly happy doing what she was doing right now, she thought, and arrived at her little cubbyhole of an office a scant thirty seconds before her boss appeared.

She was just sitting down behind her cluttered desk when the head public defender, Tony Amorelli himself, arrived in her doorway. He was carrying a file that he held out to her with a grin. "No rest for the wicked."

She reached out a reluctant hand. "What's this?"

"It's right up your alley."

Glancing down at the thirty-five case files sitting right here in front of her, all demanding her attention, she said, "Tony—"

He held up his hands. "Don't blame me. They just keep coming. By the way, how did Brown go?"

"Not guilty."

He grinned. "See what I mean? They've got your client in jail. I said you'd be right down."

'Wait!'' she said, but he was already gone.

So much for her triumphant return to the office, she thought, and resignedly gathered her things again. Trying not to think how many other clients she had already, she went to meet the newest one, a black eighteen-year-old youth named Gregory Hicks, who had been arrested in conjunction with a convenience store robbery. When she got there, he looked ready to jump out of his skin.

"Hi, Gregory," she said cautiously, keeping her distance. A uniform was right outside, but you never knew. She came to the battered table and set her briefcase on it, being careful to keep the table between them. "My name is Laura Devlin, and I've been appointed to defend you."

He promptly burst into tears. It took her twenty minutes of talking to calm him down enough so that he could tell his side of the story.

"Let me get this straight," she said at last, when he had blubbered to a stop and was wiping his face with the backs of his hands. "You say you were just going into the Seven-Eleven for a pack of cigarettes when you heard the shot. Right?"

Gregory nodded.

"How did you know it was a gunshot?"

He looked at her as though she had two heads. "You live in East Los Angeles, lady, and you know a gunshot when you hear one," he said.

Ask a stupid question, she thought . . . and said, "Okay. So the next thing you know, someone comes running out—"

"It wasn't someone," he interrupted, anxious now that he'd started to tell her all the details. "It was the Squeezer."

"The Squeezer," she repeated, and looked down at her notes. "I thought you said his name was Herman Spinklemeyer."

"Yeah, that's his name. But we call him the Squeezer."

Laura decided it might be better not to ask why. "All right. So this . . . this Squeezer comes running out—"

"Yeah, he was holdin' his arm, and I could see he was bleedin' real bad. I guess the guy inside musta shot him or somethin'. Anyway, before I could move or do anythin', he grabbed me."

"And forced you toward a car that was parked at the curb."

He nodded vigorously. "Right. He was shoutin' and cussin' by then, and all I wanted to do was get the hell outta there, you know? But he had a knife, and he told me he'd cut me real bad if I didn't get in."

"What did you do?"

He gave her that look again. "Whattaya think?"

Laura nodded and made a note. "Okay. So you got in the car. What happened next?"

He glanced away. "Well, I . . . I drove, I guess," he muttered.

She had the police report, and she flipped through it again. "It says here that you drove the car through the store's front window."

He looked at her defiantly. "If that's what it says I done, then that's what I guess I done."

"Could you tell me why?"

He shot to his feet, startling her. An officer immediately appeared at the door, but after a quick glance at her client, who was gripping his elbows with both hands and huddling by the wall, she signaled that everything was all right. She waited, and after a moment, Gregory took a deep breath and turned to look at her over his shoulder.

"I don't know why I drove through the window, all right?" he said. "I just did, that's all. I just did."

"Okay," Laura said calmly. She suspected that he'd been too scared to think what he was doing, and she couldn't blame him. If someone had held a knife to her, she would have been terrified out of her wits. "Come back and sit down."

"I'll pay for the window, honest I will, miss," he said earnestly. "I just don' wanna do no time. I didn't rob that store, I swear it. I din' even know Squeezer was in there till he came runnin' out. I don' know nothin' 'bout no robbery, you gotta believe me!"

Laura was about to reassure him that she did when she saw a glint in his eye. She paused, wondering if it had been a trick of the light. For a minute there, he'd looked almost . . . sly, and she wondered if she'd been taken in by the crying act. He seemed so scared and sincere—but then, a lot of them did when they were faced with hard time. Suddenly it wasn't a game anymore.

He leaned forward again. "You do believe me, don't you?" he asked.

Laura hesitated. Did she? She frowned, remembering that conversation earlier with Dale, annoyed with him all over again for putting these doubts into her head. Her job wasn't to believe her client, only to defend him. If he was guilty, the district attorney's office had to prove it. That's how the system worked, and until today, she'd been happy with that.

She was *still* happy with it, she told herself, and said, "I do, if you're telling me the truth."

"I am, I am!"

She'd seen this act before, too, she thought, and was ashamed of her cynical reaction. "Good," she said quickly, and then couldn't prevent herself from warning, "Because if you aren't telling me the truth, I won't be able to do you much good when your case comes to trial. Are you sure you're telling me everything?"

He made a dramatic gesture of crossing his heart. "May God strike me dead if I'm not."

Don't tempt Him, she thought, and was surprised at herself again. What was the matter with her today? Ordinarily she felt only sympathy for people like Gregory, who seemed to have been caught up in circumstances that weren't their fault, but today she seemed to be suspicious of everything anyone said.

"That's fine," she said, "but right now, the DA's the one to worry about. Even though witnesses can't place you inside the store with Mr. Spinklemeyer, two people are ready to swear that you were loitering outside during the robbery—"

"I wasn't loiterin'!" Gregory protested. "I tol' you! I was goin' inside to buy some cigarettes!"

She closed the folder. "Then you don't have anything to worry about, do you?"

He looked doubtful. "I don' know. This DA dude, he sounds like a hard ass to me."

If you only knew, she thought, picturing Dale's boss, Jim Duluth, with his uncompromising eyes and stern mouth. His scath-

8

ing opinions about how the new liberalism had ruined the judicial system were well known—certainly to the public defender's office, which had often been the target of his most acrid attacks. Especially in an election year, she thought, and stood.

"We'll just have to convince him it was all a mistake, then, won't we?" she said, and paused. "Is there anything I can get you?"

"No, I'm okay," he said, and then looked up. "Wait. There is somethin'."

"What?"

"Could you get me some cigarettes?" he asked. "This thing went down before I got a chance to buy some myself."

By the time Laura got back to her office again, it was after five. She'd been so busy getting Gregory his cigarettes, filing a motion to suppress on one case, talking to another deputy she'd been lucky enough to meet in the hall about something else, that she'd lost track of time. Maurey Webber shared her office space, and he was packing up to go home when she got there. She took one look at her watch and groaned.

"God, where did the day go?"

Maurey stopped what he was doing long enough to give her a grin. His blue eyes behind thick glasses glinted, and his receding hairline made him look older than his thirty-six years. "No rest for the wicked, I guess," he said with a shrug.

"You're the second person who's said that to me today. If you're not careful, I'll charge you with originality and send you home."

Maurey laughed. "Congratulations on Brown this morning."

"Thanks," she said, and abruptly remembered that damned conversation with Dale again. "Maurey—"

"Yeah?" He was busy adding more papers to his already overstuffed briefcase.

"I had the strangest conversation with Dale Davidson today."

"Dale? You mean the DA's advertisement for California's good life—tall, blond, tan, muscular—a briefcase under one arm, a surfboard under the other? That Dale?"

"Come on, Maurey. Stop kidding around—"

"Who's kidding?" paunchy Maurey asked, and shoved his glasses back up onto his nose. "I'm sorry. Go on."

"He asked me if I'd ever thought of joining the DA's office."

Maurey snorted. "All that and a sense of humor, too. Who would have believed it?"

"I know. But—"

When she faltered, he looked curious. "What did you say?"

"What do you think I said?"

"I don't know. What *did* you say?"

She frowned. "That I didn't think he was serious."

"Was he?"

She shrugged. "I don't know. You know Dale."

"Maybe it was his inept way of making a pass."

She shook her head. "No, he's made a pass at me before. I know the difference. No, this was—"

"When?"

"When what?"

"When did he make a pass at you?"

Rolling her eyes, she said, "Right after I started here. It didn't mean anything. He does the same thing to anyone new in skirts. You know that."

Looking despondent, Maurey plunked down on the edge of his desk. "Yeah, he scores, too, I've heard. Lucky bastard."

Laura couldn't help laughing at his expression. "He doesn't score as often as he says he does."

Maurey gave her a hopeful glance. "Really?"

"Take my word for it."

"So what did you say, about the DA's office, I mean? Maybe it's not as farfetched as you think."

"I can't believe you said that."

"Now, wait a minute," he said thoughtfully. "You're a damned good attorney, Laura; we all know it. So do you. Maybe you are wasted in this office."

"Are you?"

He shrugged. "Well, we all know about your stand on victims' rights—"

"That has nothing to do with this!"

"Maybe it does," he said stubbornly. "After all, you asked. Doesn't that mean that you've at least thought about quitting?"

"Of course I have!" she exclaimed. "But that doesn't mean I've had my eye on the DA's office. For pete's sake, Maurey—haven't you thought about quitting? Hasn't everyone around here? What about those times when the caseload is so heavy, you can't see straight, or when you're handed conviction after conviction when you've done your best? Don't you get discouraged? Don't you think about quitting then?"

Maurey held up his hand. "Hey, calm down. You're not doing

10

a summation, remember? This is old Maurey here. And I just asked.''

"Yeah, well . . .'' Throwing herself down into the chair, she took a deep breath, wondering why she'd overreacted like that. Maybe she had been thinking about quitting, without even realizing it. Lately, deluged with endless cases, burdened with the certain knowledge that most times no matter what she did, her client was going to do time, she had wondered if she'd made the right decision in joining the public defender's office right out of law school. She'd been so sure at the time, but after two years, things didn't seem so clear anymore. Especially when she remembered the terrible fight she and Jack had had about her decision. He'd wanted her to join a cushy law firm, but oh no, she'd opted for the PD. She was going to do great things, make a difference, tilt at all those windmills.

"Of course I've thought about quitting,'' Maurey said. "I guess we all have. We'd be pretty crazy not to.''

She didn't want to discuss this anymore. Sorry she'd mentioned Dale and the DA's office in the first place, she said, "You see? Case closed.''

He started to say something, thought better of it, and turned back to his desk. Watching him, she was sorry she'd jumped on his case like that; he was a friend who deserved better. "Hey, Maurey,'' she said. He turned to look at her, and she lifted her shoulders. "I'm sorry, okay? It's been a long day.''

Looking relieved, he smiled then, too. "Don't worry about it. I understand.''

When he left, she steeled herself and picked up the phone. She should have gone an hour ago; she had to call home and tell her family she was going to be late . . . again. Trying not to feel guilty, she listened to the third ring . . . the fourth . . . the fifth. She was about to hang up when her mother answered.

"Hi, Mom,'' she said, tensing despite herself. Her mother, Estelle, who had lived with them for the past two years, hated for her to be late. She also disapproved of the time Laura devoted to her work, muttering endlessly that her days would be better spent as a mother and wife. It was an old impasse, one they'd never cross, and Laura had long ago given up trying. Trying to play it light tonight, she said, "I was just about to give up.''

"Laura, where are you?''

"I'm still at work, Mom,'' she said, and wondered how that

11

particular tone could still make her feel like a child. "That's why I'm calling. I wanted you to know I'd be late."

"Again?"

She stifled a sigh. "I'm sorry, Mom. It's been a hectic day."

There was a heavy silence. Then, "I suppose you've forgotten."

"Forgotten? She tensed, her mind instantly flying over a mental calendar. What had she forgotten? It wasn't anyone's birthday; their anniversary wasn't for four months. Then she thought of it, and nearly groaned. She had promised Jack she would go to the city planning commission meeting tonight. They lived in Manhattan Beach, and as a civil engineer with his own business, Jack had a stake in the current controversy surrounding the new shopping mall. He wanted the contract desperately, but environmentalists had stalled the work, and now a public meeting had been called to decide the issue. Jack had asked for her support, and while she privately felt that the last thing the community needed was another shopping center, she had agreed to go with him. She spent so much time at the office, especially lately because of the heavy caseload, that she felt she owed him that.

With a sinking feeling, she glanced at the clock. Even if she left now, she'd never make it, and she said, "I'm sorry, Mom. I just forgot."

"That seems to be a habit with you lately, Laura. I wonder at times if you have any regard at all for Jack and the children."

This was an old song, too, but Laura still felt so guilty that she didn't argue. Hoping she could apologize to Jack before he left, she said, "You know I do, Mom. Now, is Jack there? I'd like to talk to him for a—"

"He's already gone to the meeting. He told me you'd be late, so we ate early and he left."

Suppressing a sigh, she sat back in her chair. She was too tired to fight with her mother about this, so she said, "That's too bad. Are the kids there?"

"Peter's upstairs doing his homework, and Andrea is taking a bath. Do you want me to interrupt them?"

Interrupt them? Laura rubbed a hand over her burning eyes. "No, that's all right," she said. "I'll be home soon, and I'll talk to them then."

"Oh, don't hurry on our account. There's no rush *now*."

Her mother hung up before she could reply, and she carefully replaced the receiver, staring at it for a minute, too tired to get out of the chair. At times like this she wondered if having her mother move in with them hadn't been a mistake. It had been two years now, and things hadn't improved.

She shook her head, remembering how horrified she'd been by the idea when Jack first suggested it. She was sure it would never work, even if she couldn't argue his logic. Still, as much as she hated to admit it, the move had solved a lot of problems. Laura's father had just died, and her mother Estelle was alone in her big house. She was just starting her new job with the PD, and Jack had quit his old office to start his own. They needed someone at home to watch the kids, and she couldn't deny that Peter and Andrea adored their grandmother. It seemed the perfect solution.

For everyone but her, that was. In his enthusiasm, Jack had conveniently ignored the fact that she and her mother had never gotten along. Estelle had always favored Laura's older sister, Janette, who had been just as horrified as Laura had been when she heard about the new arrangement.

"Are you out of your mind?" Janette had shrieked. "That's never going to work, not in a million years. You two are going to be at each other's throats before Mom is even unpacked!"

"I can't help it," Laura had said. "It's the best thing for everyone."

"But you," Janette had said, and wished her luck. She might be her mother's favorite, but there were times when she didn't get along with Estelle, either.

Laura sighed. In the end, of course, she'd given in to Jack—not because it was convenient, but because she felt so guilty about taking the PD job instead of going into private practice as she'd expected. He'd made no secret of his delight when the South Pasadena firm where she'd clerked offered her a position after law school; she knew he had visions of a partnership in two years. For him, it would all have been worth it then—the sacrifices, the night classes she'd attended, the responsibilities he'd had to share when she finally decided that the children were old enough for her to go back to school. She'd quit right out of college to marry, then Peter had come along the first year, and Andrea two years after that. She'd felt obligated to stay at home while they were small, but once they had started school, she was restless. It was time for her to go back to school, too.

It had taken her six years to get her degree, and up until the

13

day she took the bar, she had intended on following the career path she knew Jack approved. But when it came time to accept Edmund Ferris's offer to join Ferris, Wentworth, Carlyle and Smote, she knew she couldn't condemn herself to a life of corporate and tax law, with an occasional *pro bono* case thrown in to assuage her conscience. Her first love had always been criminal law, and she wanted to be a trial lawyer. Where better, she'd reasoned, to get all that trial experience than in public service?

Although she still wasn't sure why, since she had discussed it with him, Jack had been stunned by her decision. Her father, however, had been furious. They were still estranged when he died, and his death was still painful to her. He'd never listened; he had refused even to try to understand. He had believed until the day he died that the only reason women were put on earth was to become wives and mothers. They didn't have careers, and they certainly didn't become trial lawyers. To him, it was as simple as that.

But nothing was ever that simple, Laura thought, coming out of her reverie. Her desk was still a cluttered mess, and she quickly grabbed her briefcase and started stuffing things in. She'd loved her father, but he'd been wrong.

And you? a little voice asked. *Were you wrong, too?*

Wishing Dale had never mentioned the DA's office to her this morning, she finished with the things she needed and switched out the light. She didn't want to think about Dale right now; she had a long drive home, and she was dead on her feet.

On the way out to the car, she remembered Gregory Hicks again. She'd been playing around with the idea of pleading duress, but she couldn't get that gleam she'd seen in his eye out of her mind. Making a mental note to request an investigator to nose around, she threw her stuff in the car, got in herself, and headed toward the freeway.

An hour later she was finally home, wrestling with Andrea's bike, which had been left in the driveway, before she could pull the car in, noting the fact that Peter hadn't weeded the lawn. She heard the TV in the family room when she came in and set her briefcase on the kitchen counter before she went through to the den.

"Hi, guys," she said.

Eleven-year-old Peter and his nine-year-old sister, Andrea, turned at the sound of her voice. They were both lying on the floor in front of the set, and Peter, who had recently decided that hugs and kisses were for babies, said, "Hi, Mom," and turned around again. Looking very much like her mother, with dark hair and clear green eyes, Andrea jumped up and ran to give Laura a hug.

"You're late, Mommy."

She returned the hug. "I know, honey. I had a lot to do today."

"We had to eat dinner without you."

"So I heard," Laura said, and cast a quick glance in the direction of her mother's bedroom, off the den. The door was shut, which meant that Estelle was watching her own set. Giving thanks for small favors, she turned back to her daughter. "How was school today?"

Andrea giggled. "Great! Jimmy Anderson got caught chewing gum in class and the teacher made him stand in the corner with it on his nose! Isn't that funny?"

"A real scream," Laura said, and ruffled Andrea's long hair, exactly the color of hers. "What are you watching?"

"Something Peter wanted to see. We put your dinner in the oven so it wouldn't get cold."

She smiled. "Thanks, honey. I'll get it in a minute. Have you done your homework?"

"We only had arithmetic," Andrea said, and made a face. Math wasn't one of her favorite subjects.

"Okay, then," she said. "I think you'd better get ready for bed, don't you?"

The green eyes instantly clouded. "But Grandma said I could stay up until nine!"

Laura controlled herself. This, too, was an old argument. "That's a little late on a school night, don't you think?"

"Please, Mommy! There's a neat nature program on at eight-thirty. It's National Geographic," she added slyly, putting her arms around Laura's waist and giving her that innocent "but this is an educational program" look.

Laura had to smile. "All right," she said, and added, "But just this once."

"Thanks, Mommy!" Andrea cried, and ran back to her place.

Laura looked in her son's direction. He seemed totally involved in the set. "Peter? Did you get your homework done?"

He nodded and didn't look around.

This was a new attitude of his, and Laura didn't like it. Because she was tired, she spoke more sharply than she intended.

15

"Peter, I'd appreciate it if you would look at me when I'm speaking to you!"

Slowly Peter turned around. "Jeez, Mom, what's the matter with you tonight?"

"Nothing's the matter with me," Laura said. "I just prefer not to stare at the back of your head when I'm asking you a question. Now, did you get your homework done or not?"

He shifted uncomfortably. "Well . . . not all of it."

"What do you mean—not all of it?"

"Well, I have some science left, but jeez, Mom, this program came on, and I thought I'd do it later."

Laura was shocked. "You know the rules, Peter. No television until your homework is done!"

"Grandma said I could!"

He looked defiantly at her, the spitting image of Jack, with the same intense blue eyes and shock of thick blond hair. Already gangly, with long arms and legs, he showed every indication that he'd reach his father's height of six-two before he left adolescence; he'd grown three inches this past year as it was. But even more startling than his appearance had been the disturbing change in his temperament. Always much more amenable and easygoing than his sister, who had inherited her quick temper, he'd developed a stubborn, defiant streak this year that she didn't like. She'd always gotten along well with her son, but lately he seemed to argue with everything she said. Tonight was no exception, and she knew she should sit down and talk to him about his attitude, but she just couldn't face another argument right now, not when she still had all that work to do that she'd brought home. Promising herself she would talk to him this weekend, she said wearily, "All right, Peter. But the instant this program is over—"

Peter threw himself back down on the floor. "Okay, *okay!* I'll get it done, all right? What's the big deal, anyway? It's only a science project!"

Only a science project? She thought of his C in science so far this year, and tightened her lips. But he was already absorbed in his program—or pretending to be—and she decided to leave it alone. Sighing heavily, she went back to the kitchen. There was a plate in the oven for her, but she ate unenthusiastically and only because she supposed she should. She wasn't hungry, and the thought of all the work she had to do tonight defeated her before she even started. Deciding that maybe what she

16

needed was a long, hot bath, she took her briefcase and went upstairs.

Jack came home just as she was getting ready for bed. She'd postponed her bath after all in the hope that if she got some work done, they could have a little time together tonight, but when she realized she'd fallen asleep over some briefs, she'd given up and gone to take a shower. Wearing her robe, she was smoothing cream on her hands and thinking how tired she was when he came into the bedroom.

He stopped in pretended surprise. "Well. I see you finally made it home."

She wouldn't be drawn. She was in the wrong, and she knew it. "Yes," she said. "I'm sorry I forgot the meeting tonight, Jack. It was stupid of me."

He grunted, only half acknowledging the apology, and because she couldn't gauge his mood yet, she didn't say more. Dressed in slacks and sport shirt, with a chino jacket thrown over, he looked younger than his thirty-six years, lean and trim. He'd always been interested in sports, and had played basketball in college. It showed. He still had an athlete's body, but now it was because he ran five miles nearly every morning on the beach. Laura had seen the girls staring admiringly after him and couldn't blame them. Despite the fact that they hadn't been getting along very well these past few months, her heart always gave a little leap when she saw him. It was hard to believe they'd been married twelve years. Sometimes she felt like a teenager herself. But not tonight.

He threw the jacket down and glanced at the bed. "I see you've been working."

Guiltily she followed his glance. Since her mother had come to live with them, she'd given up the room she'd used as an office so it could be turned into a bedroom. Now this room—or the kitchen table—were the only two places in the house where she could work, and she'd spread out her files and other papers on the bed. Quickly she started to gather it up again. "Are you going to forgive me for missing the meeting?" she asked after a moment.

"It wasn't important."

She looked at him over her shoulder. "It was. But I said I was sorry." She hesitated. "How did it go?"

He sat down in the chair and started taking off his shoes. "How do those things ever go? It was stupid and pointless and

17

ultimately futile. It was obvious after the first two minutes that the planning commission had already made up its mind. Feeble as it is.''

She paused with some folders in her hands. ''So you didn't get the contract.''

''What do you think?'' he said acidly, and threw the other shoe down. ''Besides, what do you care? We both know which side of this issue you were on.''

Unable to argue that point, she silently finished clearing the bed. ''I'm sorry, Jack,'' she said finally.

''Yeah, well, so am I,'' he said, and stood to strip off his shirt, adding nastily, ''If things keep up this way, maybe you'll get your wish and I'll have to go back to McNaughten and Tate.''

She was shocked. ''How can you say that? I supported you when you wanted to start your business! You can't possibly think I want you to fail!''

''I don't know what you think anymore, Laura,'' he said, and reached out to turn on the television.

''Jack!''

''Forget it,'' he growled. ''I want to hear the news.''

''Isn't this more important than the stupid news?'' she cried.

He whirled around, his expression ugly. ''I said, forget it, all right?''

She started to say something, then thought better of it. With him in this kind of mood, they'd only fight. But she would talk to him about this tomorrow, she decided, and then suddenly felt depressed. There seemed to be a lot of things she intended to do tomorrow; when was she going to start handling her life *today*?

''I'm going to take a shower,'' he said.

She looked at him in dismay. ''But I thought you wanted to watch the news!''

''You watch it,'' he said, and headed toward the bathroom.

''Jack!''

She started after him, but as he'd begun doing lately, he shut the door. When she heard the click of the lock, she sank down on the edge of the bed.

What's happening to us? she wondered, and without thinking, glanced dully at the flickering television screen. It seemed too much effort to get up and turn it off, and because she couldn't seem to decide what else to do, she sat there and watched. The

18

commercial had ended and the oh-so-cheerful newscaster had come on again.

". . . and in the national news today, Senator Douglas Rhodes, the junior senator from Arizona, is making headlines of his own," the man said. "For the past several weeks, the Senate Budget Committee has been conducting hearings on defense spending, and now a disagreement has arisen between the head of that committee, Senator Albert Rawlings of Louisiana, and Senator Rhodes, another member, who claims alleged misconduct on the part of at least two major defense contractors. Senator Rhodes is calling for an investigation, and . . ."

A film of the senator leaving the Capitol filled the screen just then, and without realizing it, Laura sat forward. She couldn't stop herself from staring. Dressed in a dark suit, he was casually carrying an expensive-looking briefcase and looked so self-assured that she felt something stir inside her. She couldn't look away from the TV.

The clip went to close-up, and someone out of camera range asked the senator a question. He turned, and his face in profile was even more compelling: deep-set eyes; prominent nose; thick, dark hair just starting to be touched with silver. There was something magnetic about this man, something special. Without warning, she felt that jolt again.

"This is crazy," she said, and quickly reached over to turn off the set. But she sat there for a moment after she did, unable to rid herself of the feeling that something momentous had just happened to her.

"Ridiculous," she muttered, and reached for one of the files she'd left by the bedside. But it was a long time before she opened the folder, and when she finally did, she had to force herself to concentrate. The image of Senator Rhodes had faded from the television screen, but to her dismay, it remained fixed in her mind.

"Ridiculous," she muttered to herself again, and didn't hear Jack come out of the bathroom.

---⚘---

CHAPTER TWO

Douglas Rhodes was surrounded by a crowd of reporters the instant he got out of the car at Dulles Airport. Since he'd just given a lengthy interview on the Hill, he was irritated that they'd followed him, but then he reminded himself that this kind of thing came with the territory. He'd been in the Senate four years now, and if he planned to stay longer—not to mention stir up more controversy, as he had with these Budget hearings—he'd better cultivate the press. He had a feeling he was going to need them on his side. So he summoned a smile instead of a frown, and prepared for the onslaught as he led the way into the airport.

The crowd followed on his heels, pencils and recorders at the ready. One young reporter, whom Douglas recognized vaguely as a new stringer for the *Star*, pushed his way to the front of the group. Douglas had long legs, and some of the less fit had trouble keeping up with him. This one didn't.

"Greg Hastings, Senator," he said with barely a pant as they strode rapidly along. "Mind if I ask you a few questions?"

Douglas glanced sideways with a smile. "Not as long as I don't miss my flight."

Greg was new, and serious. "No problem, Senator," he said, and read quickly over his notes. "Now, you said in a Hill interview tonight, and I quote: 'The most productive breeding ground for lobbyists isn't Congress but the Pentagon.' Does that mean you're against lobbyists, or—" he looked up "—that you have something against the Pentagon?"

Douglas sighed inwardly. He should have known that statement would get turned around, and he couldn't help thinking of a fellow senator, now a good friend, Sarah Ambrose. Sarah had warned him long ago to watch what he said; in a town where the walls had ears, and telephones had bugs, and personal radar was the order of the day, reporters had developed a special antenna that started to twitch at the first sign of an incautious remark. Obviously things had twitched, and now he understood the reason for the welcoming committee at the airport.

"I have no quarrel with either one," he said. They had reached his gate, and he stopped and turned to the group so they could all hear. "The First Amendment guarantees citizens the right to petition their government, which is what lobbying is supposed to be. There's nothing wrong with that."

A new reporter came forward, Charlie Rasmussen of the *Post*. "Then is the Pentagon connection the basis for your disagreement with Senator Rawlings, the head of the Budget Committee?"

"I'm not sure what you mean by this 'Pentagon connection,' Charlie," Douglas said, with the easy smile that had made him such a favorite on the Hill. It was effective in masking his annoyance, since he really didn't want to talk about this. However, it seemed he had no choice. "My disagreement, as you put it, with my esteemed colleague Senator Rawlings stems not from lobbying or the Pentagon per se, but from the system."

"What system is that?"

This innocent question was from Darryl Ryan, a veteran reporter for the *Times*, and Douglas gave him a look. Darryl knew better, he thought, and hid a smile when the reporter saw his expression and shrugged with a "what can I say?" gesture.

Douglas decided to play the game. Turning pointedly away, he looked at the rest of the reporters and assumed a proper solemn senatorial stance. "I don't have to tell you," he said, "that the single largest item in the federal budget is defense, and has been for years—"

Greg jumped in again. "Do you believe that lobbying is responsible for that?"

Douglas had to hand it to him; he was quick. "Not solely," he said. "But it is a fact of life that all the major defense manufacturers are aware that the easiest way to get government contracts is to hire as a personal contact—or lobbyist, if you will—a retired, high-ranking military man."

"So what's wrong with that?"

"Nothing," Douglas shot back. "As long as the lobbyist is registered. Unfortunately, as you may or may not know, many are not. It seems that somewhere along the line, the executive order prohibiting a retired officer from 'selling' or negotiating contracts with his former service has been . . . ignored."

"Can you prove that?" This from Charlie, who was staring thoughtfully at him.

Douglas hesitated. Then he decided to let them have it. The report would be made public anyway, and the hearings weren't a secret. "Yes," he said, to renewed murmurs. "The committee has just received documentation that clearly states that at least ninety percent of the retired officers hired for top-level positions by the defense contractors ignore that regulation."

The veterans had pushed Greg aside. Douglas had their attention now, and he faced a suddenly serious Darryl again, who had no need to glance at his notes. "Senator, you said that it's a fact of life that the major defense manufacturers use retired military as lobbyists—"

Douglas saw immediately where this was heading. He started to say something in response, but just then the intercom erupted, and to his relief, his flight was called. People were starting to line up at the gate, and he wished he could join them. But he knew Darryl wouldn't let this go, and he didn't.

"Well, then," Darryl said, with that pouncing expression so many of Douglas's colleagues had learned to dread, "isn't it also a fact that associations exist in Washington solely for the purpose of promoting the causes of the armed forces? What do you think about that?"

Douglas had seen this coming, but he had already decided not to debate the issue of possible collusion between the service organizations and the defense manufacturers. It was a serious, highly sensitive subject that merited time and study—and proof. He'd locked horns on this very issue with Senator Rawlings— privately, of course—and had promised himself he wouldn't go public until he had more information.

"I don't think anything about it—yet," he said. "As I've previously indicated, I need to study the subject more thoroughly."

"Isn't that a cop-out, Senator?" Greg Hastings asked.

Douglas looked at him a long moment before he answered. "No, I don't think so," he said slowly. "As I said, I want to be sure of my facts before I accuse anyone of anything."

The implied rebuke caused the young reporter to flush. Douglas's reputation for straight shooting was well established in Hill circles, and his honesty and integrity had never been questioned. Still red-faced, Hastings muttered something and stepped back.

"Anything else?" Douglas asked, graciously dismissing both him and the incident with a brief smile. He was anxious now to get on the plane. His wife, Marcella, was giving him a birthday party tonight, and as much as he hated such things, he'd promised to be there.

"I have a question, Senator. . . ."

Douglas looked up in surprise at the feminine voice. He hadn't noticed a woman in the crowd before now, but as she stepped forward and introduced herself, he wondered how he could have missed her. Tall and slender, she was wearing a fawn-colored suit with a silky blouse and a wide alligator belt that showed off a tiny waist. Long, shapely legs looked even longer because of her high heels, and her thick, straight honey-colored hair fell from a center part to her jaw on either side of her oval face, framing a pair of eyes of the strangest shade of amber he'd ever seen. Those eyes held his now, and for some reason, he couldn't look away. Who was she? He didn't remember ever seeing her before.

"Dawn Van Doren," she said, in a honeyed voice that somehow matched her hair. "From the *Washington Eye*."

Douglas found his voice. He knew about that gossip rag, and he wondered fleetingly why she was working there. With her looks, she should have been a model. "Yes, Miss Van Doren?" he said politely.

She looked him straight in the eye, no notes for her. "You said a few minutes ago that an executive order had been ignored—"

"Yes."

"If you were president, what would you do about something like that?"

The question caught him by surprise. But not the fact that everyone in the group had suddenly come to attention. With the instinct that had served him so well in the Senate—and before he'd been elected, in his successful Arizona development company—he knew he'd better be careful how he answered. An incautious remark now would be picked up, pulled apart, analyzed, intellectualized, and finally be made an augury for the future, so he smiled and said, "Well, I'm not the president, Miss Van Doren. I'm just a junior senator, trying to get home to my wife. She's giving a party tonight, and I promised to be there."

As if on cue, his final boarding call sounded just then, and he

23

spread his hands in a helpless gesture. "I'm sure I don't have to tell any of you what will happen if I miss that flight," he said, and waved good-bye on the rising laughter.

A few long strides took him safely to the plane, and then he was ducking his head so he could enter. Two flight attendants with professional smiles that warmed considerably when they saw him were waiting by the door, and one of them held out her arm to take his coat.

"Good evening, Senator Rhodes," she said. "It's a pleasure to have you aboard."

The other one glanced at his tickets. "Your seat is the second on the left, Senator. We'll be serving drinks, and then dinner, about an hour into flight time."

Thinking he could use a drink now, he found his seat and sank gratefully into it. It had been a long day, and these two interviews back to back had been an added strain. As he glanced out the window, he thought that this was one of the times he wished he'd kept his own plane. He'd had a Lear jet for a while, but it had been such a nuisance that he'd finally sold it. Despite the convenience, it had seemed so ostentatious when he got to Washington. He was supposed to be a representative of the people, and as some public-minded—and no doubt envious—reporter had caustically reminded him during one of his first press conferences, the majority of the population did not go around flying their own jets. He'd been so embarrassed by the jab that he'd gotten rid of the plane and started to fly commercial like everyone else. At least these cross-country flights gave him time to get some work done, and with a sigh, he pulled down the table tray in front of him and opened the briefcase he was never without.

The file on top was stamped with an official-looking ARMED SERVICES stamp across the front, and as he took it out, he thought of Sarah Ambrose again. Sarah had been such a godsend; sometimes he didn't know what he would have done without her. Despite his own experience of running a highly successful real estate development company, he'd felt like a fish out of water when he'd first arrived in Washington, but for some reason—he didn't question it; he was too grateful—Sarah had taken him under her wing. As senior senator from Wyoming, she'd spent thirty years on the Hill and she knew her way around. She continued to deny it, but he was sure she had pulled a few strings to get him assigned to a plum committee like Budget, but to make up for it, he had asked for several less popular committees, Judiciary being one. Judiciary had lost popularity in 1974 because of the impeachment inquiry, but many of his colleagues shunned it still because the so-called social issues they dealt with, like abortion, and school prayer, and gun control, and the death penalty, were so volatile. He'd been warned by several friends not to get involved because taking a "wrong" stand on any of these issues could mean defeat in the next election. That, of course, had only made him more determined to sit on the committee. He wasn't going to shirk responsibility because he wanted to get elected again.

Elected again. With the plane starting to taxi out to the runway, he sat back and thought about that. The decision to stand for reelection seemed increasingly complicated these days, but he knew he had to make the choice soon. Even though his present term still had two years to run, he'd already been approached by an agency that wanted to represent him for the next election.

Impatiently he shook his head. It was ridiculous, this packaging of political candidates, and he resented it. He hated the thought of having to resort to any kind of advertising to get elected, and these people could call themselves what they liked: to him they weren't "political imagers"—whatever the hell *that* meant—they were advertising agencies. It was as simple as that.

"Cocktail, Senator?"

He looked up to see the smiling flight attendant, and on impulse asked for a whiskey sour. He rarely drank, but this ruminating about running for election again bothered him, and he decided it was too soon to think about it. Dismissing the problem, he attacked the files he'd brought, worked through dinner, and three hours later landed at Sky Harbor. To his delighted surprise, his son, Rob, was waiting for him when he got off the plane.

"What are you doing here?" he asked, barely restraining the impulse to give his son a hug. He had to content himself with a grin and a thump on the arm instead.

Rob grinned, too. "I just thought I'd come to meet you."

Trying to recover his composure, Douglas gave him a fond look. Rob was his and Marcella's only child, and they were both very proud of him. He wasn't ashamed to admit that his son was the light of his life, and that things would pretty much be meaningless without him. But the boy had become almost a man, and he had to hide his emotion. So he cuffed Rob on the shoulder again and said, "That's nice, but since I have a car here, I suspect an ulterior motive. You sure you didn't want to talk to me about something—in private, without your mother around?"

Rob grinned again. "You know me too well, Dad."

They were the same height, and Rob had inherited his dark hair and bone structure. But he had his mother's deep blue eyes, and the combination was striking—as Douglas had long ago learned, constantly amused by the legion of girls who continually called the house. Rob seemed to take it all in stride, much more interested in his horse when he was younger, in his car when he got to driving age. Bright, handsome, athletic, he seemed destined to go places; if his college grades were any indication, he would. Because he'd skipped a grade at the lower level in school, he was a junior at Arizona State now, majoring in business. Anticipating an M.B.A., Douglas had wanted him to go to Harvard, but Rob had insisted on staying closer to home.

"So what's the big secret?" Douglas asked as they went out to the parking lot. "You want me to increase your allowance, or what?"

Rob looked indignant. "You haven't given me an allowance since I was ten years old."

Douglas laughed, glad to be home, even happier to be walking out in the warm Arizona night air with his son. Impulsively he put an arm around Rob's shoulders. "What then?"

When Rob hesitated, Douglas had the first intimation that something wasn't right. Frowning, he glanced at his son. "Rob? What's wrong?"

"Nothing's really *wrong*," Rob said, shrugging out from under his arm. He turned to face his father, his face slightly pale under the glaring parking lot lights. Taking a deep breath, he said, "It's just that I'm not sure I want to be a business major anymore."

Douglas couldn't have been more surprised if Rob had said he wanted to quit college to be a rodeo clown. His son had focused on business from the time he was in high school; they had plans. Rob would join Rhodes and Son, the family company, when he graduated. The idea was that one day he'd take over the company. Was all that going by the wayside now? Trying to remain calm, he said, "But you only have one more year. Why are you having second thoughts now?"

Rob hesitated again. But he'd never lacked courage, so he

finally said, "I'm sorry, Dad. I guess I just wasn't interested in business administration in the first place."

Douglas couldn't believe they were having this conversation. "I don't understand," he said. "I thought that's what you wanted to do. You were the one who chose your major—"

"Only to please you, Dad."

"To please me!"

"Come on, Dad—there's the car. Let's—"

"To hell with the car! I want to get this straight right now!"

Rob took the overnighter he'd brought with him, practically wrestling it out of his stiff fingers. "Dad, please. Let's discuss this on the way home."

He was about to object again, but then he realized Rob was right. He couldn't very well start shouting right here in the lot; this was a family matter. His face a mask of anger, he headed toward the Corvette that was Rob's pride and joy, and jerked open the door. He didn't speak again until they were on the freeway.

"All right," he said, his voice tight. "Let's hear it."

Rob glanced nervously across the seat. "Are you going to start shouting?"

"Only if I have to," Douglas replied grimly.

Sighing, Rob turned back to the road. He drove the car as he did everything else, effortlessly and well, reaching out casually to downshift so he could go around a slower car, shifting back into third with barely a jerk.

"I just don't like it, that's all," he said after a moment. "I thought I would, I tried to, but I just—" he shrugged "—don't think I can do that the rest of my life."

Trying not to think what was going to happen to all those wonderful plans they'd made, Douglas was tight-lipped. "Fine. Do you mind telling me what you'd like to do instead?"

Rob winced at that tone. "I don't know," he said. "I'd like to take a year off and think about it."

Take a year off? Douglas barely restrained himself. What was the matter with the boy? This didn't make sense at all, and he could feel his blood pressure rising. Then he was struck by a sudden thought. This wasn't like Rob, and he gave him a sharp look.

"Does this have anything to do with a girl?"

To his relief, Rob laughed. "No, Dad, it doesn't have anything to do with that. It's me. Just me. I don't know—lately, things just seem . . ."

He stopped, and Douglas prodded, "What?"

"I don't know. Confused. Unclear. I don't know what I want to do."

Douglas was feeling confused and unclear himself. How could this have happened? *When* had it happened—and why hadn't he seen it coming? He and Rob had always been able to talk; if Rob was so unhappy, why hadn't he said anything until now? He didn't understand, and because he didn't know what else to say, he said, "Have you told your mother about this?"

Rob looked at him. "Are you kidding? If you went through the ceiling, imagine what she'd do."

Douglas didn't have to think about it. Even more than he, Marcella doted on Rob; she was so proud of his accomplishments—everything from his pitching at Little League to his winning the state speech competition in high school—that she had scrapbooks filled with mementos. She'd dreamed for years of her husband and son in business together; she had even insisted on Douglas changing the company name to Rhodes and Son when Rob turned sixteen. She'd had visions of Rob heading the company when it came time, married to a devoted and beautiful woman who would give them wonderful and smart grandchildren, who would then take over the company in their turn. They would all be one loving family, just like a Hallmark card. She'd had it all planned, and now it seemed that those plans were about to be dashed. Groaning inwardly, he wondered what the hell he was going to tell her.

"If you take a year off," he said carefully, "what will you do?"

Rob shrugged. "I don't know. I haven't really thought about it. Travel, I guess. See a few things."

Travel, I guess. See a few things. Douglas felt his blood pressure go through the roof, and his hands itched to reach over and shake some sense into Rob since he seemed to have lost all else. If Rob didn't have any coherent plans, why was he throwing everything away on a whim? This was unbelievable, unacceptable, outrageous. He stopped himself, breathing hard.

"I see," he said, his voice harsh.

Rob looked anxiously over at him. "Look, Dad, I know you're having trouble dealing with this, but it's not as if I've decided to drop out entirely, you know."

"Oh, really?" He couldn't help the sarcasm. "Forgive me, but it certainly seems that way to me."

"It's only a year," Rob said pleadingly.

Only a year. Douglas shook his head. When had a year become a minute to him—and all those minutes flying by, too swift to catch? When had he stopped feeling as though his entire life was spread like a feast in front of him, instead of looking back into a funnel of time? *Only a year.* Rob didn't understand.

Rob mistook his silence for acceptance. "Dad, will you help me talk to Mom?"

Douglas had briefly forgotten about Marcella. What was she going to say about all this? "I don't know what to tell her," he said dully. "Besides, don't you think you should do this yourself?"

"I will, but I still need your help," Rob said, and paused. "I helped to convince her when you wanted to run for Congress, didn't I?"

"That was different," Douglas muttered. Marcella had been shocked when he'd first started talking about running for office; she hadn't understood his sudden desire to become involved in politics. He hadn't really understood it, either, except that he'd built up the company to the point where it didn't need his constant presence all the time—and he was bored. He couldn't explain it to her; he could hardly explain it to himself. All he knew was that it was time for a change, time to make a difference. Marcella had finally accepted his reasons, but she had refused to uproot her life. She still lived in Scottsdale while he commuted when he could from the town house he'd bought in Georgetown. It wasn't the best solution, but since Marcella showed no sign of budging from their original agreement, it seemed the only one he could get.

"Why was it different?" Rob asked quietly. "I supported you; why can't you support me?"

Douglas had no answer; he was wondering what he was going to say to his wife. Glancing out the window, he saw with dismay that they were almost home, driving through a part of Scottsdale that bore little resemblance to the desert it had once been. The streets here were wide and immaculate; the landscaping could almost have been imported from Los Angeles. Even though it was night, he could see that the sloping lawns were a verdant green from sprinkler systems that were computerized to go on and off at scheduled times. Vast stucco homes perched coolly back from the street, protected from view by lattices and screens and standing walls that were softened by palms and various shrubberies. The air was practically scented with the aura of wealth. Rob turned from Bell onto their street, and Douglas knew he had to make a decision.

"You're a better politician than I gave you credit for, Rob," he said. "But remember, you can only call in a marker once."

Rob gave him a quick, grateful glance. "Then you'll talk to Mom?"

Douglas sighed. "I'll try."

"Thanks, Dad," Rob said, and reached across to punch Douglas in relief on the shoulder. "I guess this makes us even, right?"

They were in the driveway by this time, and Douglas got out of the car without answering. When he realized Rob had left the Corvette's engine running, he bent down. "Aren't you coming in?"

Rob shook his head. "This is your party," he said, and smiled as he put the car in reverse. "Thanks, Dad. I left your present on the bed. I'll see you later."

Douglas didn't have time to protest; whatever he might have said would have been drowned out by the heavy throbbing of the car as Rob backed down the driveway. He stood there for a moment, watching his son drive away, wishing he didn't have to go in. After what Rob had laid on him tonight, the last thing he wanted to do was face a party, but he knew Marcella was waiting, and so, with a heavy heart, he turned and trudged inside.

Three hours later, the party in full swing inside, he slipped out the sliding glass doors to the patio. The noise from within abated slightly as he closed the door behind him, and he stood there for a moment, hoping no one would come looking. When it seemed he had made a successful escape, he took a deep breath and looked up at the glittering night sky. The air was warm and clear tonight, and he was glad to be alone to enjoy it. Still, he knew it wouldn't be for long, and he moved quickly to the edge of the big patio.

Out here, the only sounds were the faint noises from the pool filters and the chirping of the crickets in the bushes covering the gazebo to his left. The landscape contractor he and Marcella had hired when they bought the house a decade ago had planted mock orange and bougainvillea in that area, and over the years the plants had grown so high, the gazebo had nearly disappeared. It looked like an inviting cave in the darkness, and when he remembered he still hadn't told Marcella about Rob, he was tempted to shut himself inside. He felt guilty about that, until he rationalized that he hadn't had a chance. Despite his protests that he didn't want a party to celebrate his forty-second birthday, Marcella had been planning this affair for months now, and he couldn't ruin it for her. Everyone who was anyone was here, and he probably shouldn't have left. He sighed. He'd go back inside in a few minutes, but first he wanted to see the horses.

Turning away from the house, he went down the terraced steps toward the pool. It was lighted tonight for the party from floodlights under the rim, and as he skirted the waterfall at one end, and then stepped across the little bridge that led to the whirlpool, he heard another burst of laughter from inside and shook his head. Sometimes it seemed that his life was filled with people. First the company, now his Washington office. He hadn't realized the huge staff that would be required on the Hill; so far, he'd managed to keep the payroll down to about thirty, but even that was a circus, for now, instead of dealing with secretaries and executives as he had at Rhodes and Son, he had administrative aides, legislative assistants, caseworkers, and press people to organize his life. They were the ones who kept track of the legislation he had to vote on, the meetings he had to attend, the social obligations at which he had to appear. And sometimes, when he could squeeze them in, they even penciled in time on his schedule for him to meet with constituents—the people who had elected him in the first place.

Shaking his head at the irony, he went through a gate almost hidden by oleander bushes. He was on the path to the barn then, and as he started down it, he let himself realize how tired he was and remembered the management study he'd come across the other day. It had stated, among other things, that a senator or one of his chief aides was required to respond personally to an event every five minutes throughout a ten- or twelve-hour working day. After the week he'd had, he was sure that was a vast understatement. He hadn't told Marcella, because she was so excited about the party, but he'd had a hard time getting away tonight; with those Budget hearings still going on, he shouldn't have left Washington at all. But he couldn't disappoint her; there had been too many times during the past four years when he'd begged off as it was. Tonight couldn't be one of them.

Wishing now that he had made up an excuse because of this thing with Rob, he came to the barn and was immediately greeted by soft whickers along the aisleway. Because Scottsdale weather was so good, he had built only a half barn, and in the moonlight, he could see heads poking curiously out over the stall doors. One in particular caught his eye and he went there first, chuckling when the stallion inside nuzzled him and took his jacket sleeve in his mouth. The horse was looking for a carrot, and he'd forgotten to bring one.

"I might have known I'd find you here," someone said.

He recognized his sister's voice, and turned with a smile. "I was just heading back," he said, and added hopefully, "Unless you want to go for a ride."

Deidre laughed and came out of the shadows. She was wearing a long, sequined gown with a slit halfway up the thigh and a lot of bare shoulder on one side. Blue-eyed, with titian hair that was no stranger to Clairol, she was better-looking at forty than she had been at twenty, and strict attention to diet and exercise had made her body the envy of the women at her tennis club. With her straight nose and the uncompromising Rhodes chin, she couldn't be called beautiful, but as Douglas gazed at her in the moonlight, the word "handsome" came to mind.

"I don't think I'm really dressed for it, do you, Doug?" she said. She was one of the few people who called him that; as a general rule, he detested the nickname, but she'd been calling him Doug—or Dougie, he thought with a wince—since they were children. It was hopeless to break her of the habit now, and he didn't try. But sometimes he retaliated by calling her Dee.

"That never bothered you before," he said.

"We didn't have an image to uphold before," she said lightly. "Now, come on, what are you doing out here? Skipping out on the party already?"

He stroked the horse's long forelock. "No, I just needed some time to myself, I guess."

"Would you like me to leave?"

Giving the stallion a last pat, he put his hands in his pockets. "Don't be silly. It's time for me to get back anyway. Did Marcella ask you to look for me?"

"No, but in about two minutes she might have. I was going to talk to you about something, but I turned around and you were gone. Since I've never known you to object to social occasions, it must be the birthday that's giving you the problem."

"No, it's not that. I really don't mind turning forty-two."

"Lucky you," she said, sounding envious. "I dreaded forty, and every year seems to get worse. Why is it that when men age, they're considered distinguished, but women somehow just turn into old hags?"

"I'd hardly call you an old hag."

"Spoken like a true politician," she said. "Now, do you want to go back to the house, or should I tell Marcella I couldn't find you?"

"No, I'm coming," he said, and looked longingly at the horse. Maybe he could go for a quick ride this weekend before he caught a return flight.

"Okay, you might as well tell me," Diedre said as they started back. "You know I'll bug you until you do."

"Tell you what?"

"Come on, Doug. This is me. Normally you're the life of the party, but tonight you're hiding out in the barn. What gives? You used to confide in your little sister, remember?"

He did remember. Unlike many brothers and sisters, he and Deidre had always been close, even as children. They'd had to be: with a frail mother who spent most of her time in bed, and an absent father who spent every waking minute at the office, they were often left to their own devices. He had loved his father, but sometimes he didn't think Ian Rhodes even noticed he had a family; he'd been too busy building his empire.

People at the time had scoffed, but Ian had been a visionary who had foreseen a population boom even before the Southern Pacific Railroad had connected Phoenix with the East in 1926. He'd been twenty-five at the time, and had already started buying as much property as he could, borrowing himself heavily into debt, but managing somehow to stall his creditors until the first influx. When the boom he had predicted had arrived, he owned thousands of feet of office and commercial space that was rented or leased, never sold, to all the business and industrial companies that flocked to the new mecca. By the time Douglas was born, Ian was a millionaire several times over, and when Douglas had joined the company seventeen years ago, Rhodes and Son had been the largest real estate developer in the state. It still was.

Deidre interrupted his meanderings through the past. "Well,

are you going to confide in me or not? You can tell me it's none of my business, you know."

He smiled, amused at the thought of trying to convince his strong-willed, quick-tempered sister that. "There's nothing to confide," he said. "I'm just tired, I guess. It's been a long session this time."

"The Budget hearings?"

"Those and everything else."

She took his arm. "Well, if you can't stand the heat—"

"—get a microwave, I know," he finished, and they both laughed.

Diedre sobered. "But it's not only that, is it, Doug?"

He hesitated, then shook his head. Sighing, he admitted, "No, I'm afraid not. Rob told me tonight he wants to quit school and take a year off."

"I don't believe it!" Deidre had stopped in sheer surprise. She and her husband, Brad, didn't have children of their own, and she had always doted on Rob. "But he's a junior," she said. "How can he quit now? What's he going to do?"

Douglas thought of that incredible conversation, and said, "He doesn't know. He wants to—and I quote—'travel a little. See some things.' End quote."

"What does that mean?"

"You tell me."

"Does Marcella know about this?"

He shook his head. "I haven't told her yet. Rob asked me to talk to her." He glanced at his sister. "Any ideas?"

She quickly shook her head. "Not me, big brother. I don't have any kids, remember?"

"Would you like one?"

"I wouldn't mind," she said lightly. "But I don't think Marcella would give him up. And speaking of Marcella, I think we should get back before she sends a posse out for both of us, don't you?"

"Wait a minute—what did you want to talk to me about?"

She laughed. "It wasn't important—not in view of this news about Rob. I just wondered if you had decided if you were going to run for office again. The last time we talked, you weren't so sure, remember?"

"I still haven't decided," he said with a sigh, and looked forlorn. "It seems I'm losing control in every part of my life, doesn't it?"

She laughed again and took his arm. "Oh, you'll handle it," she said confidently. "You always do. Now, come on, you have to go inside and do your thing with the birthday cake."

He looked at her in horror. "She didn't get me a cake!"

"She did. Complete with forty-two candles, I might add—all of which you'll be expected to extinguish with one mighty senatorial blow."

He groaned, and tried to pull back, but she giggled like a girl and relentlessly tugged him inside. Marcella saw them the instant they came in, and practically flew across the room, a bright-colored bird in Galanos trappings. Deidre relinquished his arm with a smile and a wink, and Marcella pulled him aside. "Where have you been, Douglas? It's time to cut the cake!"

He was caught. "I'm sorry, Marcie," he said. "I needed some air."

She looked up at him with instant concern. "Aren't you feeling well?"

"I'm fine," he said, and gave her a reassuring smile before he turned her toward the kitchen. "Go get the cake. I'll warn everybody."

She looked back at him in puzzlement. "Warn everybody? What do you mean?"

Suddenly he didn't want the party to end. He knew that when it did, he was going to have to tell her about Rob. So he laughed and said, "About the fire. There is going to be one, isn't there, when you light all those candles?"

Her expression cleared, and she laughed the musical laugh he loved, and which he heard so seldom. "Oh, Douglas!" she said, but he could see that she was pleased as she headed toward the kitchen. He turned to gather everyone around.

"Okay, all," he called over the noise. "Get your fire extinguishers ready; the cake's about to appear."

There was a chorus of catcalls and jests, and then Deidre turned the lights down as Marcella came from the kitchen, proudly carrying the blazing cake. Someone started the birthday song, and as he gazed at his flushed and happy wife, Douglas remembered the present Rob had given him, and felt a pang. He'd found the present on the bed when he came in—a first edition of the Jefferson-Adams letters. Thomas Jefferson had always been one of his heroes, and the book had been a wonderful gift. Wondering how it was that Rob could be so thoughtful at times, and then do something like this, he shook his head.

Marcella carefully placed the cake on the table, and he leaned over to blow out the candles.

"Don't forget to make a wish, darling," Marcella whispered.

A dozen things to wish for came to him, but as he bent to the cake again, he wasn't thinking of Rob or his wife or any of his family. Inexplicably the question that woman reporter—what was her name? Dawn . . . Dawn Van Doren—had asked was suddenly uppermost in his mind.

"If you were president, Senator Rhodes," she had asked, "what would you do?"

Shaking his head to dispel the sudden, tantalizing thoughts of such awesome power at his command, Douglas took a deep breath and blew out the candles to a round of applause.

CHAPTER THREE

Some two thousand miles away from Douglas Rhodes's birthday party, Lenore Deering-Kirk had gathered together four friends to watch television in the den of her Connecticut estate, Deer Hollow Farm. The fact that Deer Hollow wasn't a farm, and hadn't been for nearly sixty years, since her great-grandfather had raised Thoroughbred horses in the early twentieth century, was beside the point. The place had been in the family for three generations, it had been christened Deer Hollow, and that's what it would stay. Lenore liked it that way; it gave her a sense of continuity, of history. And that's what she thought was about to be made this night, in the den at Deer Hollow Farm.

She was a small woman, barely five feet, but she seemed taller because she carried herself so well. As a young girl, she had been forced to sit with a broom handle taped to her back, and good posture had carried into adulthood. Standing or sitting, no one had ever seen her slumped, and her little body was as lean and hard now as it had been fifty years earlier. Her hair had once been a glossy chestnut, but it was white now, waving back from a high forehead. There were wrinkles, too, around her eyes, but the eyes themselves were still as bright, and the mind that never stopped was as sharp. She walked four miles a day, rain or shine, and an invitation to one of her parties was as coveted as the Nobel Prize.

"Turn that thing off," she said impatiently, waving a beringed hand in the direction of the television set. She and her guests had been watching a tape of the interview with Douglas Rhodes; as someone leaped to obey, she sat back and gazed expectantly at the others. "Well, what do you think?"

Jonathan Gage Bartholomew glanced around. As the newly appointed chairman of the Federal Reserve Board, he felt the initiative should be his, so he cleared his throat and said, "Well, the man certainly has charisma."

Lenore made a rude sound she could well afford. Bartholomew might arguably be the second most powerful man in Washington, but as the daughter of one of the most famous Speakers of the House, Hudson Stafford Deering, she had been raised on politics, and felt she had no little cachet herself. At nearly seventy, she had entertained those on the Hill for almost five decades, first as Debutante of the Year in 1928, then briefly as a young matron, the wife of the up-and-coming new senator, Ashford Kirk. Ash had been tragically killed on a rhino hunt in Africa only a year after they were married, and Lenore had never married again. Once was enough, she said, and Ash, as wonderful as he'd been, couldn't compare to her daddy. When Leila-Elaine Deering, Lenore's mother, had succumbed to tuberculosis in the forties, Lenore had become her father's hostess, an arrangement that suited them both admirably. She had carried on alone when Hudson had died, and she had long been regarded, not necessarily with fondness, as Washington's hostess *extraordinaire*—a title not lightly dismissed by anyone in the know.

It was said, most often by Lenore herself, that more political careers had been built—or destroyed—between the walls of Deer Hollow Farm than in the halls of Congress. Whether or not that was true was beside the point: everyone trod carefully where Lenore was concerned. Whatever else might be said about her, her sharp and sometimes malicious tongue was no myth. She enjoyed manipulating people, and always knew, disconcertingly, where all the bodies were buried, and whose grave was likely to be dug next. She'd been around so long, she was practically an institution herself, and despite what people might think about her personally, her opinion was respected. Her judgments about people and events were astute and shrewd, and she was rarely wrong about anything, from foreign policy to the federal debt. All four of the men in the den tonight owed their careers in some measure to Lenore, and of the four, three were painfully aware of it.

"The man has charisma," Lenore repeated. "Is that all you have to say?"

As Gage reddened, someone else spoke up. Hugh Redmond, the undistinguished senior senator from Illinois, who was wondering why he'd been included in the group tonight, stretched his neck and ventured almost timidly, "He reminds me of another John F. Kennedy, Lenore—"

Lenore gave another snort. "God, I hope not. We only needed one."

Hugh flushed, too, but he persisted, "Don't you think that's—"

"No, I don't," she said shortly. "We're talking about Douglas Rhodes here, not another JFK!"

It was time for someone else to step in. General Harding Aspinall—old Hard Ass, as he was known affectionately by his fellow members of the Joint Chiefs of Staff—shifted his considerable bulk in the delicate Queen Anne chair he'd been forced to take, and said, "I don't know, Lenore. He's been giving us all a pack of trouble with these damn—begging your pardon, ma'am—Budget hearings. From what I've seen, he might be a little hard to—"

He paused at the look she gave him. General Aspinall had served in three wars and advised in one; he had a chestful of medals, a wall of awards and commendations, and he had clawed his way to chairman of the Joint Chiefs. Thinking he'd rather face a horde of red devils than that look on his hostess's face, he finished awkwardly, "—control."

"We're not worried about *control*, Harding," she retorted. The famous blue-gray eyes, like chips of glacier ice, flashed. "We're here to gauge his . . . marketability. Could he take the nomination? And would the country vote for him?"

The one man who hadn't said anything so far, the Speaker of the House, Caleb Young, turned back to the room. Tall and lean and white-haired, he was a contemporary of Lenore's who had been standing by one of the long windows, staring somberly out into the night. Now his eyes met hers. Long ago, he'd been one of her beaus, and although she had rejected him—a relief to them both—their friendship had endured, mainly because Caleb was fond enough of her to pretend to take her seriously. Most times, he had to admit, it was no pretense. Lenore had always possessed a fine mind, and he respected her opinion—if he didn't act on it as often as she wished. He knew she believed the country was run at times from Deer Hollow Farm, and it amused him to allow her the fantasy. But he also knew how conniving she could be, and so he said calmly, "Don't you think you're rushing this a bit, Lenore? The man has only been in Washington four years."

"More than long enough to be bitten by the bug," she answered in a flash. "Now, don't give me a hard time about this, Cal. I'm just suggesting that we keep an eye on him, that's all."

"That's rarely all with you, Lenore," he said calmly, hiding a smile at her choice of pronouns.

Annoyed with him—with them all—Lenore dismissed the group. As they filed out with the appropriate thanks for an interesting evening, Cal winked and pecked her cheek with a kiss. She made a moue and pushed him out the door—but gently. Then she went back to the den to finish her tea and summon her butler-houseman-general factotum. Chester had been with her for years; they knew each other very well, and his loyalty to her was complete. He had carried out many tasks for her in the past, a number of which it was better not to mention, and when he came into the den, she gestured toward the television.

"I want you to watch that tape with me," she said, and waited impatiently until it came to the place she wanted, the interview at the airport. When the woman in the fawn-colored suit stepped forward to ask a question, she ordered, "Stop it right there."

Chester obeyed, and they both leaned forward. "Do you recognize that reporter?" Lenore asked.

The butler studied the face in freeze-frame. He'd worked for Lenore for twenty years, and he knew all the people who mattered in the Capitol. He never knew what task his mistress might ask of him, and he prided himself on being up-to-date. But this one stumped him, and he reluctantly shook his head.

"No, madam, I'm afraid I don't."

"Hmmm. Neither do I," she said, annoyed that a new face had appeared on the scene and she didn't know who it belonged to. "She said her name was Dawn Van Doren."

The butler turned and met her eyes. The same thought occurred to him as it had to her, and he inclined his head slightly. "I presume you would like me to find out more about her."

"I think that would be helpful, Chester," she said with a smile, and poured herself some more tea.

Dawn Van Buren, nee Gloria Mae Wannamaker ("Hey, hey, there's Gloria Mae . . . Whaddaya say, ya wanna make her?"), originally from Steel Town, Pennsylvania, now resident of Washington, D.C., by a long and circuitous route, got home from the airport at nine. Traffic had been crowded on the thruway, and her ancient car had overheated again. She'd been forced

40

to pull over and wait until it cooled down, and by the time she let herself in, she was tired, exasperated, and ready to scream. The sight of her cluttered studio apartment made things even worse, and as she kicked off her high heels and went to the refrigerator for a beer, she swore a colorful curse. Popping the top, she took a long swallow of the beer, then another. Then, holding the can, she went to the window and stared through the blinds down at the street.

Her apartment was on the third floor, and a streetlight was just below her. In the weak pool of light it shed, she could see the trash cans lining the curb for pickup tomorrow. The split bags, the leaning cans, the garbage spilling out, reminded her of home, and her mouth tightened. She hated to think of home; she'd trained herself not to remember. Most of the time she could banish the memories, but for some reason they came crowding in tonight, maybe because she was so tired. She took another long swallow of beer. God, she'd hated that town! Soot and piss and dirt, that's all it was: cold as shit in winter, hotter than hell in summer, and nothing in between.

Her lip curled. Except the long lines of men trudging off to the mills every morning, each carrying a steel lunch pail packed by a tired-looking wife with circles under her eyes, sagging breasts, and too many kids hanging on to her. Her own mother had been one of those women, and like so many of her neighbors, Mary Margaret Wannamaker had learned to shush the children when the old man came home drunk again. She could hear her mother now, quieting her brother, smoothing salve on his back because the old man had taken his belt out again.

Hush, Donnie. Your father works hard to provide for us. He's not to blame if his temper gets the best of him at times. You shouldn't make him mad, that's all.

Dawn shut her eyes. She'd been fifteen before she'd had the courage to stay the old man's hand. But there had been one time too many when she'd seen his big fist raised toward her, and something had finally snapped. She'd grabbed his arm with a strength she hadn't even known she had.

"Don't you *dare* touch me again!" she'd hissed.

He stared at her in loutish surprise. As always, he'd stopped at the bar on the way home from work, and he reeked of booze and sweat and the soot embedded in his skin. They all had it; dirt in that town was everywhere, even on those who didn't work down in the mines. It rimed fingernails, clogged pores, stuck to

41

hair, made clothes a dull gray. There had been times when Dawn thought she'd never be clean again. She hated that town, hated everyone in it, especially her father, who was so astounded at her defiance that he had stared at her with raccoon eyes. The safety goggles all the men wore protected their eyes, but not the rest of their skin; he always came home with big white rings. She would have laughed at the surprise on that brutish face if her mother hadn't tried to interfere and had been roughly pushed aside.

"Dick . . ." she'd pleaded. "The girl doesn't know what she's doing."

Big Dick—how she had laughed at that at times—Wannamaker had looked scornfully at his wife out of those ringed eyes. "Doesn't know what she's doin', eh? It's all over town that she's been playin' fast and loose with that Eddie Gentry—"

She couldn't have been more terrified if her father had suddenly turned into the devil right before her eyes. How had he known? When had he found out? She and Eddie had been so careful. Then she knew. It was Eddie himself who had bragged. He'd always been full of himself; she knew that. But what was she going to do? She'd been too frightened to say anything, but she was carrying his child. She'd been fifteen at the time.

Her Catholic mother had looked at her in horror. "Is that true?"

Dawn might have hated her father, and there were times when she was contemptuous of a woman who could be so weak and foolish about a man. But she couldn't despise someone who had been so loving, and when she saw the hurt and betrayal on her mother's face, she lied and said the first thing that came to mind. And how she'd paid for it.

"It wasn't Eddie at all," she said. "It was . . . Bud. Bud Hilliard."

To this day, she didn't know why she'd named Bud instead of Eddie. But the instant she saw the look on her father's face, she wanted to call back the hasty words. She didn't have time. The old man had grabbed her and hauled her right up to the Hilliards' house and threw her in their startled faces. He'd seen a way to get her out of the house, and he'd taken it. He'd already married her older sister off at sixteen to a man three times her age; he'd driven her two older brothers out to make their own way at the mines downstate. Only Dawn and a younger brother were left, and after that day, she was gone, too.

"You had your way with her," he'd roared to the surprised Bud. "Now act like a man and do the right thing!"

Bud had. She never understood why, except that she knew he'd always been gaga over her. Cow-eyed Bud, her girlfriends had teased in school, and that night she'd been glad. The irony of it was that she'd miscarried a month after the wedding. She hadn't even started to show yet. Sometimes you had to wonder.

She took another swig of beer, but the bottle was empty, and she moved away from the window and the sight of all those garbage cans, still thinking of Bud. He was kind and gentle, and he hadn't deserved what she'd given him. Sometimes, when she remembered his innocent blue eyes, and the cowlick in his brown hair, she wanted to cry. She could imagine his reaction when he read the note she'd left him; she'd lasted a year, and then she'd had to fly. Steel Town was no place for her; she wanted something better.

Glancing around the cluttered apartment, with the couch that folded out into the bed that she hadn't made up this morning, at the clothes scattered around, and remnants of last night's Chinese dinner, her mouth twisted. Was this what she had run away for? She'd been so sure that her star was on the rise once she left that town, but it was six years later and as many other towns in between until she'd landed in D.C. Now she had a run-down old apartment where half the time the plumbing didn't work, an ancient car that overheated when she drove over ten miles an hour, and a job at a fleabag gossip rag.

Oh, she'd come a long way, hadn't she? she thought bitterly, and flung the empty beer bottle into the trash.

CHAPTER FOUR

When Laura saw Dale Davidson in the hall as she came out of court, she stopped to wait for him. It was six months after the Olivia Brown trial, and she had just successfully defended another, this one involving a young man named Eduardo Salazar, who had made the mistake of intervening in a street fight between two brothers. When he had ended up being charged with assault with intent to kill, she had been assigned. Eduardo maintained that he had been trying to separate the men when one brother pulled a knife and went after the other; by the time the police arrived, one man was bleeding profusely from a deep stab wound and both brothers claimed that the knife had been Eduardo's. The situation seemed bleak for her client until today, when she had managed to make the witness, the uninjured brother's wife, admit on cross that the knife belonged to her husband. The case against Eduardo had been dismissed, and she should be happy. She wasn't. Dale saw her expression and stopped.

"Bad day?"

"No, my client just won his case."

"Your enthusiasm is a little underwhelming, then. Do you feel better when you lose?"

"No, it's just that I had to play pretty dirty with a witness just now, and I feel—"

"Pretty sleazy yourself?"

"How'd you guess?"

"Even the opposition has feelings, Counselor," he said with a wink. "Despite what you think, we're not total ogres."

"Did I say you were?"

"I'll have to remember that the next time you and I lock horns. Come on, cheer up. Let's go have a cup of coffee."

She wanted to, but she didn't have time. "Thanks anyway,

44

but I can't. I have to interview one of those expert witnesses for an upcoming case."

He rolled his eyes. "Lucky you," he said. "What kind does this one claim to be?"

"A playground expert," Laura said, and sighed. All of them, prosecution and defense alike, were starting to get irritated by the proliferation of so-called expert witnesses. All you had to do these days was pick up the classified pages in any law publication to find anything from "addictionologist" (a physician who offered, for a fee, naturally, testimony on drug and alcohol issues) to zoologist—someone who might be an expert on zoos instead of animals. Counsel was available on bicycle accidents, bottle explosions, balloon mishaps, and thousands of other categories. Someone had told Laura just the other day that there was now a nationwide list of about ten thousand experts for some four thousand categories. All of which proved that no matter who you found to buttress your case, opposing counsel could find someone else to counter it. The result was that witnesses just canceled each other out and everybody was back to square one. Still, they seemed to be a necessary evil these days, and so she had to grit her teeth and interview the one waiting for her down the hall.

"Better you than me," Dale said. "But before you go, what did you decide about Marion Higgins?"

That was another irritant. "Prepare yourself, we're going to trial."

"Can't convince him, huh?"

"Not a chance," she said. They'd already discussed this when she'd first been assigned. Marion Higgins was a thirty-year-old black man who had been arrested for carrying a gun—an automatic felony since he was out on parole at the time. When she had reviewed the circumstances, and his file, she had advised him to plead guilty. He refused. He insisted the search was illegal because the arresting officer didn't have probable cause; in vain, she had pointed out that because he was an ex-con, reasonable suspicion was sufficient. He still wouldn't listen. He wanted to have his day in court, and he claimed he could prove the cop had rousted him without reason. He hadn't told her yet how he planned to prove that.

Dale shook his head. "Did you explain the facts to this guy?"

"I told him, but he still insists that search was illegal. He wants to go to court."

"More fool he, then," Dale said, shrugging.

"Yes, well . . ." She couldn't hide her annoyance, and he grinned.

"Hey, don't worry about it. We all catch it sometimes. Right now, for instance, I'm going to court on a new version of a domestic disturbance."

"Oh? What?"

"Mayhem and assault with a deadly weapon."

"There's nothing new about that."

"When the weapon is a hair curling iron?"

Her eyes widened. "You're kidding."

"As God is my witness."

She couldn't resist. Sure he was joking, she said, "What did the defendant do—curl someone's hair to a crisp?"

"Burned the sucker some forty times."

Her smile vanished. "Lord."

"Yeah, well, we all have different ways of taking out our aggression, I guess. Angelica Simone is just another example, isn't she?"

"Who's Angelica Simone?"

"Don't you read the morning paper over there at the PD's office?"

"We're too busy going over our caseloads. Who's Angelica Simone?"

"Come on. She's the one who was arrested last night for shooting her next-door neighbor."

"Oh, well, unfortunately there's nothing new about that kind of thing, either."

"Not until you hear about the original stand she's taken. She claims self-defense."

"So what's different about that?"

"Only the fact that she took a gun, went next door in the middle of the night, and shot the guy while he was sleeping in bed."

"You sure you got your facts straight?"

"I better have. I caught the case."

"Obviously you don't buy the self-defense."

"No, I think we'll probably go for murder one," he said mockingly. It was obvious. "Beasts that we are, we take it to the hilt. Justice be done, and all that."

"Cute, Dale," she said. "Who's defense?"

"Guess."

"She's been assigned?"

"What else?" he said, and gave her an evil smile. "I hope you catch it, Laura. We've jousted with the small stuff; I think it would be fun to face each other over a big one. You're ready, don't you think?"

Laura was already planning her approach. *I can do it,* she thought excitedly, and started to marshal the arguments she'd present to Tony. She had the experience; she had the knowledge. She'd point to her dismissal record: she'd remind him of all the acquittals. If she had to, she could assemble results on all her cases. She had an impressive file, and she had been waiting for this chance. She'd put in her time; she'd done everything she was asked. The dismissal this morning would buttress her argument, and she'd ignore that business with Gregory Hicks, the junkie who claimed he'd been coerced into driving the getaway car during that convenience store robbery six months or so back. She had finally decided to go to trial on that one, but only two weeks after the preliminary hearing, he'd OD'd in his cell. She didn't know where they got the stuff, inside like that, but he'd managed somehow. She'd blamed herself for days afterward, feeling that she should have seen it coming, thinking that if she hadn't been so busy, she would have realized he had a habit and applied for a withdrawal program. Tony had been nice about it, assuring her it wasn't her fault. But she still felt responsible, until he'd finally called her into his office.

"These things happen," he said briskly. "You're not omniscient, and you weren't his keeper. He didn't ask for rehab, did he? It was his call, and he called it. Don't you have enough to worry about without taking on that?"

She hadn't been able to argue, and in the months that followed, Gregory Hicks had faded from her mind. She didn't know why she remembered him today; she had long ago accepted that it was as Tony had said: these things happen. Besides, he was right. She had more than enough to worry about.

Her home situation was one, she thought, when she and Dale said good-bye. And as she headed toward her playground expert interview, she knew the problem was Jack. Pausing by a water fountain to take a drink, she recalled how hostile he'd been lately, how quick to take exception to everything she said and did. It was like living with an ogre. She felt as though she were walking around on eggshells, and didn't even know why. He wouldn't tell her what was bothering him, and they'd had an

47

argument about it just the other night—again—when she'd tried to find out.

"Jack, what's wrong?" she finally asked. He'd come home from work, turned on the TV, and buried his head in the newspaper while he waited for dinner. Estelle had bridge club that night, so she'd been in the kitchen fixing the meal. It hadn't been a good day for her, either; she had been late again and hadn't even gone upstairs to change when she came home. The sight of him lounging on the couch while she worked in the kitchen irritated her, but she masked her annoyance because she wanted to talk to him. It was more important to find out what the problem was.

"Nothing's wrong," he said, and threw down the paper. "Do I have time for a quick run before dinner?"

She tried to hold on to her temper. She hadn't had time to change clothes, and she wanted to go for a run before they ate.

"Jack, I'd like to talk about this," she said.

"There's nothing to talk about."

"I think there is. I want to know why you've been so—so hostile lately. It seems that everything I do or say is wrong."

"That's ridiculous. You're imagining things," he said, but he wouldn't meet her eyes.

"Then why—?"

"Look, do we have to talk about this now?" he asked impatiently. "I haven't had time to run these past few days, and I'd like to get a couple of miles in, anyway."

She didn't want to leave it like this, but it seemed she had no choice. Tight-lipped, she went back to the kitchen, half hoping he'd follow her. But when she heard him leave a few minutes later by way of the sliding glass doors to the deck, she carefully put down the spoon she was holding and told herself she would not cry.

Dinner had been a tense affair, the children quiet and alert, sensing something in the air; Jack eating quickly without looking at anyone, excusing himself practically before he'd swallowed the last mouthful with the claim that he had work to do upstairs. Silently she'd cleared the table and tried to concentrate on her own work until her mother came home. By then the kids were in bed, and the house quiet. She didn't know what Jack was doing; she hadn't seen or heard from him since he'd gone upstairs.

"Hi, Mom," she said tiredly when she heard Estelle at the back door. "Did you have a good time?"

Estelle grunted. "I won the prize, if that's what you mean. No thanks to that partner of mine. Honestly, I don't know why Maxine insists on playing bridge. She should stick to gin rummy."

Since this was an old complaint, Laura murmured something sympathetic and turned back to her work. It took her a few seconds to realize that her mother was still standing there, and she looked inquiringly over her shoulder.

"Something wrong, Mom?"

"I just don't understand you, that's all."

It was going to be another one of those nights, and Laura sighed. "What do you mean?"

"You know exactly what I mean, young lady. Must you work *all* the time? Your father and I didn't raise you to be like this. Why, your sister, Janette, never wanted to go out and get a job. She's been perfectly happy staying home and taking care of her husband and raising her children. Why can't you be the same way?"

This, too, was an old argument, one Laura knew from bitter experience that she couldn't win. "Janette and I have different needs, Mother," she said carefully.

"The only need you should have is to care for your family!"

Laura started to gather her things from the table. "I really don't think we should discuss this now," she said quietly. "We're both tired, and we might say something we don't mean."

"Well, fine," Estelle sniffed, injured. "But all I can say is that you're certainly not the same sweet girl you used to be. You've changed, since you took this awful job."

It was tempting to point out that Estelle had never considered her a sweet girl, but she knew it would only lead to further argument. Ignoring that sniff, she closed the file she'd been working on, and took her coffee cup to the sink. "I'm sorry you feel that way," she said, reaching for the dish towel.

"I just don't want to see your marriage break up. You have two beautiful children—"

Slowly she turned to look at her mother. "What do you mean? My marriage isn't breaking up."

"Isn't it? Well, perhaps you'd better look a little more closely, dear. In case you hadn't noticed, Jack is unhappy, and has been for some time now."

49

She forgot her annoyance. What was this? She couldn't imagine Jack confiding in his mother-in-law, but in the mood he'd been in lately, anything was possible. "Has Jack talked to you?" she asked. "Has he said what's bothering him?"

"No," Estelle answered. "And I haven't asked. It's none of my business."

"But you said—"

"I *said* Jack was unhappy. Anyone can see that—who cares to look, of course."

"Are you accusing me—"

"I'm not accusing you of anything, Laura," Estelle said. "I'm merely suggesting that you take a good look at things around here—before it's too late."

"Too late!"

Estelle gave her a significant look. "A word to the wise . . . ."

She was too angry to reply. Gathering her things, she went upstairs. Jack was already asleep, crowded against the edge of the bed on his side, his back to her. As she stood there and looked at him, her anger disappeared and she began to feel frightened instead. Was her mother right? Maybe her marriage was falling apart right before her eyes and she couldn't see it. No, no; that was absurd. Things weren't that serious; they were just going through a rough patch right now. The situation would smooth out; everything would be as it had been before. They had a good marriage; they loved their children, their home. Every family went through times like this; she wasn't going to panic just because her mother had been trying to stir up trouble.

But she was troubled despite herself as she got ready for bed, and it didn't help that Jack moved away from her when she tried to get close. Near tears because it had been such an awful day, she lay there for a few minutes, hoping he'd come to her in his sleep, but when he hadn't, she had moved slowly to her own side of the bed. It was a long time before she slept, and when she did, fragments of that conversation with her mother chased themselves through her dreams all night. Feeling as though she hadn't rested at all, she got up early the next morning to fix pancakes, hoping they'd all sit down to breakfast together. But Jack wasn't hungry, and the kids wanted cereal, and in the end, she'd finally thrown the batter down the drain and dragged herself to work.

"Excuse me."

Laura returned to the present with a jolt. A man was standing behind her, and when she gave him a blank look, he gestured toward the drinking fountain. She was blocking the way, and when she realized what he wanted, she moved aside with an embarrassed apology. Belatedly remembering that her playground expert was waiting, she started off in that direction. But she couldn't help wondering as she walked quickly along if it was time to make a few changes. Maybe with all the work she'd been doing lately, she'd lost sight of a few priorities.

The only problem, she thought unhappily, was how to rearrange things. She couldn't shirk her work, not when everyone else handled as many cases as she did; and she couldn't stop bringing work home. She had been so snowed under lately—they all had—that it was impossible to get everything done at the office no matter how hard she tried. It was inevitable that things spilled over, and she couldn't just ignore it. But what could she do? Quit her job?

The thought startled her, and she forced herself to examine it briefly before she shook her head. That was a drastic measure she'd just as soon save for a last resort. There had to be another way to handle this, and she suddenly thought of private practice.

She frowned. Where had that idea come from? She hadn't consciously considered that as an alternative since she'd graduated from law school. She didn't know why it had occurred to her just now.

Maybe she was experiencing some kind of burnout; many of her colleagues did. It was so hard to keep going, to feel optimistic, to believe that you were making a difference when things just kept getting worse. Courts were so crowded that plea bargaining was the order of the day, and even she had long ago stopped feeling triumphant when she was able to plea one of her clients down to a lesser charge. They all knew that most of the time it had nothing to do with right, or justice, but simple expediency. Trial schedules were filled to bursting, and they all were only human. There simply wasn't time, or resources, or manpower to do it differently. A corner cut here, another one there, and pretty soon that was the only way to do business.

Feeling really out of sorts now, she stopped outside the conference room where her expert witness waited. Normally she wasn't so discouraged and depressed, and she wondered if those remarks her mother had made the other night were the cause. No, that wasn't the total reason; she'd been feeling this way for some time now. Maybe she needed a big case—an exciting

51

case—to get her mind off things, she thought, and remembered Angelica Simone. That would do it, she decided, and promised to pay Tony a visit as soon as she finished here. She could talk him into it, if she really tried.

That decided, she opened the conference room door and went inside. A little man was sitting by himself at the long table, and he stood when she entered. He was wearing a gray pinstripe suit, a red bow tie, and round glasses. She didn't know what she had expected, but he didn't look like a playground expert to her, and she said uncertainly, "Hello, I'm Laura Devlin. You must be—"

"Reginald Shotz," he said, and took off his glasses. His eyes were a bright, hard blue. "My fee is two hundred dollars an hour, and you're five minutes late. Shall we get started?"

Thirty-five minutes later, not knowing whether to laugh or be irritated, she got back to her office. Maurey was already there, his shirtsleeves rolled up, looking as though he might disappear behind a mound of paperwork. Setting her briefcase down, she sank wearily into her own chair, saying, "Don't tell me that's the same stuff you were working on this morning."

He gave her a dazed look. "As a matter of fact, it is—" he started to say, and then looked at her more fully. "You look the wrath of God."

"Thanks," she said, rubbing her neck. "I just came from a very expensive interview with the playground expert for the Menzies case."

"And?"

She glanced up. "Don't ask."

"Okay," he said agreeably, and returned to his work. "By the way, the boss wanted to see you when you came in."

She straightened. "Do you know why?"

He was busy making notes. "Beats me. He'll probably tell you, if you ask."

"Very funny," she said, and despite herself, felt a stab of excitement. "Maybe he wants to talk to me about the Simone case."

Maurey looked up. "Our gun-wielding temptress? You want that case?"

"Are you kidding? Don't you?"

"Not particularly. It's a loser."

"Why do you say that?"

He glanced at her over the tops of his glasses. "Self-defense when she offed the guy in his sleep? Come on. Besides, I think Tony already gave it to Clay."

"But he gets all the good cases!"

"Maybe that's because he's got the most experience."

"That may be so," she said. "But he's not necessarily the best."

"That's a matter of opinion. All you have to do is ask him."

She stood. "I'm going to ask Tony instead."

"Atta girl," Maurey said, and gave her a thumbs-up before he returned to his work.

Tony's office was at the end of the hall. Laura stopped a moment outside the door to smooth her skirt, fiddle with her hair, and gather her thoughts. When she was ready, she knocked and went in. Tony was sitting at his desk; he glanced up briefly, gestured her to a seat, and went on with what he was doing. Halted at the starting gate, so to speak, she took the chair and waited in a fever of impatience. She knew she was going to have to talk him into letting her have this case, especially if he was already thinking of assigning it to someone else. She had her arguments all ready by the time he looked up again, and she launched right into it.

"Tony, I've got something to ask you. Now, before you say now, let me present my argument, all right?"

"Is this about Angelica Simone?" he asked.

"Yes, as a matter of fact it is. Now, I know that Clay has more experience, but—"

Wordlessly he handed her the file he'd been working on.

"What's this?" she asked.

"The Simone case," he said without cracking a smile. "The DA's not going to bargain on this one, and I figured it was time for you to get your feet wet. Anything else, or will that do?"

She took the file. "No," she said faintly. "I think this will do just fine."

She managed to escape with a little dignity intact, and she stopped briefly by her own office again before she went to visit Angelica Simone. Maurey was still wading through his stack of paper, and she waved the file at him from the doorway.

"Guess what?" she said with a broad grin.

He shook his head. "You got it."

"You bet I did."

"You just went in there and told him you deserved it and wouldn't accept anything else, right?"

"Well, sort of."

Smiling broadly himself, he gave her another thumbs-up sign. "Congratulations."

"Thanks," she said, and went to see her new client.

She didn't know what she had expected Angelica Simone to look like, but when her client was brought in, she had to hide her surprise. Angelica was petite and blond and ethereal, with pale skin and terrified blue eyes. Dressed in the sacklike dress that was the uniform of all female prisoners, she seemed even smaller than she was, the coarse material hanging on her slender body like a burlap sack. Nervously she took a place opposite Laura and clasped her hands tightly in her lap. Wondering what could have driven this delicate-looking woman to kill someone, Laura debated how to begin and finally said simply, "Hello, Angelica. My name is Laura Devlin. I'm from the public defender's office, and I've been appointed to defend you."

Angelica raised bruised-looking eyes to her face. She tried to say something, but her throat convulsed, and she had to close her eyes and try again. "I know . . ." she said, her voice shaking, "I know I did a terrible thing, and I'm sorry. But I couldn't help it. Are they going to . . . to send me to prison for a long time?"

Since the woman looked ready to faint, Laura decided not to be too blunt. "Why don't we worry about that later?" she said. "Right now I think you should tell me what happened. Exactly. Don't leave anything out."

Those terrified eyes caught hers again. "But where should I start?"

"At the beginning," Laura said, and took out her notes.

Angelica stared at her for a moment, obviously trying to gather her thoughts. Arranging her legal pad, Laura gave her an encouraging smile, and the other woman swallowed. "I didn't mean to do it," she said finally, in a voice so low, Laura could barely hear. "But he was after me all the time. I was so frightened, even in my own house. I couldn't go anywhere or do anything, because he was always there."

Now that she seemed to be getting herself together, Laura hated to interrupt the flow. But she had to have her facts clear, and so she said, "Who are you talking about, Angelica? Who was always there? Your husband?"

The woman shook her head. "No, Mike. Mike Marino."

Laura frowned. "The victim?"

Angelica looked down. She seemed to stumble over the word. "Yes, the . . . the victim. He was my—our—neighbor, he and his wife, Ilene." Dropping her head, she broke into tears. "I forgot about Ilene."

Silently Laura handed over a Kleenex. Angelica took it, tried to thank her, gave up, and dabbed at her eyes. Controlling herself with a visible effort, she said, "I'm sorry. It's just—"

"That's all right," Laura said. "I understand. Let's go on, now." She leaned forward. "Angelica, I'm sorry to put you through this, but I have to know. Did you shoot Mike Marino?"

Angelica's answer was a whisper. "Yes."

"Why?"

That pale face blanched even more. "Do I . . . do I have to say?"

Thinking how much she hated to do this, Laura nodded. "I'm afraid so, Angelica," she said, and then put her hand quickly on the other woman's arm to reassure her. "But remember— whatever you tell me is confidential—"

Hope flared in those shadowed eyes. "We won't have to tell it in court?"

Laura shifted uncomfortably. "Well, that's not exactly what I meant," she said. "We'll use whatever we have to to put on your defense. But Angelica—" she looked at her client directly in the eyes "—I have to know the truth. Otherwise, I can't help you. Do you understand?"

There was a silence during which the other woman was obviously struggling to come to grips with the situation. Finally her shoulders slumped. "I know you're right," she said haltingly, and then gave a shudder. "But I'm so afraid. My husband has such a temper, and if he knew the whole story, he would blame me, and then . . . and then . . ." She couldn't finish, and Laura put her hand briefly on her arm again.

"Let's start with that night," she suggested. "Just tell me what happened."

Angelica raised those tragic eyes to her face again. "But it didn't start with that night," she whispered. "It started months ago—when Mike raped me the first time."

Laura thought at first that she hadn't heard correctly. "The . . . first . . . time?" she echoed.

And then the whole story came out. Once Angelica started,

she seemed unable to stop, and Laura's pen flew over the legal pad, taking down all the incredible, sordid details. The rapes had begun months ago, when the neighbor, Mike Marino, was out of work. He'd come to the house one day when he knew Angelica was alone. Her husband and his wife worked, the children were in school, and no one was around to stop him. He'd taken her by force on the kitchen floor and threatened to kill her if she told anyone. She knew he meant it; she'd seen his collection of guns. He liked to play with them, take them out and clean them, point them at people, and laugh when they shrank away. She'd seen him shoot stray cats and dogs that wandered into the yard; he took them all target practicing in a canyon and set up a scarecrow, using his wife's clothing. Oh, she had no doubt that he'd do it; he hadn't been the same since he came back from Vietnam.

So she'd been afraid to tell anyone, and the visits had gone on for months, sometimes once a week, sometimes more. She had endured because she was frightened of him—and because she was accustomed to abuse. She'd been raised by an abusive father; she'd married an abusive man. The pattern had been formed at an early age, and had just . . . gone on.

Laura took it all down, her expression betraying none of her churning thoughts; only the occasional tightening of her fingers on her pen, or the turning down of her mouth, indicating her true feelings. Finally Angelica's recounting brought her up to that tragic night.

"He had come to the house that day," she said, her voice strained. "It was as always, but I let him have his way." She looked at Laura, her eyes faraway. "It seemed easier, somehow, if I didn't think about it. Just get it over with, and go on with what I was doing." Her glance focused, and she saw Laura's expression. She looked away. "I know that sounds crazy, but . . . but I think it was the only thing that kept me sane. After a while, I just wanted to pretend it wasn't happening."

Laura couldn't help herself. "But it wasn't your fault, Angelica."

The woman looked at her again, the wisdom of ages in her eyes. "That wouldn't have mattered," she said quietly. "You know, and I know, that in these things, it is always the woman to blame, never the man. That's the way the world sees it, and even I, after listening to my own story, believe it. People will ask: why didn't I do something? Why didn't I fight? Why didn't

56

I run away?'' She stopped and searched Laura's face again, then she nodded. ''You see? Even you are thinking it.''

''No, I—'' Laura protested, but Angelica briefly shook her head.

''It's all right. I understand. There were times when I wondered such things myself. I wanted to go, but I couldn't. I had to think of my children. I couldn't go without them, and I couldn't take them with me. I tried once, and my husband found us and brought us back. He said that if I tried to leave a second time, I would never see them again.''

Laura couldn't imagine a life like this. She shook herself, focused on what she was supposed to be doing. Glancing down at her notes in an effort to pull herself together, she said, ''Tell me what happened that last day.''

Angelica nodded, relieved to be at the end. ''It was as I said— he came, but he was different. I could see that right away, and at first I thought he had finally tired of me. I was glad, until he said—'' She stopped, her voice catching. She had to force herself to go on. ''Until he said that I bored him now and that he wanted someone young and pretty.'' She swallowed, the cords of her neck standing out. ''My daughter.''

Laura looked up. ''My God.''

''Miranda,'' Angelica said, ''is eleven.'' She briefly closed her eyes, her voice sinking to a whisper. ''That's when I knew I had to stop him. And so . . . I shot him.''

Laura knew what her strategy was going to be. There was no doubt in her mind that Angelica had acted in self-defense. She said as much, and as her grateful client was led away and she stood up stiffly herself, she promised them both fiercely right then that she was going to prove it.

57

CHAPTER FIVE

As much as the woman had touched her, Angelica Simone was only one of Laura's cases. Thinking how different the two clients were, Laura went to court the next day with her gun-toting ex-con, Marion Higgins. She couldn't help thinking of the frustrating interview she'd had with him about filing the motion to suppress. She'd been so angry that she'd nearly walked out. When she had tried to convince him to plead guilty, he had sat there with a stubborn look on his broad face and refused to listen.

"No, I ain't gonna plead guilty to somethin' that isn't right," Marion had said, shifting his heavy bulk on the battered chair. "That sumbitch cop had no right to search me that night, and you're gonna prove it."

She was still trying to be patient at that point. "Marion," she said again, "I can't prove it if you won't tell me the whole story. If I file a fifteen thirty-eight point five motion, we have to prove the gun was illegally seized."

He sat back, picking his teeth. "I can prove it, all right."

She wanted to throttle him. "How?"

"All right, I guess the time is now," he said, nodding his heavy head. He motioned her to come closer. She obeyed, her nostrils contracting involuntarily at the odor of stale sweat, nicotine, and unwashed flesh that wafted over to her as he pulled his chair up to the table. Glancing around to make sure they weren't overheard, he whispered, "You know why that cop had a hard-on for me that night?"

She gritted her teeth. "Come on, Marion. I don't have much time."

His black eyes flashed, but he held his temper, something she knew from his rap sheet was foreign to him. She ignored the glare he directed at her. She had a job to do, and she was doing it. He knew the score, but so did she.

"Okay, then," he said. "The reason I *know* that search was illegal was because that cop was involved with my woman, don't you see? He and Daisy had been goin' at it like a stud and a bitch in heat."

Laura looked impassively back at him. "You mean they were sleeping together."

Marion grinned, a silver-capped incisor glinting in the overhead lights. "Oh, they was doin' more than that, missy. I'll fill you in on *all* the dee-tails if you like."

"That won't be necessary," she said, ignoring the leer he gave her while she went over possibilities. It seemed pretty weak to her, and she said so.

He shook his head vehemently. "No way, missy. That prick had it in for me, and this proves it. He wanted to get me out of the way so he could get it on, you know what I mean? Now all you gots to do is get that cop to admit it. Then this bogus case will be thrown right out of court and I'll be a free man."

To go back and beat up on Daisy? She nearly spoke the words aloud, but bit her tongue instead. Through her investigator, she knew all about Marion's reputation as a man who slapped women around; knew, too, that his connection with sweet Daisy was as her pimp. But as Maurey had reminded her, that was none of her business. Proving that Marion's civil rights had been violated was.

Hoping that her expression didn't betray her disgust, she glanced down at her notes. But she couldn't help remarking, "You seem to know a lot about this, Marion. You must have spent a lot of lockup time in the prison library."

He was too pleased with himself to be offended. Smirking, he flashed that silver tooth at her again and said, "Oh, you bet, and it paid off, didn't it? Maybe I should be my own lawyer, what do you think?"

She didn't want to tell him what she thought. "I think that's up to you," she said, and glanced at her watch. "You have about thirty seconds to decide."

That wiped the smile off his face. "Hey, wait a minute. Let's not get hasty here, missy. You're the one with the license. You gotta do it for me."

Recalling that conversation, Laura entered the courtroom that morning, prepared to defend Marion Higgins's civil rights. She saw the arresting officer sitting at the back of the court as soon as she came in, and when their eyes met briefly, and she saw the rage and disgust in his, she turned quickly away. She understood how he felt, but it was too late. Trying not to feel guilty and revolted by this as well, she became angry instead. The cop was at fault here, too. Investigation had turned up proof that Marion hadn't lied when he said the officer was involved with Daisy; witnesses placed him in her apartment several times over the past few months. As much as she hated to admit it, Marion had a case.

But that didn't make her own participation in this any less repellent, and even after the motion had been granted and the gun was suppressed as evidence, she felt little satisfaction. In fact, after leaving the grinning Marion behind and taking the elevator to the nineteenth floor, she felt sick.

Not exactly the way defense counsel is supposed to feel, she thought when she reached the office, and was glad that Maurey was gone so she'd have the tiny space to herself. Throwing her briefcase down, she sat behind the desk and put her head in her hands. She knew she'd done the right thing by her client, but that didn't help. This was one of those cases where legalities and morals butted heads, and she couldn't rid herself of the feeling that she'd be sorry for what she'd done. Pushing her hair back from her face, she sat up and tried to tell herself she was being ridiculous. She'd done her job; that was that.

But the queasy feeling persisted, and she glanced at the phone. Her desk was piled high with work, but on impulse she decided to call Jack. She couldn't stay here; she had to get away. It had been a long time since they'd played hooky together, and she needed to be irresponsible for once. Reaching over the stacked files, she picked up the phone and called his office.

His secretary, Maureen, answered. "Devlin Engineering."

"Hi, Maureen, this is Laura. May I please speak to Jack?"

There was the tiniest of silences. Then Maureen said, "I'm sorry, Laura, but Jack . . . isn't here."

"Oh. Well, when do you expect him back?"

"Uh . . . I'm not sure. I don't think he intended to come back to the office today."

Already feeling guilty, Laura was paging through her calendar, not really paying attention. "I see. Did he have an appointment?"

"I really couldn't say, Mrs. Devlin."

Couldn't say? Frowning slightly, Laura shoved the appointment book impatiently away. Her impulse to run off had vanished, and she said, "All right. It wasn't important anyway. If he comes in, please tell him I called, Maureen."

"I will, Mrs. Devlin."

Annoyed, Laura replaced the receiver. How typical it was, she thought, that on the one day she decided to take off early and meet Jack somewhere, she couldn't get hold of him. Now what?

Glancing at the work on her desk, she made a face and started to reach for it when she changed her mind again. She wasn't going to give up this unexpected hour; she deserved it, and she was going to take it. She'd been working hard, and it wouldn't hurt to steal some time for herself. With the caseload she had, and now the Simone case, she was going to be even busier the next few months, and God knew when she'd get another chance like this. Grabbing her things, she left.

Traffic at this time of day was almost light. For once she beat the rush hour, and as she pulled up in her driveway, she actually grinned. She'd surprise the kids, go for a walk on the beach, maybe even talk Jack into going out for junk food when he got home. They used to do these things once. Quickly she got out of the car and went inside. To her dismay, no one was home.

"Mom?" she called, throwing her things down on the kitchen table. "Peter? Andrea?"

When no one answered, she went into the living room and looked out the sliding glass windows, hoping they'd gone to the beach. But the only people in sight were two early sunbathers who were trying to get a tan, and she turned away from the window with a frown. Throwing herself down on the couch, she wondered where everyone had gone.

She wasn't going to find them sitting here. Jumping up again, she checked the kitchen bulletin board for a note, found none, and went to the refrigerator to peer restlessly inside. She reached for a bottle of soda, looked at it, put it back again. She didn't want anything to drink; she wanted her family. Where were they?

Still restless, she went back to the living room. The sunbathers were still there, joined now by a man running with his dog. Sunlight sparkled on the waves behind him, and the sight was so lovely that she opened the door and went out to the deck. Leaning against the rail, she saw two more beachcombers a long way down, walking hand in hand. The sight reminded her that she still didn't know where her family was, and she sighed. It

61

seemed a shame to waste such a beautiful day, and she went back inside to change. It had been ages since she had gone for a run on the beach, and she decided to take the opportunity. Maybe by the time she got back, everyone would have come home.

An hour later, aching and exhausted, hoping she could make it the last few yards to the house before she collapsed, she finished her run. The wind had stiffened during the time she'd been gone, but even so, sweat had stuck strands of hair to her face. Wiping her eyes with her forearm, she was chagrined to realize how out of shape she was. Her only consolation was that two teenage boys had given her the eye when she passed them half a mile down, and when she thought how incensed she once would have been to hear those wolf whistles following her, she grinned. How things had changed. Now that she was approaching thirty-five, she felt flattered.

Getting her second wind, she turned and started up the sand toward the house. She didn't notice Jack standing on the deck until she was almost there, and she waved.

"You're too late!" she called. "I already ran my ten miles!"

"That'll be the day!" he yelled back. "If I know you, you were lucky to make it down to the lifeguard station and back!"

Since the lifeguard station was about five hundred yards away, she thought that was a low blow and told him so as she climbed the steps to the deck.

"Hey, you're the one who never has time to run anymore, remember?" he said.

She didn't want to get into a fight about work, so she said, "Well, I had time today. I called your office, in fact; to ask if you wanted to play hooky with me."

"You did? When?"

Was that her imagination, or had he suddenly tensed? It was hard to tell, for he was wearing aviator sunglasses that hid his eyes. "About three, I guess. You'd already gone."

He glanced away, suddenly absorbed—or pretending to be— in the wind-reddened sunbathers just now gathering their stuff. "Yes," he said. "I . . . I had an appointment."

"So I gathered," she said.

He turned back to her, still wearing the glasses. "If I'd known, I would have canceled. I can't remember when you've left the sanctum sanctorum early like that. Weren't you afraid the building would fall down, or all the jail cells would open and the convicts come pouring out?''

She wasn't going to be drawn into a fight. ''I decided to chance it,'' she said lightly. ''I was hoping we could all go on a picnic, or something, but then I got home and found everyone gone.''

He seemed relieved at the change in subject. ''Yeah, your mother took the kids to the mall after school,'' he said. ''Come on, let's go inside and get a drink.''

She didn't know why, but she was suddenly angry. ''I don't want a drink,'' she said. ''How do you know Mom took the kids to the mall?''

He'd already started inside. Turning back to her in surprise, he said, ''She told me this morning.''

''Why didn't she mention it to me?''

He stared at her, his eyes hidden behind those damned glasses. ''Jeez, Laura, I don't know. What difference does it make?''

She didn't know herself. She didn't even know why she was making such a big deal out of this, but she couldn't seem to help it. ''It makes a difference because she could have told me for once!'' she snapped. ''Why does she always confide these things to you?''

He was really surprised at that. ''For Christ's sake, Laura, what's the matter with you? Going to the mall didn't exactly require a *confidence*, you know. She just mentioned that's what she wanted to do. You weren't here, so—'' He shrugged.

Without warning, she was close to tears. Horrified because she hated to cry, she turned away from him and tried to pull herself together. What *was* the matter with her? She felt him come up behind her and turned farther away. He put his hands on her shoulders and gently turned her to face him.

''What is it, Laurie?'' he asked.

His eyes in the setting sun were very blue; she realized then that he'd finally taken off his sunglasses. But she couldn't hold his glance and she looked down at the beach, her eyes filling with tears. ''I don't know,'' she said, and didn't have the faintest clue.

He put a hand under her chin and made her look up at him. ''Know what I think?''

She searched his face. He had never seemed so handsome to her as in that moment when the fading light gilded his face. ''What?''

"I think we need to get away—just the two of us, for a few days. What do you say?"

She didn't know what to say. She had never expected him to say that, and she was at a complete loss for words. "I . . . I don't know," she said uncertainly.

He pulled her persuasively toward him. "Come on, Laurie," he murmured. "We haven't been away in a long time, just you and I. Don't you think it's time we just took off?"

She hated herself, but she couldn't help it. Thinking of her heavy caseload, she had to ask. "For how long?"

"I don't know. For however long the spirit moves us. Do you realize we haven't gone away—just the two of us—in . . . I can't remember how long, can you?"

She couldn't remember, either. For six years there'd been law school, and she'd started at the PD's office right after that. Time was at such a premium then that the only reason she'd taken a vacation was because she'd been forced to. Neither of them had felt right about leaving the kids behind, and so it was always a family thing, brief trips here and there, staying home mostly to enjoy the beach. But as for she and Jack getting away by themselves . . . She shook her head.

"No, I can't remember the last time," she said, and without warning thought of Angelica Simone. She tensed. She couldn't take time now, not with a murder trial coming up. But how was she going to explain that to Jack? She hadn't even told him about Angelica yet; there hadn't been time.

Before she could say anything more, Jack pulled her a little closer to him. "I thought maybe we could go up to Monterey or Carmel for a few days, get a motel room there, and just spend some time together. We could wander through all those shops and get fat at all those restaurants, and make love every night. What do you say?"

Despite herself, her heart leaped at the thought. It had been so long since Jack had said anything like that, so long since he had made a gesture like this. Angelica's pale face floated into her mind, and she hated herself.

"It sounds wonderful, Jack," she said. "But—"

He pulled her even closer, started nuzzling her neck. She closed her eyes. "No buts," he whispered. "I'll make the reservations tonight."

She wanted to tell him to go ahead, but she couldn't make herself say it. She would have given anything to abandon all responsibility for once, but she couldn't. Angelica was depending on her, and she couldn't let her down.

"Jack, I—" she started to say weakly.

His lips moved from her neck to her ear. "Don't say anything," he murmured. "If you're worried about the kids, your mother can handle them for a few days. We'll send her over to Las Vegas for the weekend when we get back. She could go on one of those tours. You know how she loves Vegas."

She had to stop this. With an effort, she pulled away. "I wasn't thinking of that, Jack," she said miserably.

"What, then?" he said, a warning in his voice. He knew what she was going to say before she said it.

She had to tell him; it was too important to hide. "Jack, I know what you're going to say, but I've got a new case—"

His eyes darkened. "There's *always* a new case."

"But this one is different," she said pleadingly. "Jack, I've been appointed to defend a woman against a murder charge, and I can't just leave!"

"Let somebody else take it! In this town, there will always be more."

"But this is my first one!"

"And it's more important than going up to Carmel with me?"

She hesitated. It was only for a split second, but Jack saw the indecision on her face, and his jaw tightened. "Well, that's great. You'd rather spend time with a homicidal maniac than your husband."

"Angelica isn't a homicidal maniac! She's an abused woman who defended herself by—"

"Who cares?" Jack shouted. "Who gives a fuck what happened anyhow? For all we know, she deserved it!"

She looked at him, shocked. "You don't mean that!"

"The hell I don't! You think I give a damn about some woman who offed someone? I don't care if she went on a rampage and killed everyone in sight! Why do you have to defend her?"

"Because it's my job!" she cried. Why couldn't he understand?

"Your *job*," he spat. "Don't give me that. Ever since you started at that damned PD's office, you've acted like you're on some kind of crusade."

"Crusade! I don't know what you're talking about! You're not being fair!"

He looked at her incredulously. "*I'm* not being fair? Haven't you got that backwards?"

She couldn't believe this was happening. Feeling that the situation had gotten completely out of control, she tried again. "Jack, please listen to me. You know I'd love to go. I wouldn't have hesitated last month, or last week, or even yesterday. But that was before—"

"Before you got this big break in your career, right?"

She flushed. "I wouldn't put it like that—"

"How would you put it, then, Laura? It's obvious that this case means more to you than I do, so maybe we'd just better forget it."

He started to brush by, but she put a hand on his arm and stopped him. "Why can't we just postpone going away for a while?" she asked.

He gave her a withering look. "For how long, Laura? A month? Two months? A year? The rest of our lives? No, like I said, just forget it."

He pulled away and reached for the sliding glass door, jerking it so furiously that it rattled in the track. Without thinking, she followed him and saw with dismay that he was reaching for the coat he'd thrown over the couch.

"Jack, we're not finished with this!"

"The hell we're not!" he said, pulling on the jacket. "I was a fool even to ask, I see that now. Don't think I will again."

"Where are you going?"

"What do you care?" he hurled at her, and slammed out the front door.

"Jack!" she cried, but she was too late. She heard the truck's engine start and knew it was too late to stop him, that it would be foolhardy to try. Wondering what had happened, she slumped against the edge of the couch, trying not to cry. She was still sitting there when her mother and the kids came home. She heard them in the driveway and quickly brushed the tears from her eyes just as Andrea came rushing in, her arms full of packages. A few months ago she had abandoned the childish "Mommy," and now with the single-mindedness of youth, she cried, "Mama, Mama, look what Grandma bought me!"

Over Andrea's head, Laura met her mother's eyes. Estelle said, "Was that Jack I saw leaving?"

She didn't want to go into it now. "Yes," she said, wiping furtively at her face. "He had an appointment."

"He seemed in quite a hurry."

Their eyes met again. She said, "He was."

"I see," Estelle said, and turned away.

"Mama!"

Relieved at the interruption, Laura turned to her daughter. Andrea had opened one of the packages and was ecstatically holding up matching blouse and pants. "Remember that outfit I liked at the mall, Mama?"

Despite her worry about Jack, Laura remembered it very well. She also recalled telling Andrea it was too expensive. Her face darkening as she recognized the same garments now, she said, "I thought we discussed this, Andrea."

"Yes, but Grandma said it would be all right." Andrea looked uncertainly from her mother to her grandmother. Laura followed her glance. She'd also discussed this with Estelle, who knew her views about labels and young children.

"Mother?" she said.

Estelle looked up impatiently from her own packages. "I thought it would be all right."

Laura knew that she should discuss this privately with her mother, but after the fight with Jack, her patience was at an end. "Well, it's not," she said. "You know how I feel about designer clothes for kids."

Estelle looked even more annoyed. "Oh, for heaven's sake, Laura. What difference does it make? It's my money, and I know how much she wanted it."

"That isn't the point, Mother, and you know it. There's no reason for Andrea to get everything she wants. You're spoiling her rotten."

Sensing trouble, Andrea looked from one to the other again. "Does this mean I have to take it back?" she asked. Her lip trembled, and she looked on the verge of tears.

Laura knew it was too late now. But that didn't make her any the less angry, and after glaring at her mother, she looked down at Andrea. Her daughter was gazing at her so pitifully that she felt herself weakening despite her resolve. But she had to say, "No, you don't have to take it back—this time. But don't try this again."

Andrea knew what she meant, and her face crumpled. "I'm sorry, Mama," she said, clutching the clothes. "But I wanted it so *bad*. I promise, I'll never ask for anything again." She looked up. "Would you like me to try it on? Maybe if you see what I look like in it, you won't be so mad."

Despite her anger, Laura had to laugh. What would it hurt, just once? Relenting, she gave Andrea a hug. "Yes, go ahead. I want to talk to your grandmother, anyway."

Andrea rushed off, but before Laura could turn to her mother and tell her what she thought about this, Peter came in. He'd grown again and couldn't seem to get enough to eat; he'd stopped in the kitchen on the way in from the garage to make a peanut butter sandwich, and he was carrying a bag of chips. Annoyed because it was so close to dinner, Laura was about to say something when she realized he was wearing a new jacket—this one sporting, as had Andrea's new outfit, a well-known logo. She looked at Estelle.

Her mother stared calmly back. "Well, I couldn't buy Andrea something and ignore Peter, could I?"

Laura felt at the end of her rope. She didn't have the energy to deal with this right now, and without saying anything more, she went into the kitchen to start dinner. Jack came home smelling like beer sometime in the wee hours of the morning, and she lay awake long after he was snoring. They didn't discuss the vacation idea the next morning, or any morning after that, and after a while it was only a memory. But things weren't the same between them after that, and Laura knew that neither of them forgot.

CHAPTER SIX

Douglas Rhodes shifted restlessly in the back of the limousine as it sped along the freeway toward Century City. His flight had just arrived in Los Angeles, and he was supposed to take another to Phoenix tomorrow after his appointment with Malcolm Tanner tonight. He tried to settle back against the plush seat, but he was too annoyed to get comfortable. Glancing across at his chief administrative assistant, Irving Mayhew, the man responsible for his being here, he wondered why he had allowed Irv to talk him into this. Malcolm Tanner was a political consultant. He might be the best, but to Douglas, he was still an ad man.

Irving felt his glance and shifted position. Brown-haired, with light blue eyes behind wire-framed glasses, Irving Mayhew was a man of medium height and giant intellect. He had an awesome grasp of politics, and Douglas sometimes thought there wasn't anything he didn't know *something* about. He had a ready answer for just about everything, it seemed, and if by some rare chance he wasn't completely sure of his facts, he found out. In a business where a nose for politics and an eye for detail and an ear for gossip were practical necessities, Irving was a rare find, and Douglas knew it. Normally he trusted his chief aide's instincts completely; tonight, he wasn't so sure.

"Something wrong, Senator?"

Douglas sighed. He'd already told Irving how he felt about this media packaging of political candidates; it seemed pointless to belabor that now, especially since he was here. But he couldn't help saying, "It's just that I'm not sure this is right for me, Irv. From what I've heard, this Tanner is a real hired gun."

Irving smiled at Douglas's use of the "in" phrase. "If by that you mean he sells his talents to the highest bidder, you'll get no argument from me," he said, and added dryly, "And probably not from him, either."

"Then why are we consulting someone who has no political ideology?"

"Because his political affiliation isn't the issue here, Senator, his expertise is. And no matter how you feel about him personally, no one denies that he gets people elected."

Douglas couldn't argue that. He'd read Tanner's dossier, and he couldn't deny the man's abilities. Still, he was ambivalent about hiring a political consultant who was known for working both sides of the fence. What had happened right here in Los Angeles was a case in point: After waging a fierce mayoral campaign against the incumbent some years before—and losing—Tanner had directed the present mayor's campaign to beat back a recall vote three years later. He'd followed that by orchestrating Don Buswell's successful bid for Congress against Maxine Duprey, only to announce recently that he'd been hired to plan her gubernatorial bid in the fall. If the man did any more jumping around, they'd have to follow him with a net, Douglas thought grumpily, and turned to look out the window.

"I don't know," he muttered. "I'm not sure I can hire a man who stated in a *Fortune* interview that *he* chooses who to work for, and not the other way around."

Irving hid a smile. The senator had been muttering along these same lines ever since they'd caught the flight out of Dulles. "Well, we're almost here," he said. "Why don't we see what the man is like, and then decide?"

Douglas shot him a glance. "Don't you have that backwards? From everything I've read about this man, we're not going to decide anything. He's going to check *us* out."

The aide laughed as the car pulled to a smooth stop in front of the twin towers of the Century City office buildings. They got out, Douglas noting the slight breeze that was tainted with only a whiff of acrid smog tonight. At this time of night, the fading light tinted the sky a pink-mauve-gold, and everything seemed bathed in a gentle light that softened the harsh outlines of buildings and never-ending cement. He looked in the direction of the ocean, remembering his undergraduate days at UCLA. He loved the beach; he wished he were there right now.

Realizing that Irving was looking at him questioningly, he sighed and turned toward the building. The offices of Malcolm Tanner, Inc., occupied the entire fifteenth floor, and as the elevator whisked them smoothly upward, he chided himself for disliking the consultant before they'd even met. Resolving to keep an open mind, he was immediately annoyed again when the elevator doors opened and his eyes were treated to a panoramic view of the immense Tanner logo: a glossy, flamboyant, multicolored phoenix, the mythical bird that consumed itself by fire and then rose again from its own ashes. He was wondering cynically which of them—Tanner or himself—the bird was supposed to represent, when he suddenly recalled that the phoenix was also a symbol of excellence. Irritated anew, he preceded Irving into the office.

A beautiful young woman looked up when they came in. She was seated behind a vast horseshoe-shaped desk that perched elegantly on plush carpet so dense, it looked like an unbroken sea of beige grass. The desk itself looked like a space capsule console, with telephones and buttons and an array of electronic equipment that was surely the ultimate in high tech. No obligatory ficus trees in brass tubs were scattered around here; verdant living plants clustered in marble planters were strategically placed, and another phoenix logo was repeated in a gigantic painting that took up one vast wall. For visitors' comfort, several seat groupings were placed at intervals, with telephones on low tables in front, and there wasn't a magazine in sight. Douglas took it all in with one swift glance. If this was the outer office, he couldn't wait to see the rest.

Irving stepped up to the desk. "Senator Douglas Rhodes and Irving Mayhew to see Mr. Tanner," he said, trying not to goggle. The girl was one of the most beautiful women either of them had ever seen.

"Yes, of course," she said. "Excuse me, I'll tell him you're here. I won't be a moment."

Wondering why she didn't just buzz through on that elaborate console in front of her, Douglas glanced at his watch as she disappeared. He had read somewhere that truly important people worked at their own pace and assumed others would wait for them, and because he was already annoyed at being here, he decided to play the game, too. He was usually above such conceits, but since he was becoming more and more positive this was a mistake, he checked the time. It was one minute to the hour; Tanner had exactly sixty seconds to appear.

Irving was aware of that glance, and he said, "I'm sure she'll be back in a moment. Our appointment is for seven."

The girl reappeared right on schedule. Offering them a brilliant smile and a careful toss of perfectly coiffed long blond hair, she said, "Right this way, gentlemen."

Although he'd seen pictures of Malcolm Tanner, meeting the man in person was still a surprise. He looked much younger than his forty years; much younger than the photos Douglas had in his file. With his blond hair in a choirboy cut, gray eyes, and round, babylike face, he looked like a mail clerk who had wandered into the office by mistake, not the owner and president of a highly successful political imaging firm. He was sitting behind a desk that Douglas couldn't help noticing was not nearly as large and grand as the one in the outer office, but which held an even more bewildering array of equipment, and when the girl ushered them in, he stood at once.

"Senator," he said warmly. "How nice to meet you."

His handshake was firm and decisive, and when he turned to Irving, Douglas had time for further study. He was wearing a brown suit with a blue shirt and striped tie, all of which looked almost slept in, and after the introductions, he grinned boyishly and said, "Please excuse my appearance. I haven't been to bed for forty-eight hours, and I didn't have time to go home and change before your appointment. Would you like some coffee? Perhaps a drink?"

"Coffee would be fine," Douglas said, starting to like the man despite himself. There was no doubt; he had a certain charisma.

"For me, too," Irving said.

"That makes three of us," Tanner said, and punched a button on the elaborate console. "Coffee please, Dora," he said into some hidden microphone, and smiled at his guests again. "I gave up the booze a couple of years ago—along with three packs a day." He grimaced. "But sometimes I wonder which is worse—the cure or the disease."

Douglas found himself saying, "I know what you mean. I was a smoker once myself. I still crave it, and I haven't had a cigarette in fifteen years."

Tanner grimaced. "You mean I have that much more time to look forward to?"

As though she'd been waiting outside for the opportunity, the secretary came in just then carrying a tray upon which she'd arranged the coffee things. She glanced around. "Where would you like me to serve this, Mr. Tanner?"

Tanner indicated one of the seating arrangements at the end

of the office. "There will be fine. We'll serve ourselves, Dora. That'll be all."

The girl nodded and left. Tanner gestured them toward the couch. "Shall we?" he said. "Oh, and I hope you don't mind my recording our meeting. It makes things so much easier that way."

For whom? Douglas wondered, and then gave a shrug. He didn't care if the meeting was recorded or not.

"I don't believe in beating around the bush, Senator," Tanner said, getting down to business with the pouring of the coffee. "I'm sure you'll agree that time is money, and the more we waste, the more we spend. I understand that you're going to run for reelection and that you want me to manage your campaign."

Douglas took a sip from the Spode cup. The coffee was fresh-brewed, Kona, excellent. It didn't change his mind. "I am going to stand for reelection," he agreed, and set the cup down. "But the reason I came is to find out if I want you to manage my campaign."

"I see," Tanner said, and smiled. Suddenly he didn't look quite so youthful. He sat back, balancing his coffee cup on his knee. "Well, that sort of clears the air, doesn't it? As I said, I like the direct approach, and since you obviously agree, I think we should establish up front that my fee for a campaign is one-fifty. Plus expenses, of course."

Douglas couldn't prevent a slight lift of an eyebrow. "You don't come cheap, do you?"

Tanner met his eyes. "You wouldn't consider me if I did," he said, and then laughed with genuine amusement. "Besides, it's not so much when you consider that I charge three times that for a presidential bid. Plus expenses, naturally."

"Naturally," Douglas said.

Smiling at his dry tone, Tanner set his cup on the table. "Since you haven't walked out yet, would you like me to explain what you get for all that money?"

Douglas admitted he was curious.

Suddenly serious, Tanner said, "Well, the first thing you get is—me. And by that, I mean my undivided attention. If you need me to ride horses with you in Scottsdale, I'll be there. If you need me for a fund-raiser in Georgetown, I'll pack my tux and go. In short, Senator, I'll be wherever you need me—and where I'll do the most good. Most of the time, I admit, that will be here. Would you like me to show you why?"

Deciding he had nothing to lose—except a hundred fifty thousand dollars, Douglas thought wryly—he gestured to the consultant to lead on. With a solemn Irving following close behind, they went on the Cook's tour.

As they'd already discovered, Malcolm Tanner, Inc., occupied the entire fifteenth floor. Once they had a glimpse of what was behind all the closed doors, they understood why. Tanner had his own photography studio, video display and editing room, graphic arts room complete with typesetting equipment, and a dozen private offices used by full-time employees. In a room all to itself was a state-of-the-art mainframe computer, and despite himself, Douglas was impressed.

"The equipment you've just seen is the result of new innovations in campaign techniques," Tanner explained when they were back with fresh coffee again in the main office. "And one of the most exciting of those is the new degree to which voters can be broken into identifiable demographics."

"Why is that?" Douglas asked.

"Well, in the past, cities and counties were divided into precincts, which were considered liberal or conservative, depending on which way that precinct voted as a whole in the previous election. But this generalized approach never could differentiate between individual voters."

"But you can now."

"Yes, especially since computers have made gathering information so much easier. We can collect data from all sorts of different government offices, such as the Registrar of Voters, and the tax assessor." He smiled. "Even from the DMV—as long as their computer isn't down."

"What does all this information tell you?"

"It tells us such things as race, sex, whether a voter is a homeowner or a renter, what his, or her, sexual preference is."

Douglas couldn't hide his surprise. "You need to know a voter's sexual preference?" The idea shocked him, but Tanner didn't seem to find it strange at all.

"In this business, we collect as much data as we can," he said. "You never know when you might want to target a particular group—gays, for example."

Douglas had no comment to that; he wasn't sure he wanted to pursue it. Tanner saw his expression and smiled.

"As you've seen, I have all I need to give my clients the best right here, on this floor," he said. "We have everything from computer analysis and demographic statistics to direct mailings and fund-raising."

Irving asked curiously, "Does all that video equipment mean you make your own commercials?"

"Sometimes. It depends."

"On what?"

"On whether we're going to use television advertising or direct mail, or a combination of both."

Feeling that he was rapidly getting out of his depth, Douglas asked, "How do you decide?"

Tanner grinned. "Well, it's a complicated process that starts when a client comes to me and asks me to design a campaign for them. The first thing we do is conduct early polling—not so much to see if the client is ahead, but to identify strengths and weaknesses."

Noting that Tanner had said, "when a client comes to *me*," Douglas nodded. "Go on."

Tanner obliged. "After the polling, we start to create a campaign theme. This is usually something simple and direct—catchy, if you will. Something that associates some quality with the candidate, so that the phrase sticks in the voters' minds. Then, using the computer-generated lists I told you about earlier, we design brochures, targeting each one for a specific audience. Sometimes we use radio, sometimes television, or newspaper advertising, depending on which the computer determines is best." He paused fractionally. "And on how much money is available, of course."

"And assuming the money is available?" Douglas asked.

Tanner gave that grin again. "Then the sky's the limit."

Douglas turned to his aide. "What do you think, Irv?"

As though he'd been waiting for the opportunity, Irving said, "I'd like to ask a question if I may."

"Fire away," Tanner said.

"What is the difference—in effect, I mean—between direct mail campaigns and television advertising?"

"Good question," Tanner said, and got up to get something from his desk. He returned with a file folder and removed a series of glossies that he spread out on the coffee table. "This is a good demonstration," he said. "They're from a congressional campaign I did last year. What do you think?"

Douglas didn't know what to think. The mailers were high-quality photographs of supporters for the candidate. The pieces were identical—except for the races of the people in the pictures. On one, blacks predominated, on another, Asians, and still another, Hispanics. He looked at Irving, who was frowning, too.

Tanner saw their expressions and said, "Televised messages must appeal to a broad spectrum of voters, all with different political beliefs. As you can see, direct mail campaigns do just the opposite. Instead of making the candidates mean all things to all people, as on TV, DM stresses the strengths most likely to appeal to the target audience."

Douglas looked up. "Doesn't that make it difficult for voters to determine where candidates stand on the issues?"

Tanner shrugged. "I don't try to change people's minds, only to enhance what's already in them. We present the best possible picture to all the people we can. We just do it differently in some areas than in others. There's no harm in that. The candidate is still the same person."

"How can voters be sure?" Irving asked. "You've altered that perception by appealing to different target groups."

"I see your point, but my argument remains the same. Think of it this way—you and I have a different perception of Senator Rhodes, don't we?"

Irving cautiously agreed that they did.

"Okay, the reason for that is because we have a different relationship to him, for one thing, but also because we *want* to see different things. He represents something different to each of us, doesn't he?"

"Yes, but we know the senator. The voters don't."

Tanner smiled that smile again. "They will when I get through with him."

Douglas wasn't sure he liked this. "Yes, but how well will they know me?" he asked. "From what you've said tonight, I'm beginning to feel as though a candidate—any candidate—is just a package to you people. It doesn't matter what we stand for or think, only what the demographics say."

"Not true," Tanner denied. "When you sign with me, we do an in-depth interview—lights, cameras, recorders, the works— while you tell me everything you ever thought about, or hoped for, or wished. Then, when I'm familiar with you, the man, we'll get to Douglas Rhodes, the politician, and go through the same thing again. By the time we finish, I'll know you better than your own mother, and as a double check, every word written, every sentence spoken, every picture taken, has to be approved by you. I don't work any other way.''

Douglas nodded, but he couldn't help wondering how much of what Tanner had said was true, how much hype. He still didn't like the attitude that *he* had to pass muster instead of the other way around, and he decided he had to think about this. He stood, holding out his hand. "Thank you for your time," he said, and smiled a little smile of his own. "As they say in your business, I'll get back to you."

His eyes glinting, Tanner returned the handshake. "They say that in any business, Senator," he said, and saw them out.

On the way down in the elevator, Irving shook his head. "Wow. I feel like I've been in a whirlwind. Tanner has something; no doubt about it."

"He seems to know what he's doing," Douglas said grudgingly.

"He does, that. Those offices were pretty impressive."

"So what do you think?"

"He's supposed to be the best, Senator."

"Yes, so you said."

Irving looked at him as they walked toward the car waiting by the curb. "I take it you didn't like him."

"No, I didn't like him," he admitted. "But that's not really the point, is it?"

Irving hesitated. "Shall I set up another appointment?"

He considered it. "No, let's wait a few days," he said. "I want to think about it."

Irving was heading on to San Francisco to visit his family, so they went their separate ways. Douglas planned to spend the night in L.A. before flying home for a few days; since he was here, he wanted to get together with an old friend, Jim Duluth, who was starting a reelection campaign to retain his seat as DA. He and Jim went back a long way, and he'd called ahead to see if Jim could clear some time. As always, his old friend had been expansive.

"I think I can manage to squeeze you in," Jim said. "Are you going to be here for dinner? This old town still has a little life in her, and I'm sure we could scare up a good time."

Remembering previous "good times," Douglas laughed but had to beg off. "Afraid not," he said. "I've got an appointment the night I get in, and I don't know how long it will take. I plan

77

on flying to Phoenix the next morning, but can we make it breakfast instead?''

"Breakfast," Jim repeated distastefully. "You sure about that? Let's make it brunch instead. I've got an early meeting, but I can go after that."

They had agreed to meet the next morning, and as Douglas asked the chauffeur to take him to the Biltmore, he wished he'd invited Jim for a drink tonight. He was still hyped up from that meeting with Tanner, and when he realized it was ten o'clock, he was shocked. He hadn't eaten yet, but that would have to wait. After checking in, he sat on the bed to call Marcella, who would be waiting, wondering what had happened to him. He'd promised to call as soon as he got in.

The phone rang just twice before Marcella picked it up with an anxious "Douglas?"

"Yes, it's me," he said. "I'm sorry it's so late, but the meeting with Tanner took longer than I expected."

"Did it go well?"

He heard the reservation in her voice and suppressed a sigh. He'd told her who Tanner was and knew she wasn't happy that he'd decided to stand for reelection.

"I guess so," he said. "I haven't decided about him yet."

"I see," she said, sounding even more subdued. He found out why when she added, "Douglas—Rob called tonight."

He tensed. It had been less than a year since Rob had dropped the bombshell about his wanting to quit school for a while and travel; since then, their relationship had grown steadily worse. Rob had been home several times, each time looking scruffier and more unkempt than the time before, and his last visit had been a disaster. Douglas couldn't help himself; they'd had a terrible fight and, for the first time in their lives, ended up shouting at each other.

The scene had been so unbelievable that he still couldn't think of it without wincing. He had never dreamed they could say such things to each other; it hurt even now to think how much they'd grown apart. But he couldn't understand what was happening, and he wanted to try.

"What's to understand, Dad?" Rob had said. They were in the kitchen at the time, where Rob had been wolfing down a sandwich as though he hadn't eaten in weeks. He looked as though he hadn't; he'd lost a lot of weight. Equally alarming was that he'd changed in other ways. Once so well groomed, so

. . . so all-American, he resembled a refugee from the tenderloin, his hair long and down to his shoulders, a three-day stubble of beard, his jeans almost stiff with grease and dirt, his shirt with holes in it.

"What's to understand?" he'd echoed disbelievingly. He wanted to grab Rob by the collar and haul him over to the mirror. "What do you mean, *what's to understand?* Have you looked at yourself lately?"

Rob sneered. "Haven't you always said that clothes don't make the man?"

The only reason he hadn't throttled his son was that Marcella was upstairs, crying. She didn't know what was happening any more than he did. Somehow he had controlled himself. "We're talking about more than your appearance, Rob," he said, tight-lipped. "You aren't the same person, and your mother and I would like to know why."

Rob shoved the nearly eaten sandwich away and washed down the last mouthful with a swallow of beer. "There's nothing to know," he said. "I found out a few things, that's all."

"What . . . things?" Douglas asked, distracted by the sight of his son wiping his mouth with his sleeve. He'd never seen Rob do that, not even on the many camping trips they'd taken together.

"I don't know—things," Rob said, and reached into his pocket. When he started to roll a cigarette, it was a moment before Douglas could speak.

"When did you start to smoke?"

"A while ago," Rob said with a shrug. He held out the pouch. "Want one?" He saw Douglas's expression and put the pouch back in his pocket. "No, I guess not."

There was a silence while Rob fashioned the cigarette, rolled it into a straight tube, wetted it with his tongue, and stuck it into his mouth. Douglas waited until he had struck a match with a fingernail. He wasn't really paying attention; he wanted to work this out.

"You were saying?" he asked, his voice tight.

Drawing in a deep lungful of the smoke, Rob held it and said, "All right, you asked for it. For one thing, I found out that all politicians are ripping us off. And that big business is screwing the public and no one's doing anything about it." He exhaled slowly, squinting through a cloud. "And I found out that the oil

79

crisis was engineered by men who got *very* rich by playing on people's fears. You want me to go on?''

Douglas couldn't reply; he was in a state of shock. He couldn't believe that Rob was saying these things, that he apparently believed them. What had happened to him? Where had he been?

With an effort, he pulled himself together and said carefully, ''No, that's not necessary. I can't believe you honestly think that, but that's not the issue. Something more important than politics is going on here, and—''

Rob laughed again and blew out a smoke ring. ''What's more important to you than politics?'' he sneered. ''Except maybe business? You're so involved with both, it's no wonder you can't see the light.''

Douglas couldn't believe they were having this conversation. ''I'm not so sure you've seen the light, either, Rob,'' he said. ''To my mind, you're talking like a naive child.''

Rob had been sitting back in his chair, balancing on the two rear legs. Now he leaned forward so that the two front legs crashed to the floor. Suddenly he wasn't laughing, and Douglas was shocked anew by the sheer contempt on his son's face. ''You know,'' Rob said, ''the best thing I ever did was quit school and find out what the real world was like. Until then, I never realized how . . . sheltered I was, how ignorant of the way things really are. But you—you've never learned, have you?''

With supreme self-control, Douglas managed to say, ''Since you're so enlightened now, maybe you should tell me.''

But Rob had sensed his anger, and held up his hands in mock surrender. ''Hey, don't pay any attention to me. After all, what do I know? I'm just a kid, and kids don't have any right to opinions.''

He'd had enough. He'd tried to understand, to give Rob the benefit of the doubt, but his son's contempt was too much. ''I've never heard such drivel in my life. Until now, I've always valued your opinion!''

''Only because it happened to go along with yours, Dad,'' Rob said, his eyes narrowing as he took another drag off the almost-finished cigarette. ''As long as I agreed with you, everything was fine.''

''That's absurd! There have been times when we haven't agreed, but it wasn't like this!''

''You're right about that,'' Rob said, and ashed the cigarette into his hand, which he'd been doing all along. Douglas hadn't been paying attention; he'd been in shock. But he looked suddenly at that cigarette and his hand shot out.

"What is that you're smoking?" If he'd been angry before, he was furious now.

Rob tried to laugh. "What's the matter, Dad? Finally recognize the sweet smell of cannabis?"

He'd been filled with so many conflicting emotions, he couldn't even speak. Incredulously he'd looked from the roach in Rob's grimy fingers, to the stubbled, handsome face, and for an instant he wanted to clench his fist and—

The thought of violence against his son shocked him even more than the idea that Rob had been smoking marijuana right in front of him—and that he'd been too self-involved to notice. Appalled, he willed himself under control. What was happening to him—to them? He felt like he was in a nightmare; he didn't know what to do.

Rob saw his expression and his own face changed. Looking a little frightened now, he said, "Hey, Dad, if I'd known—"

"Get out," Douglas said. He hardly recognized his own voice.

"But—"

"I said . . . get out." It seemed the only thing he was capable of saying.

"Dad, if you'll just listen—"

He'd stood, but only because he could no longer endure sitting there, staring at this boy he didn't recognize as his own. "There is nothing," he said, his voice shaking despite himself, "you could say to me to justify your behavior just now. You *know* how your mother and I feel about drugs; you *knew* what my reaction would be to having them in the house!"

"Dad, please let me explain—"

His own face white, Rob got to his feet, too. His eyes were on the same level as his father's, his pupils dilated. That was the only visible effect; the euphoria produced by the drug had vanished with the realization that he'd gone too far. "Dad—"

"No, there is no explanation," he'd said unequivocally. "Unless it's that somewhere in your *travels*—" his voice dripped scorn "—you have learned contempt for everything I stand for. That's the only explanation for your outrageous behavior tonight, and that is the reason you're going to leave."

"But, Dad!"

Rob looked so agonized that he nearly relented. But he knew

81

if he surrendered, Rob would never respect him again. His own heart pounding, he said, "Get out, Rob. And don't come back."

Rob's pale face blanched even more. "Never?"

He almost said it. He was furious enough to banish him right then. But he couldn't do it, and when he heard a sharp intake of breath behind them, he was glad he hadn't. They'd been so intent, they hadn't heard Marcella come into the kitchen, and when she uttered a sound, they both whirled around.

He saw her face and warned, "This is between Rob and me, Marcella."

It was obvious she'd heard most of the argument, and she looked imploringly from Rob to him. "Douglas, don't, please."

He hesitated. The power to disinherit his son was his, but he couldn't do it. The interruption had brought him to his senses, and without a word, he'd turned and left the kitchen.

Rob had been gone when he got up the next morning, and neither he nor Marcella had mentioned the incident again. That had happened three months ago, and they hadn't heard from Rob until now.

"Douglas, are you still there?"

The images of the night faded with Marcella's voice, and he blinked. "Yes, I'm here," he said, and had to ask. "What did he want?"

"To let us know that he was . . . well. And that's he's in Seattle now, staying with friends."

Again, he couldn't help himself. "I see. Does he have a job yet?"

She hesitated. "He said he's looking for one."

Grimly he held on to the phone. "I hope so. I can't imagine what he's living on, unless he's sponging off his friends."

"Oh, Douglas!"

He heard the reproach, but ignored it. They had already argued about this, the night he'd struck Rob's name from all the credit cards and checking accounts. When Marcella had protested, he'd replied in a cold fury that since Rob was so contemptuous of their life-style, he shouldn't be forced to participate in it. If he wanted money, he could work for it. Then, knowing what a soft touch she'd always been where Rob was concerned, he'd warned her not to subsidize him. Rob couldn't have it both ways, and it was time he learned a few tough lessons.

Now he wondered just how much Rob had learned. His tone

sharp, he said, "You haven't been sending him money, have you?"

He knew she had been even before she admitted it. "Well, yes, I have, Douglas," she said in a small voice. "But can you blame me? He's our son! I can't let him starve!"

"He won't starve," he said harshly. "When he gets hungry enough—or runs out of friends—he'll find work."

"But it's not necessary, Douglas!" Marcella cried. "We have so much—"

"So could he," Douglas said inexorably.

"Why are you so hard on him?" Marcella shrilled.

"Because life is hard," Douglas replied, his voice cold. "And until he learns that, he'll never be a man."

"But he's only nineteen!"

"Old enough," Douglas said, and then, because he was in danger of losing his temper, he ended the conversation with a brusque "Room service just came. I'll see you tomorrow."

He was still out of sorts the next morning when he left the hotel for his brunch meeting with Jim. His old friend had two sons of his own, and as he took the elevator to the eighteenth floor of the Criminal Courts Building in downtown L.A., he hoped Jim would be able to give him some advice on how to handle this situation with Rob. He hated the breach between himself and his son, but he didn't know how to cross it. Preoccupied, he was just approaching the big double wooden doors with the guard in front and the impressive logo of the district attorney centered above, when the door opened and Jim came out with a woman who had her back to him. Preoccupied in conversation, they didn't see him right away.

"Thank you, sir," she was saying. "I appreciate the time."

She turned just then, and before he could move aside, she nearly ran into him. She jumped back, obviously embarrassed. "Oh, I'm sorry! I didn't see—" she started to say, and then recognition dawned in startling green eyes. "Aren't you—?"

"Senator Douglas Rhodes," he said, forgetting that he always felt slightly pompous using his title. He was hardly aware that he had; for some reason, he couldn't look away from her face.

"Yes, of course," she said, getting herself under control. "I'm so pleased to meet you, Senator. My name is Laura Devlin. I'm with the public defender's office."

He took her hand with the feeling that something momentous had just happened; he didn't know what. "A pleasure," he

83

murmured, and couldn't understand why she was having this effect on him.

"And I'm Jim Duluth," a voice boomed from somewhere to his side. "Remember me?"

Embarrassed, he quickly dropped her hand and turned to his old friend. But he was aware that she was still staring at him when he said heartily, "How can I forget? How are you, Jim?"

"Never better," Jim said, and looked it. He was a big, barrel-chested man with brown, tightly curled hair and steely blue eyes. Many a defense attorney had been intimidated by that icy gaze, but as Douglas glanced briefly at the woman beside him, he doubted she was one of them.

As though that were her cue, she smiled and said, "It was nice meeting you, Senator. But I'm due in court, so if you'll excuse me . . . ?"

Suddenly he didn't want her to go. Incredulously he realized he was about to invite her to come with them, but he bit his tongue. "My pleasure," he forced himself to say, and had to drag his glance back as she walked away. Jim was looking at him in amusement, and he tried not to sound too defensive when he demanded, "What's with you?"

Laughing, Jim pushed him toward the elevator. Punching the button for the first floor, he rocked back and forth on his heels and said innocently, "I haven't seen you tumble like that since you fell for Denise Aznevor in college."

Had he been that transparent? "I don't even remember a Denise Aznevor!"

"Yeah, but I'll lay you odds you won't forget a Laura Devlin!"

Convincingly, he hoped, he made some indignant denial, and to his relief, Jim let it go. But he couldn't prevent a quick look back when they left the building. Feeling guilty at the thought, but unable to repress it, he couldn't help wondering if he'd ever see Laura Devlin again.

CHAPTER SEVEN

Dawn Van Doren slammed her apartment door shut, kicked off her high heels, glanced at her watch, and groaned. She had barely thirty minutes to get ready for what might be the most important night of her life, and after the day she'd had, it wasn't going to be nearly enough. Glancing into the mirror over the hall table, she grimaced. She looked like a hag.

It was all Barnaby's fault. As publisher *and* editor of the *Washington Eye*, he handed out assignments, and when she got to the office this morning, he'd given her a list of charity events he wanted her to cover today. The *Eye* was a gossip rag, and he hoped that one of the rich dames attending these events would let something slip. If that happened, she was supposed to be there to catch it. So, not one to argue, especially with a society editor byline dangling enticingly before her eyes, she'd grabbed the list and started running all over town. Far too late this afternoon, she raced back to the office with what little she'd gleaned, only to find the new computer system down. That meant she had to type everything out on a *typewriter*, for God's sake, and it had ruined the manicure she'd gotten especially for tonight. God, what a day.

Realizing that she'd just spent two minutes grousing in front of the mirror, she grabbed the heels she'd kicked off and started toward the bedroom. The living room archway caught her eye, and despite her hurry, she stopped. She could come home a million times to this place, she thought, and never stop feeling a thrill. She'd been promoted to permanent status at the *Eye* six months ago, and the first thing she'd done was to leave that cramped studio apartment behind. Smiling to herself, she padded across the wall-to-wall and looked out the living room window to the glimpse of park she had between the trees. This still wasn't fashionable Dupont Circle, but it would do—for now. She hadn't given up the idea of living at that oh-so-chichi area between Massachusetts and Connecticut Avenues, and if things kept going the way they had been, it wouldn't be long before she'd be moving again.

Hugging herself gleefully at the thought, she turned away from the window and went to get dressed. As she did, she thought about her date tonight and smiled again. Six months ago she wouldn't have dreamed a feature reporter for the *Post* would ask her out. Of course, she'd done everything but stand on her head to make him do it, but still . . .

Feeling pleased with herself, she went into the bedroom, shedding clothes as she went. Stripping off her slip, she stood in bra and panties in front of the mirror and gazed critically at her reflection. Not bad. All the equipment was there: small waist, long legs, good boobs. If she was objective, she could see why so many people thought she should be a model. She had the bones and the figure to try, but she'd long ago realized that looks didn't last forever. Power was what counted, and God knew, there was plenty of that in this city.

Making a face, she went to take a shower. She could always have been a call girl—or, excuse me, *escort*, to employ the euphemism in use here. She'd had plenty of opportunity for that, too, and if she'd been able to stomach the thought of banging it with all those old goats, she could be making ten, twenty, thirty times the money she was making now. She made another face. Who needed it? She'd never understood the big deal about sex, but she had long ago accepted the fact that it was another coin of the realm, something to be bartered with if you didn't have anything else. Shrugging, she stepped under the steaming water. If she didn't hurry, she was going to be late.

Lee was on time, but by some miracle, so was she. He rang the bell just as she was blotting her lipstick, and she took a quick second check of her appearance before she went to answer the door. After debating, she had finally decided on the tight white satin with all that beading laboriously done. It might be a tad extreme for one of Lenore Deering-Kirk's parties, but she had decided to take the chance. She'd heard the old lady had been a little wild herself in her day, and she wanted to make just enough of an impression. Besides, she'd spent months wrangling this date, and she wanted to leave Lee panting for more. She'd orchestrated everything so carefully, and as she pirouetted slowly before the mirror, she was satisfied.

Wondering what all the old dowagers she was going to meet

86

tonight would say if they knew she'd also made her gown—
knew, in fact, that she made all her clothes—she laughed to
herself as she left the bedroom and turned out the light. It was
amazing what you could do if you put your mind to it, and she
had vowed long before she'd left the godforsaken steel town
behind that even if she couldn't afford the best, she was still
damn sure going to look as if she could. Miraculously, her
mother had owned an ancient sewing machine, and she'd taught
herself to use it. She'd pored over every fashion magazine she
could find, hiding them from her father, who would have burned
them just to be mean, and when he wasn't home, she would turn
out designs that looked as though they'd come right from the
pages of those magazines. It was a talent she had, and if the
sewing machine was newer now, and the gowns she turned out
much more sophisticated, she doubted that anyone—even those
old biddies she would meet tonight—could tell she wasn't wearing a designer original.

Lee didn't seem able to tell the difference, either. His eyes
widened when she opened the door, and he let out a low whistle.
"Wow, you look great."

"Why, thank you, kind sir," she said, and gestured for him
to come in. "I'd hoped this would be suitable. After all, I've
never been invited to one of the famous Deering-Kirk parties
before."

"You haven't missed much," he said, his eyes still traveling
over her. Before she realized what he was going to do, he grabbed
her and pulled her toward him and gave her a moist, deep kiss.
She responded, but only because she wanted to cultivate him.
Later, of course, things would be different.

"Wow," he said again, his mouth still on hers. When one of
his hands wandered to her breast, she firmly pulled away.

"You're going to wrinkle my dress," she pouted.

His eyes gleamed. "There's not much to wrinkle, I'd say."

"Perhaps we should have a drink," she suggested. She hated
to be pawed, and only endured it because she needed something
from him.

Successfully diverted, he considered it, but then reluctantly
shook his head. "No, much as I want one to fortify myself, we'd
better get going. Lenore doesn't like people to be late, and it's
a long drive to Deer Hollow Farm. But I'll take a rain check, if
you know what I mean."

Dawn knew very well what he meant. "Fine with me," she

said lightly, and took her wrap from the chair where she'd left it before. "Shall we go?"

"Tonight?" he persisted.

Wondering how she had ever found this man remotely attractive, Dawn reminded herself that she shouldn't think about what he was, but who, and she said huskily, "Why not?"

His eyes gleamed again. "Then let's get going," he said, and put a hand on the curve of one buttock as she led the way out to the car.

At Deer Hollow Farm, things were in readiness. Lenore abhorred the informality of some Washington parties, where guests actually came in casual dress and sat about on the floor—the *floor*, she thought with a shudder; it was unbelievable. She never permitted that here, and as she inspected the buffet table in the long drawing room, she was satisfied. The linen was crisp and starched and blindingly white, and the silver and china and crystal gleamed. Baccarat and Waterford glistened on the sideboard, and matching decanters were placed inconspicuously under the bar. In memory of her beloved father, who had been known to tip more than his share or two, Lenore stocked everything from Amaretto to Zinfandel at Deer Hollow, but because it was well known that from the age of five she had been taught that champagne was the only drink for the civilized, it was the rare guest who asked for anything else.

Now, everything prepared and ready for the several dozen guests, the staff of twelve had retired to the kitchen to wait until they were needed. Everyone except Chester, of course, who was standing by, waiting to review the guest list with his mistress. This was a long-standing custom, for even though she really had no need to go over details, Lenore liked things to be firmly fixed in her mind. She hated to be surprised.

Aware that Chester was waiting, Lenore smoothed the gray silk taffeta she had chosen for tonight, touched her white hair, and took her customary seat in her winged chair. A cup of comfrey tea was by her hand, and she lifted the cup.

"All right, where were we?" she asked.

Chester had no need to consult his notes, either. "We were discussing Lee Walker and his date for the evening, Miss Dawn Van Doren," he said.

Lenore's bright little eyes gleamed. "Ah, yes, so we were. I'm so pleased that Lee took my little hint and invited her. I've been anxious to meet this enterprising young woman." She looked, birdlike, at him over the rim of the cup. "I plan to ask her how she likes her new job."

Chester allowed himself a smile. "Yes, of course—her advancement from . . . er . . . swinger . . . to reporter."

Lenore chuckled. "Stringer, Chester," she said, and cocked her head. "Although now that I think about it, maybe your description is better. From what you've told me, it seems Miss Van Doren is more than adept at looking out for her own interests."

"A useful quality at times, do you not agree?"

"I do indeed," Lenore said with another cackle. "I like a woman who knows where she's going."

"And how to get there."

"With our help, of course," she murmured, her eyes gleaming again. Then she dismissed Dawn with a wave of her hand, except to say, "So far my plans for Miss Van Doren are proceeding exactly as I envisioned. Let's move on to Douglas Rhodes."

"Oh, yes, the senator from Arizona. I understand he's decided to stand for reelection."

"Does that surprise you? Given his record so far, it would be more astonishing if he didn't."

Chester was impassive. "Yes, but I understand there is some family pressure."

"Yes," Lenore said thoughtfully. "Although I can't imagine why."

"The rumor is that his wife, Marcella, is not fond of Washington."

Lenore gave a brief, impatient shake of her head. "Impossible to believe, isn't it?"

"Indeed," Chester agreed. "Still, it seems that Mrs. Rhodes prefers Arizona to the capital."

Lenore shuddered. "My God. All that cactus. Is the woman out of her mind?"

Chester smiled. "There is also difficulty, I understand, with the only son."

"Yes," Lenore murmured. "What is his name?"

"Rob, I believe," Chester said. "It seems that the boy has decided to . . . to drop out, as they say."

Lenore rolled her eyes again. "Oh, yes. He wants to *find* himself—is that the term?"

"I believe so, yes."

"And has he done so yet?"

"No, it seems that he is still looking."

"I see," she said thoughtfully. "Well, this puts a different complexion on things, doesn't it? Do you think it might influence our Senator Rhodes to stand down?"

"It's difficult to say, madam. I understand that he dotes on his son."

"Yes, but he also seems to like it here, doesn't he?"

"So it seems. Hasn't he performed admirably at those budget hearings?"

Lenore gave him a calculating look. "Yes," she murmured. "You're absolutely right. I believe I'll have to do something about that."

Realizing the interview was over, Chester stood. An admiring expression on his face, he bowed slightly and said, "You have always been adept at dropping a word or two where it will do the most good."

Lenore smiled in acknowledgment of the compliment. "Yes," she agreed. "I have, haven't I?"

When he was gone, she calmly finished her tea. Then, her plans made, she went to greet the first of her guests. Later that night, Hugh Redmond was flattered to receive Lenore's undivided attention for a few moments. Everyone in Washington knew that a smile and a nod from Lenore Deering-Kirk, or a whisper in someone's ear, could enhance or impede a career, and when the senator was seen leaving her library wreathed in smiles, raised eyebrows went around. He received many phone calls over the next few weeks, many invitations to parties. And at Deer Hollow Farm, Lenore observed all this flurry of activity, and smiled.

CHAPTER EIGHT

"Penny for your thoughts," Janette said to Laura. It was April, and the two families had met at Point Magu for a picnic. Even with the beach right outside their door, Jack had insisted on driving up the coast for this get-together; probably, Laura thought, so she wouldn't be tempted to sneak back into the house and work.

"Shouldn't you be offering me a quarter?" she said, thinking as Janette came up to her how different they were. Older by three years, Janette was petite and blond, with very blue eyes and a motherly air that endeared her to nearly everyone she met. They were also worlds apart in temperament, but they had always been close—well, not *always*, she had to admit. There had been times growing up when they could have strangled each other. But they were friends now.

"Boy, am I out of condition," Janette said, fanning her flushed face. Then she added in typical Janette-style non sequitur, "You're right. I should have added for inflation."

"Maybe not. Even with that allowance, my thoughts aren't worth a whole lot today."

"Boy, you sound dour. What's wrong?"

"Oh, nothing," she said impatiently, and started off again. Now that everybody had eaten, she'd gone for a walk by herself, pretending to look for shells, but really just happy to be alone. Then she was ashamed of herself. She welcomed her sister's company; she was glad Janette had joined her.

They walked in silence for a few minutes, enjoying the day, the pounding of the surf, the sight of the huge rocks strewn here and there along the beach. Finally Janette couldn't stand it any longer. "So are you going to tell me, or what?" she exploded. "Come on, Laurie, what gives? You've been quiet the whole time we've been here. Didn't you want to come?"

"No, it's not that," Laura said, wondering how to explain.

She stared out to sea, and the breeze lifted her long, dark hair. Her face looked tanned . . . and tense.

"What is it, then?"

She shook her head. She knew Janette was going to press her until she confessed, but she really couldn't put her finger on what the problem was. "I'm sorry, Jan," she said with a faint smile. "I know what a sacrifice this is for you. I'm sure you'd rather be back there reading. But I don't know what's wrong. I'm not sure anything even is."

"Something is," Janette insisted. "You know what I think? I think you're feeling anxious about taking this time off, that's what. You're always so wrapped up in your work that you can't even enjoy just an afternoon of hanging out. How's that for an armchair analysis?"

"Pretty good, I guess," Laura admitted gloomily, and couldn't help thinking of all the cases she had on her desk, the people who were depending on her, in jail, or waiting for trial. She started walking again. "But I'm here, aren't I?"

Grunting, Janette caught up with her. "Are you? You're so preoccupied, you might as well have stayed home." She searched Laura's face. "Maybe you wish you had."

"Don't be silly," Laura muttered, but she couldn't help a quick glance back the way they'd come. Both their families were there, the children playing at building a sand castle, Janette's husband, Frank, starting a fire for the kids to roast marshmallows. Jack was tinkering with his diving gear, and her eyes lingered on him for a moment, her expression becoming sad and frustrated at the same time. They hadn't been getting along very well lately, and part of the reason was the problem they'd been having in bed. For the first time in their marriage, Jack was impotent, and although she assured him it was temporary, that these things happened to all married couples, that she wasn't worried about it, and that he shouldn't be, either, nothing she said did any good. It was getting to the point where they were both reluctant to initiate lovemaking, and she had decided the other night when the same thing happened again that if they didn't overcome this hurdle soon, she would suggest counseling. But not yet, she thought hurriedly; neither of them was ready for that.

Her eyes moved on to her mother, who was sitting on a sand chair, and her glance narrowed. She was only too painfully aware what her mother would say if she knew about the problem; she'd made her feelings clear on other issues. In Estelle's opinion, all her and Jack's difficulties would be solved if she'd quit work and stay home like a good wife should. Thinking things were never that easy, she gave a sigh.

Janette followed the direction of her glance. "Mom giving you a hard time?"

Trying not to sound bitter, she said, "Mom always gives me a hard time."

"She just doesn't understand how important your work is to you, Laurie."

"I'm beginning to wonder how important it is, period."

"You, having doubts?"

"You make it sound as though that's some surprise."

"Well, it is. You never have doubts about anything." Spying a big piece of driftwood a few feet ahead, Janette grabbed Laura's arm and dragged her over to it. "Here. Sit down, and let's talk about this. You don't sound like yourself at all."

"I don't feel like myself."

"So what's wrong?"

Laura hesitated. "Look, don't take this the wrong way, but I'm not sure you'd understand."

Janette paused. "Because I don't have the same drive to prove myself that you do, you mean?"

Annoyed with herself, she said, "That's not what I meant at all."

"Maybe I put it wrong, then. Look, I've always admired how ambitious you are. I wish I was."

"You do?"

"Now you sound surprised," Janette said with rare irritation. "What do you think? That I never wanted to go out and get a job? A real job, I mean, not just clerking part-time at Penney's in high school or something. I even used to dream about having a career—just like you."

Laura had never heard Janette talk like this; she hadn't had any idea. "But you never said anything."

"What was there to say? I just wasn't cut out to be a career woman, I guess. I never really had the . . . the drive. Not like you. You knew what you wanted from the time we were small," she said, and laughed. "Remember how you used to talk me into playing lawyer and judge, so that you could act out some imaginary case of yours? I'll never forget the time you defended the cat on an attack charge against that crow." She laughed

93

again. "Thank God the bird got away, or we would have had a murder trial!"

Laura had to smile, but the comment had brought Angelica Simone too sharply into her mind, and she sobered. She was due to start trying the case soon, and this one wasn't a game.

"I remember," she said. "But what does that have to do with this?"

"I was trying to prove my point. I always envied how even as a little girl, you knew what you wanted to be."

"Yes, and I got sidetracked."

"But you went and did it anyway, didn't you?"

"You could have done the same thing," Laura pointed out. "Except that the only thing I ever remember you saying you wanted to be was a housewife—" without realizing it, Laura glanced back at the family group, and her voice changed despite herself "—like Mother."

Janette turned to look, too, and as they watched, Estelle picked up the thermos and offered coffee to the men. Laura frowned when she saw Jack reach for the flask he'd slipped into a jacket pocket; as she watched him pour a measure into the coffee mug, she realized he'd been drinking a lot lately. *I should talk to him about it,* she told herself, and then thought that there were a lot of things they should talk about. Why didn't they? Was she the one who was reluctant, or was he? Maybe neither of them wanted to get into something they didn't care to finish, she thought, and turned abruptly away.

"Yes, like Mother," Janette said. Now she was the one who sounded bitter, and Laura glanced quickly at her sister's face. Janette saw her expression and tried to laugh it off. Shrugging, she said, "It's what was expected, wasn't it?"

Laura knew what she meant, and her mouth tightened. "Because of Dad, you mean."

This was a painful subject, one they both normally stayed away from. "Yes," Janette said. "Because of Dad."

Laura looked down at the sand. "Yes, well, you might admire what I've done, but don't forget that Dad never did. He died telling me what a fool I was."

"Maybe he was the fool," Janette said, her voice soft.

She was grateful for the support, but the pain was still too raw. "You couldn't tell him that."

"No. But he never understood that most of us just dream, Laurie, but a few—like you—go out and get things done. You should be proud of yourself for that. *I'm* proud of you," she finished, a little shakily.

On impulse, Laura gave her a hug. "I'm proud of you, too," she said, and then, meaning it, added, "What would I ever do without you?"

Embarrassed, Janette started to reply, but just then a series of indignant shrieks erupted from the campsite area. They both looked quickly in that direction, and saw Andrea, and Janette's youngest daughter, Amy, running toward them.

"Mama!" Andrea yelled, getting there first. "Did you see what Peter and Randy did?" Randy was Janette's oldest son, close to Peter's age. "They kicked the sand castle down, and you promised us we could watch the water come in and dissolve it! They ruined all that work! What are you going to do?"

Laura met her sister's glance over Andrea's head. Thinking the same thought, they sighed and started back. The defiant boys were standing nearby, and Laura had to wonder if there was something symbolic in this. She'd thought for a long time that if life was as simple now as it used to be when she was a child, she could manage better. But as she looked down at the castle and the main turret, which now had a fist imprint in it, she wondered if that was the answer after all. Maybe the problem was that there were always sand castles; it was just as you got older, they got bigger—and the potential for destruction was that much greater.

Depressed at the thought, she reached down and tried to re-form the turret. It leaned haphazardly to one side when she finished, but as she wiped her hands on her shorts, she knew it was the best she could do.

She was still thinking about that conversation with her sister the next morning on the way to work. She had meant it when she told Janette she didn't know what she'd do without her; sometimes it seemed as though her sister was the only one who cared about her problems, the only one who really understood. Remembering the short, acrid argument she'd had with Jack when they got home about his drinking, she decided that Janette was the only one she could talk to. Then she sighed. Jack had been in such a bear of a mood lately that she should have known he'd turn her concerned comment into a personal attack.

"Who says I'm drinking too much?" he'd asked angrily.

95

"I didn't say you were drinking too much, Jack," she'd replied. "All I said was—"

"Yeah, well, you handle things your way, and I'll handle 'em mine," he'd sneered, and slammed out of the bedroom to get himself a brandy. She'd known better than to pursue it when he was like this, but she was starting to feel desperate. What was wrong? Why wouldn't he talk to her? Why couldn't they communicate anymore?

A horn sounding loud behind her made her jump, and she looked quickly into the rearview mirror in time to see the driver make a rude gesture. Hastily she moved out of the way and he shot by, glaring at her as he did. She felt guilty, knowing he was right to be irritated. She hadn't been paying attention to her driving, and she forced herself to concentrate the rest of the way to work. She had a lot to do today, and she had to keep her wits about her.

Maurey was already there when she arrived, blearily rubbing sleep out of his eyes. He took one look at her face and said, "What's the matter with you? Get up on the wrong side of the bed this morning?"

Because she was already irritated, she started to snap at him, and bit back the words just in time. She wasn't mad at Maurey, but with herself. "Yes," she said instead. "I guess I did."

"Dare I ask about the weekend?"

Trying to put her annoyance out of her mind, she shrugged. "The weekend was okay. My family was over and we all went to the beach."

"You *live* at the beach."

She shook her head. "No, I meant Point Magu."

"Jeez, I haven't been there in years," Maurey said, sounding wistful. "When I was in high school, everybody used to go up there and drink."

"That sounds productive," she said dryly, staring to unpack her briefcase.

"Hey, we were kids; what did we know? Besides, I bet you did the same thing."

She thought about it. "No, with my crowd, it was Zuma."

"Zuma was for surfing."

"No, that was Malibu."

"Malibu was where all the rich kids went."

"No, that was Balboa."

They laughed together, and her good humor was restored until

96

she found a note she'd tucked into a desk drawer and had forgotten. It concerned Marion Higgins, her gun-carrying ex-con, and she frowned. That case was now long in the past, but she had never rid herself of bad feelings about it, and she sank down into her chair, holding the note. She looked over at Maurey, who was staring blankly down into his coffee cup, still trying to wake up.

"Maurey, do you remember Marion Higgins?"

He glanced up vaguely. "Marion Higgins. Was that the ex-con, illegal search, motion to suppress? What about him?"

Marveling at his memory, she said, "Well, I just found this old memo about him, and I still wonder if I did the right thing."

"Isn't it a little late for second thoughts?"

"Yes, I suppose so, but—"

Maurey sighed. "I thought we had discussed this—endlessly, I might add—when you were agonizing about filing that motion."

"We did discuss it," she said stubbornly. "But I thought at the time there was something wrong with the law. Maybe the point is that Marion *was* carrying a gun, whether it was found illegally or not."

Maurey looked scandalized at such heresy. "No, the point is that there was a Fourth Amendment violation—which you proved, I might add. The judge agreed with you, remember?"

She was still unconvinced. "I remember," she said reluctantly.

His expression firm, he started gathering his things. "Enough," he said. "You did your job, the judge did his. Case closed, and now I've got to get to court for one of mine. See you for lunch?"

She agreed absently, her mind on what he'd said. She supposed he was right, but she couldn't rid herself of the feeling that something was wrong here. Frowning, she crumpled up the memo and dropped it in the wastebasket.

You'd be better off nailing these creeps instead of trying to clean up the mess they leave behind.

Involuntarily the words Dale had spoken to her so many months ago flashed into her mind. He usually made some joke or comment about her joining the opposition every time they met, and at first she'd answered with a smart remark herself. Lately, though, it hadn't been such a joke, and there were times when she had wondered if she really wanted to take him up on the offer. She'd been so confused and unsure of herself lately; she couldn't rid herself of doubts.

Impatiently she shook her head. She was being ridiculous, imagining things because of her tense home situation. She didn't really want to change jobs; if she had doubts, all she had to do was think of Angelica Simone. She'd really put herself on the line for this one, and she'd had to do some fast talking to convince Tony of her strategy. It would have been foolish as well as negligent not to run a simultaneous plea, and so she had filed both not guilty and not guilty by reason of insanity. But as she'd told Tony, and anyone else who had asked, she was determined to get an acquittal. She was positive Angelica had acted in self-defense, and she intended to convince the jury of it. When Dale had heard, he'd raised that eyebrow of his and wished her luck.

And now, several weeks later, she wondered if she was going to need it. She really didn't know why these things happened to her, but as it had before, this case had become a minor cause célèbre, and from the morning the trial opened to the final climactic day when she rested her case, she was right in the middle of controversy. It started the first day of trial, when she was accosted in the lobby of the Criminal Courts Building by a group of unfriendly reporters.

She'd hardly entered the building before they were shoving a bristling bouquet of microphones in her face, and she had no choice but to stop as they pressed forward.

"You're the PD on the Angelica Simone case, aren't you?" someone asked aggressively.

"Yes, I—" she started to say, but before she could complete the sentence, someone else was piping up.

"How can you in conscience allow your client to plead not guilty?"

She started to turn to the second speaker, but a third was already demanding, "How can you justify that when the woman shot her lover in cold blood?"

She gave up. The final question was an annoying "Do you really expect the jury to believe that story?"

It was that tone of scorn that got to her. Like all attorneys in public service, she had quickly learned to deal with the press, and she knew the folly—and futility—of getting angry. But this was too much, and she looked over the heads of others to find the last speaker.

"What was that?" she asked.

"I'll be glad to repeat it if you like," a man said, stepping forward. She didn't recognize him, but that didn't mean anything. He was fat, balding, and wearing a belligerent expression that annoyed her even more. With an effort she maintained a neutral expression as he said, "I asked how you expect a jury to believe this woman's story. As I understand it, she took a gun, went next door, and shot the guy when he was asleep in bed."

Her eyes went very green, always a dangerous sign. "I don't expect the jury to believe a *story*, Mr. . . . " She paused, and he supplied his name. "Mr. Ruskin. I expect the jury to deliberate the facts and make their judgment accordingly."

That brought the others to life, but she had decided not to answer any more questions. Moving away, she was lucky enough to catch an elevator just as the doors opened, and she slipped inside, leaving the mob behind. She hadn't noticed, but Dale came in right behind her, and he murmured, "You handled *that* well."

She gave an impatient shake of her head, directed at the press. "Thanks," she said. "You could have come to the rescue."

"And have them accuse the prosecutor and the defense of collusion?"

She gave him a look. "Fat chance of that."

"You never know."

"That's true. After all, you might have come to tell me you'd decided to dismiss."

"Fat chance of *that*!"

Feeling better, she smiled. "Well, it was worth a try."

He cocked an eyebrow. "Always the optimist, aren't you? Well, you're going to need it to get through this trial."

"Don't count your chickens, Dale," she warned.

The elevator stopped on their floor, and as the doors opened and they exited, he gave a doleful shake of his head. "I always admire confidence—even if it is misplaced."

"Speak for yourself," she replied haughtily. "See you in court."

"I'll be there," he retorted.

"So will I," she said, and started off with more confidence than she suddenly felt. So much depended on this, she thought, and felt the cold wind of doubt. Then she was annoyed with herself. She might not be too sure about her personal life right now; she might even feel confused about her job. But one thing she didn't doubt was her legal ability. That resolved, she lifted her head and marched in to do battle.

A week later, she felt as though she'd been battling forever. She knew she looked it when she stopped in at the office one night to get her messages and Maurey was there. They hadn't seen much of each other since the Simone trial started, and he took one look at her and gave a low whistle.

"Wow. You look like the wrath of God."

"Thanks," she said dryly. "I needed that."

"I just meant you look like you're having a rough time of it."

"I am," she said, sitting tiredly in her desk chair. Suddenly she hadn't the energy to go through the message slips. "Dale isn't giving me an inch."

"You wouldn't want him to."

"No," she agreed with a sigh. "But still."

"I understand," he said sympathetically. "It's not as if this is the only case you have to worry about."

"That's true," she said, and made herself sit up to look through the slips of paper she held. Several requests for call-backs, a continuance . . . nothing urgent, thank God. Realizing that Maurey was still sitting there, she glanced across at him. "What?"

He shrugged. "Well, I was wondering how it was going."

She thought about it. "Okay, I guess."

"You guess?"

She smiled. "Well, better than okay, I guess."

He smiled, too. "I knew you could do it."

"I haven't done it yet," she warned.

Grabbing his briefcase, he stood. "You will. I've seen you in action, dearie. You're going to have that jury eating out of the palm of your hand."

She sat back, her expression wistful. "God, I hope so."

He grinned, hefting his heavy briefcase in preparation for going home. "Just tell me when we can break out the champagne."

"Don't worry," she said fervently. "If there's cause for celebration, you'll hear the rockets going off from here."

"We're counting on you, kiddo," he said, and left.

Her smile disappeared as soon as he was gone. Thinking that Angelica was counting on her, too, she went through the messages once more, then with a weary sigh, she followed him out the door.

The case dragged on. Angelica's pale face and the pleading in those wide blue eyes drove Laura over the next weeks, and one consolation was the knowledge that she was giving Dale as good as she got. But neither of them could be sure what the jury was thinking—not until the day she called the victim's wife to the stand. To Laura's surprise, Ilene Marino had appeared in the office one day and offered to testify for the defense. Knowing what a powerful psychological weapon this could be in her case, she had immediately taken a statement and then agreed to use her as a witness. Questioning had been proceeding according to plan when Ilene suddenly became agitated.

"Your Honor, I want to make a statement!" she cried. Her face turned red, and she burst into a storm of tears. "I want to say something!"

The judge leaned down. "Counselor?"

But Laura didn't have a chance to reply. Before her startled eyes, Ilene suddenly leaped to her feet. The next few minutes were chaos, for over the banging of the gavel, and Laura's own pleas to sit down, Ilene screamed, "No, I won't be quiet! I was quiet for too long! Angie wasn't the only woman my husband raped; he got one of my girls! He would have got Angie's daughter, too. He threatened it; he told me he would! He was a bad man, a mean man, and I'm glad Angie shot him. I wish to God I'd had the courage to do it myself!"

Pandemonium broke out, the judge instructing Laura to calm her witness, Laura herself trying to get Ilene to sit down. Angelica sat white-faced at the defense table, and Dale took one look at the jury box and put his head in his hands.

The papers the next day were filled with headlines, WIFE TESTIFIES GLAD HUSBAND WAS SLAIN; WISHED SHE'D DONE IT HERSELF being typical. Laura didn't have time to worry about it. Closing arguments soon followed, and then the case went to the jury. She went back to her office that final afternoon wondering if this was really the longest day of her life, or if it only felt like it. Tony met her in the hall, took one look at her face, and said, "Here."

She glanced down at the envelope he was holding out to her, then suspiciously back up to his face. "What's this?"

He gave her a winning smile. "An invitation to a fund-raiser for our man of the hour, Jim Duluth."

She shook her head, shoving the envelope back at him at the same time. "No, thanks. I don't want it."

He smiled again. "You don't seem to understand, Laura. I want you to take it."

"Oh, no, you don't—"

"Oh, yeah, I do," he said blithely. "Since you've been such a media hit lately, I decided you'd be the perfect representative for this office."

"But, Tony . . . !"

"You'll have a good time," he said unconcernedly, and waved as he went off down the hall.

Left standing there, she stared after him, trying to think what to do. Maurey came along, saw the envelope she was holding as though it were a snake that might bite, and said, "What's that?"

She made a face. "An invitation to a fund-raiser for Jim Duluth."

"Oh. That sounds like fun."

"You want to go?" she asked hopefully.

He held up his hands. "No, thanks. I've got other things to do."

"What things? You don't even know when it's going to be held."

"That's okay," he said, backing hastily away. "I'm sure I've got something planned."

"You're a real friend, you know, Maurey?" she called after him.

He'd already disappeared around the corner.

Sighing heavily, she went to her desk and sat down. Tossing the embossed invitation down in front of her, she was just thinking how much she hated things like this when she suddenly realized how long it had been since she and Jack had been to a fancy party. Her expression thoughtful, she picked up the envelope again and tapped it against her palm. Maybe this was just what they needed, she thought: a chance to dress up and go someplace nice. . . . She checked inside to see where the fund-raiser was being held, and raised an eyebrow when she saw the Beverly Hills Hotel.

That decided her. That hotel was a famous landmark, and she'd only been there once, long ago, for some event in college. It was obviously time to go again, she thought, and wondered how Jack would feel about making a night of it. They could take a room. It would cost the earth, but who cared? They hadn't done anything impulsive and fun like this in longer than she

102

could remember, and if it put things right between them again, it would be worth an evening of office politics. Besides, Jim Duluth wasn't a bad guy; she actually liked him at times.

She was smiling as she took her purse out to put the invitation away, but as she tucked the envelope inside, she suddenly thought of Douglas Rhodes. Her hand froze. Why had she remembered him now? She'd tried so hard to put that single meeting with him out of her mind, and until now, she thought she had succeeded. Then she was impatient with herself. Why shouldn't she think of him? It was an obvious connection: this fund-raiser for Jim Duluth, and recalling that brief introduction outside the DA's office that morning. It seemed so long ago now—counting back, she realized with surprise that it had been several months. So much had happened since that day, and when she found herself wondering if the senator would come to the fund-raiser for Jim, she hurriedly shoved the invitation into her purse, and put the purse back into the desk drawer. Slamming the drawer shut, she pulled some files toward her, intending to get to work. She had a lot to do while she waited for the verdict on Angelica Simone; she couldn't waste time just sitting here.

But for some maddening reason, she kept picturing Douglas Rhodes's face as she tried to read police reports on an upcoming case. Without wanting to, she recalled the way his dark hair grew back from a widow's peak, and how distinguishing silver was just starting to appear at his temples. She remembered the high cheekbones, the prominent nose. But most of all, she remembered his eyes. So dark as to appear almost black, they seemed to burn—

As her cheeks were burning right now. Muttering impatiently under her breath, she shifted position and wondered why she was remembering all this in such meticulous detail. She'd met him once. There was no reason to get all shiny-eyed and weak-kneed. That decided, she pulled the files more firmly toward her, switched on the desk light, and willed herself to concentrate. The afternoon dragged on.

The jury returned a verdict that night, just before closing time. When Laura heard they were in, she glanced at her watch in surprise. They'd only had the case three hours and twenty-seven minutes, and she was still trying to figure out whether this was a good or bad sign when Maurey came in.

"The jury's in," she said.

"I heard."

"What do you think?" she asked.

"Who knows?" he said. Like everyone else, he didn't want to second-guess, and he shrugged. Then he saw her expression and added, "Hey, not to worry. You did a great job."

She nodded, unconvinced now that the moment was at hand. When she stood, Maurey put an arm around her shoulders. "Come on, chin up. You did your best."

She gave him a glum look. "There's just one problem with that."

"What?"

"Dale did, too."

Grinning, he shoved her toward the elevator. She gave him a bleak smile before the doors closed, and the first person she saw when they opened again was Dale, standing outside the courtroom, in deep conference with a man she recognized as one of the investigators from the DA's office. Intending to squeeze by without interrupting, she started inside, but Dale reached out and stopped her as he gave last instructions to his investigator. Then he turned to her.

"However it goes, I just wanted you to know that you gave me a real run for the money," he said.

"You weren't so bad yourself," she replied.

"I did my best," he said, bowing.

She had to relieve the tension she felt. "You know what I've always liked about you, Dale? You're so modest."

"Why, thank you," he said, smoothing his hair with a grin. Then his expression sobered. "All joking aside," he said, "you were really good in there. You sure you don't want to come downstairs one floor? We could use you on our team, you know."

Going down one floor meant she would be moving her office to the prosecution side of the street. She couldn't think about that, not right now. "I'll let you know," she said, and went inside. Ten minutes later, as she was holding a sobbing Angelica Simone in her arms, Dale approached her again, but this time to offer his hand. When the jury had returned a not guilty on all counts, she'd hardly been able to believe it herself. She'd won, she thought blankly. And then, more important: Angelica had won. With the woman still weeping on her shoulder, she accepted Dale's handshake.

"Congratulations," he said, and gave a little shrug. He was too good at what he did, too experienced, to feel resentful. It was part of the job; win one, lose one. And Laura had a sneaking suspicion that he'd sympathized with Angelica anyway.

"Thanks," she said.

"You think about what I said, will you?"

Preoccupied with her weeping client, she promised vaguely she would. But as soon as Dale went off, she forgot about him and gently held Angelica away. During the course of the trial, the woman had told her more than she wanted to know about her sad home life, the abusive, alcoholic husband, the nights of fights and fear. She hadn't said anything until now because she knew Angelica had enough to handle with the trial, but she couldn't just walk away without offering a helping hand, and so she said quietly, "Angelica, I want to ask you something—"

To her embarrassment, the woman grabbed her hand and kissed it. "Anything!" she wept. "Anything! I know I'll never be able to thank you enough. I'm so grateful. If there is anything I can do, ever, I will!"

"I'm glad to hear you say that," Laura said, and gently made the other woman sit down. They were alone in the courtroom, but she spoke quietly nonetheless. Taking Angelica's hands, she said, "Have you thought about what's going to happen now?"

Angelica looked puzzled. "I will be able to leave jail—I won't have to go to prison!" Despite herself, she shuddered, and her eyes filled again. "I can't believe it even now! I was so afraid, so afraid. My children . . ."

Seizing the opportunity, Laura said, "That's what I wanted to talk to you about—your children."

The blue eyes flashed fear. "What about them? Has something happened? Did—"

"No, no, they're fine," Laura said quickly. "I was talking about their future—*your* future. Have you thought about that?" She hesitated. "Do you really want to go back and take up where you left off?"

"You mean with Leo," Angelica said faintly. Leo was her husband, and she shuddered again. Her voice was nearly a whisper. "No, I don't want to go back. But I don't know what to do. I have no money, no place to go—"

She was trembling, and Laura gripped her hands more tightly. "There is someplace," she said.

Angelica jerked her head up, her eyes filled with sudden hope. "Where?"

Laura told her about the women's shelter she'd found out

105

about; she gave her the name of the woman to call. "I've already spoken with her and told her about your situation," she said. "She's expecting to hear from you."

Angelica looked disbelieving. "You . . . did this . . . for me?" She seemed so incredulous that Laura felt a pang. "But . . . but how did you know? Were you so certain the jury would let me go?"

Laura thought of all the nights of tossing and turning, the uncertainty she'd felt, the endless poring over law books, the final marathon of polishing her summation to the jury. She could hear an echo of herself even now:

The district attorney has tried to paint a picture of a vengeful murderess, she'd said at one point, turning to look each juror individually in the eye, *a woman without conscience, who shot a man in cold blood while he was sleeping in bed. But I say to you, ladies and gentlemen, that Angelica Simone is not a cold-blooded murderess, but a desperate woman fighting for her life— and the future of her eleven-year-old daughter. Yes, she did go next door with a gun, yes, she did shoot Michael Marino. She has admitted this to you in the hope that you will understand that these were the acts of a woman who believed—who was CONVINCED—that she and her daughter were in peril.*

The echo faded. Angelica was gazing at her anxiously, and she said, "I never doubted your innocence, Angelica. My only concern was to make sure the jury didn't, either."

Her face working, Angelica glanced down at the card for the women's shelter Laura had pressed in her hands. "No one ever believed in me before," she whispered, and looked up again, her eyes swimming in tears. "I'll call them. . . ."

Angelica's sister, Rosalie, came forward then, and as the two women went away, wrapped in each other's arms, Laura felt the sting of tears. Hefting her heavy briefcase, she left the court-room and went home, feeling as though she were walking on air. She couldn't wait to share her victory with her family.

Her euphoria lasted even through the gridlock on the San Diego Freeway. For some reason traffic was blocked, and they all crept along until suddenly the way was clear again. She was going to be late anyway, but tonight it didn't matter. She had already decided she'd take everybody out to dinner, and to cap off her celebration, she stopped at the liquor store to buy cham-pagne. Even Peter and Andrea could share; this was a night to celebrate.

106

Her family had other ideas. Andrea was in tears when she got home, and Peter was upstairs, throwing things around as he hunted angrily for his soccer leg guards. Jack was nowhere to be seen, and her mother was tight-lipped in the kitchen, sitting in front of a cold cup of tea.

Laura walked in and was engulfed.

"Mama!" Andrea wailed as soon as she saw her. "Betsy asked me to stay over tonight, and Grandma won't let me! Can I go? Please, can I go?"

Peter came thumping down the stairs, one cleated shoe on, the other swinging by a broken lace. "Mom," he said impatiently, "where's the extra shoelaces? Didn't you get any at the store? I asked you last week, and we've got special practice in fifteen minutes!"

She still hadn't left the kitchen. She hadn't even had time to rid herself of the heavy briefcase, or set the champagne down. Glancing from one whining child to the angry other, she happened to meet her mother's eyes.

"Don't talk to me," Estelle sniffed. "And don't ever mention your sister's name to me ever again!"

Sighing, she put the bag containing the champagne on the counter. She hardly dared ask. "Where's Jack?"

"And that's another thing!" Peter erupted. "Dad said he'd be home in time to drive me to practice, but he hasn't shown up yet. What am I supposed to do—walk?"

She was just starting to reply sharply that if Peter could run around a soccer field for two hours, he could certainly walk to practice, but Andrea burst into tears.

"Mama, you never said I could go to Betsy's! She's waiting for me to call, and her mom said we could have pizza and everything! I'll just die if I can't go, I'll just die!"

The phone rang at that moment, adding to the din. Before Laura could answer it, or even decide if she wanted to, the back door burst open and Jack appeared. He was carrying an armful of plans and blueprints, some of which spilled from his hands. They scattered all over the kitchen floor, and he shouted, "Goddamn it to hell! First some cretin nearly rear-ends me on the freeway, and then I come home to find your car blocking the drive, Laura! Haven't we talked about that?"

The phone rang again. Estelle rose from the table. "If that's your sister," she said, "please tell her I have nothing to say to her."

"Mom, what about the shoelace?" Peter demanded.

"Mama, *can* I go? Please . . . pretty please!" Andrea whined.

"Enough!" Laura cried, her hands clenched. Everyone stopped and stared. She didn't care. Turning from one to the other, she said, "The shoelaces are in the top drawer of your dresser, Peter, which you would have known if you'd taken the trouble to look." And to Andrea: "Stop whining! You know you're not allowed to sleep over on a school night!" She bent and picked up one of the rolls of plans Jack had dropped and held it out. "I hope this is a plan to enlarge the driveway, since obviously you feel you have more right to park there than I do." And finally, to her mother, over the maddening ringing of the phone, "If that's Janette, you tell her yourself you don't want to talk to her. I've had it. I'm going upstairs to take a bath. I won a big case today, and I was going to take you all out to dinner tonight to celebrate, but I'm not in the mood any longer. Don't anyone follow me, because *I just want to be left alone!*"

And before anyone could respond, she turned and swept out of the kitchen. For once, not even a protest followed her; there was only startled silence behind. She didn't care. She didn't go back and apologize as she always did. She marched right up the stairs, into the bedroom, and slammed the door. Grimly she went into the bathroom, determined to pamper herself to spite them all. Turning the water on full force, she took out the precious bath salts Jack had given her for Christmas, and which she saved for very special occasions, and defiantly added a handful. For good measure, she added some more. Then she stripped off her clothes and stepped into the tub. Only when the scent of Pavlova drifted up to her did she begin to relax. She glanced at the closed bathroom door. Maybe she'd overreacted, she thought guiltily. It was so *quiet* down there.

Then she got angry all over again. Let them stew for a while, she thought, and sank down into the water up to her chin. The strain of the past few weeks caught up to her without her realizing it, and she was almost asleep when the knock came softly on the bathroom door.

"What?" she said grumpily. She still wasn't ready to forgive anyone.

"Laurie, can I come in?" Jack said tentatively from the other side of the door.

She thought about it. "What do you want?"

Instead of answering, he opened the door. She was just about to erupt again when she realized he was completely naked except for a tie around his neck and a towel over his arm. In one hand he held the chilled bottle of champagne she'd brought home; in the other, a tray of cheese and crackers with two glasses precariously balanced.

She didn't know whether to laugh or be amazed. "What's this?"

He bowed. "Room service."

Their eyes met, Laura's with a question she couldn't hide, Jack's with confidence. "Then in that case," she said, her voice suddenly husky with anticipation, "do come in. I only have one question."

"What's that?" He shut the door with a deft kick of his foot.

"What took you so long?"

He grinned a grin she hadn't seen in a long time. "I had to find the right outfit."

She looked at the burgeoning erection beneath the tie and smiled. "Well, you did," she said. "Would you care to join me?"

"I'd be delighted," he said, and stepped into the water with her.

CHAPTER NINE

By making a superhuman effort, Douglas Rhodes managed to leave his office on the Hill just after seven that night. His day was already twelve hours old, but the thought of having dinner with Sarah Ambrose revived him, and he ordered himself to unwind as he drove to the restaurant where they were to meet. Once he had time to take a breath, he glanced around and couldn't help thinking that there was no city in the country more beautiful than Washington in the spring. It was May, and the cherry trees were in bloom—the millions of white blossoms that attracted tourists like hummingbirds to nectar, and which imparted a certain fragrance to the air. As he arrived at the restaurant and got out of the car, he breathed in deeply, and was reminded suddenly that the scent competed with another heady perfume that was always present here: the scent of power.

Evidence of that was everywhere, encountered at high-level meetings, such as the one he'd attended today, or even by glimpses of powerful people, seen here and there. In one way or another, they were all affected by it; power was almost a tangible, a hum never far from the surface, symbolized by the monuments that had been erected in homage. From the Capitol building, arguably the most famous structure in the United States, to the Washington Monument, one of the most identifiable, it was all here, and if he was honest, he never tired of it.

Just as he never tired of Sarah. She was waiting for him when he entered the restaurant, a Scotch already in her hand. As he seated himself opposite her, she said in her husky voice, "I ordered for you—whiskey sour, if I remember right."

"You do," he said, and added, "Thanks for coming tonight. But I could have come for you, instead of meeting you here."

"And have someone report that we're wasting taxpayers' money by touring around town in a limo?" she said tartly. "No, thank you. I'm perfectly capable of driving myself."

He wouldn't dream of arguing with that. Although she was in her late sixties, no one ever realized it. She was still a handsome woman, tall and almost painfully slender, with iron-gray hair worn in a trademark smooth cap. Douglas knew from experience that those bright blue eyes never missed anything, and she attributed her energy and stamina to her cattle drover father. She had shuttled back and forth to Washington for six terms now, and despite her sex, was by far one of the most influential members of the Senate. But her official address was still the Circle A, a vast cattle ranch in northern Wyoming.

She'd told Douglas many a story about the ranch, including the fact that she still participated in roundup whenever she could, riding with the cowhands, bucking her horse out in the morning with the rest, lining up at the chuck wagon. Douglas didn't doubt it for a second; he'd always thought that she was one of Wyoming's most valuable resources, the kind of tough, savvy, smart frontier woman who helped build this country, and who, in many ways, was still helping to preserve it from her seat in the Senate. The number and importance of the bills she had authored or sponsored was legion; few could match her sterling record. She was known for taking up unpopular causes, and she had more than once single-handedly pushed through the passage of some legislation or other by the sheer force of her considerable personality. Because they'd become such firm friends, Douglas had asked her once why she hadn't consolidated her position into one of greater power.

"I prefer doing battle from the main lines, not the general's tent," she'd said with asperity, and then winked. "Besides, it's more fun that way."

The waiter came to take their orders, and when he'd gone, she leaned forward and said with her usual directness, "I know you didn't ask me to dinner to discuss Commerce's problems with the attempted takeover of that airline—or the ethics violations we've uncovered because of it. We talked about that today, after session. So what's the problem?"

Smiling, he said, "I really wish you wouldn't mince words, Sarah."

"Don't try to be disarming, Douglas," she retorted. "I know you, and you've been troubled about something for some time." She gave him a keen look. "Is it Rob again?"

He winced despite himself. He'd told her about his problems with his son some time ago; his pain had been so great when

111

Rob had quit college and gone off that he'd had to confide in someone, and Sarah had seemed the perfect person. Although she didn't have children of her own, he had sensed that she would somehow understand what he could hardly put into words, and his instincts had been right. She'd been sympathetic but not maudlin, and had told him it was too soon to worry. She'd heard that kids these days did this kind of thing all the time.

"But not my son!" he'd protested.

She'd looked him straight in the eye. "Why not?"

He had no answer to that, but for some reason he'd felt better. But that was then; this was now. "Yes, it's Rob," he said, his voice low. He shook his head, not realizing how bewildered he looked—or sounded. "I don't know, Sarah. I guess I'm like any other parent who believes he's done the best for his child and can't understand why it wasn't good enough."

Studying his face, she sat back. "He still hasn't come home."

He shook his head again. "Not since that last time when we . . . when we quarreled. And I—" He stopped. The admission was hard for him to make. "I don't know where he is."

"And Marcella does."

"I don't know." He'd been so furious when he found out about Marcella sending Rob money after he had cut him off that he had decreed they weren't going to discuss their son.

"And you haven't asked."

"I can't," he said painfully. "I told Marcella that I didn't want to hear Rob's name until he came to his senses. How can I beg for information now?"

Sarah uttered an exasperated sound. "Men!" she said. "I'll never understand you if I live to be a hundred and sixty! This is your *son* we're talking about, Douglas—not some stranger you don't care about! Is your pride too great to see that?"

His face burning because he knew she was right, he tried not to feel like a schoolboy brought to task when he said, "No, of course not. It's just that I don't understand his behavior at all! I mean, it's not as if he's ever wanted for anything—"

"Maybe that's not the problem."

He looked up quickly. "What do you mean?"

She shrugged. "Look, I'm no expert, but it seems to me that Rob isn't the only child of a prominent, successful man who feels overshadowed by his father. I'm sure thousands of other kids feel the same way."

"But why should he feel overshadowed?" Douglas asked,

bewildered. "I've never demanded that he imitate me. All I ever wanted was for him to be his own man!"

"Then let him be, Douglas," she said softly, her hand on his arm. "Let him work it out. He just needs time to realize that."

Douglas realized suddenly that their salads had been served. He hadn't touched his, and he pushed the plate away with distaste. Instantly the waiter appeared.

"Is something wrong, sir?"

His mind still on what Sarah had said, he glanced up. "No— just take this away."

Expressionless, the man removed the plate. Sarah gestured, and he took that one away, too. "Now that we've discussed Rob," she said, "you want to tell me what else is bothering you?"

He would never cease being surprised by her. "How did you know . . . ?" he started to say, and then saw her expression. Giving up the attempt, he sighed. "You're right. There was something else I wanted to talk to you about," he said, and took the plunge. "Sarah, have you ever felt ambivalent about your political career?"

To his surprise, she burst into laughter. "I feel that way every day I'm here!"

"No, I'm serious," he said. "Sometimes I wonder if I'm really making a difference here at all."

She was serious, too. "Oh, you're making a difference, all right, Douglas," she said softly. "Don't you doubt that."

He smiled briefly to acknowledge the compliment, but said, "I do doubt it, Sarah; that's the problem. Lately I wonder if I really want to do this the rest of my life."

"Aha," she said knowingly.

"What does—"

But the waiter appeared just then with their entrées, and he had to wait until they were served. Waving the man away as quickly as he could, he said, "Would you mind explaining that cryptic remark?"

She started on her own pepper steak. After examining the meat critically, and muttering, "What I'd give for some of my own beef!" she looked up with a sly smile. "Gladly. It means that you're getting the reelection jitters."

He stared back at her. Then he gave an impatient shrug. "That's ridiculous."

"Is it?"

"Yes, absolutely. That's not it at all."

"Then what?"

He thought about it. "I don't know. I'm not sure how to explain."

She speared another forkful of beef. "Try."

But he had tried, ever since the first doubts had appeared, right after that last terrible argument with Rob. Maybe his indecision had begun that night right there in the kitchen, when Rob had condemned the kind of man he was and the work he did. Maybe it had always been there, in the back of his mind. He didn't know, and at this point, it didn't seem to matter. The doubts were there and wouldn't go away. And as time went on, and his estrangement with his son continued—and the strain between him and Marcella increased because of it—he couldn't help wondering if his drive to succeed in politics was worth all the sacrifice it entailed. He'd begun to wonder if he shouldn't just give up his dream, go back to Arizona, and take up the reins of his company once more. He'd been happy there once; he could be again—couldn't he?

Realizing that Sarah was waiting for his answer, he said, "I'm sorry, Sarah. I don't even know what I'm trying to say. It's just that everything seems very complicated right now."

She nodded sagely. "As I said—the reelection jitters. I know— I've felt them myself. Especially as I get older."

"Yes, but you're still here," he said glumly. "You didn't have any doubts."

"About devoting my life to politics? No. I knew it was right from the time I first took my seat on the Cheyenne city council, and that was—" she shook her head "—more years ago than I care to count."

"I wish I could be as positive as you are," he said with a sigh. "But I'll have to make up my mind one way or the other soon. I've got another appointment with Malcolm Tanner later this month, when I'm in Los Angeles for that fund-raiser for a friend of mine. I told him I'd let him know by then."

"Malcolm Tanner, the kid who's made all the headlines?"

Douglas winced. The Los Angeles–based political consultant had been a key figure in a runoff between two state legislators, and even here, the headlines had been full of the bitter battle. Tanner had been right in the thick of things, and his candidate had won. When he'd heard, he'd almost been sorry. Tanner on the losing side might have made his own decision a little easier.

"I'd hardly call him a kid," he said, "but yes, that's the one."

"One thing I can say for him—he's good."

"Yes, he is," he agreed glumly.

His expression was easy to read. "But that doesn't make things easier, does it?"

He shook his head. "Unfortunately not."

"Ambition is a hard taskmaster, Douglas, as I'm sure you've found out—first in your real estate business, now in the Senate. It's difficult for all of us to balance things. Sometimes—" her expression became faraway "—sometimes you wonder if all the sacrifice is worth it."

He'd never heard her talk this way, and he looked at her in surprise. "You sound as though you have regrets."

She came back from wherever she had gone. "We all have regrets," she said softly. "One of mine was that I never took the time to have a family. But Lester and I were so busy then—"

Lester had been her husband, a man who had died in his prime. Douglas had often thought that he must have been quite a man, for Sarah had never married again. "Go on," he said quietly.

She took a deep breath, her face softened by the memories. "We wanted to have a family, but as I said, it wasn't the right time. We'd just bought the ranch, and then I started getting involved in politics. First at the local level, but then higher. I liked it, you see. . . ." She smiled sadly. "I guess I always wanted to be important, to make a difference, and soon I ran for the state legislature, leaving Lester and the ranch behind, except for the times I could get away. And then, after Les died . . . well, it was too late to do anything about a family."

Douglas knew the rest of the story, how together Sarah and Lester Ambrose had made the Circle A one of the biggest cattle ranches in Wyoming. He knew more from what Sarah hadn't said about it that the marriage had been loving and strong enough to survive the inevitable separation while Lester stayed behind at the ranch, and she fulfilled her duties in Cheyenne. But then, on the eve of their twelfth anniversary, when a big party had been planned, Les had been killed in a fall from a horse. He'd gone out that day and had been trying to rescue a calf that had been stranded down some ravine.

He'd been appalled when he'd first heard that part of the story; he'd tried to express his sympathy. But Sarah had just shaken

115

her head and told him that Lester had died the way he lived—doing something he loved. No one could ask for more than that, even the ones a loved one left behind. She had decided to run for Congress then, and had been in Washington ever since. A trusted manager handled the ranch in her absence, but she'd said she would never sell it. She came back to the Circle A for rest and sustenance, and memories of the husband who had left her too soon.

They sat there in silence for a moment, then Sarah stirred. Brisk again, she said, "But all that's in the past, Douglas, and I take responsibility for the choices I've made. We all have to, in the end." She paused, and looked at him shrewdly before she added, "You have to—and so does Rob."

He agreed with that, but the thought still made him glum. "You're right, I know," he said with a sigh. "But somehow, that doesn't make it any easier."

She was at her tart best again, refusing to let him feel sorry for himself. "Correct me if I'm wrong, but whoever said it was supposed to be easy raising a kid? You want them to be individuals, but then when they are, you take exception."

He had to defend himself. "Is it so wrong for me to want the best for my son?"

"Absolutely not," she said, and gave him that look again. "But maybe the problem is that you and Rob haven't agreed on just what that is."

He was about to answer that charge, but before he could, someone stopped by their table. He recognized her at once; who could forget? But for some reason, he couldn't remember her name.

"Senator Rhodes," the woman said. She had a throaty voice, and her amber eyes rested on him a moment longer than necessary before she turned to Sarah. "And Senator Ambrose. How nice to see you."

A change had come over Sarah; she had a chilly look in her eyes, and her tone was definitely frosty. "Miss Van Doren," she said.

The name jogged his memory, and Douglas wondered how he could have forgotten her name. They'd met before, at the airport, he recalled, and she worked for that insipid gossip rag, *The Washington Eye*. He glanced at Sarah. Now he knew the reason for the chilly reception. Sarah had been a target in that paper herself, and Douglas vaguely recalled something about raddled old ladies clinging to the remnants of power. Looking up at this beautiful young woman, with those strange-colored eyes and the thick, honey-colored hair, he wondered if she had written such tripe. It didn't seem possible, and yet he had been here long enough to know that things weren't always what they seemed—especially in this town.

But even if she had written the column, he could hardly ignore her. Seemingly oblivious to the reception from the other side of the table, she turned to give him a blinding smile, and he forced himself to recall his manners. Only half standing, he murmured, "Miss Van Doren . . ."

She seemed delighted at the recognition, increasing the wattage of that smile. Douglas was wondering why when she suddenly remembered she had an escort. Dragging the man forward, she said, "Senators, may I introduce Gunther Norse, the undersecretary to the German ambassador. Gunther, please meet Senator Sarah Ambrose and Senator Douglas Rhodes."

The young man practically clicked his heels together as he bowed. In a heavily accented voice, he acknowledged the introduction, and then stood stiffly aside. Dawn seemed amused—until she saw the steely look in Sarah's eyes.

"Well, don't let us interrupt your dinner," she said, and treated Douglas to another brilliant smile. "It was so nice seeing you again . . . Senators."

With a gesture to her escort, she moved away. Douglas found his glance following her, thinking despite himself how attractive she was. Then, dismissing her, he turned back to Sarah and saw with surprise that she was glaring at him.

"Well," she said. "You seem quite taken."

He raised his eyebrows. "She's a beautiful girl."

"With an instinct for the jugular."

"Yes, I know. I remember that piece about you in the *Eye*. But that still—"

She waved her hand dismissively. "I'd completely forgotten about that," she said. "If I paid attention to all the things that have been written about me over the years, I would have slunk out of Washington with my head down and my tail between my legs years ago."

He sometimes thought he'd never understand women. "Then what?"

"I can't explain it, but if I were you, I'd watch out for that one. As we say in Wyoming, she's a snake in high grass."

He couldn't imagine what danger Dawn Van Doren represented to him, but he wasn't about to say so. "She's probably one of that army of young women who came here to snag herself a rich politician," he said, and shrugged. He was tired of Dawn Van Doren, and he reached for the dessert menu.

But to his surprise, Sarah wasn't ready to abandon the subject. "Oh, she's here to snag herself something, all right," she said, her glance going over his shoulder and narrowing. "But it's not a rich politician—at least, not in the way you meant. She's out to make a name for herself, Douglas. I've seen her kind before."

Wondering why they were going on about this, he said, "So have I. So what?"

Sarah looked at him again. "I've heard rumors," she said.

Wishing they could just leave off, Douglas made himself ask, "What rumors? About what?"

"About her and Lenore Deering-Kirk. She's not just another of those girls who come here looking for a rich husband, Douglas. You mark my words."

He appreciated her concern, but he was really getting tired of the subject. Placing a hand over hers, he gave her fingers a brief squeeze and said, "Thanks for the warning, Sarah. But I assure you, it's lost on me."

"I hope so," she said darkly.

He'd had enough. Pointedly he said, "Are we going to have dessert?"

Sarah saw the annoyance he couldn't hide, and suddenly looked contrite. Now she was the one to place a hand on his arm. "I'm sorry, Douglas. I don't mean to insult you. It's just that I've seen so many promising political careers ruined because of sweet young things like her. I'd hate to see that happen to . . . to a friend."

He put down the dessert menu. "I'm grateful for your concern, Sarah, but I'm afraid it's misplaced. I'm a married man; I don't indulge in trivial affairs." Realizing what he'd said, he laughed. "I don't indulge in affairs, period. Besides, I've got too many other things on my mind. Remember, I still haven't decided about standing for reelection."

To his relief, she let it go. Finally dismissing Dawn, her face cleared and she sat back again. "Oh, you'll run, Douglas. You have to."

He was amused. "And why is that?"

It was her turn to finger the menu. "Because if you don't,"

she said, reading over the dessert list with an innocent expression, "when the time comes, we won't be able to nominate you for president."

He laughed until he saw her expression. "You're not serious!"

"I don't joke about things like that," she said calmly, and ordered a chocolate almond mousse.

---⎐---

CHAPTER TEN

Dawn made some excuse and asked Gunther to take her home early. She got rid of him as soon as she could manage to shove him out the door, then she went to the phone to call Lenore. She'd long ago memorized the number, and as she listened to the ringing at the other end, she thought how ironic life could be at times. She'd been furious all those months ago when Lee hadn't called to ask her for a date after that party at Deer Hollow Farm; she thought at first that she'd made a terrible mistake going to bed with him that first night. He had been her entrée to the power people, and the idea that she'd blown it had been enough to make her gnash her teeth. Then Lenore had called, and she forgot that Lee had ever lived.

She still remembered that occasion very well. She'd been in a bitch of a mood from a rotten day at work, and the phone had been ringing when she walked in the door. She hadn't wanted to answer it; all the way home she'd looked forward to running a long, hot bath and mixing about a gallon of martinis to take into the tub with her. She'd recently learned to drink martinis because she thought it was better for her image than beer, and to her surprise, she actually liked them better now.

So she hadn't wanted to talk to anyone, even the president himself. She didn't know why she'd picked up the phone, but she was glad she had; oh, was she glad!

"Miss Van Doren?" the voice said.

She hadn't recognized the voice right away, although she knew instantly she should place it. "Yes," she said cautiously.

"This is Lenore Deering-Kirk."

She almost died on the spot. Wondering why in the world Lenore Deering-Kirk was calling her, she pulled herself together. She'd only met the woman briefly at her party, and that had been several weeks before. Since they'd only exchanged a few words, she hadn't thought her hostess would remember her at all. Now the obvious fact that she had was exhilarating and frightening at the same time. What did one of the most recognizable and influential women in Washington want with her?

She was about to find out. Although she knew she had written one, she told herself again that she had definitely mailed a thank-you note after that party. Women like Lenore Deering-Kirk expected such things, and she had learned a lot these past few years. "Yes, of course," she said, managing at last to get herself in hand. "How nice to hear from you, Mrs. Deering-Kirk. This is a pleasant surprise."

"We have met before," the woman reminded her.

"Indeed we have," Dawn agreed. She was better now, under control. "Lee Walker escorted me to a party of yours several weeks ago. I was delighted. You have such a beautiful home."

"Why, thank you," Lenore said, as though it should be a surprise.

Dawn wasn't sure what to say next. She had no idea why a woman of Lenore's stature was calling, and she decided to take a chance. "But you obviously didn't call to hear me compliment your home, Mrs. Deering-Kirk. I know how valuable your time is, so what can I do for you?"

She hadn't realized she was holding her breath until her caller laughed. Relieved, she sank into the nearest chair. Her gamble that Lenore appreciated the direct approach had paid off.

"How refreshing," Lenore said. "Someone who gets right to the point. I like that, my dear. And since you ask, the reason I'm calling is to invite you to luncheon tomorrow."

She couldn't have been more surprised if Lenore had invited her to roll Easter eggs on the White House front lawn, but she said at once, "Why, how lovely. I'd be delighted, Mrs. Deering-Kirk."

"Excellent," Lenore said. "I'm so glad you're able to accept on such short notice. I do so enjoy luncheon, don't you? It's such a relaxing way of getting to know someone. I'll send a car for you at noon."

Dawn had seen that distinctive cream-colored Rolls-Royce; her eyes gleamed. But for form's sake, she had to protest. "Oh, that won't be necessary—"

"Nonsense," Lenore said. "Chester loves to drive, but I'm such a recluse that he hardly gets the chance anymore. He'll be delighted to collect you."

She was still dazed when they said good-bye. Lenore broke

the connection, but she just stood there staring at the instrument before replacing the receiver herself. Hoping she hadn't dreamed that conversation, she decided to splurge on a new outfit. Nothing in her crowded closet seemed right; she had the feeling that this was going to be the most important luncheon of her life.

Chester came the next day as promised, pulling smoothly up to the front of her apartment building in that gorgeous cream-colored car. He emerged correctly in uniform and held the door, and as she sank into butter-smooth leather seats and saw the console with the chilled champagne in front of her, she was sure she had died and gone to heaven. At that moment, Gloria Mae Wannamaker seemed to have been banished forever.

The drive to Deer Hollow took an hour, far too little time. She luxuriated in the backseat, feeling like a princess as they rolled through the countryside. She was so elated at her good fortune that she wanted to drink the entire bottle of champagne, and only stopped herself by imagining what her hostess would think if she arrived tipsy. Someday, she thought with a sigh, someday . . .

Someone picked up the phone at the other end, interrupting her thoughts. "Deer Hollow Farm."

Dawn recognized the voice as Chester's, and as she kicked off the heels she had worn to dinner with Gunther, she said, "This is Dawn, Chester. I'd like to speak to Mrs. Deering-Kirk."

"Of course," he said in those measured tones that sometimes drove her crazy. "If you will hold a moment, I'll see if she is able to speak with you."

"Please do," she said, rolling her eyes. They'd been through this every time she called; it was an irritating ritual she had never managed to find a way around. Doomed to wait until Chester asked Lenore her pleasure, she occupied herself by thinking of the house. She'd been there several times since that first unsettling luncheon with Lenore, but she never tired of seeing that beautiful place—or discovering new things about it. She'd taken a course in architectural styles and periods so she wouldn't act completely ignorant, but even after all these months, she knew she could live to be a hundred and never be comfortable with what people like Lenore took for granted. There was a genuine Aubusson on the drawing room floor, for example, and silk draperies lining the paneled walls. The linen was Irish cutwork, and she thought she recognized a Lannier sideboard. She'd been so nervous the day she first went there for lunch that her knees shook, and for a horrifying moment she wasn't sure as she paused on the drawing room threshold that she could walk across that floor to greet Lenore.

Then an image of the girl she'd been flashed through her mind, and she took courage. She'd come a long way from Gloria Mae Wannamaker; that persona had been abandoned, along with a dreary life and a featureless future. In her place was someone completely different, someone with a new identity, a whole new outlook, and vastly improved prospects. In that moment, she knew instinctively that all she had to do to make that bright new future happen was to get through the next hour without a slip. Gloria Mae Wannamaker couldn't do it, but Dawn Van Doren could.

Then Chester announced her, and it was too late for retreat. Lenore had been facing the window, but when the woman turned that appraising glance her way, Dawn knew the time had come. Taking a deep breath, she smiled and said, "Good afternoon, Mrs. Deering-Kirk. How nice of you to invite me."

"Good afternoon, Miss Van Doren," Lenore said. "How nice of you to come."

Thinking uneasily that Lenore was even more formidable than she remembered, she crossed the acres of space between the door and the sofa her hostess indicated. There was a different Aubusson in here; the soft shadings in cream and rose and blue made her feel as though she'd stepped into a garden. She was glad now she'd sprung for a new outfit; the linen suit with the honey-colored heavy silk blouse seemed just right. She was wearing her trademark high heels, but her one departure from tradition was an interesting free-form design pin that looked like a streak of lightning in gold.

"What a lovely suit," Lenore said.

"Thank you," Dawn replied. "I was just thinking the same thing about your dress."

Lenore was wearing a blooming pink chiffon that nauseated her, but since the woman was richer than Croesus, who was she to judge?

"Thank you," Lenore said, and gestured toward a table that had been set up near the French doors at the end of the room. "Shall we?"

She hadn't had time to notice the table yet—a good thing, since when she saw it, she was tempted to laugh at the coyness

123

of it all. Like Lenore's dress, it seemed to be made of pink and white crystal, and as she took the place her hostess indicated, she saw that not only were the shell-shaped candy dishes made of mother-of-pearl, the place mats were, too—as well as the handles on the silver. Pink porcelain plates carried the shell motif, and in the center of the table a single water lily floated in the thinnest of pink crystal bowls. The bowl was a perfect match for the tall, thin-stemmed pink glasses for the white wine, and it was all so much that Dawn had to struggle for something to say. She finally managed, "What a beautiful table."

Lenore gave it a dissatisfied glance. "You think so? This service belonged to my mother, and I've always thought it a bit overdone myself."

Dawn didn't know how to respond to that, so she murmured something and took her place with relief. Lenore sat opposite and removed the elaborately folded pink napkin from the wineglass. As she spread it across her lap, she said, "I know you're wondering why I invited you here today, so I'll get right to the point. The reason I wanted to see you is because I think we have a mutual interest."

Feeling as though she'd just stepped into a pink and white minefield, Dawn held her composure. "Oh? And what is that?"

"Power," Lenore said, and lifted the small silver bell by her hand. She gave it a quick jerk, summoning two servants who brought lunch.

"Miss Van Doren?"

Chester's voice broke into her reverie, and she banished the memory of that tense meal. A lot had happened since then, and she said, "I'm still here, Chester."

"I'm afraid Mrs. Deering-Kirk can't come to the phone at the moment. May I take a message, or will you call back?"

Dawn knew how futile it was to try and play this game; she'd been bested too many times. Lenore could hold out much longer than she could, and so she said resignedly, "No, I'll give you a message. Just tell her that when I was out to dinner tonight, I happened to run into Senators Ambrose and Rhodes."

"Yes, miss. Is that all?"

"No," Dawn said with a satisfied expression. She knew this was going to bug Lenore, and so she drew it out. "Tell her also that the word 'president' was being bandied about. And I don't mean the incumbent. You got that?"

124

He was as imperturbable as ever. "Indeed I do," he said. "I'll relay the message exactly as you said."

"You do that, Chester," she said, and hung up.

The word seemed to be the operative topic that night, both in Washington and at Deer Hollow Farm. Even though it was May, a fire crackled brightly in the magnificent Adam fireplace in one of the sitting rooms there, and Lenore was seated right beside it, in one of her favorite wing chairs. Glimpsing the sheen of perspiration on the face of her guest, she was immediately irritated. If the man was so damned hot, he should either say so or take another chair.

"Are you too warm, Hugh?" she said abruptly.

Hugh Redmond was a big, solid, stolid man in his late fifties, who very much resembled Gerald Ford. He'd been pleased with the comparison when someone from Lenore's inner circle mentioned it; when he found himself, amazingly, included with that group, he'd taken up a pipe. He was sure that the likeness to the former president was that much greater when he had a stem clamped between his teeth. He wasn't smoking tonight. Wondering why Lenore had to have it so damned *hot* in here, he smiled at his hostess and shook his head. "No, of course not. I'm just fine."

Lenore was feeling testy. "Well, you look a little hot to me, Hugh."

"Not at all," he insisted, wary of offending her. "In fact, I was just thinking how cozy it is in here."

She was diverted, glancing around in satisfaction. "It is, isn't it?"

Privately he thought this was one of the least coziest rooms he'd ever been in. Because he didn't know why she had summoned—there was no other word for it, he thought uncomfortably—him here, the brown felt-lined walls seemed ready to close in on him. He knew it was his imagination, but all those gilt-framed portraits of Deerings and Kirks appeared to frown, and he hastily reached for the coffee cup on the table in front of him. Lenore still hadn't told him what she wanted, and he'd had to cancel a black-tie affair tonight to come to Deer Hollow at the last minute. His wife, Nora, already dressed in a new Givenchy gown he'd paid a fortune for, had been furious.

"But why do you have to go out there *now*?" she'd demanded. They had practically been ready to walk out the door.

He was already getting out of his tux and into a suit. Still unnerved from that unexpected phone call, he'd snapped back. "Because when Lenore Deering-Kirk calls, everybody listens!"

Nora had been too upset to listen to him. She'd been looking forward to this party for the French ambassador for weeks; she'd even taken private lessons in French so she could say a few words to him in his own language. "I still don't understand why you couldn't have said you had another engagement!" she pouted. "For God's sake, Hugh, we're due there in twenty minutes!"

Feeling his blood pressure rise, he'd made an effort to control himself. They'd been married nearly twenty-five years, and sometimes, for the life of him, he couldn't think why.

"If you have to ask that, Nora, after being in Washington all this time, then you wouldn't understand the answer anyway," he said. "Give my apologies to our hosts, but this can't be helped."

And now he'd been here more than twenty minutes, and apart from the obligatory small talk, Lenore still hadn't told him why she wanted to see him. Wishing she had offered him something stronger than coffee, he took a sip.

Lenore put down her own cup of tea and without preamble said, "Hugh, have you ever thought about running for the presidency?"

He didn't know what he had expected her to say, but it wasn't that. For a wild moment he nearly choked with nervous laughter, but he managed to say with a big grin, "Who hasn't?"

"I'm serious, Hugh," Lenore rebuked, and remembered that Cal had tried to warn her.

"He's not ready yet, Lenore," the Speaker of the House had told her when she'd had her brilliant idea and called to tell him about it. To her disappointment, Hugh's name was already being discussed.

"I suppose you'd prefer someone like Douglas Rhodes," she'd said.

"He does have potential," Cal remarked calmly.

She was being sarcastic; already she'd heard—and seen—that Senator Rhodes would be difficult to manage. Were they actually considering him? "So does Hugh Redmond," she said.

"Have you been listening to gossip again?" Cal teased. "I appreciate your input, my dear, but why don't you leave the selection to us?"

She hated it when he said things like that to her. They'd been friends for nearly fifty years, and at times like this she wondered why. "Because you men don't know everything!" she'd replied tartly. "I'm going to invite him here to find out for myself."

"Another of your famous interviews?" he said, amused.

She wasn't laughing. "If you're going to be so nasty, I'm going to hang up right now."

He gave in, as he usually did. "All right, all right. Check him out if you like. I admit, he is a possibility."

"I knew it!"

So she'd been right. Satisfied, she realized that Hugh was staring at her, and she said impatiently, "Well?"

"I'm very flattered, Lenore," he said hastily, and then, looking as though he'd rather not, added, "But isn't this conversation a little premature? Our incumbent has only been in office two years."

Cal's dry laugh echoed at the back of her mind, and she irritably shifted position. Damn Caleb Young, she thought: she'd show him! "I'm aware of that. But we all know I helped get the man elected, don't forget!"

Hugh tactfully didn't reply to that. Lenore was powerful in her own little circle, to be sure; she was respected, and in some cases feared for the damage she could do. But she wasn't *that* influential—he didn't think. Even so, it paid to be cautious, and he said warily, "What are you suggesting?"

"I haven't suggested anything yet," she snapped. "Let's not get ahead of ourselves, please."

Feeling confused, he sat back. "In that case—"

Wondering if she'd been wrong about this man, she raised a hand. "Let's confine ourselves to hypothetical situations, all right? Suppose I did call you here tonight to discuss the nomination. What would you say?"

It was obvious he didn't know what to say. "I'd . . . I'd be honored, of course," he said hesitantly, and then added with a smile, "In any situation, hypothetical or not."

She glared at him. He was not taking this seriously, and it was all Cal's fault. Sternly she said, "You might be amused, Hugh, but believe me, the Speaker takes such things very seriously."

At this oblique reference to her very well-known friendship with the powerful Caleb Young, Hugh sobered. "The Speaker has said something—?"

Satisfied she had his attention now, she leaned back. But even she didn't dare speak for Cal, so she merely said, "Your name has come up, yes."

He couldn't hide his rising excitement. "I'm honored," he said.

Thinking he should be, she replied, "There is a problem."

He frowned. "Problem?"

She gave him a look of exaggerated patience. "You're not known, Hugh," she said. "Illinois might have sent you to Washington for three terms now, but even you have to admit you're a stranger outside your own state. And in many places there, as well. You just haven't . . . distinguished . . . yourself."

"I can change that."

"How?"

He couldn't give her specifics, but he'd been around long enough to know there were ways. He also knew there was a reason for her support—and a price for it. But what a prize! he thought, and said, "And in return . . . ?"

She gave a satisfied smile. "Oh, I'll think of something . . . when the time is right. Good night, Hugh. This has been a pleasant, and productive, chat."

Hoping it had been, he left the room. Lenore forgot him before the door shut. Now that that was settled, she could think about Dawn's earlier phone call and the message she'd left. If the girl's information was correct, she was even more glad than ever that she and Hugh had had their little chat. But there were still problems ahead, and no one knew that better than she.

"Hellfire and blast," she muttered, using one of her father's favorite sayings. Tapping her fingers on the arm of the chair, she pondered the real reason Douglas Rhodes and Sarah Ambrose had dinner together tonight. She knew, because she made it her business to know, that her old enemy Sarah had taken the junior senator under her wing; it was rumored that Sarah regarded him almost as the son she'd never had. Tongues had wagged gleefully over that one, but Lenore hadn't dismissed it lightly. Sarah Ambrose had been here a long time; her power base was secure. Worse, she was known to be incorruptible. There wouldn't be any secret midnight visits with Sarah, no secret negotiations, no private promises—oh, no, not with the good witch of the West. If Sarah planned to support Douglas Rhodes, it would make things difficult.

Well, so be it. She had always enjoyed a challenge, and she never avoided an opportunity to put a spoke in that woman's wheel. Now, with Hugh, she had a chance to do just that. Gleefully she rubbed her little hands together. She'd call Cal tomorrow and ask him to lunch. He couldn't refuse her, and they had much to discuss.

CHAPTER ELEVEN

If Laura had doubted the dress would be a success, Jack's face as she came down the stairs told her all she needed to know. She was pleased even before Andrea rushed up, crying, "Oh, you look beautiful, Mama! Doesn't she, Daddy?"

"She does indeed, pumpkin," Jack said, looking at Laura. "Where did you get that dress?"

"I picked it out, Daddy," Andrea said proudly.

"Is that so?"

Nodding happily, Andrea reverently touched Laura's long, emerald-green satin skirt with the slit nearly to the thigh and looked up at her mother. "I told you he'd like it."

"And you were right," Laura said, bending to give Andrea a quick hug. "You've got great taste."

"And you've got—" Jack started to say, but she silenced him with a warning look. He subsided with a grin, and she realized then that he'd had a few. *Don't get into it,* she told herself, and turned to make one last check in the mirror. She'd put her hair up for the occasion, and the smooth chignon banished the harried, harassed public defender for the night. In her place was a completely different woman—or so she thought, until she caught the whiff of alcohol on Jack's breath when he came up behind her to nuzzle her neck. Fortunately Peter distracted her by coming in just then from the kitchen. He was carrying one of his favorite peanut butter and jelly sandwiches, and when he saw them he grimaced. "Yuck."

Jack turned. "Is that a comment on the way your mother looks?"

"Nah, she looks okay," Peter said around a mouthful of bread. "It's just that all this romantic stuff is the pits."

"I'll bet you won't say that in another five years," Jack commented, winking at Laura. Peter would be seventeen then, almost a man.

"Yuck," Peter said again, dismissing the possibility as remote. "Can I stay up to watch *Nightmare on Elm Street*?"

Laura had been watching Jack, trying to remind herself that things had been better between them lately. But at Peter's question, she glanced at him. She'd heard about this movie. But sometimes she felt she was too hard on the kids, so she said cautiously, "What time does it end?"

Peter didn't want to say. "About midnight, I guess," he mumbled.

She glanced at Jack, who shrugged. "All right," she said, deciding one time couldn't hurt. "As a special treat."

"All *right*!" Peter exclaimed, and took off, shouting for his sister. "Hey, Andy, I get to stay up—"

His voice faded as he dashed upstairs, and Laura sighed. "Be prepared," she said, and was vindicated a few seconds later by Andrea's wailing cry, "Mama! Peter says—"

"Would you handle that?" she said quickly to Jack. "I've got to say good-bye to Mother."

"Coward," Jack grinned, and turned toward the stairs as their daughter came thundering down.

Leaving them to it, Laura headed toward the bedroom, where Estelle had vanished earlier to watch the nighttime soaps. Knocking on the door, she said, "Mom? Jack and I are going to leave now, okay?"

"If you have to," said a small voice from the other side of the door.

Recognizing that tone, she sighed. Wondering if she could just walk away, she made herself say, "Is something wrong?"

"No, it's all right."

She could tell it wasn't. Resigning herself, she said, "Mom, can I come in?"

"Go ahead. It's all right."

Estelle was sitting on the edge of the bed, the television on, but the sound turned down. She looked so forlorn that Laura sat beside her. "What is it?"

Estelle wouldn't look at her. "Nothing. It's not important. You look wonderful, darling. You and Jack go and have a good time. Don't worry about me."

She knew *that* tone, too. Closing her eyes, she sought strength. *Why now?* she wondered, and said, "I can't leave with you just sitting here. Now, please, tell me."

"There's nothing to tell," Estelle said in that little voice.

131

"Your sister just doesn't want me to visit her this weekend, that's all."

Surprised, she said, "I'm sure that's not true! You know Janette likes you to visit. You always have a good time."

Estelle sniffed. "Then why did she call to tell me that this is the weekend of Brad's company party at Great America, and that they have to go? She said she forgot, but I'm sure that's just an excuse because she doesn't want me to visit."

Laura was silent, wondering what had brought this on. Deciding that maybe Estelle felt a little left out, she said, "I'm sure you misunderstood, Mom. You know Janette can't remember her own name at times. If she doesn't look at the calendar, she'd forget her own birthday."

"That's no excuse."

This wasn't getting her anywhere. Knowing Jack would be wondering what had happened to her, she said, "I'll call her. I'm sure there's been some mistake. I know she would have invited you."

"Well, she did," Estelle admitted, and added quickly, "But only because she had to. I said I couldn't intrude."

There was no dealing with her mother in this mood. Resigned to straightening it all out tomorrow, she said, "I'm sure Janette would love to have you, but if you don't want to go, we'll do something here. Maybe we three—Andrea and you and I—can go shopping, or something. Andy would love it."

"Are you sure that wouldn't be too much trouble?"

"Of course not," she said, resolutely putting aside the thought of all the work she'd brought home from the office that she'd planned to do tomorrow. "You think about it. But I really have to leave now, or Jack's going to have a fit. Okay?"

Estelle took her hand. "You're a good daughter, Laura," she said, smiling faintly.

"Thanks, Mom," she said, bending to give Estelle a quick kiss. "Now, I really have to get going. You sure you're going to be all right?"

"I'll be just fine."

"Good," she said, relieved, and went out to the car, where Jack was waiting. He gave her an inquiring look as she got inside, but she shook her head. "Don't ask."

"I wouldn't dream of it."

She sat back as they started off, trying not to think of all the problems she'd left behind, but of how much she was looking

132

forward to this evening. She and Jack hadn't been out in longer than she could remember, and she glanced covertly at him, trying to gauge how much he'd had to drink. She suspected that he'd had another while he was waiting, and she debated about discussing just how much he was putting away lately. But she didn't want to get into another fight, not tonight; they'd already had too many fruitless arguments about it as it was. He claimed to be under pressure at work, and it was true that he was busier than he'd ever been. Now, as often as not, she was home before he was, and often she couldn't get hold of him at the office because he claimed to be out in the field so much. Telling herself he'd taper off when his work settled down, she decided just to wait it out—and hope that he'd had his limit for tonight.

Reminded of something she'd been wanting to talk to him about, she said, "Jack, I've been thinking about something—"

"So have I," he said, leering at her. "Why don't we take a room at the hotel tonight so we don't have to drive all the way back to the beach?"

She was surprised into forgetting what she'd been about to say. "I was going to suggest that, too. Then I remembered what rooms go for at the Beverly Hills, and I thought it would be too expensive."

"Who cares?" he said grandly. "Just think of all that history!"

This was the Jack she loved. Eagerly she fell into the game. "You mean all those stories about the movie stars!"

"Like the one when Tallulah Bankhead fell into the pool, fully dressed—"

"And was rescued by Johnny Weissmuller—"

"Tarzan," he reminded her. "Get it right."

She laughed, remembering this as a game they had played when they were first married. Because they had so little money, they'd entertained each other with trivia. "Okay," she said, "I've got one for you. What famous couple used to sneak into this hotel to meet secretly?"

"That's easy," he scoffed. "Gable and Lombard. But who was the comedian who always ordered a table for two? And tell me why."

She was stumped at that one. "I don't know—who?"

"W. C. Fields," Jack said, and grinned. "For himself and a man-eating plant."

"You're making that up!"

"I swear to God," he said, and added, "So what do you say?"

"I give up. You always were best at remembering these stories."

"No, I mean about spending the night," he said, turning in to the driveway of the famous pink stucco hotel. "We don't have to get a suite. We can stay in an ordinary room."

Glancing at all the tropical grandeur that surrounded them, she said, "I don't think any of these rooms are ordinary."

"I hope not," he said, and leered at her again.

She didn't have a chance to answer, for the valet leaped to attention as they came to the entrance and whipped open the door. A gloved hand helped her from the car, and after Jack had handed over the keys, he took her arm and murmured, "Just keep walking. Maybe they'll think the Volvo is a Cadillac in disguise."

"Or that we're movie stars researching a role," she suggested.

"For what movie—*Oliver Twist*?"

Surrounded by all this wealth and glamour, not to mention the Mercedeses and Jaguars lined up ahead and behind them, Laura had to laugh. They went inside without looking back.

"What were you going to ask me before?" Jack asked as they started toward the ballroom where the fund-raiser was being held.

She'd almost forgotten. "Oh, well, I was thinking that since your birthday is coming up, you might like a car phone."

He stopped so suddenly that she was nearly thrown off balance. "A car phone! What in the world for?"

She couldn't understand why he looked so upset. "Well, since you're out of the office so much lately, I thought—"

"Are you trying to tell me you want to keep track of me?"

She looked at him in surprise. "Don't be silly. I just thought—"

"Look, Laura, I don't need a car phone. If I did, I'd get one myself."

"Okay," she said, beginning to get irritated herself. "It was just a suggestion, all right? Why are you acting like this?"

"I'm not acting any way! I don't question where you are at work, so don't question me!"

She couldn't believe this. "I wasn't *questioning* you, Jack. I told you that it was just an idea. In fact, if you must know, it wasn't even my idea. Andrea saw a display of car phones when we were shopping the other day, and said how much fun it would be to talk to her daddy from the car.''

She was so annoyed that she pushed past him and headed alone toward the ballroom at the end of the corridor. He caught up within a few strides and took her elbow. She had to face him or jerk her arm away.

"I'm sorry, Laurie," he said. "I don't know why I snapped at you like that. I guess you just surprised me, that's all. Can we forget it?"

Still angry, she was about to snap back a reply. Then she remembered he'd already had a few and decided not to push it. "All right," she said stiffly, and swept ahead of him into the ballroom.

The first person she saw was Dale—thank God. He appeared out of a swirling mass of humanity and handed her a compliment that went a long way toward lifting her mood.

"Jeez, you look beautiful!"

"You don't look so bad yourself," she said, and couldn't help thinking that in black tie, he looked like a blond movie star. Realizing Jack was by her elbow, she said, "Jack, you remember Dale Davidson—"

Jack had obviously decided to be as disagreeable as possible. "Yes, we've met," he said rudely, and glanced around. "Where's the bar? I'd like a drink."

Unruffled, Dale gestured. "It's over there."

Giving a brief nod, Jack disappeared into the crowd, and without realizing it, Laura sighed.

"Trouble in paradise?" Dale asked.

"Not exactly," she said. She didn't want to talk about it.

A waiter passed by with a tray of champagne just then, and Dale took a glass off the tray. He was already holding a highball of his own, and he handed her the glass, saying, "Here, you look like you could use this."

Telling herself one wouldn't hurt, she nodded her thanks and glanced around. Jack was nowhere to be seen in the crowd, and she said, "Where's the man of the hour?"

Dale gestured with his head. "Over there by the dais."

"*What* dais?" She could hardly see through the crush of people.

"You want me to lift you up so you can see?" he asked with a wicked smile.

She gave him a look that made him laugh. Before they knew it, several other members of the DA's office had joined them, and as always when attorneys got together, the conversation quickly turned to legal anecdotes. Everybody always had a story to tell, and a woman who had left the PD's office and gone into private practice took the stage first. Her name was Nadine Fellows, and she had a habit of speaking in italics, widening her eyes at the same time. Laura didn't know whether to be more fascinated with what she was saying or how she was saying it.

"It was my first case," Nadine began, "and I was really nervous, as you can imagine. It didn't help that I'd drawn Judge Blending—" a sympathetic murmur from the group, who had all dealt with Blending before "—because I'd already heard how tough she was."

"Tough?" someone murmured. "Like cold nails and shoe leather, if you ask me."

"Yes, I found out," Nadine said, her eyes widening. "There I was, a brand new member of the PD, terrified of the bench but determined to defend my client, and all of a sudden the judge leaps up. *Leaps* up—can you imagine the terror? I thought she was having a fit or something. Anyway, she starts shouting at me that the presumption of innocence is a legal fiction, that she knows my client is guilty, that *I* know my client is guilty, that the entire *city* knows my client is guilty. I was so scared, I didn't know *what* to do!"

Someone asked, "So what *did* you do?"

Nadine's round eyes widened again as she spread her hands open. "What *could* I do? I took a deep breath and said, 'Your Honor, if my client's guilt has already been decided, why are we here?' "

"So what happened?" someone else asked.

"She threatened to cite me with contempt, of course, but before she could, my client grabbed my arm and started shouting himself. He said that the judge couldn't know he was guilty, and he wanted to know where she got her information from. Then he went on to yell that if his friend Alonzo had told her, he was going to get him with an ice pick. Well, you can *imagine* the pandemonium. Blending was shouting at me to control my client, and I was trying to get him to shut up because he was incriminating himself right *there* in front of the *judge*, for God's sake, and then all hell broke loose. He started screaming threats at Blending, who seemed to know all about him in some mysterious way, and then he tried to jump the rail. The bailiffs grabbed him, but it took three to subdue him, and he was still screaming that he was going to get the scumbag who ratted as he was hauled away.''

They all burst into laughter, and then as new people joined the group, the conversation turned to the Code of Professional Responsibility. This was an old argument between prosecutors and defense attorneys because it stated in part that a lawyer could not knowingly use perjured testimony or false evidence.

"The problem is that the code leaves unclear just what 'knowingly' means," someone said.

"Not in my view," another objected. "It's clear that a defense attorney should refuse to question a client who plans to lie. And further, that he shouldn't refer to that client's testimony in summation."

This was too simplistic for Laura, and she said, "What about the federal court decision that a defense attorney can't refuse to argue a case to a jury because he believes the client is guilty? To do otherwise violates that defendant's right of due process."

"What about perjury, then?" a deputy asked. "You expect someone who's guilty to lie. Don't tell me you're one of those who responded by survey that they would question a perjurious client in normal fashion."

She'd read that survey. Reluctantly she said, "I'd have to. If I didn't, that would amount to telling the judge and jury that the defendant *is* guilty."

The deputy persisted. "So even though you *know* your client is guilty, you'd still question him as if he weren't?"

Feeling as though she'd just been pinned in a spotlight on an unfriendly stage, she said, "It's not for me to decide whether my client is guilty; my job is to defend him. It's *your* job to prove he's guilty beyond a reasonable doubt. That's what due process is all about."

There was a general mutter from the other side at that, and she caught Dale's wink. She knew she'd bested the deputy on that one, but it was a hollow victory because she wasn't sure she really believed the answer herself. Wondering where *that* feeling had come from, she realized uneasily that the group had abandoned standards and had moved on to the exclusionary rule.

This was another of those endless debates from both sides of the fence. The occasional suppression of evidence and consequent dismissal of charges against an apparently guilty defendant upset a lot of people who didn't understand the finer points of law—and some who understood them very well. She was one herself. She hadn't forgotten her gun-toting ex-con, Marion Higgins, for whom she'd evoked the exclusionary rule herself to suppress his gun as evidence. Because of that, the case against him had been dismissed, but because she still had doubts about that, she stepped back from the group. She didn't want to discuss suppression of evidence.

Remembering suddenly that she hadn't seen Jack since he'd disappeared to get a drink a good half hour or more ago, she glanced around. There, not ten feet from her, was Douglas Rhodes. He was looking at her, and when their eyes met, she just stared. She'd wondered if he'd be here tonight to support Jim Duluth, but she hadn't really expected to see him. When he smiled and started toward her, she caught her breath. For some reason, she seemed rooted to the spot.

"Hello," he said, coming up. "We meet again. I'm Douglas Rhodes. We met outside Jim's office—"

Did he think she'd forgotten? "Of course I remember, Senator," she said. "How nice to see you again."

"And you," he said, with another smile. "Please, call me Douglas."

"Douglas, then," she managed. He was just as charming as she'd remembered. "And I'm Laura."

"Yes," he said, and glanced at her empty glass. "Would you like another drink?"

She looked blankly down. She didn't remember drinking the champagne, but she must have. Suddenly thirsty, she nodded. "Yes, please."

He looked around. Instantly a waiter appeared beside him with a full tray, and he tilted his head at her. "Champagne, or something else?"

"Champagne will be just fine," she said, wondering what was wrong with her. She'd never had a man affect her like this; she felt like a silly teenager, and she started looking around again. As ridiculous as it was, she thought she'd feel more secure if Jack were here.

To rescue her? She felt her face flush and told herself she was being absurd. But she still couldn't stop glancing around, and Douglas said, "I'm sorry. You seem to be looking for someone. Can I help?"

Feeling foolish, she tried to laugh. "Actually, I was looking for my husband. He went off to get a drink some time ago, and I haven't seen him since.''

''Well, I'm sure nothing has happened to him,'' he said, smiling.

She felt even more idiotic. ''It's not that,'' she said quickly. ''I just wanted to introduce him. I know he'd be disappointed if he didn't get to meet you. It's such an honor to meet a United States senator. . . .''

Realizing she was babbling, she trailed into silence. To her relief, he seemed not to notice her embarrassment when he said, ''I don't intend on leaving right away, but if you could tell me what he looks like, maybe I can spot him from here.''

''Oh . . . he's tall and lean and . . . and blond,'' she said, and briefly shut her eyes. She sounded like a blathering idiot. Then she made it even worse. ''He should be at the bar.''

He looked in that direction. He was so tall, he could easily see over the heads of the crowd, but after a moment he shook his head and glanced at her again. ''The bar is about twelve deep. I probably couldn't see him if he were waving a flag.''

She smiled, and he smiled with her, and without warning, their shared glance made something change. A spark leaped between them, and for an instant she had the absurd notion that they were the only two people in the room. Then she blinked, and mercifully the illusion vanished. Shaken, she drained the last of her champagne. When he finished his just as quickly, she knew that he had felt it—whatever it had been—too. ''Another?'' he said, gesturing toward her empty glass. His voice sounded different.

She shook her head. She'd had enough. His glance suddenly seemed too intent, and she didn't know what she was feeling. Startled by an almost overpowering urge to touch him, she tried to think of an excuse to get away. Hoping that a breath of air would restore her equilibrium, she said, ''I think I'll step outside. Would you excuse me?''

Of course he offered to go with her. Of course she couldn't refuse. But she moved quickly ahead of him so that he couldn't gallantly take her arm, as he obviously intended on doing. She had the feeling that if he touched her, she would lose what little composure she had left. Trying not to think what might be happening to her, she started toward the door. Just as they got there and Douglas started to make a path through the throng blocking the way, there was a stir and an excited shout.

"Hey! Some guy just fell into the pool! He's yelling that he's Tarzan, and he wants Tallulah to come and join him!"

Laura stopped dead. *Tallulah and Tarzan?* She shut her eyes, willing it not to be true. It couldn't be. It was a coincidence; it had to be.

But fragments of the conversation she and Jack had in the car flashed into her mind, and she could hear them laughing about this very thing.

Just think of all that history! he'd said.

You mean the stories about all those movie stars?

The one, for instance, where Tallulah Bankhead fell fully clothed into the pool—

And was rescued by Johnny Weissmuller!

Tarzan, you mean. Get it right.

Douglas interrupted her racing thoughts by taking her arm and shaking it slightly. "Laura? Are you all right?"

"Hey!" the guy at the door shouted again. "You ought to come and see this! This guy's a scream! Now he's taking off his shirt and doing a Tarzan yell!"

She didn't know what to do. She was so mortified, she couldn't make a sound. Douglas was looking at her in concern, and she didn't have to go outside to know there was no doubt. "I . . ." she said, and cleared her throat. How was she ever going to get through this? "I think that's my husband in the pool," she said faintly.

Douglas didn't hesitate. He started instantly toward the door again, and by some miracle, people scattered at his approach. Her heart thudding, she followed in his wake. As they went outside, she was almost afraid to look, but then she heard the yelling and the splashing, and knew she couldn't hide any longer. Taking a deep breath to steady herself, she stepped around Douglas and gasped.

Her worst fears were confirmed. It was Jack, all right—along with about four uniformed waiters who were all treading through the shallow end of the pool in an effort to rescue him. He didn't want to be rescued. Leaping and jumping away from them, he was obviously so drunk, he didn't know what he was doing. It was all she could do not to turn around and slink away. She had never been so mortified in her life.

"Is that—" Douglas asked.

She couldn't look at him; she nodded.

To her relief, he took charge. She'd seen people jump at someone's command before, but the hotel employees who were standing around just watching practically leaped to obey when he said, in a quiet voice that somehow carried over the splashing and commotion in the water, "Get that man out of the pool."

Two more uniformed attendants dove into the water at that, but it was a few minutes before the six men could subdue Jack and drag him to the side. Jack looked up and saw her as they were hauling him out and gave her a drunken wave. "You're late, Tallulah," he said. "I started without ya."

And then, to her horror, he doubled over and passed out.

"Take him to my suite," Douglas said.

Somehow she pulled herself together. "Oh, no, please—you can't. Let me have the car brought around, and I'll just drive him home."

He looked down at her. "You won't be able to manage."

"Yes, I—"

Someone came running up just then. "Excuse me," he said. They both turned. "Yes?"

The man looked at her. "Are you Laura Devlin?"

She couldn't imagine what now. "Yes."

"You have an important phone call."

She immediately thought of her children and felt a stab of fear. "Who is it?"

"I'm sorry, ma'am, I don't know."

She didn't know what to do. Jack was passed out by the side of the pool and she didn't want to leave him. But she couldn't ignore the phone; it might be her mother.

Douglas solved the problem for her. "Take the call," he said, and gestured to the dripping attendants to remove the limp form of her husband. "We'll get him dried off, at least."

Briefly she clutched his arm in thanks before turning to the attendant. "Where do I go?"

There was a phone in the manager's office, a light blinking in the row of buttons. The attendant showed her in, and she stabbed at the flashing button even before he left her alone. "Yes?"

"Laura?"

She was so disoriented that for a moment she didn't even recognize Tony's voice. She had been expecting her mother. When she realized who it was, she cried, "Tony! What are you doing? I thought something awful had happened at home! You scared me to death!"

He wasn't his usual bantering self. "I know. I'm sorry. I

141

wouldn't have called except I knew you'd want to know right away.''

She heard the door open and turned distractedly. Douglas was standing there, and she gestured for him to come in before she turned back to her call. "What is it?"

"It's Marion Higgins," Tony said. "He's just been arrested for murder."

She thought she hadn't heard right. "What?"

"They just booked him," Tony said, sounding more reluctant than ever. "I hate to tell you this, Laura, but he shot the cop who pulled him in on that gun-carrying charge."

She was so shocked, she sank into the chair. Tony knew how she felt about that case; this was why he had thought it important enough to call her here. Blankly she looked up as Douglas came over. He saw her pale face and wordlessly put a hand on her shoulder. It was the most comforting gesture she'd ever felt.

"Laura?"

It was Tony again, wondering what had happened to her. She forced the words through stiff lips. "Yes, I'm still here."

"Look, Laura, I know this is a shock. I know how you felt about this. Come in early tomorrow and we'll talk about it."

She never wanted to talk about it again. "Sure," she said, and dropped the phone as she was trying to replace it in the cradle. Without a word Douglas took it from her and replaced it himself. Then he turned to her and drew her gently to her feet. His hands on her shoulders, he looked deep into her eyes and said simply, "How can I help?"

She couldn't speak. She felt numb with shock, stunned by the awfulness of what had happened, appalled by her part in it. She was responsible; how was she ever going to live with this? Stricken, she shook her head. Then, unable to help herself, she put her cheek against his broad chest and squeezed her eyes shut as if she could also shut out the horrible pictures that rose in her mind. With a blessed sense of comfort and relief, she felt his arms tighten around her, pulling her close, and almost without volition, she let him. Almost.

And then, for a while, the room was silent except for the slow ticking of the clock.

CHAPTER TWELVE

Douglas wasn't sure what to do next. He realized, too late, that embracing Laura was a mistake, but he seemed helpless at the moment to correct it. He didn't know what was wrong, but that phone call had clearly upset her, and he tried to tell himself that his gesture had been instinctive. That wasn't true. He'd wanted to do this all evening, from the moment he saw her enter the ballroom. Now he was caught. He never should have let himself get off the track like this; he couldn't understand how he had allowed himself to lose all sense of decorum, or control. Worse, now that he was holding her, he didn't want to let her go. The scent of her perfume wafted up to his nostrils, and the feel of her body in his arms stirred something more inside him than friendship, no matter what he wanted to pretend. He was still trying to decide what his next move should be when he heard the office door open, followed by a sharp intake of breath. He turned.

"I'm sorry, sir. I didn't realize anyone was here."

He recognized the assistant manager at once. His name was Johnson, and they'd met when he and Irving arrived tonight. Despite the deliberately expressionless face, he knew instantly that the man was lying. He had known someone was here, and now that he'd found out, he seemed to be debating the wisdom of going or staying. Douglas decided to give him some help.

"I'm glad you're here, Mr. Johnson," he said briskly. "I know this is a private office, but there's been an emergency. My aide's name is Irving Mayhew. Please page him and have him meet me here. Thank you so much."

He turned away, effectively dismissing him, his attitude such that he didn't doubt Johnson would hurry to obey. The man had no choice but to withdraw, but Douglas saw speculation flash quickly across his face, and he knew his brusqueness had probably been a mistake. Well, it couldn't be helped. Laura was

143

more important, and as the door closed again, he made a mental note to see that Irving took care of any awkwardness before they left. Laura had moved away from him during the exchange and was standing by the desk looking pale, but more composed.

"I'm sorry," she said, her voice low. "I usually don't allow myself to lose control like that. But that phone call just now—" She stopped, shuddering despite herself.

"I understand," he said, and hesitated. "Would you like to talk about it?"

She started to shake her head, changed her mind, and said faintly instead, "Yes, but I . . . I think I'll sit down. . . ."

He held the chair for her, and as she sank into it, he couldn't help thinking again how attractive she was. It wasn't only her physical beauty, but something inside. He'd thought when he first met her that there was something special about her, and tonight had only confirmed that opinion. The soft light from the desk lamp illuminated her face, and it was an effort not to reach out and touch her. Hastily he averted his eyes and looked around for a place to sit. The chair closest was a spindly-looking thing that seemed too fragile to hold his weight, and he sat down gingerly.

Laura took a deep breath. "Who was that man?"

He grimaced. "The assistant manager."

Her shoulders slumped. "I'm sorry, Douglas," she said, her voice even lower. "I should have realized how that would look. I hope—"

He knew what she meant, but it had been more his fault than hers, and he said quickly, "Don't worry about it. There was nothing to see."

Their eyes met, and for some reason they both looked away. He had to think of a safe topic, so he said, "I gather it was bad news just now."

That seemed to depress her even more. "Yes, I'm afraid it was. That was my boss, Tony Amorelli. He called to tell me—" her voice faltered, but she controlled it and went on "—to tell me that a man I defended a while ago was just charged with murder."

"I'm sorry," Douglas said. He wasn't sure what else to say.

She gave a brief dejected shake of her head. "You don't understand. The man he shot and killed tonight was the officer who arrested him a few months ago for carrying a gun." Her voice threatened to fail her, and she steadied it this time with a

144

visible effort. "I was the one who proved the search was illegal."

There was a silence while he digested the implications. Finally he said quietly, "And you feel responsible."

"Wouldn't you?"

She looked in such pain that without realizing it, he reached for her hand. "You did what was right, didn't you?"

"Right?" she repeated with an anguished shake of her head. "I don't know right now. I did what I was supposed to, but if it hadn't been for me, that police officer would still be alive."

Feeling totally inadequate, he said, "But you don't make the laws, Laura. You did what you had to for your client, didn't you?"

She gave him a bitter look. "Oh, yes, I did that. I'm good at what I do, Douglas. Look what I did—freed an ex-con who shouldn't have been carrying a gun at all, so he could go out and kill the cop who arrested him for having it in the first place. I did a great service on that one, didn't I?"

She looked ready to cry, and he wanted to take her in his arms again. He didn't dare. Instead he said intensely, trying to make her see, "It wasn't your fault, Laura. You were doing your job."

Glancing away from him, she drew in a shuddering breath. "Then maybe it's time to change jobs."

He didn't know what to say to that, and because he didn't trust himself to do anything else, he patted her awkwardly on the arm. "You've had a terrible shock," he said. "It might be wise not to do anything rash."

The clumsy gesture made her smile—shakily, but a smile—and she put her hand over his. "Thank you, Douglas," she said simply. "If you hadn't been here, I don't know what I would have done."

Their eyes met again, and this time neither of them could look away. Without realizing it, he took her hand in his and held it. The simple gesture seemed suddenly more than that, fraught with peril. Even the air seemed to electrify, as though before a storm, and he felt the hairs at the back of his neck prickle. He was finding it difficult to breathe, his face felt on fire. An ache throbbed in his loins, and without realizing it, he leaned slowly forward, intending to—

He never found out. A stir at the door broke the spell, and he was just reeling himself back when Irving stumbled in. His aide looked as though he'd come at a dead run, and before he realized

Douglas wasn't alone, he said, "Senator, someone said you—"

He skidded to a stop, looking uncertainly from Douglas to Laura. Then, his face turning bright red, he straightened himself and his jacket and said, "I'm sorry. I was told it was urgent."

"It . . . was," Douglas said, with a glance at Laura. He'd used the interruption to compose himself, and he was relieved to see that she had, too. Now, although still pale, she seemed in control, and he turned back to Irving. "I think we need some coffee here."

"Oh, no—" Laura said at once.

Douglas turned to her. "I'm sorry. I didn't mean to be presumptuous. If you have to go to your office, we can have someone drive you there."

She shook her head. "No, I've got a car. And in any case, that can wait until morning." She looked embarrassed again. "But I still have to do something about Jack."

Douglas had forgotten all about the husband. He turned inquiringly to Irving, who looked at Laura and said, "Your husband is . . . resting . . . comfortably in the senator's suite, Mrs. Devlin."

She was grateful for his tact; they all knew that Jack had passed out. "Thank you," she said, and took a breath. "But I can't leave him there. I should take him home."

Douglas knew when his aide was unhappy about something, and when he saw Irving's worried expression, he said, "What's wrong?"

Irving sighed. "I'm sorry. I tried to talk those photographers into giving up the film they took of the . . . the pool incident, but they refused."

Laura looked stricken. "Photographers were there?"

"I'm afraid so."

"Oh, no! What now?"

Douglas shook his head. "I'm afraid there's not much you can do. You know the press."

She shut her eyes as though seeking strength. Faintly she said, "Yes, I do."

"Maybe it will all blow over," Irving said hopefully. But they all knew that was too much to expect, and Laura stood.

"I want to thank you both so much for everything you've done—"

Douglas got up, too. "You're leaving?"

"I can't stay here. As much as I'd rather not run the gauntlet, I've got to get Jack home." She hesitated. "Could I ask you one more favor?"

"Anything!" Irving said.

She looked at him in surprise, and he flushed bright red, stammering, "I mean . . . I'll be glad to do what I can."

Douglas saw what the problem was. He had already come under Laura's spell; he knew Irving had, too. Giving his flustered aide a chance to compose himself, he turned to Laura. "What would you like us to do?"

She seemed embarrassed again. "I don't think I can get Jack to the car by myself. If you can help, I'd be so grateful."

That was when he nearly offered to let her spend the night with Jack in the extra bedroom in his suite. Realizing what he was doing, he managed to stop in time, but he was upset with himself. Wondering if he'd lost his mind, he took action and supervised the transfer of Laura's half-awake husband to the backseat of the car. The valet was carefully expressionless the entire time, and in reward, he gave the boy a generous tip that made him grin.

"Thank *you*, sir! Anything else I can do?"

Wishing there were something more *he* could do for Laura, he dismissed the valet and turned to her. She was going to go, and he couldn't stop her. Shouldn't *want* to stop her, he told himself, and held the car door open. Irving had already departed, and she gave him a shaky smile.

"I'm in your debt, Douglas," she said, clutching the car keys. "I know I keep saying it, but I don't know what I would have done without your help tonight. If there's anything I can do—ever—all you have to do is call."

And Douglas, who could have said much more and didn't dare, said, "It was nothing. I'm glad I could help."

Then he watched her climb gracefully into the car. The husband was snoring in the backseat as she gave a little wave and drove away, and he stood under the portico and waited until the Volvo's taillights disappeared. Then he went slowly inside.

Early the next morning, he had an appointment with Malcolm Tanner, and as he and Irving took the limo to Tanner's office, they carefully avoided each other's eyes. Douglas hadn't slept well and he wasn't in the best of moods. As ridiculous as it was, he couldn't get Laura out of his mind. He had played and replayed that scene in the manager's office in his head until he thought he'd go mad, and finally he'd given up about five this morning and gone outside. The air had been filled with that heavy, almost pregnant silence that was peculiarly Southern California in early morning before the hum of activity began, and he had watched the sun come up to touch the tops of the palms before taking a quick swim. The exercise hadn't improved his mood, and Irving took one look at his face and wisely decided to pore over business papers on the way downtown.

They were met by a cheerful Tanner, who immediately offered them that excellent coffee and some fresh-baked croissants. Douglas accepted the coffee, refused the croissants, and watched in fascination as Tanner made small talk and lighted one cigarette off another he already had smoldering in an ashtray by his elbow. Some hidden mechanism sucked the smoke into a receptacle every time he put the cigarette down, and after a moment Tanner noticed his attention and looked abashed.

"I wasn't smoking the last time you were here, was I?" he said.

Amused, Douglas shook his head. Once he had decided to hire Tanner to manage his campaign, he'd been prepared to try and like the man. To his surprise this morning, he wasn't finding that as much of an effort as he'd imagined. The smoking lapse made Tanner seem more human, and he smiled as he said, "No, as I recall, you told us you'd given it up."

The political consultant reddened. "Yes, well, as you can see, that attempt didn't last long, either," he said, and took a hefty drag off the cigarette before replacing it in the ashtray. "But at least I'm trying to spare you my secondary smoke."

"I see," Douglas said. "What is that thing?"

"Something the NASA engineers dreamed up for me," Tanner said, sounding as though that were the most natural thing in the world. "They're very efficient at getting rid of smoke and things, you know."

"Nice," Douglas said. "But what do you do outside the office?"

Tanner laughed. "Take the portable unit they designed for me, of course," he said, and took another drag off the cigarette. "Now. Shall we get down to business? Now that I'm going to be working for you—"

Douglas couldn't help smiling at the change in structure. The last time he'd been here, Tanner had implied that Douglas would be part of his stable; now it seemed as though Tanner would be working for him. Approving the change, he let his glance meet that of the political consultant's. Tanner saw his expression and grinned. Douglas decided then that he liked this man more and more, especially when Tanner winked at him and then went on without further acknowledging the shift in their relationship.

"As I was saying," he said, "I'd like to join you at home in Scottsdale for a weekend soon. I want to get to know Douglas Rhodes, the man, before coming to Washington to become acquainted with Senator Rhodes, the politician. . . ."

They agreed to meet a few weeks hence, and the meeting ended on a much more cordial note than the first one had. He was still smiling as he and Irv separated at the airport—the aide on his way back to Washington; he to fly on to Phoenix. As he waited for his flight to be called, he was glad he had decided to hire Malcolm to manage his campaign. He didn't know why, but he had the feeling that Tanner was going to play a much larger part in his life than as political consultant.

Thinking what an eventful trip this had been, he caught his flight. He'd already called a worn-out and slightly hung over Jim this morning to say good-bye and wish him luck, and suddenly remembered the stab of guilt he'd felt at promising to visit again soon. He'd wondered at the time if he wasn't just making up excuses to come to L.A. more often on the chance that he'd see Laura, and although he tried to tell himself not to be absurd, he found he couldn't dismiss the idea as completely as he would have liked. Such weakness annoyed him, and he made himself open his briefcase and get to work.

To his surprise, Marcella was among the waiting crowd when his flight arrived, and even before he saw her face, he knew something was wrong. It had to be. Marcella hated crowds, and airport parking was a horror she avoided at every opportunity. Her aversion was one reason he kept a car here, and he felt his stomach tighten as he came down the ramp. His first thought was that something had happened to Rob; he couldn't imagine what else would have driven her here to meet him.

"What are you doing here, darling?" he asked when he came up to where she was waiting. He bent down and gave her a quick kiss, trying to gauge the situation at the same time. He couldn't rid himself of sudden dread. If something had happened to Rob while they were estranged, he'd never forgive himself.

"Oh, I just thought I'd meet you," she said, and brushed her lips against his cheek. She wasn't a demonstrative person, es-

149

pecially in public, but she took his hand as they started out, and this disturbed him even more. Remembering the last time a member of his family had met him like this, and the disaster that ensued, he tensed even more. Unable to bear the suspense, he drew Marcella aside as they left the terminal. "Marcie," he said. "What is it? You never come to meet me. Is something wrong?"

She laughed and avoided his eyes. "How suspicious you are, darling," she said. "I thought you might like to be met for a change."

"Marcella—" he warned.

She suddenly crumpled. "All right, Douglas," she said with a sigh. "You're going to have to know sooner or later, I guess."

Another stab of fear thudded through him. He tried to tell himself that Marcella wouldn't be this calm if something truly disastrous had occurred, but even so, his voice was tight when he said, "Know what? Tell me, Marcella. Has something happened to Rob?"

She looked shocked. "Oh, no! I'm sorry, Douglas; it's nothing like that. Rob is fine. Just . . . fine."

His relief was so great that he snapped at her without realizing it. "What a scare you gave me for nothing! Do you know what I thought when I saw you standing there? You never come to meet me, and I was sure something terrible had happened. For God's sake, don't do that again!"

He rarely spoke so harshly to her, and tears filled her eyes. "I'm sorry, Douglas," she said contritely. "It's just that I thought I should warn you."

Anxiety again. "*Warn* me?" he said sharply. "About what?"

She glanced nervously around. "Someone will hear you."

He controlled himself with an effort, cursing the necessity of holding himself back. But he was in a position now for things to be picked up, distorted . . . misconstrued, he knew, and suddenly an image of himself holding Laura in his arms last night flashed through his mind. Wincing, he remembered the expression on the assistant manager's face. In all the excitement, he'd forgotten to ask Irving to follow up on that, but he knew his aide, and he was sure it was taken care of. Wondering why he was thinking of that now, he thrust the thought and the possible consequences out of his mind. Marcella was gazing at him unhappily, and he managed to say, more calmly, "All right. I'm listening. What has Rob done now?"

When she hesitated, he knew he wasn't going to like it. "He hasn't really done anything, Douglas," she said, and then despite herself, became animated. Clutching his arm, she said, "He's home, Douglas! Rob came home!"

He couldn't believe it. There had been no warning, he thought, and then: *he'd* had no warning. He didn't know anymore what went on between his son and his wife; he and Marcella didn't talk about Rob at all because she was so sympathetic that he always became too furious with her to discuss him.

"Home?" he said, and then had to ask. "For good?"

Marcella looked up at him, her eyes determinedly bright. "I don't know, Douglas. I was just so happy to see him that I didn't ask." She searched his face. "Aren't you happy, too?"

He didn't know how he felt, or what his reaction should be. He and Rob had parted under such ugly terms last time that he wasn't sure what they had to say to each other. He'd tried to project how it would go if Rob came home again, but even though he had rehearsed the scene a dozen times in his mind, he realized now that he didn't have the faintest idea what he was going to say. He wasn't sure if too much hadn't already been said, or if the schism had gone so deep now, it could never be repaired. Could they go back again? As much as he might want to, he doubted it. If he still felt the sting of all those hurtful words, he knew Rob hadn't forgotten, either.

But maybe Rob had changed, he thought with sudden hope. Maybe that was why he'd come back—to say he'd been wrong, to apologize, to . . . to take up his life again where he'd left off. Was that it? He shut his eyes, overcome by his intense longing to have his son back again. If Rob had come back, he'd forgive him anything.

"He's brought someone with him," Marcella said, interrupting his racing thoughts.

Alerted, he looked down at his wife. He was familiar with that false brightness, that determined glow, and he knew instantly that this was the reason she had come to meet him. Rob had sent her, or she'd come on her own; it didn't matter. She was here to break the news gently, to introduce him to something he was going to find unpalatable, to give him a chance to get used to it as they drove home. He knew then that he wasn't going to like whoever Rob had brought with him.

"Who?" he asked, trying to be calm.

Marcella took the plunge. "Her name is Calypso, Douglas,"

151

she said, as though she couldn't quite believe it yet herself. She was still holding that bright smile, but above it, her eyes sought his, begging him to—to what? He didn't have time to ask. "She's pregnant," she added. "With his child."

CHAPTER THIRTEEN

"Congratulations, Mrs. Wannamaker." The doctor beamed at Dawn. "You're pregnant."

Dawn didn't say anything for a moment; she was trying to digest the not-so-unexpected information and decide just how unwelcome it was. There had been a chance, until now, that she'd made a mistake; those home pregnancy kits weren't a hundred percent reliable, and so she'd made an appointment with a Baltimore clinic using her own name. She didn't want anyone getting any bright ideas about tracing her whereabouts today, especially since it seemed that she was going to have to deal with this after all.

She looked at the doctor, who was one of those young, bright, enthusiastic sorts. From his expression, he apparently assumed it would be good news, for he was beaming at her, eager to help. He saw her glance and smiled. "Do you have any questions, Mrs. Wannamaker?"

She didn't. She just wanted to get dressed and get out of here. But she didn't want to arouse his suspicions, or have him wonder if she'd show up here again, so she made herself smile. "I'm sure I will. I guess I'm just a little . . . overwhelmed."

That was putting it mildly. Wondering how she'd ever let herself get caught in such a stupid position, she pulled the paper gown around her, hoping the doctor would take the cue and get the hell out of here. Instead he said eagerly, "Now, I don't want you to worry about a thing, Mrs. Wannamaker. You're young and healthy and everything seems just fine. I'll want to see you in a couple of weeks, but if you have any questions in the meantime, please don't hesitate to call."

"I won't," Dawn assured him, thinking that was the last thing she intended to do. "Thank you."

Finally he left. She dressed, paid the bill in cash so there wouldn't be any trace, and went out to the car. She was on the expressway back to Washington before she allowed herself to think about it, and she frowned. Now that her suspicions had been confirmed, she had to figure out what to do. The first thing, she supposed, was decide how to turn this to her advantage.

Of course, she knew who the father was. In fact, she thought as she glanced in the rearview mirror to make sure she'd remembered to put on lipstick, she remembered the exact night it happened. It had been the night . . .

Distracted by the sight of the car behind her, she looked from that mirror to the one attached to the car door. She hadn't really been paying attention, but wasn't that the same green sedan that had been parked outside the doctor's office? She watched it for a moment, dividing her attention between the reflections and the traffic ahead. After a moment she frowned again. She was *sure* that was the car. She remembered seeing it when she left the clinic; it had been parked right outside. But why was it following her?

Then she felt foolish. What made her think she was being followed? This pregnancy must be making her paranoid, or something. And speaking of that, she'd better get back to the matter at hand. She still hadn't decided what she was going to do, and this was the kind of thing that just didn't go away with wishful thinking.

She was just smirking at the thought when she glanced in the rearview mirror again and saw the green sedan pull out. As it went around her, she couldn't help giving it a tense glance, but the two men inside didn't even look her way. The car passed, accelerated, and soon disappeared in traffic, leaving her feeling even more foolish. Annoyed because she usually didn't let her imagination get the best of her, she forgot the damned car and tried to concentrate on the real problem.

Now that she was sure, she remembered exactly the night it had happened. After months of not hearing from Lee Walker, he'd finally called to ask her to one of those Power Parties. Oh, they called it a "little dinner" in this town, but it was really a chance for some hostess to show off. This was accomplished by bringing two Important People together who, in access-oriented Washington, either hadn't managed to meet yet, or who hadn't wanted to seem too eager to do so. The hostess ferreted out this information and used each as bait for the other. Once acceptances were in, the "little dinner" was born.

Some little dinner, Dawn thought. It was currently fashionable for the guest list for one of these shindigs to number twenty-four, two of which had to be media people. That's why Lee had been invited. He was a feature writer for the *Post*, and word had to get around somehow, didn't it? Why go to all the trouble of planning one of these soirees if no one knew about it except the people who attended? It was all so transparent, she had to laugh.

She had also been eager to go. When Lee called, she didn't know whether to be more pleased that he was asking her out after all this time, or excited at the idea of attending one of these power functions. She'd immediately seen it as a chance to impress her own boss, Barnaby, who *still* hadn't given her a column, the bastard. But with all those important people in one room, someone was sure to let something slip, and so she had accepted. But that meant that she had to pay for the invitation, and *voilà!* Now she was carrying the result.

Realizing suddenly that the car in front of her was going a snail's pace, she changed lanes. The little old man driving honked furiously at her when she whipped into the lane in front of him, but she tossed a curse backward and dismissed the old fart. Catching sight of something green ahead, her heart leaped into her throat. Was that the same green sedan she'd thought was following her? Then she saw it was a truck, and she cursed again. What was wrong with her? That stupid car was long gone, and she couldn't understand why she was still preoccupied with it. *Forget the damned car,* she told herself angrily, and whipped around another slow vehicle.

On track again, she drummed her fingers against the steering wheel and thought about that particular party. She was sure that was the night she'd gotten pregnant; she'd been so looped when Lee brought her home that she'd completely forgotten about safeguards. Even so, it had been worth it. She'd learned so much circulating that night that this was a small price to pay.

Thank you, Lord, for inventing the miniature tape recorder, she thought, and grinned. If it hadn't been for that clever little machine she carried in her purse, she wouldn't have taped those conversations, and Barnaby would never have believed her, much less given her the chance to write the story. It hadn't led to a regular column yet, but it was a start. Better than a start, she thought with a smirk. She'd caused quite a furor when those items came out: the one about the senator who was a passionate advocate for the rights of American workers, and who had gone to the White House to plead their case for banning all imports—

155

wearing his Guccis . . . the item about the Moral Majority senator who had met with a waiter in the Longworth Building's men's room . . . the conversation she'd overheard—and taped—about the goings on at Rehoboth, the chichi Delaware beach resort, where guests at a private party had been treated to a real show between a highly paid government figure and a transvestite he'd brought with him to the ball. She hadn't named names, of course; there was always the threat of libel. But she had given the items just enough genuine flavor to make the subjects readily identifiable, and Barnaby had been so pleased at the uproar she'd caused that she figured her own byline wasn't in the too far future.

Lee had been amused that night, too, she remembered, when she played the tape for him. But then, they'd both been pretty well oiled by the time they got back to her apartment, and obviously, one thing had led to another. What would he say when he found out the result now? Maybe he'd offer to marry her, she thought with a disdainful smile, and didn't believe it for a minute. Even if he did do such an uncharacteristic thing, she wouldn't accept. She had other plans for her future, and they didn't include a husband and a stupid kid.

A face flashed into her mind just then, startling her. She frowned, instinctively thrusting the mental picture away. She didn't want to think about Bud just now; she never wanted to think about him again.

But those kind blue eyes wouldn't leave her, nor the earnest expression, the sensitive mouth. Despite herself, she remembered Bud's arms around her, his hands so gentle on her body, his lips so tentative on hers. She could feel him trembling against her with love and desire; even though she hadn't been there to see, she knew he'd cried when she'd run away. He deserved better, but she couldn't help it. She'd always be grateful to Bud for marrying her—for rescuing her when she was pregnant—but she couldn't look back. Not now, not ever again. Bud was part of the buried past, and it had to stay that way.

Grimly she willed Bud's face from her mind by concentrating on her driving. She had moved again, and her new apartment was on Wisconsin Avenue. Leaving the parkway, she pulled up in front of her building, wondering how long she'd stay here. She still hadn't forgotten her vow to move to the more fashionable Dupont Circle, but in the meantime, she had other decisions to make.

The message light was glowing on her answering machine, but she ignored it for the time being and kicked off her heels. Padding over to the liquor cabinet, she poured herself a stiff shot, which she tossed back, then poured another, which she took to the window. It was October now, and the leaves were turning color. The trees outside were a blaze of gold and red and yellow, but she really didn't see the sight; she was thinking of Lee and wondering what he'd say if he knew about the baby. Then her eyes hardened. He wasn't going to know, was he? She had no intention of telling him; this was strictly her own business. Turning away from the window, she was just reaching for the answering machine to see who had called when the phone itself rang. She let it ring for a second time before she picked it up.

"Hello?"

"Miss Van Doren?"

She recognized that voice right away; she should, she thought: she'd talked to him often enough these past few months, relaying all those messages for his mistress.

"Hello, Chester," she said, resigned. What did Lenore want now?

Lenore's butler didn't waste time. "The reason I'm calling is to tell you that Mrs. Deering-Kirk would like to see you. Today."

Bristling at the peremptory summons, she said immediately, "I'm afraid that's not possible. I have other plans."

"Nothing quite as important as this, I'm sure," he said with that assurance that had irritated her from the start. It was as though they all waited for him to pick up the phone and tell someone that Lenore wished to speak. "Shall I pick you up in— say, an hour?"

"No, you shall not!" she snapped. "I told you, I can't—"

"Would you like me to relay that message to Mrs. Deering-Kirk?"

"Yes, and you can tell her—" She stopped abruptly, realizing in the nick of time that she was about to go too far. As much as she detested being ordered around like this, she wasn't stupid. She knew how unwise it would be to offend Lenore, especially at this point, so she gritted her teeth and said instead, "Never mind. I'll be there."

"Splendid," Chester said, as though she'd volunteered. "I'll be there with the car in—"

Determined to assert what little independence she could, she interrupted, "No, thanks. I'll drive myself."

There was a little silence. Finally he said stiffly, "As you wish."

"I do," she said coldly, and couldn't resist adding, "And furthermore, it will probably take me an hour and a half. Because despite what Lenore thinks, I *do* have a life, and I must make some arrangements."

She could almost see that condescending little bow. "As you wish," he said again. "I will relay the message."

"You do that," she said nastily, and hung up.

It was tempting to be late, but she didn't dare make Lenore wait too long. Still, she couldn't go out to Deer Hollow wearing the jeans and sweater she'd worn to the clinic, so she went into the bedroom to change. Stripping off her casual clothes, she was just reaching for a jersey dress hanging in the closet when she caught sight of herself in the mirror. Did she show? Straightening, she went closer to the mirror and turned sideways. No, it was her imagination. Her belly was as flat as it had always been, and why shouldn't it be? She was only two months along, after all. Without realizing it, she put her hand on her stomach. A fragment of conversation she'd had once with Lee flitted into her mind, and she frowned.

"Yeah, I'd like to have a family one day," he'd said. *"You know, a wife . . . kids, the little vine-covered cottage and all that shit."*

He'd laughed as though cynically amused at himself, but she'd glimpsed the quickly hidden longing in his eyes, and as she stared at herself in the mirror, she wondered herself—just for an instant—what being part of a real family would be like: a couple who loved each other, children who weren't terrified of their father. Maybe she and Lee could have that, she thought, and was surprised at the sudden yearning she felt. Quickly she turned away from the mirror. What was the matter with her, was she crazy or something? Family life wasn't for her; she didn't want to get tied down to any man. She'd seen what married life was like, and no thanks. She must have been out of her mind to consider it even for a second. This was getting too weird. She'd better make an appointment for this abortion right away.

Muttering to herself, she finished dressing and had managed to get herself back on the track again by the time she returned to the mirror. Now, that was better. She looked just the way she wanted to look: cool, competent, and totally in charge of her life. And in a few days, once she got rid of her little problem, she would be. Satisfied, she grabbed her purse and got going. If she didn't hurry, she really would be late.

She'd hoped that a drive in the country would make her feel better, but the farther she got from the city, the more resentful she became. She *hated* kowtowing to Lenore like this, but she felt helpless to alter the situation at present, and she was seething by the time she reached the huge wrought-iron gates that led to Deer Hollow Farm. The gatekeeper waved her in, and as she drove through and glimpsed the huge house beyond the thinning leaves, far up the curving drive, her resentment increased. She'd once been so impressed by this show of wealth, but she wasn't much moved by it anymore. For too long, Lenore had reminded her of a spider in a very elegant web. She might look like a helpless little old lady, but she knew from bitter experience that appearances were deceptive. She was an example of it herself. No one would ever confuse the amber-eyed, confident-appearing blonde she was now with the hostile and defiant dark-haired girl who had piled all her belongings into a cardboard suitcase and left home on a train at one in the morning. And if she could alter appearances so much, so could Lenore—in spades. She might look like everyone's ideal of a kindly old grandmother, but she was about as far from that as a scorpion is from a butterfly.

Grimly staring at the house as it came fully into view, she thought of the stories even she could tell about Lenore. Oh, she'd seen things, all right, right here—things even she didn't dare publish. It was amazing what a word or two from this old hag could do. She might not have the power she thought, but she did have clout, no doubt about it.

Chester opened the door two seconds after she rang the bell. If she didn't know better, she would have thought he was standing just on the other side, waiting for her to get here. Then she shrugged. Maybe he had been.

"Ah, Miss Van Doren," he said, and stepped aside with a polite smile.

She didn't smile in return. She'd known about Chester right off the bat. But then, she conceded, she'd met a lot of Chesters in her life: cold-eyed, coldhearted men who would do anything for the right amount and the right person; the two went hand in hand. She'd met them in Steel Town; she'd seen them in bars and streetcorners and department stores and offices many times since. They were the oil of a certain part of society, the ones who weren't afraid to get their hands wet. Necessary, evil, the kind to watch out for. Far more easily spotted than the Lenores of the world, and almost as deadly.

"Mrs. Deering-Kirk is in the library, Miss Van Doren," he said. "Follow me, please."

She'd had enough of him. "I think I know the way," she said sarcastically, and brushed by him. She could feel his eyes on her as she started across the vast football field of an entry, and her head came up. Let him think what he liked; she didn't care. Lenore was waiting, as promised, in the library.

Long ago, when Dawn had first been given a partial tour of the house—partial, because there were so many rooms that a complete tour would probably have taken several hours—she'd been awestruck by this room. For one thing, it was octagonal, something she'd never seen before, and six of the walls were covered, floor to ceiling, with books. All were housed on mahogany shelves behind beveled-glass doors, and bound in morocco leather and detailed with gold leaf. A huge and ancient globe stood to one side, and grouped around were seatings for several visitors at once. Each leather, brass-studded chair was presided over by a Tiffany lamp, and the diamond-patterned parquet floor shone with polish and a daily dusting by maids who accomplished the task on their knees. The scent of lemon and beeswax was in the air, and in the middle of it all, reinforcing Dawn's earlier image of a spider, was Lenore. She was sitting on one of the big leather chairs, her feet barely touching the floor, holding one of the books in her lap.

"Ah, here you are at last," Lenore said, setting aside the book. "I was beginning to wonder if something had happened. Would you be a dear, please, and close the French doors?"

The doors were at the opposite end of the room, and as Dawn crossed to obey, she vowed she wasn't going to make excuses about being late. Aware of Lenore watching her, she started to say, "Nothing happened. I—"

She stiffened. The library was situated at one end of the house, where the drive curved around to what had once been the carriage stables at the back. And there, parked at the curb, in plain sight, was a green sedan. *The* green sedan. She was sure; she would have staked her life on it.

160

"You were saying, my dear?" Lenore asked.

Dawn barely heard her; she couldn't stop staring at that car. For a few breaths, she felt totally disoriented, and then, when she realized what had happened, she became furious. How *dare* Lenore have her followed! And even worse, how dare she make it so obvious! She was so angry, she couldn't even speak.

"Is something wrong, Dawn?" Lenore asked. "I'm sorry, but you look as though you've seen a ghost."

With tremendous control, Dawn reached out and closed the French doors. In that bare space of time she had already decided how to handle this, and she turned back to the room. "Not a ghost," she said, "but two of your henchmen. You really should hire better quality spies, Lenore. I had them spotted the instant I left the clinic."

Lenore laughed. "Touché, my dear," she said. "I'm having tea brought in. Or would you prefer something stronger?"

Dawn stared at her. She couldn't believe this. She'd just accused Lenore of having her followed, and they were talking about tea? "Didn't you hear what I said?"

"I heard," Lenore said calmly, and glanced in the direction of the car. "And you're right. I really should get rid of those two." She shrugged. "But good help is so hard to find these days, and they have been with me a long time. Now, about that drink—"

Before Dawn could answer, there was a quiet knock on the door and one of the maids came in with the silver service. "Ah, Theresa," Lenore said. "Just put it right there, please. And you may leave. I'll pour."

"Yes, Mrs. Deering-Kirk."

A low table stood between Lenore's chair and one other, and Theresa obediently set the tray on it, straightened an immaculately starched linen napkin, and departed. As soon as the door closed behind her again, Lenore reached for the Georgian teapot. "Now, you were saying?"

Dawn didn't know what to say. The interruption had given her a few seconds to assess the situation, and she realized that Lenore had wanted her to know about the men in that car all along. It was the only explanation. The woman was rich enough to hire the best; if Lenore hadn't wanted her to spot them, she wouldn't even have known they were there. But why this elaborate charade?

161

"You look confused, my dear," Lenore said. "Why don't you sit down and let me serve?"

Confused wasn't the word for it, Dawn thought, and gave Lenore a suspicious look as she took the chair opposite. "Lenore—" she started to say, and had to wait until the pouring ceremony was complete.

"Now, then," Lenore said comfortably. She had poured one transparent china cup, then a second, which she held out with a smile. "First, I'd like to thank you for coming all the way out here on such short notice. I do appreciate it."

Gritting her teeth, Dawn accepted the cup. Obviously they weren't going to talk about the men in that damned green sedan, and she put the cup down, untouched, and waited.

Lenore took a sip and nodded. "Ah, that's good," she murmured, and then glanced, birdlike, at her guest. "I know how busy you are, my dear. Shall I get right to the point?"

Dawn clenched her hands. "Please."

To her surprise, Lenore laughed again, a merry little sound that sounded to Dawn like tacks on a blackboard. "I see that you aren't amused by my little game," she said, gesturing to the car outside. "But aren't you curious about why I had you followed?"

Feeling as though her nerves had been stretched to the breaking point, Dawn figured she had nothing to lose. "I really don't give a damn, Lenore," she said. "As you say, you have your little games."

For an instant she thought she'd gone too far. Lenore's eyes narrowed, and suddenly she didn't look amused. "This wasn't exactly a game."

Dawn willed herself to meet that glance. "Your words, not mine."

Lenore's eyes flashed at this insubordination, and despite herself, Dawn nearly cringed. "You're being difficult," Lenore said, as though speaking to a recalcitrant child.

Marveling at her audacity, Dawn said, "I always am when someone invades my privacy."

To her surprise—and relief—Lenore laughed again. "Well spoken," she said. "I always knew you had backbone. Now then, the reason I had you followed is obvious, I think. I thought I might find out something interesting, and of course, I did."

Dawn decided to brazen it through. "All you found out is that

162

I visited a clinic," she said with a shrug. "That information can't be of much value."

"Ah, but I found out more than that, my dear."

She'd been about to take a sip of tea. Her lips suddenly stiff, she paused with the cup halfway to her mouth. "What?"

"Let's not beat about the bush, shall we?" Lenore said calmly. "I have quite a bit of time and energy invested in you, my dear, and I'd like to know what you intend to do about your pregnancy."

Dawn's cup clattered in her saucer. "You can't know about that! That information is confidential!"

Lenore laughed. "Not anymore."

"You had no right!"

"Perhaps not," Lenore agreed. "But that's beside the point, isn't it?"

"That's exactly the point!" Dawn cried. "What business is it of yours?"

"Oh, come now, Dawn. You're not naive. You certainly know the score."

"What score? What are you talking about?"

Lenore gave her a severe look. "If you'll kindly stop shouting, I'll tell you."

"I'm not shouting!" Dawn cried, and made a fierce effort to bring herself under control. But she was so furious, her hands were shaking, and she put the cup on the table with a clatter. Gritting her teeth again, she said, "I'm listening."

Again that maddening incline of the head. "Now, then," Lenore said, as though preparing to lecture. "You're angry that I had you followed, and I suppose that if I were in your shoes, I might feel the same way. But you have to understand that I have an investment to protect—"

Dawn couldn't control herself. "An investment! But you've been well paid for everything you've done!"

"So have you," Lenore said sharply. "And if you want that arrangement to continue, you'll do me the courtesy of listening without further interruption!"

Dawn hesitated. Finally she said sullenly, "Go ahead. I'm listening."

"Thank you. Now, as I was saying, you do have *some* potential, or I wouldn't be bothering with you. I'd hate to see you throw it all away because of this . . . this inconvenience, and I

163

asked you here today to make sure you intend to do the right thing.''

''And that is?''

Lenore looked at her as though she'd lost her mind. ''An abortion, of course! What else?''

She didn't know why, but she couldn't stop herself. ''And if I choose not to have one?''

Even Lenore was momentarily stymied by that one. ''You wouldn't be so stupid.''

She took a chance. ''Lee might not think it's so stupid.''

''Surely you don't think you can get him to marry you!'' Lenore exclaimed. She looked so incredulous that Dawn flushed. She knew Lenore was right. ''For heaven's sake, girl, think what you're saying. Why, you can't even prove the child is his! Besides, what about your career?''

Dawn was too embarrassed to look directly at her. ''What about it?'' she said sullenly. ''You have nothing to do with that.''

''Ah, but I might. If I choose, I can decide how long you stay there, how far you might rise, and so on. All it takes is a little call. Barnaby and I have known each other for years.'' She paused. ''I hope I make myself clear.''

Wondering how this had all gotten turned around, Dawn clenched hands in her lap. ''You do,'' she muttered, and forced herself to look up. She still had a little fight left in her, and she said, ''I still don't know why any of this should matter to you.''

''It does,'' Lenore said complacently. ''Trust me. Everything will become clear in time.''

''And all I have to do is do what you want, is that right?''

''And continue to do so, when I ask,'' Lenore agreed. ''And in return . . .''

She paused, deliberately, tantalizingly, drawing it out. Dawn had to ask. ''And in return—what?''

Lenore shrugged. ''Well, what would make you happy? Let's see. How about your own column at the *Eye*?''

Dawn couldn't help it; her longing flashed quickly across her face. But she said, ''And all I have to do for that is get rid of my . . . problem . . . and keep reporting to you, is that it?''

Lenore inclined her head. ''That's all.''

Dawn tried to think about it, but ambition was getting in the way. What the hell, she thought: she'd already decided to have the abortion anyway. This was turning out a lot better than she'd hoped, or dared expect, and she stood. "You've got a deal," she said.

"Splendid," Lenore replied, and took an envelope from the book she'd laid aside. She held it out, gesturing when Dawn gave it a suspicious look. "Go ahead, take it. Consider it a bonus. To show you how very much I appreciate your . . . services."

Two spots of color burned on Dawn's cheeks. She couldn't believe she'd been taken in like this. "You had it figured out all along, didn't you?"

"I'm an old woman, my dear," Lenore said with a shrug. "I haven't lived to this age without knowing something about people. Good-bye for now. Chester will show you out."

As though by magic, the butler appeared. Dawn had no choice but to leave, but as soon as the door closed behind her, Lenore laughed and shook her head. The girl had put up a fight, but she'd done as expected in the end. She might have gone unwillingly just now, but she hadn't left without that envelope.

---*⊘*---

CHAPTER FOURTEEN

"Mama," Andrea said to Laura, "tell me about your new job."

Laura glanced across the counter. She was making sandwiches for lunch, and she paused, mayonnaise knife in one hand, slice of bread in the other, distracted for a moment from the question by how much her daughter had changed in the past year. Just the other day, it seemed, Andrea had been inclined to chubbiness, her cheeks full, her body round and undefined. Now, almost overnight, she'd lost that baby fat, and even at ten was showing tantalizing glimpses of the young woman she would be all too soon. She'd never lost her love of shopping, but lately that particular interest had been supplanted by another: boys. Shaking her head at the thought of what was still to come, she answered the question.

"It's not exactly a new job," she said. Then, because it had been over six months since she'd quit the PD, she asked curiously, "What made you ask?"

Andrea seemed to have inherited a love of peanut butter from her brother, and the jar was open on the counter. Averting her eyes from her mother's disapproval, she took a swipe with her finger and said with a shrug, "I don't know. I guess it was something Dad said."

Laura started spreading mayonnaise again, deliberately casual. "What was that?"

Helping herself to another taste from the jar, Andrea shrugged again. "I don't know. Just that instead of defending creeps, now you were persecuting them."

Despite herself, Laura smiled. "*Prosecuting*, Andy," she said, and reached for another slice of bread. But she felt tense when she asked, "How did Dad seem to feel about that?"

"About per—*pros*ecuting all those creeps? Okay, I guess. He said that was better than getting chummy with all those lowlifes you had in court before.''

"I see," Laura said. She could imagine him saying just that. "And how do you feel about it?"

Andrea levered herself onto one of the bar stools opposite the kitchen side of the counter. Her expression serious, she said, "I'm not sure. I don't know what the difference is."

"Between prosecuting someone and defending them, you mean?" Laura asked, and glanced around for the meat tray. Her children were the only ones who wanted peanut butter; everyone else was having ham or turkey. Reaching for one of the deli packages, she said, "Well, when someone is accused of a crime, it's the job of the defense attorney to convince the jury he didn't do it, and it's the job of the prosecutor to prove that he did." She smiled. "Does that make it easier to understand?"

"Yeah, I guess. But what if the person really did it?"

Laura glanced quickly down at the package she held. It had been eight months now, but she still felt a stab of guilt whenever she thought about Marion Higgins killing that policeman. She'd awakened for weeks afterward from nightmares in which she tried to wrestle the weapon from him and failed; every time the gun went off in her dreams, she bolted upright, drenched in sweat, a cry on her lips. She wouldn't be able to get back to sleep for hours afterward, and finally Jack had become so impatient, he'd threatened to move to the couch until she resolved it. She knew he was right, but she couldn't help feeling resentful that he wasn't being more supportive. She'd wrestled with the problem for weeks and had finally gone to Tony to tell him that she'd decided to quit.

He hadn't really looked surprised. "I'm sorry to hear that," he said, sounding as if he genuinely was. "Have you decided what you're going to do?"

"I'm not sure," she'd admitted painfully. "I've been thinking of giving up criminal law altogether."

He had been surprised at that. "Laura, you can't let one case get to you like this."

She knew he was right, but she couldn't seem to help herself. The knowledge that she was responsible, however inadvertently, for that cop's death had eaten away at her for weeks. Her professional life as well as her personal life had been affected; her work here had suffered because of her guilt and uncertainty. Cases she would have approached confidently before terrified

167

her now, and at times she was so afraid of doing something wrong that she felt too paralyzed to do anything at all. Tony, bless him, had been understanding; he'd assigned someone else to defend Marion Higgins. She couldn't have defended him if her life depended upon it; even the sight of the man revolted her, and all she could think about was that police officer's sobbing wife and uncomprehending children when she'd gone to the funeral. She didn't understand how this had happened any more than they did.

Finally she'd come to the conclusion that she wasn't effective here any longer, and that's when she'd tendered her resignation. Tony hadn't been happy, but he claimed to understand.

"Hey, this happens sometimes, Laura," he said. "I sympathize, but we're going to miss you like hell. You had the makings of a fine defense attorney."

Wondering what kind of attorney she'd make now, she'd left Tony's office and gone back to her own. Maurey was there, and he took one look at her face and knew.

"You did it, huh?"

"I had to."

He looked so dejected that she put a hand on his shoulder. "Hey, it's not that bad—"

He looked even more glum. "Yes, it is."

She tried to cheer him up—she, who felt like crying even though the conviction was growing in her that she'd done the right thing. "Look at it this way," she'd said. "There's a bright spot."

"What?"

She tried to smile. "You'll have the office all to yourself."

Neither of them had laughed.

That hadn't been her last day, of course; she still had other cases pending, obligations to Tony to give him enough notice to replace her. But finally the time had come, and after an office party at which they'd all been determinedly cheerful—and which Jack had missed—she'd said good-bye to her days as a public defender. She was just leaving when Dale came by for a farewell drink.

"I think there's still some punch," she said, pleased to see him.

"Punch wasn't what I had in mind," he said gruffly. "I came to take you out for a real drink."

She couldn't refuse him; she was too depressed. They went

to a little bar close by, and he had barely waited until the waitress had left with their orders before he said, "Okay, so now what are you going to do?"

She gave a shaky laugh. "Take a vacation, of course. I need some time off after these past three years, don't you think?"

"I don't know. It's been so long since I've had a vacation myself that I've sort of forgotten what they're like."

Feeling that if she didn't keep up the patter, she would dissolve in tears, she said, "I haven't. It's where you sleep until noon, then get up and sun yourself for the rest of the day on the beach, reading all the novels you promised yourself you'd get to when you had time."

"That sounds boring as hell."

"I don't know; it sounds pretty good to me."

He shrugged. "Okay, so what are you going to do the second day?"

"I don't think you've gotten the point, Dale," she said with a laugh. "A vacation is more than one day, you know."

He was serious. "For other people, maybe. But not for you. You're not the kind to sit around painting your toenails and reading the latest fiction trash. You'll be bored out of your gourd in five minutes. So—now that that's out of the way, tell me what you're really going to do."

She couldn't keep up the pretense. Sobering, she stared into the drink the girl had just brought and said honestly, "I don't know, Dale. I don't know what to do. Right now I'm so confused, I'm just taking it one step at a time."

He surprised her by reaching for her hand. His fingers were warm and comforting as they closed over hers, the gesture of a friend. Without warning, she felt the sting of tears in her eyes again and looked away.

"Everybody in this business has a Marion Higgins in the basement, Laura," he said quietly. "You can't let it get you down."

She couldn't hide her bitterness. "Easy for you to say."

"Not really. The same thing happened to me once," he said, and shrugged when she looked at him quickly. "Oh, the circumstances were different, but the effect was the same. I felt all the blame and guilt you're feeling now." He gave her a keen glance. "You want to hear about it?"

He had her attention, and she leaned forward intensely. "Yes."

169

"Well, it was when I was with the DA's office in San Diego—right out of law school, still green, and wet behind the ears." He looked wry. "When I was gung ho, and still believed I could charge in and save society by sending all those sickos away."

"Go on."

"It was my first big felony trial, my chance to prove that I had what it took. You know the feeling." He glanced at her for confirmation and received a rapt nod. "And I was determined to win, at any cost. The defendant had an alibi a baby could punch holes in, and I was sure I could nail him. He'd been accused of stabbing someone to death outside a bar, but even with two eyewitnesses, he denied being anywhere near the place. He claimed instead that he'd been playing poker with some friends, but when we questioned them, they refused to corroborate his story."

"It sounds pretty basic to me," Laura said.

Dale downed the last of his drink. "That's what I thought. The only thing I didn't have were fingerprints on the weapon, but that didn't bother me; prints can be wiped off, right? So I went after this guy with everything I had. I had forensics, the eyewitnesses, the weapon, everything I could want to get a conviction. I was going to make a name for myself, and no one was going to stop me." He set the glass down.

She leaned forward again when he paused. "So what happened?"

"Oh, I convicted the guy," he said. "He went to prison, where, after being 'initiated' by the boys, he was torn up so bad inside, he died. I didn't find out until then that he'd been telling the truth all along. He hadn't been near that bar when the stabbing took place; he'd been with his so-called friends. But it wasn't for a poker game."

"What, then?"

"The three of them were doing a drug deal—a big one—and when this guy got busted, they didn't want any ties to them. It was safer to lie about where they'd been and what had happened. After all, they figured the guy wouldn't do too much time. What's the sentence for manslaughter—seven years? It was the first arrest, first conviction. With good behavior, he could've been out in five or less."

"So who tipped you to the drug deal?"

"One of the men there after he got burned by his dealer. He

rolled over, and as an added bonus, he dropped the information on the stabbing.''

''But what about the eyewitnesses?''

Dale shook his head. ''Friends of the dealer.''

''Lord,'' Laura muttered, and because he looked so unhappy, tried to comfort him. ''But he would have gone down on the drug deal, Dale.''

''Yeah, but he didn't, did he? He caught manslaughter instead, and paid a hell of a big price for my mistake.''

Laura thought of her own agonizing about Marion Higgins and knew nothing she said could make any difference. They both stared into their glasses for a few moments, then Dale stirred. ''There's a lesson to be learned in all this.''

''I hope so,'' Laura said morosely.

''Well, all we can do is our jobs,'' Dale said. ''The law is clear, remember. We present the case, but it's up to the jury to decide guilt or innocence.''

She had a faraway look in her eyes. ''I used to think that.''

''You still do,'' he said firmly.

''I'm not so sure.''

''Well, you'd better be by nine Monday morning.''

This was Friday. Wondering what he was talking about, she looked at him curiously. ''What's Monday?''

''Your appointment with the DA.''

''What!''

''Oh, don't be coy. You know you've been thinking about it for months now. I just decided to get the ball rolling by making the appointment for you.''

She looked at him in horrified dismay. ''What are you talking about? You can't do that!''

''I certainly can.''

''This is outrageous!''

He grinned. ''I know. But I knew that someone had to get you off your butt and back to work or else you'd just mope around feeling sorry for yourself.''

Suddenly comprehending, she narrowed her eyes. ''You made up that whole story just now, didn't you?''

''I most certainly did not!'' he said indignantly. ''Check the records if you don't believe me. The defendant's name was Gary Bentwhistle.''

Despite her turmoil, she nearly laughed. ''You're making that up!''

"I am not! Check it yourself."

"I will!"

"Good," he said with a grin. "But make it after Monday at nine, will you? Duluth doesn't like people to be late."

"I'm not going to keep that appointment, Dale," she warned.

"Oh, yes, you will," he said confidently, and ordered another drink to celebrate.

She had kept the appointment. As much as it galled her to admit it, Dale was right. She *had* been thinking about this; she just needed the impetus. Dale had provided it, and exactly at nine Monday morning, she presented herself at the district attorney's office for her first interview. To her surprise, considering how nervous she suddenly was at the prospect of turning her career plans completely around, it went very well. Because they knew each other, Duluth waved aside most of his opening speech and came right to the point.

"I don't need to give you the big tour, Ms. Devlin," he said. "You're as aware as anyone else of the number of applications we receive to this office every year." He winked at her. "We're a pretty elite group around here, but after being with the PD, you know that yourself."

She had to smile at his manner. "I can't argue that. I've come up against many of them in court."

"And acquitted yourself well, I might add," he said, and winked again. "No pun intended. How long were you with the PD?"

"Three years."

"Let's talk about that a little, shall we?"

She'd known this was coming, and she nodded. "If you like."

He sat back. "At the risk of seeming presumptuous, let me guess why you originally applied for public defender service. To put it in a nutshell, you saw it as a way to insure social justice, to make sure the scales were balanced, to see that poor people were furnished with service that others could pay for. Am I close?"

She didn't know why she felt like squirming inside; she hadn't detected even a gleam of condescension. Still, when he put it like that, it made all her reasons for becoming a public defender childish and naive and almost silly. Thinking how much she had changed, she made herself say, "I'm not sure I thought about it quite like that, but yes, I suppose I agree."

"And is it your experience that attorneys who choose legal

aid, no matter how well they perform, are still on the outside? After all, legal aid is not the government, and however we might rail against it, society still tends to stigmatize people who represent rapists and murderers.''

She couldn't help it; she immediately thought of Jack, who felt exactly that way. He'd never understood her desire to defend criminals, either, and she'd never been able to impress upon him that defendants weren't criminals until they were found guilty. It had been a poor argument, especially when one of her clients had a rap sheet as long as her arm, but she hadn't realized how uneasy she'd been about that part of it until now.

"Yes, I have to admit that's true," she said. "But I also have to say that prosecutors only see the victims. The public defender has to deal with the defendants, and most of the time the defendants are sad cases, too.''

"I agree," he said. "But that brings me to another point: the qualities that make a good prosecutor. First, and most obvious, naturally, is a commitment to public service. But equally important is what I call the judgment factor. As you're also aware from your own experience, so much of a deputy's job involves decision making—whether to reduce charges, for example, and by how much; how cases should be handled, if witnesses are telling the truth. But you've dealt with all that, too.''

"Yes, I have," she agreed.

"And well, I might add," he said, gesturing toward a file with her name on it that sat in the middle of his desk. He sat back, tenting his hands in front of his chin. "But what you might not be aware of is that I also want to see some signs of humility here, no matter how corny that sounds. The reason is that I give my staff a lot of power, and I want to make sure everyone who works for me is going to use that power with good sense and without arrogance. Does that make sense?''

"Yes," she said, and didn't realize how surprised she sounded until he smiled. She flushed with embarrassment, but to her relief, he didn't seem to notice. He was already going on.

"I guess it all comes down to the desire to try cases, Ms. Devlin," he said. "The most challenging part of this job, naturally, is going to trial, putting all the pieces of a case together for the jury, insuring that the evidence establishes the defendant's guilt so that the jury will vote guilty. It's something that you haven't pursued from the defense table, something that only you can decide if you want to pursue from the prosecution's side.''

She started to say something, but he held up his hand. ''I don't want your answer yet. I assume you've devoted some thought to this, or you wouldn't be here.'' He smiled and reached for a file under hers with a little shrug. ''This is the point where I like to get some idea of how you'd handle a case. Here, why don't you read this while I go get some coffee, and we'll discuss it when I come back. Would you like some?''

She shook her head. ''No, thanks.''

He stood. ''I'll be back in a few minutes.''

She was already absorbed in the file when he closed the door, and by the time he returned, she had a thoughtful expression on her face. He took a seat behind the desk and grinned. ''So. What do you think of our Bigfoot case?''

Fortunately, she'd heard of it before. The case involved a charge of child stealing against the defendant, one Homer ''Chip'' Andrews, who had been arrested on the charge of abducting a fourteen-year-old girl named Sharon Quinlan. The two had been camping at Lake Arrowhead, and when he had returned without the girl, the parents had brought the abduction charge against him. When the police had investigated, Andrews claimed that Bigfoot had abducted her. Psychiatrists' reports indicated the man was able to stand trial, but the problem now seemed to be whether to go ahead and prosecute. Duluth was asking her opinion about what she would do if she were the deputy who'd caught the case.

''Well?'' Duluth asked. He was sitting back now, but under the grin and the apparently lazy gaze, his eyes were intent. She didn't have to be told that the next few minutes would decide her own case.

Deciding just to go for it, she took a deep breath. ''I'd drop the charges.''

The grin disappeared, and for a horrible second Laura was sure she'd made an irretrievable error. ''You mind telling me why?'' he said.

She'd started, now she had to go on. ''Well, for one thing, the girl hasn't been found, has she?''

''No, the sheriff's investigators have searched the entire area, and people here have interviewed practically everyone she knew. No sign, no trace.''

He was staring at her intently, but even though that steady

gaze was unnerving, she knew her instincts were right. "Okay, then I think the charge should be dropped because if the girl's body is ever found, we could pursue a homicide investigation instead."

He looked thoughtful. "Yes, but suppose the body isn't found? Wouldn't it be better to go for a child-stealing charge and then bring him back for the homicide?"

Now she knew she was right. "No, I don't think so. If we went to trial on child stealing, and then the body *is* found and we retry for homicide, we have a potential for double jeopardy. I know, because if I was acting as defense, I'd file it myself."

"Interesting approach," he said, and her heart sank as he sat back, still staring at her. "Are you sure that's what you'd do?"

He was giving her a chance to change her mind, but she couldn't take it. Carefully she put the file back on the desk. "I'm sure," she said.

He'd sat there a few tense seconds longer, then a slow grin spread across his face. "Good," he said. "Because that's probably what I'd do, too." He stood and held out his hand. "Thanks for coming in, Ms. Devlin."

She stood, too. The words were out before she could stop them. "That's all?"

"The rest is up to you," he said with a smile. "You think about it awhile, but if you decide you'd like to be part of my staff, I'll be glad to have you aboard."

She was so pleased she'd done well, that it was over and she hadn't committed some awful blunder, that she laughed. With the laughter had come her decision. Even so, she waited to discuss it with Jack, who lately had been too preoccupied with his own concerns to think of hers. When she came home that night, he was just getting off the phone with an Arizona contractor who had offered him a job. To her dismay, she learned that he was going to be gone six months.

"You didn't even discuss it with me?" she asked in disbelief. The tentative gains they'd made had been lost that horrible night at the Beverly Hills fund-raiser, but she hadn't believed they were this bad.

"I think we both need some time, Laura," he said without meeting her eyes.

"Yes, but do we have to get it in different states?"

He had no answer. He'd left at the end of the week, and she had taken the position with the district attorney. That had been six months ago, and now that the Arizona job was winding up, he was due to come home. She wondered how things would be between them, how much time it would take to get used to being together again. They'd never been separated for such a long time, and while he'd flown home several weekends during this period, he never wanted to talk about what was going on. She had been forced to put her marriage on hold until he came home for good, and in the meantime was thankful for her work. Now she had finished with what she privately referred to as her probationary period, and she was eager to move on.

And her marriage? What was she going to do about that? A picture of Douglas Rhodes's face flashed into her mind just then, and despite herself, she felt a pang. She'd never forgotten what he'd done for her that night Jack had jumped into the pool; she'd thought about calling him so many times, but hadn't dared to pick up the phone.

"Mama?"

Jolted out of her thoughts by Andrea's insistent voice, she looked at her daughter, sitting across the counter from her, then at the slice of ham in her hand. She'd been so lost in thought that she'd forgotten she was supposed to be making lunch, and she hurriedly finished the sandwich she'd been working on and laid it on the plate with the rest. The back door slammed just then and Peter came in. He'd been playing volleyball on the beach and looked flushed. She wanted to reach out and give him a quick hug, but at twelve, such gestures had long been beneath his dignity. She ruffled his hair instead, noticing that it had been bleached nearly white already by the sun. He pulled his head back and made a sound of disgust.

"Aw, Mom," he said in protest, and spied the plate of sandwiches. Grabbing one, he bit into it before Laura could stop him and said, "Guess what?"

"What?" she said, and resignedly reached for the loaf of bread again. At the rate she was going, she'd never finish making lunch, and her sister was waiting for her down by the water. Janette and her husband had come over with the kids for the day, and because Janette looked so tired, she had insisted on taking care of the food.

"There's a dead dolphin down by the water. It's really gross."

Laura turned to look at him. "Did you call the lifeguard?"

He took another bite of sandwich. "Nah, somebody else already did,'' he said, and grinned. ''Aunt Janette nearly had a fit! You should have seen her face!''

Andrea jumped off the stool. ''I want to see it!''

''No, you don't,'' Laura said, catching her daughter's arm as she started to rush by. ''You just leave it alone.''

''But Mom, Peter saw it!''

''That was an accident. And I'm sure there's a big enough crowd by now; you don't need to add to it. Let the people in charge do their jobs.''

''Aw, gee, I never get to do *anything*!''

''Not true,'' Laura said calmly, grabbing Peter's hand as he reached for another sandwich. ''You can call everybody for lunch.''

''Oh, Mom!'' Andrea wailed, but she stomped off. The screen door banged behind her, and seconds later, Laura heard her calling everybody shrilly from the porch. Closing her eyes, she shook her head. She hadn't meant for Andrea to stand outside and yell.

Peter lingered in the kitchen. ''Mom . . . ?''

Busy piling sandwiches on a plate to take out to the deck, she answered absently. ''What?''

''When is Dad coming home?''

She stopped for the barest instant, then continued with the food. ''I don't know. Why?''

When he didn't answer, she turned to look at him. He was standing there uncomfortably, and his blue eyes, so like his father's, struck a chord in her heart. ''Well, because he's been gone so long, I guess.''

''Yes, he has,'' she agreed. ''But he told you before he left how important this contract was to him. It's just taking longer than he expected.''

''Yes, but . . . '' Peter glanced away. Absently tracing a pattern on the counter with a grubby finger, he said, ''Is he ever coming back?''

''Of course he's coming back! What makes you say a thing like that?'' Horrified, she put the plate of sandwiches on the counter. Now she knew why he'd been so quiet lately, so withdrawn. But why was he thinking such things? How . . . ?

Her eyes narrowed, and suddenly she knew who had been filling his head with these doubts. Her mouth tightened and she came around the counter and put her hand under his chin, forcing him to look up at her. ''Who told you that?''

177

He tried to free his chin. "Come on, Mom. No one told me," he protested.

She knew him so well; she could tell he was lying. "No one?" she repeated.

He succeeded in jerking his head away. "No, Mom, I told you! Leave it alone, all right? No one said anything, I just guessed!"

But she knew that wasn't true, and as he tried to push past her, she took him by the shoulder. With everyone coming in soon for lunch, she didn't have time to discuss this as fully as she wanted, and in any case, she was too angry with her mother to approach this calmly. But she wanted to reassure him, and so she said, "Listen to me, Peter. I admit that your father and I are having a few problems right now, but it's nothing we can't work out. Do you hear me? *It's nothing we can't work out.* So I don't want you to worry, or . . . or think that your father isn't coming back. He loves you; we both do. We wouldn't do anything to hurt you. Do you believe me?"

He glanced away sullenly and shrugged. "Yeah, I guess."

It was all she was going to get from him; she had to be content with that. But her expression was grim as she watched him run out, and she expelled a harsh breath. Why did her mother do things like this? What purpose did it serve? She knew Estelle blamed her for Jack's absence, but why fill the children's heads with fears? Did her mother *want* to hurt her?

She didn't have time to answer that; maybe she didn't want to know. Just then everybody came in from the beach, and she involved herself in serving lunch. She was just unwrapping the potato salad when her mother came in, and her lips tightened when Estelle tasted it and immediately reached for the pepper. She met her sister's eyes across the kitchen, and when Janette winked, she just threw up her hands and left the kitchen.

"You shouldn't let her get to you, Laurie," Janette said, joining her on the deck, where she'd gone to cool off. "You know she does things like that just to bug you."

"Yes, well, she does a good job," Laura muttered, turning to look at Janette from her leaning position against the rail. "Why, does it show?"

Janette laughed and took a bite of ham sandwich. "Only to a trained observer. Forget it. You worry too much."

"Easy for you to say. You don't have to live with her."

"Thank God. I've only been here since one, and already I've

had it up to here with her remarks today about my weight, the way I raise my kids, how I don't take care of my husband, how I really should put more effort into cleaning my house, et cetera, et cetera. I think if I hear one more criticism, I'm going to commit—what's the word, when you rend someone from limb to limb?''

"Mayhem," Laura said. "Does Mom really criticize you like that?''

"Not in your hearing, of course. But yeah, she does," Janette said, and held up a forkful of potato salad. "Didn't you hear what she said when I took some of this?''

"No, I was busy getting the kids settled. What did she say?''

"It wasn't exactly what she *said*; it was the way she looked at me. You'd have thought I'd just buried my face in the whole bowl instead of taking a spoonful—'' Janette looked down at the mound of salad on her plate with a wry expression. "Or two. But speaking of mayhem," she went on, "tell me about the job. You still like it as much as you did?''

Laura smiled. "Yes, I still like it.''

Janette squinted up at her. "I'm glad. It sort of makes up for Jack's . . . shall we say . . . lack of enthusiasm?'' She took a bite of ham. "When's he coming home, anyway?''

"I'm . . . not sure," she said. She really didn't want to talk about it. To her relief, Janette picked up on her mood and set aside her empty plate.

"I'm going to get some cake. You want anything?''

Laura shook her head. For some reason, her appetite seemed to have fled. She caught a glimpse of her mother, sitting inside on the couch, and knew why. Averting her gaze, she looked at her sister, standing expectantly by the door. "No, thanks; you go ahead. But check the kids, will you? I told Andrea she had to eat lunch before she started in on dessert.''

Janette gave her a mocking look. "And you thought she'd do it with Mother there, egging her on to have some of the cake she'd made?'' she said. "You incurable optimist.''

"Well, try, anyway," Laura said resignedly, and turned back to her contemplation of the beach when she was alone again. Mention of Jack had brought back memories of the mortifying experience in Beverly Hills, and she knew it would be a long time before she could forgive him for his appalling behavior that night. He had never apologized, and she knew that he somehow blamed her for what had happened. Whenever she thought about it—which was as seldom as possible—she felt embarrassed all over again, and when she remembered how kind Douglas Rhodes had been, she wondered what she would have done without him.

Her cheeks reddened when she remembered something else. She rarely allowed herself to think about it, but there were times—like now—when without warning she recalled the feel of his arms around her, and how he had held her that night. She never should have allowed that loss of control; she'd tried to tell herself that if she hadn't been so upset about Jack, and then about that phone call from Tony, she wouldn't have dreamed of letting herself be embraced by another man. Then she knew that wasn't true. She had been attracted to Douglas Rhodes from the first time they met, and she had wondered that night what it would feel like to be in his arms.

Now she knew. Worse, she knew, too, that if circumstances were different . . .

Quickly she shut her eyes, trying to banish the tantalizing pictures that rose in her mind. What was wrong with her? Why couldn't she forget him? They were both married, for God's sake; they both had *lives*. This preoccupation was unhealthy, unbecoming; she had to stop it.

But how? she wondered dismally, and to her horror suddenly felt near tears. Wondering what was happening to her, she was trying to get herself under control when Janette poked her head out the door.

"Hey, you! I could use some help in here!"

Relieved to have something mundane and ordinary to do, Laura sniffed and turned away from the rail. Janette saw her face and said in concern, "What's wrong with you?"

Laura didn't know how to explain. "Nothing. I guess I'm just feeling blue."

"Maybe you miss Jack," Janette said uncertainly.

She tried to smile. "Maybe I do," she said, and knew it wasn't true.

CHAPTER FIFTEEN

To the uninitiated, criminal court could be an assault on the senses. A tumult ensued before the judge appeared, a persistent din made by people trying to get something done. Laura had heard that in Manhattan it could be even more of a madhouse, with prosecutors and defense lawyers haggling over prospective plea bargains down by the bench so they would be able to hear their case called, six or seven attorneys clustered around the docket clerk, handing in appearance forms or examining court files as they urged the clerk to pass their case forward to be called next, all with witnesses milling around, asking plaintively what to do. Police officers, summoned for testifying, could be lined up in pairs against the walls, many of them in from the twelve-to-eight shift for the bail hearings on their nighttime collars, sipping coffee in an effort to stay awake, and everybody trying to hear themselves through the noise. Always so much noise.

Here in Los Angeles, she reflected, things weren't much different. Each day's schedule in the criminal court system typically included a mix of petty larceny, burglary, possession of a weapon, possession of narcotics, rape, indecent exposure, resisting arrest, assault, picking pockets, mugging, shoplifting . . . murder.

This particular morning, things were the same as they had been since she started work. As the first case was called—"Charles Edward Damian: burglary and possession of stolen property"—she searched through her stack of files. She saw the defendant out of the corner of her eye come forward with his attorney, and knew the judge would turn to her soon, so she thumbed through the pile more quickly, trying to find the right one. Today, lo and behold, the file she needed was here. Pulling it triumphantly from the bottom of the stack, she scanned the contents quickly: an affidavit by the arresting officer, information that the defendant was burglarizing the apartment complex where he lived, a warrant that led to the discovery of stolen stereo equipment in the defendant's apartment, his arrest . . . and the fact that the witness hadn't been able to pick him out of a lineup.

Great, she thought, and turned to the yellow sheet. Thinking how quickly her caseload had increased, so that she was in the same position here as she'd been with the PD—awash in files she didn't have nearly enough time for—she scanned the arrest record. She'd been handed this case when she came in this morning, and she hadn't had time yet to go over it. When she saw that the sheet listed numerous burglary, B and E, and possession convictions, she closed the folder. The defendant was a career burglar who was pleading innocent to the charges, and this was a hearing to determine whether there was probable cause. According to his file, she had the physical evidence to prove that he'd been holding stolen goods, but nothing to show that he'd stolen them.

She didn't have time to think about it. The judge was already addressing opposing counsel. "What's your motion, Mr. Latham?"

Hiram Latham was a private attorney, an unctuous little man she disliked. "We are ready to proceed, Your Honor," he said, and gave a little bow that irritated her even more.

When the judge turned expectantly to her, she said without preamble, "May I approach the bench, Your Honor?"

The judge gestured for both counsel to come forward, and when she and Latham were standing before him, she said, "Your Honor, we're ready to make a disposition on this case right now."

Judge Hemmelbacker nodded. He liked things done this way, quick and clean. "Go ahead."

"We'd be willing to drop the burglary charge if the defendant agrees to take a guilty plea on the charge of criminal possession."

The judge turned questioningly to Latham, who said, "Sounds good to me."

"The defendant must also agree to maximum time," she added.

As she'd expected, Latham protested. "But that means a year in jail!"

She wasn't sympathetic. "Your client should have thought of that before."

He drew himself up. "And if we don't agree?"

"Then we'll go to trial on both burglary and possession," she said. "And since we'll probably win on possession, at least, that's going to mean maximum time for your boy. But we could also get lucky and win on burglary, in which case, your client is going to be looking at a lot more time."

"Let me discuss it with Mr. Damian," Latham said hurriedly, and went back to the defense table. The two had a quick conference, and then the attorney glanced up. "Your Honor, we're ready to proceed."

The judge nodded. "Any motions, Ms. Devlin?"

Laura glanced at defense counsel. "Yes, Your Honor. The state wishes to drop the charge of burglary against the defendant."

"Charge dismissed," Judge Hemmelbacker decreed, and glanced at Latham.

Right on cue, the defense attorney said, "Your Honor, my client wishes to change his previously entered plea of not guilty, to guilty of the crime of criminal possession of stolen property."

"So ordered," Judge Hemmelbacker said. "I sentence the defendant to a year in prison."

Bang, the gavel came down, and they were on to the next case.

The morning wore on, with Laura searching through her files, scanning them quickly as they came up to refresh her memory, and making fast decisions about accepting or suggesting pleas. When she had time, she marveled that she felt so comfortable doing this; it hadn't been so long ago that she'd been on the other side of the room. She seemed to have found her niche, all right, even if the morning was exhausting. Following Damian, there was an assault, with the same change in plea, one-year sentence. Then another assault, with no defendant present; bench warrant issued. A shoplifting case with a very well dressed woman huddled at the defense table hidden behind a hat with a black veil. Two hundred hours community service. Another assault, no witnesses.

"Where are the witnesses?" Judge Hemmelbacker shouted. As Laura had found out, he had a tendency to get excited.

Nobody knew where the witnesses were. She sent an assistant out to find out what had happened, requesting the case be put on the bottom of the calendar. With a glare in her direction, the request was granted. They went on to a mugging, a little old lady with blue hair hobbling to the witness stand leaning heavily on a cane, looking terrified. The defendant went up for a year, minus time served and good behavior. Laura shook her head as the old woman hobbled painfully back to her seat, the kid who had mugged her smirking behind her back. She knew he'd serve nine months, maximum, before he'd be out and prowling behind some other helpless old person, but she couldn't dwell on it; she had to go on.

Thirty-five cases later, it was noon and they recessed for two hours. She knew she should go back to her office to familiarize herself with the afternoon cases, but she felt claustrophobic. Taking her carton of yogurt and the apple she'd brought for lunch, she went outside to get some fresh air.

There wasn't any; the day was hot and smoggy, and an awful stench arose from the so-called tent city, an area of moving crates and hanging blankets and God knew what else, set up by the homeless beside the Criminal Courts Building. Her nostrils pinched, she went across the street to a tiny grassy area, resolving to eat as quickly as she could and get back to work. Trudy Mankiller, an LAPD narcotics investigator she'd met some time ago, and with whom she had developed a friendship, was there, just finishing a bag of potato chips. They waved at each other, and Laura came over and sat down.

"You look like the grapes of wrath," Trudy said. "Rough morning?"

Wearily Laura nodded. "And more to come."

"I know what you mean. We've got the special unit going out today—another big drug bust, God grant. I'll probably be on surveillance until my fanny goes numb. Did you bring anything good for lunch?"

Smiling, because Trudy proudly claimed herself to be the Queen of Junk Food, Laura held out the yogurt and the apple. "Here. Take your pick."

Trudy made a horrible face and took out a candy bar. She saw Laura's expression and shrugged. "Hey, to each her own, right?"

"Absolutely," Laura agreed, and sat there, without energy to eat.

Munching, Trudy said, "So what's new in your corner of the world? It's been a while since I've seen you."

"Just work," Laura said. "The stream is never-ending."

"How true, how true," Trudy said, and offered her one of the Twinkies she'd also brought.

"No, thanks," Laura said. She was no food purist, but she shuddered. "Do you know those things have a shelf life of six years?"

Trudy winked at her. "Then maybe I'd better stock up, in case the price goes up. What do you think?"

"I think you're going to be one big preservative if you're not careful."

"Hey, the body needs energy, and sugar is the best," Trudy said.

They ate in silence for a few minutes, then Trudy wadded up her refuse and lobbed it all in a ball toward the trash can. It sank without a trace and Laura gave her a glance. "I didn't know you could do that."

Trudy grinned wickedly. "Hey, don't let these fake glasses I wear for undercover, and frizzy hair and rotund body, fool you. There's a lot of things I can do. Besides," she added, "I played basketball in high school."

"You must have been pretty good," Laura said, thinking that for not-so-tall Trudy, basketball must have been quite a feat.

"Yeah, well, you learn a lot when you've got four brothers."

"I suppose so."

"That's what made me want to be a detective, in fact."

"They all joined the police force?"

Trudy laughed. "Are you kidding? They wouldn't know a badge from an auto insignia unless it was pointed in their direction. No, they're all into athletics in some form or another. One owns a sports store, another a gym, a third is a sportscaster, and my youngest brother plays for the Rams."

"But what does that have to do with the police force?"

"Nothing!" Trudy erupted with infectious laughter. "And that's just the point, don't you see?"

Laughing, too, Laura finished her lunch. Then, on impulse, she tossed her trash into the trash can, too. When Trudy looked surprised, she shrugged as though it were no big thing. "Hey, I played a little basketball, too."

"You!" Trudy was incredulous. "I don't believe it!"

"Oh? And just why is that?"

"Because you're so . . . so . . ." Words failed her, and she had to search. She finally came up with: "So . . . ladylike!"

Laughing, Laura said, "You make it sound like a disease or something."

"No, no; it isn't that. It's just that you're definitely not the kind of woman who gets slapped on the shoulder by a guy, you know? Or who has to worry about her slip showing, or a run in her panty hose or things like that."

"You'd be surprised," Laura said dryly.

Trudy put her hands on ample hips. "What guy has ever slapped you on the shoulder?" she demanded, and then nodded knowingly at Laura's expression. "You see? Case closed."

"Speaking of cases," Laura said reluctantly, "I guess I'd better get back to work."

"You would mention that," Trudy said with a sigh, and waved as she went off to her surveillance.

Dale poked his head into her office just as she got back. "Got a minute?"

She'd just sat behind her desk and reached for the first file of her afternoon cases, but she looked up with a smile. She'd never told him, because she wasn't quite sure how he'd take it, but during their association these past few years, she had always thought of him as a brother. She admired his intelligence, she respected his grasp of the law, and she loved his sense of humor. Better, they could disagree—and had, violently, at times—and still remain friends.

"For you?" she said. "Any time."

"That sounds promising," he said lightly.

"Don't get your hopes up," she said as he came in. She decided to tease him a little. "What's the problem? Another Gary Bentwhistle?"

He looked blank. "Gary Bentwhistle?"

"Aha!" she cried. "I got you, didn't I? I *knew* there wasn't a Gary Bentwhistle! You concocted that whole story that night just to cheer me up!"

Comprehension dawned. "I did not," he denied, caught in the act. "You can check it yourself!"

"I did," she said. "And there's no Gary Bentwhistle listed on any police report, nowhere, nohow. You tricked me, Dale—admit it!"

He drew himself up to his full height. "You have a suspicious mind. You know I wouldn't do a thing like that. And besides—wait a minute. Did you say *Gary* Bentwhistle?"

She narrowed her eyes. "That's what *you* said!"

186

"Oh, well, then, you must have heard it wrong," he said nonchalantly. "The guy's name wasn't Gary, it was Harry."

"*Harry* Bentwhistle?" She looked at him incredulously. "You've got to be kidding."

"I swear to God," he said, and started backing, red-faced, toward the door. "Check it yourself."

"I will," she warned. "Wait a minute. Where are you going? You said you wanted to talk to me about something."

"It wasn't important," he said, and escaped.

She laughed as the door closed quickly behind him. "Gotcha," she murmured, and glanced down at the files in front of her. Her smile disappeared, and thirty minutes later, she was back in court for the afternoon session, the Honorable Samuel Hemmelbacker still presiding.

The first case was another assault—was there no end to them? she wondered at times—with a defendant who'd had no priors, a steady job, and who had been released on his own recognizance. For once, faith in the system was justified, for the man actually showed up, and the judge was so pleased, he gave him probation and fifty hours of community service. They weren't so lucky on the next case, an indecent exposure, another ROR. This defendant failed to show, and a standard bench warrant was issued, but without much hope. It was always chancy releasing people on their own recognizance, but she knew judges had to play the odds. Jail space was at a premium and had to be reserved for the more serious offenses, and as a consequence, tens of thousands of people were released every year on their own; of those, thousands were never heard from again unless they happened to be arrested on another charge. She knew that it was every judge's secret fear that he'd release some jerk who would turn up later in the news as the next serial killer, but with so many people and cases moving through the clogged justice system, sometimes they all had to take a chance.

The afternoon wore on. As they labored at dispensing justice, she wondered at the sheer numbers. A recent report had circulated revealing the statistics that of the thousand and some cases arraigned every week, almost seventy percent were removed from the courts immediately, either through plea or skips after release. Of those that got past arraignment, only about three percent were ever brought to full trial, the rest being plea-bargained away. It seemed to Laura that afternoon that the statistics had somehow been reversed and that they were slogging

187

their way through the entire thousand for that week. Long before Hemmelbacker rapped the gavel down for the last time until tomorrow, she had developed a fierce headache. It had been one of those days.

She still had some loose ends to catch up on before she left, so she took a couple of aspirin when she got back to her office and started in. The headache was still hovering, but not as bad, when someone knocked on her door. Thinking it was Dale again, she called permission to enter without looking up. She had to finish this deposition; there was something wrong with it, and she wasn't quite sure what—

"I'm sorry," a voice she would never forget said. "I hope I haven't come at a bad time."

It was a moment before she could look up. When she did, her heart nearly leaped into her throat. She hadn't dared believe it was he until she saw him standing in the doorway, and to her embarrassment, her voice came out a croak. "Senator . . . what a surprise. I'm afraid you caught me a little off guard."

He smiled. "I'm sorry," he said again. "Would it be better if I came back later?"

Now that he was here, she didn't want him to go. "No!" she exclaimed, so eagerly that she was embarrassed again. Her cheeks reddened, and she tried to pull herself together. "Please, that's not what I meant at all. Come in—sit down."

He pulled up her only other chair, a horrible metal thing she knew would be uncomfortable for him. She was so unnerved, she nearly offered him hers, but he seemed not to notice the sparse seating arrangements; he was obviously waiting for her to sit down again, and when she did, he followed suit.

"I thought you were going to call me Douglas," he said with a smile. "But since you're being so formal, perhaps I should call you Deputy Devlin."

She reddened again. "Don't be silly. Laura will do just fine . . . Douglas. And I'm sorry. I guess it's just been a long day."

"I can imagine. Work never stops around here, does it?" he said. "Well, I won't take much of your time. I just stopped by to visit Jim, and when I heard that you'd joined the staff, I thought I'd come and wish you well."

She was flattered and embarrassed at the same time, uncomfortable at the idea that he and Jim had been talking about her. "Thank you," she said, and tried to make light of it by gesturing at the files piled haphazardly all over her desk, and at the blow-

188

ups of maps and sections of town and crime scenes that were stacked on the floor against the walls. "As you can see, I need it."

He glanced around. "It reminds me of my office in Washington."

She laughed, and some of the tension she felt inexplicably vanished. She could still hardly believe he was sitting right here, across from her, and she suddenly realized she hadn't a thing to offer him. She'd let Dale borrow her little coffee maker for some visitors this morning, and typical Dale, he hadn't returned it. "I'm sorry," she said. "I can't even offer you any coffee."

He held up a hand. "Oh, that's okay. At this point in the day, I'm pretty well coffeed out. To tell you the truth, I was thinking of something a little stronger, and since Jim bowed out, I wondered if you could join me instead." He smiled that engaging smile. "I'd much rather buy you a drink than Jim, any day. Since it's late, we'll make it a quick one if you like."

She was about to refuse; she knew she had to refuse. It was madness to accept, especially when she couldn't deny that he was one of the most magnetic men she'd ever met. Even his voice sent shivers through her, and he had a way of looking at her that made her pulse start to race. She knew it was absurd and ridiculous and in the realm of fantasy, but she couldn't help herself. It was folly to go anywhere with him, even for such a simple, innocent thing as a drink after work.

Tell him you can't, and just go home, she ordered herself, and reached into the desk drawer for her purse.

"I'd love to," she said, and tried to ignore the panicky little voice inside her head that asked her what she was doing. "Where would you like to go?"

He smiled with such genuine pleasure that she felt those silly shivers again. "I don't care," he said. "This is your town—you pick the spot."

What are you *doing*? that voice asked in alarm. She slammed the desk drawer shut on it. "In that case, let's go to Angel's Flight," she said, boldly naming one of the growing landmarks in town. The bar atop the Hyatt had a revolving rooftop that presented a circular view of the city. She'd only been there once, but she'd loved it. "It's a few minutes from here, but worth it."

"I know where it is," he said, and looked even more pleased at her choice. "I've got a car."

This is it! the voice commanded. *You can't go in his car!*

She listened this time. "Why don't we take both cars?" she said, and heard a little sigh of relief inside her head as she reached for her suit jacket behind her chair. "It'll be easier that way."

"Whatever you like," he said easily, and reached out to help her on with the jacket. His hands lightly touched her shoulders as he did, and she was horrified at the impulse to lean back, just slightly, into him. She shrugged quickly into the jacket instead and looked down at her desk. Files were scattered all over, and without glancing through them, she shoved as much as she could into her briefcase and snapped it shut.

This is a mistake, that nagging little voice told her sternly as she looked up at Douglas. *I know,* she answered, and said, "Are you ready?"

"Whenever you are."

She thought of her family then, and said guiltily, "Just a minute. I'd better call home and say I'll be just a little late."

"I'll wait outside," he said, and disappeared.

She didn't give her mother a chance to spoil it tonight. When Estelle answered, she merely said she was going to be late because she had a business meeting with a friend of the district attorney. It wasn't exactly a lie, but when she hung up, she knew she hadn't told the truth. Well, it couldn't be helped. Her mother wouldn't have understood, and she hadn't wanted to quarrel about it over the phone.

Douglas was waiting for her when she came out. "Everything all right?"

"Everything's fine," she said with a smile, and wondered again if she was doing the right thing.

It's only a drink, she told herself as they went down in the elevator to the ground floor. Nervous again, she arranged to meet him at the Hyatt and went out to her car.

The view atop Angel's Flight was just as spectacular as she remembered it. The setting sun was starting to gild the high rises around them as they went to a table, and far down in the canyons created by the tall buildings, lights were starting to twinkle on. She imagined a glimpse of ocean in the distance, and as Douglas seated her, she was glad she had come.

"What will you have?" he asked.

Thinking of her long drive home, she said, "I think I'd better stick with white wine."

"I'll have a whiskey sour," Douglas told the waiter.

She waited until the man had gone before she teased, "The house specialty is a margarita. I thought everybody from Arizona liked tequila."

He smiled. "Does everyone in Los Angeles drink bottled water?"

"Touché," she said, grimacing. "My daughter would die before she'd drink anything with minerals in it. I have to say I'm just as glad. Label worship is rampant enough as it is."

"You obviously don't have patience with status symbols," he said, and then looked at her curiously. "How many children do you have?"

"Two. My son, Peter, is twelve now, and Andrea is ten. But don't worry," she said with a smile. "I promise I won't haul out a three-foot-long photo folder to show them off."

"You must carry pictures."

"Not a one," she lied. "How about you? Do you have any children?"

"Just one, a son, Rob. He's nearly twenty now."

Something about his tone warned her not pursue it. Instead she said lightly, "Well, I want you to know that my daughter is going to be thrilled when she finds out I had a drink with the famous Senator Rhodes. She's seen you on television and thinks you're quite the hunk."

He seemed amused. "Should I take that as a compliment?"

"Definitely."

"Too bad she's not old enough to vote."

The waiter came then with the drinks, and when he had gone again, Douglas raised his glass. "To you," he said. "And your new career with the district attorney. The public defenders' loss is their gain."

Accepting the compliment with a pleased smile, she touched her glass to his and made a toast of her own. "And to your long and illustrious career in the United States Senate."

They drank. When Laura put her glass down again, she knew she had to mention the incident the last time they met. If she didn't, it would hang over her, overshadowing and spoiling this precious time they had together. Deciding just to get it over with, she said, "Douglas, about that business with Jack the last time—"

"Forget it," he said quickly. "That's in the past—over with. At least with me."

191

But then she met his glance and she knew that he might have put aside that unpleasantness with Jack, but like her, he hadn't forgotten that electrifying moment in the manager's office. It would always be a treasured memory, a shared recollection between them . . . unfinished business.

Shaken by her yearning reaction to that last thought, she dropped her eyes. She knew it was too dangerous to pursue it, and so she said inanely, "Thank you, Douglas. But you know I'll always be grateful to you for what you did that night."

He seemed to be struggling for composure himself. "I told you before, I was glad to help."

She had to look up at him. "I'm glad you were there."

Something leaped in his eyes, quickly suppressed. "I'm glad, too," he said.

They sat in silence for a moment, each wanting to say something more, neither daring to speak. The waiter came again and replenished their drinks, and Douglas ordered hors d'oeuvres. They were both grateful for the interruption; it gave them time to get back on track, and for a while they discussed innocuous subjects: how beautiful the city looked, their mutual love for the beach, her surprise that he'd attended UCLA. Politely he inquired after Jack; just as politely she mentioned that he had been in Douglas's own home state for a while, working on a job. Then they moved on to something else; neither of them wanted to talk about Jack. She wanted to ask about his wife, but the subject of his son had obviously disturbed him, so she stayed away from mention of his family. It didn't matter; after that one awkwardness, they didn't lack for things to talk about, and one subject led easily into another, once they had silently agreed to avoid the dangerous pitfalls of attraction. Finally Laura said, "You mentioned that you had stopped by to see Jim. Old school ties? They must be very strong if you come to Los Angeles just to visit."

He looked wry. "We're good friends, all right—but I didn't come here just to see Jim. I had an appointment with Malcolm Tanner—an image consultant who's going to manage my next campaign."

"An image consultant?" She was incredulous. "But why?"

"I asked myself the same question, but apparently that's the way it's done these days. Everything is scheduled and polled and statisticized until nothing is left to chance—not even the candidate. And God forbid that any of us have an original thought in our heads—during the campaign, anyway. And after that—'' he shook his head ruefully ''—it's too late. Sometimes that lack is carried right into office, I'm sad to say. I've been guilty of it myself at times.''

"I don't believe that for a minute.''

He was pleased at the compliment. "You'd make a wonderful politician yourself, you know that?''

"Me?'' She was genuinely amused. "You're kidding.''

"No, I mean it. Have you ever thought about running for office?''

"Never!''

"Maybe you should. We need more women like you in government—strong, independent: women who aren't afraid to speak their minds and say what they believe in.''

"You make me sound like a cross between Joan of Arc and Joan Rivers,'' she said dryly, and then happened to glance at the time. Somewhere between the first white wine and the second and the hors d'oeuvres, the time had flown. Now she was horrified to see that it was nearly ten. Where had the night gone?

"My God,'' she said, quickly searching for her purse. "I didn't realize it was so late! I'm sorry, Douglas, but I have to go.''

He seemed just as dismayed that the evening had vanished. "But we haven't had dinner,'' he said lamely, not wanting her to leave.

She didn't want to go, either. But she thought of her mother waiting up, and trying to explain to the kids in the morning, and she just couldn't stay. "I'm sorry, Douglas. I can't.''

"I know,'' he said, his voice suddenly soft. "I just don't want the evening to end.''

She stopped her frantic gathering of possessions and looked at him. "I don't either,'' she said, a catch in her throat.

He hesitated. His hand was on the table and she was seized with an intense longing for him to touch her. Quickly she glanced away, down at the car keys she was holding so tightly, they were beginning to cut into her hand. "I had a wonderful time tonight, Douglas,'' she said.

"Maybe we can do it again.''

Their eyes met. "I'd like that,'' she said.

He held her glance. "So would I.''

He walked her to her car. As she stood there, trying not to fumble with the keys, fighting a yearning just to turn and throw herself into his arms, she said, "Well, I guess this is good night."

"I guess it is."

She couldn't find the door lock; he took the keys and opened the door for her. Before she could tempt herself further, she climbed inside and looked up at him, safe at last on the inside. "Good luck with your media consultant," she said shakily.

He seemed just as off balance as she was. "I might need it. I think he intends to change everything about me."

The words were out before she thought. "Don't let him," she said. "You're perfect just as you are."

Then, feeling as though she'd made a terrible fool of herself, she quickly started the car. A glance into the rearview mirror as she drove away told her he was still watching her, and it took all her willpower not to turn the car around and drive right back to him. The bulk of the Hyatt Hotel rose up behind her, beckoning, and for an instant she was sorely tempted. Who would know?

She would, she thought, and clung grimly to the wheel. She was so tense and exhausted by the time she got home that she didn't fool with the garage door but parked by the curb. Wanting only to undress and fall into bed, she wearily let herself in to the house. Someone moved in the shadows of the living room as she headed toward the stairs, and she nearly screamed. Then she saw who it was and stiffened in disbelief.

"Well," Jack said, after an absence of six months, "I see things haven't changed while I've been gone. You're still working late, and I'm still waiting here, all alone."

CHAPTER SIXTEEN

For all his size, Douglas could move through a crowded room almost unnoticed. He'd perfected the technique long ago because he disliked large social gatherings, quickly becoming bored and feeling the need to escape, even for a few minutes. Tonight was no exception. The large drawing room at Deer Hollow Farm was filled to capacity to celebrate Caleb Young's birthday; Lenore had invited a few friends. It was an invitation Douglas couldn't have—wouldn't have—refused. For one thing, he liked and respected the aging Speaker of the House, and for another, one just did not refuse to attend one of Lenore's little parties.

But he'd done his duty now for several hours, and it was time to get some air. Smiling and nodding, pretending he had to visit with someone across the room, he made his way through to the French doors, and finally, out to the terrace. Thank God. He'd been feeling claustrophobic.

It was much nicer out here, and he breathed in deeply of the cool September air. His glance took in the dark bulk of the stables far off to his right, and even though he knew they were empty, he was tempted to visit. He shook his head. Better not.

Glancing over his shoulder, he saw that the party was going on just fine without him. Even Sarah hadn't noticed his disappearance yet, and he checked his watch. He'd stay out here for a few minutes to fortify himself, then he'd go in.

Moving slightly away from the illuminated glow of the windows in case anyone looked out, he leaned carefully against the stone rail, wishing he had a cigarette. Smoking used to relax him, and after talking to Marcella earlier, he still felt agitated. He always did now after a conversation with his wife; even though they carefully avoided any mention of Rob and that . . . that girl, the subject was never far from either of their minds, and after what had happened last time, it was a black cloud hanging over them both. He wished he could talk about it with her, because he knew she wanted him to, but he just . . . wasn't ready. Every time he thought of Rob and Oriole or Crystal or whatever her name was, he got furious all over again. He couldn't stand the thought of that girl bearing his son's child. After meeting her, he wasn't even sure the baby was Rob's.

Marcella had been horrified when he'd said that, but he didn't know why she should be so shocked. He'd taken one look at that girl—*Her name is Calypso, Douglas, and you know it!* Marcella had shouted at him in a rage when he had refused to call her by name—and knew she was nothing but a cheap little opportunist. He seldom thought such things, but he knew the Rhodes name wasn't exactly unknown in Arizona, and after meeting this Calypso, it was obvious to him that she was after all she could get. He'd told Marcella so, but she had argued that the girl was shy. *Shy* was one thing little Calypso was not. He'd seen the avid gleam in her eyes, and he knew his son was a fool.

Pained at the thought, he shifted position again and caught a movement out of the corner of his eye. A woman inside had come to one of the windows and was gazing out; for an instant, he thought she was Laura. His heart stopped. What was she doing here?

Then the figure moved away and he realized it wasn't Laura at all. What was happening to him lately? This wasn't the first time he'd made such a mistake; it had happened twice now, and once he had made a fool of himself by going up to a woman on the street, only to retreat in embarrassed apology when he realized he didn't know her after all. She'd looked at him as though he were demented, and he was beginning to think he was. He'd never felt this way before, not even as an oversexed teenager.

But then, he'd never met anyone like Laura, either; that was the problem. In addition to being so beautiful, she was intelligent and warm—and funny. Remembering the story she'd told him the last time he'd seen her, he chuckled. That time at Angel's Flight back in May had only made him want to see her again; since then he'd devised several excuses to stop in Los Angeles. Thank God he'd decided to hire Tanner, Inc., to manage his campaign. At least these visits to L.A. seemed logical; he always managed to see Malcolm about something when he was there.

But he knew those were only excuses; his real reason was that he hadn't been able to keep away. He'd be all right for a while;

he wouldn't even think of Laura that often. But then, suddenly, he would, and he'd call Malcolm to ask how things were going. He'd gone to L.A. just the other day, and naturally, had stopped by Laura's office to visit. As was getting to be the pattern, they went out for a drink.

"But only a quick one, Douglas," she'd said with that wonderful smile of hers.

He hadn't cared; he just wanted to see her, even for a few minutes. They went to a little bar they'd found not far away from city hall, where a pianist played old movie tunes in the background, and she'd told him the story about her first day on the new job.

"It was my first case of the day," she said, her eyes sparkling—with amusement at the story she was about to tell, or from pleasure at seeing him; he couldn't tell for sure. He hoped it was the latter, and found himself smiling when she laughed. He loved her laugh.

"You know the story," she went on. "Low man—or woman—on the totem pole always gets the low-priority cases, and this was no exception. I hadn't even had time to go over the file before court convened; someone handed it to me when I went in. I saw it was an assault, and I was just thinking, oh yes, another one, because unfortunately they're so commonplace around here, and then I saw what the weapon had been. Guess."

He blinked. He'd been so absorbed in watching her expressive face that he hadn't been paying strict attention. "I don't know—what?"

"A windshield wiper," she said.

"Is that a bona fide weapon?"

"Anything is a bona fide weapon if it's used to assault someone," she said with a shrug. "But this was a little different. We're not talking street gang here; these were two ordinary citizens, neither of whom had ever been in trouble before."

"So what happened?"

She leaned forward. "To make a long story short, Mr. Jones's car stalled one night after work on a busy street in the middle of one of Los Angeles's famous downpours. Since our transportation system isn't always geared for that type of thing, traffic started backing up for blocks. Horns were honking and people were getting irate and starting to scream at Mr. Jones to move his car. Well, Mr. Jones is an accountant, not a mechanic, and he's just been to his therapist for stress. All the shouting and

197

noise were making him terribly nervous, so he gets out of the car and looks under the hood to see if he can find anything wrong. He doesn't have the faintest idea what he's looking at, and he's starting to pray for deliverance when Mr. Smith arrives.''

"Ah," Douglas said. "The Good Samaritan. I didn't think L.A. had any of those."

"We don't," she said. "Not in this case, anyway. Smith is a yuppie in a three-piece suit who has a date and wants Jones to move his car so he and his BMW can be on their way. But since he knows as much about cars as Jones does, and since the radiator is steaming in the rain, he suggests—"

"Do I really want to hear this?" Douglas asked.

She laughed. "—he suggests that Jones should check the radiator. Which he does. With his bare hand. Now Jones is hopping around with burned fingers, screaming at Smith about poor advice, and Smith is screaming back that no one could be so dumb as to touch a hot radiator like that, when Jones—to use his own words—just 'loses it.' Horns are still honking and people are still shouting, and Smith is calling him an idiot, and it's too much. He grabs the windshield wiper and uses it to stab Smith.''

"Good Lord."

Her eyes twinkled. "I think Jones was almost a little proud of himself for ripping the wiper off the car like that, and I have to admit that all of us in the office sort of sympathized. But Mr. Smith took a different view and pressed charges for assault, claiming that Jones came at him like a madman and in a maniacal fury stabbed him in the hand." She laughed. "At that point he was probably lucky Jones didn't go for his heart."

"So what happened?"

"Well, charges were brought, so we had to prosecute. Smith did have a doctor's report, after all, even if the terrible wound he claims to have suffered required but one stitch. But now, in addition to criminal charges, he's also bringing civil suit against the city for allowing the street to be flooded, against the makers of the windshield wiper for designing something that could be used as a weapon, and against the auto industry for God knows what—designing the car, I suppose. And that's just the beginning. If he has his way, I'm sure the case will go all the way to the Supreme Court."

"And this was your first case of the day?"

"My first case with the DA," she corrected, and grinned. "The day went downhill after that."

"But things are better now."

"Oh, much better. I haven't had a windshield wiper assault since."

They had laughed together, but Douglas knew she was just being modest. He followed her career, and one case in particular—the Bigfoot case—had caused quite a furor. It had been in the papers, and so had Laura when she had first dropped the charges on Homer "Chip" Andrews, the man who had been accused of abducting a young girl during a camping trip to Lake Arrowhead, but who claimed Bigfoot was responsible. As it had when she'd been with the public defender, publicity seemed to follow Laura, and she'd been raked over the coals for letting Andrews go. But when the girl's remains had been found a few weeks later, and the district attorney's office brought murder charges, Laura tried the case and was awarded a guilty verdict. Predictably the press reversed themselves, and made her the heroine of the hour.

And she deserved it, Douglas thought. Jim had told him the last time they'd talked that he was pleased with her, and thought she had a bright future as a prosecutor—if she didn't turn to politics. Remembering how surprised she'd been at the idea when he had first mentioned it to her, he said he doubted it. But Jim said there had been rumors about trying to talk her into running for higher office.

How high? he wondered, and felt a thrill at the idea of Laura in Washington. She would make a wonderful congresswoman, he thought, and then brought himself up short. She'd told him herself that she was happy with her job; she hadn't indicated at all that she would consider politics, so he could just get that idea out of his head.

"Good evening, Senator."

Startled, he turned to see who had addressed him. He'd been so preoccupied that he hadn't heard anyone come out to the terrace, and he squinted against the backlight, unable to see who it was. The woman laughed and joined him at the rail. As soon as he saw her amber eyes and the thick blond hair, he knew who she was. "Oh, good evening, Miss Van Doren," he said.

"Why, Senator," she said coyly. "You remember."

He could hardly forget, he thought, and debated about congratulating her on her new column in *The Washington Eye*. The only reason he knew about it was that one of his secretaries avidly read every issue, and had been so excited when he'd been honored, if that was the correct word, by a mention several times himself.

The moment to say something passed. Dressed in a long gown made of some material that sparkled even in this dim light, she took out a cigarette from a glittery little bag she carried and said huskily, "Do you have a light?"

He sounded stiff and couldn't help it, but for some reason she made him nervous and he wanted to go back inside. "I'm sorry, I don't smoke."

"Lucky you," she said, and took out a pencil-slim lighter from the little purse. He was just reaching automatically for it when she snapped the cover and a little flame appeared. She slanted a glance up at him as she touched the flame to her cigarette, and in the tiny circle of illumination, her face appeared disembodied. Their glance held for a second or two, then she flicked the lighter out and replaced it in the bag. Expelling a long stream of smoke, she leaned against the rail and closed her eyes. "I've been dying for this ever since I came," she murmured.

Despite himself, he felt a sneaking sympathy. He knew Lenore wouldn't allow cigarettes inside the house; anyone who wanted to smoke had to go outside. But since he didn't have anything to say to this woman, he didn't want to start a conversation, so he said nothing at all. After a moment, she opened her eyes and smiled at him.

"I'm sorry, Senator," she murmured in that husky voice. "I didn't mean to intrude. Perhaps you wanted to be alone?"

He would have felt churlish admitting that he did, so he said, "No, I just came out for some air. But it's getting chilly now; perhaps we should go back inside."

"Why, Senator," she said with light mockery. "You sound like a true Southern gentleman."

He couldn't help himself. He didn't know what her game was, but he didn't want to play. "Hardly," he retorted, "having been born in the Arizona desert."

"Oh, yes, I know all about you," she said, and before he could reply, started ticking off a few facts on her long fingers. "Although you keep a home here in Washington, your primary residence is in Scottsdale, where your wife, Marcella, still resides. Although you no longer have it, you once owned a ski lodge at Lake Tahoe, and one of your first loves is still horses. I believe you keep four—or is it five?—in Scottsdale, and until recently, you and your son, Rob—"

He'd heard enough. He didn't want to talk about Rob; he didn't want her to talk about him. "You seem to know quite a bit about me, Miss Van Doren."

She smiled. "Dawn, please. And of course I do. You're very newsworthy, Senator, and news is my business."

He couldn't help himself. The thought that she had been digging through his files, or whatever, repulsed him, and he said, "News? Isn't gossip a better word?"

She laughed, unfazed. "I suppose you're right. And since gossip *is* my business, perhaps you'd like to confirm a story for me."

"I don't think so."

She waggled a finger at him. "Now, now, there's no need to get offended," she said, her eyes gleaming in that faint light. "I just wanted to know if it's true that you've signed Malcolm Tanner, of Los Angeles, to manage your campaign for reelection."

How did she know about that? He felt a flash of irritation at the thought that someone in Tanner's office had given out such confidential information, until he realized that Malcolm wouldn't let that happen. He was sure no one on his staff had said anything, so that left . . . who? Uneasily he glanced in her direction. How *had* she found out? Good Lord, he thought suddenly: was he being followed?

The idea was so absurd that he dismissed it at once. It had to be someone on one of their staffs—either Malcolm's or his. But then, unwillingly, he thought of Laura and how those seemingly innocent little after-work drinks of their could be misconstrued, and because signing Tanner no longer seemed to be a secret, he asked sharply, "How do you know about that?"

She smiled a catlike little smile. "I'm a reporter, Senator," she said. "I have my ways. So it is true, then?" She paused the barest fraction. "That certainly explains all those visits to L.A., doesn't it?"

He felt as though someone had clubbed him between the eyes. What did she really know about his visits to Los Angeles? Before he could think how to respond without sounding guilty as hell, someone else came out onto the terrace. Mercifully it was Sarah, and he turned to her with relief.

"So this is where you've been, Douglas," she said. "I should have known I'd find you out here."

"I'm sorry, Sarah. I just needed some air. Please join us. You remember Dawn Van Doren, of course."

"Of course," Sarah said, her voice turning thirty degrees cooler. "How are you, Miss Van Doren? Enjoying the party, I hope."

Dawn took the hint. "Yes. In fact, I was just going back inside." She turned to Douglas with that catlike little smile. "It was so nice chatting with you, Senator. And thanks for the confirmation."

"What confirmation?" Sarah hissed as Dawn sauntered off. "What did you tell her? You know everything she hears gets printed in that damnable rag!"

Smiling at her protectiveness, he wished she'd arrived about five minutes earlier. "Calm down, Sarah. She just asked about Malcolm."

"How did she know about that?"

He forced himself to give a casual shrug. "Someone on the staff must have said something. You know how it is."

"I do indeed," she said, her lips tightening. She glanced inside, to where Dawn had stopped to talk to someone. "I'd suggest you find and plug that leak."

He was feeling a little grim himself, and his glance followed hers. "You're way ahead of me."

She let it go at that. "Speaking of Malcolm—how is the new campaign going?"

Relieved to change the subject, he said, "Fine, I guess. Malcolm has decided to try something completely novel this time."

"What's that?"

"We're going to run a positive campaign."

"That's novel, all right. How is your opponent handling this innovative approach?"

"Not well," Douglas said with a laugh. "He's already accused me of having something up my sleeve. But that's his problem. I never have liked this trend of negative campaigning. There's something repugnant about proving your fitness for office by hammering on your opponent's character or personality flaws instead of how he stands on the issues."

"Unfortunately not everybody wants to play that way."

He grinned down at her. "You're thinking of Nelson Wyndom, perhaps?"

Nelson Wyndom had challenged Sarah during her last reelection campaign, and had been so soundly defeated that it would be a wonder if he ever took anybody on again—especially Sarah. His "youth versus seniority" theme had been such an abysmal failure that he was probably still licking his wounds.

Sarah had been outraged when she'd learned that the thirty-two-year-old Wyndom was insinuating that she was growing too frail to continue her senatorial duties. She was in her late sixties, but age had never been an issue for her, and she was infuriated that someone could question her abilities because of it. She'd wanted to launch an immediate counterattack showing herself at work—both in the Senate and at home on the ranch. Among other things, she planned to film the annual fall roundup at the Circle A, where she participated in riding and roping and branding her own steers.

Fortunately, cooler heads had prevailed at Switzer and Associates, the firm she had reluctantly hired to help her with the campaign. Since she was chairman of several committees and ranking member of several others, they decided to use this to her advantage. Douglas had always liked the last ad they'd done the best. It had depicted a disheveled, windblown, frantic young person pedaling furiously down some road, while a split screen showed a serene Sarah strolling calmly down Pennsylvania Avenue, stopping at a flower vender on the corner to buy a rose for her lapel. Another glimpse of the exhausted, perspiring youth wobbling on his bicycle, then back to a close-up of Sarah's face. She had smiled into the camera and said, "Ah, youthful exuberance. I feel it myself when I'm out riding, too—something I plan to do after I finishing chairing today's meeting of the Commerce Committee."

Sarah won by a landslide. Wyndom disappeared without a trace, and Sarah stayed home for a week or two to help finish breaking the spring crop of colts. She had one particular favorite that had to be bucked out every morning, rain, snow, or shine. She called him Nelson, and when Douglas asked why, she told him, "Because you can't ever forget the Nelson Wyndoms of this world. If you don't watch out, they'll sting you every time."

He hadn't forgotten that advice, even after everyone started telling him his reelection was such a sure thing. But he knew from Sarah's experience that there weren't any guarantees. As Malcolm himself had said, it wasn't over until the last vote was counted.

As though she could read his mind, Sarah said, "I hope Malcolm Tanner does as good a job for you as Switzer did for me."

He smiled. "Tanner *always* does a good job."

"So I've heard," she said briskly. "I've also heard he does the kind of job you let him do. So you be careful, Douglas."

"Don't worry about that. I've got my eye on him."

"Is that why you're taking all those trips to L.A.?"

He wanted to groan. Did everyone know about those? He hadn't wanted to sneak around, because then people would be sure he had something to hide, but now he wondered if he should have been just a little more discreet. *But I haven't done anything!* he thought, and asked himself how he'd feel if someone like Dawn started speculating in her column. The damage to Laura's reputation would be incalculable—not to mention what it would do to *his* career. Wishing everyone would just mind his own business, he said, "That's one reason. The other is that I have friends on the coast. L.A.'s district attorney, Jim Duluth, and I went to school together. We still keep in touch."

"You don't have to explain anything to me, Douglas," Sarah said mildly. He gave her a quick look, but she was gazing neutrally at him. "I just wanted to be sure you knew what this Malcolm was up to. I've seen a lot of good candidates ruined because they trusted the wrong people."

Telling himself he was being too suspicious, he put his arm around her shoulders and gave her a quick hug. He really was grateful for her support, and he said, "I know. I've seen that happen myself. Don't worry; I've got my eye on Malcolm, and he knows it."

"Good," she said, patting his arm before he removed it. "Because you have to win this election. Anything else is untenable."

He was amused. "So you've said."

"It isn't funny, Douglas!"

"I'm not laughing," he said hastily. "It's just that I think you're getting ahead of yourself, Sarah."

She turned him toward the window and pointed at Hugh Redmond, who was holding forth about something or other to a group of cronies inside. "Maybe you'd like *him* to be president?" she said.

"No, of course not," he protested. They had talked about this before, but he still felt it was too soon to think about it. Or maybe, he thought uneasily, he just didn't want to think about it because the idea was so overwhelming. Douglas Rhodes for president. It didn't even seem real to him . . . yet. Quickly he added, "But the election we're talking about is six years away, Sarah. A lot can change in that time."

"And it certainly will if you don't get reelected," she said crisply.

Patting the hand she had put on his arm for emphasis, he said softly, "Let's just take it one step at a time, all right?"

"Men!" she said impatiently. "Don't you understand there are plans to be made?" She glanced back into the room, her eyes seeking Lenore, who was standing off to one side, deep in conversation with Caleb Young, the guest of honor. She jerked her head, making Douglas look, too. "You don't think they're talking about cherry blossoms, do you?"

Following Sarah's glance, he shrugged. He respected Lenore because he knew what a sharp tongue she had—and an awesome grasp of politics. But he'd never understood why so many people seemed to be intimidated by her. "Everyone has plans," he said lightly. "Not all of them bear fruit."

"That's true. But there's no sense leaving things to chance."

"I'm not going to leave anything to chance," he soothed. "But Sarah—"

"All right, all right," she said tartly. "But I'll tell you one thing. As sure as I'm standing here, if Hugh Redmond gets that nomination—not to mention the presidency itself—I'm going home and raise mutton."

"Sheep?" he said, hiding a smile. He knew full well the Circle A was a cattle ranch. "Isn't that a little melodramatic?"

"Not a bit of it! I'm telling you, Douglas, if that man gets elected, I'm going to sell every cow on the ranch and buy a flock of sheep. Because that's what we'll all be if he gets into office, a nation of sheep!"

He heard the fierce note in her voice and knew she wasn't kidding, so he dropped his teasing manner. "I'm sorry, Sarah," he said seriously. "I don't mean to joke about this, but it just seems so unreal. I honestly don't feel I have the experience."

Her own expression softened. "Not yet," she agreed. "But you will. You will."

He didn't see how. But then, when he thought about it, he wondered if anyone was ever ready to take on such awesome responsibility, no matter how experienced he was. He shook his head. It was all so far in the future anyway; he couldn't worry about it now. First things first, he thought: he still had a reelection campaign to wage. But Sarah was waiting for him to say something, and he smiled and took her arm. "I hope you're right," he said. "Now, can we go inside?"

She smiled, too—a Cheshire cat–like grin he found unsettling. "I was hoping you'd ask."

He looked at her suspiciously. "Why?"

She started toward the door. "Because Hugh's been going on for fifteen minutes about something, and he should have dug himself in pretty deep by now. I want you to see for yourself just what kind of man might be president."

"Oh, Sarah—"

"Don't 'oh, Sarah' me," she said. "I'm going to prove to you that the future isn't all that far away."

He had no choice but to follow her inside, and they came in at the tail end of one of Hugh Redmond's rhetorical questions. Redmond was known for his filibustering style, and Douglas prepared himself for a long siege.

". . . will it end?" Hugh was saying. "Just the other day, for example, one of our esteemed junior colleagues on Judiciary announced his intention to seek legislation concerning the trucking industry. The *trucking* industry! That's something that belongs entirely within the province of the Commerce Committee. What does Judiciary have to do with trucking?"

There was a general murmur of agreement, but as he and Sarah took an unobtrusive place along the fringes of the group, Douglas saw that it came from Hugh's tight-knit group of friends, and was amused. The junior colleague to whom Hugh was referring was himself; he and Hugh had gotten into a battle about this subject just the other day. Resigned, he sat on the arm of the couch and folded his arms. Sarah saw the movement and glanced at him significantly. He shrugged and waited.

He didn't have long to wait. Hugh had never needed much encouragement to continue, and he said, "I ask you now. What if this junior colleague of ours succeeds in passing this legislation? What will happen next? Will he then want to take a bank merger act away from the Banking Committee, or political action away from Rules? I say again, where will it end?"

Hugh's eyes met his just then and held for a fraction of a second before they moved away. Douglas sighed inwardly. He'd thought when they first came in that Hugh hadn't seen him, but he'd obviously been mistaken. Redmond knew exactly what he was doing, and he thought that if Hugh wanted to make their private disagreement public, that was fine with him. As Sarah had commented fondly to him some time ago, he never was one to sidestep an issue, and he stood.

"There's nothing wrong with a little healthy competition, is there, Senator?" he said mildly.

The older man turned to him, a gleam of satisfaction in his eyes. He'd been planning this, and he obviously thought he'd just hooked his fish. "That's not healthy competition, that's outright thievery!" he declared. "Our committee system was formed for a purpose; each has its stated goal." His eyes narrowed. "Unless you don't believe in the committee system in the first place, sir!"

Douglas became aware that they had the attention of practically everyone in the room. People were drifting over, and he wished he'd never started this. But then he caught Sarah's eye and knew he had to go on. Sighing inwardly, he said, "I certainly do believe in the committee system. Both houses would have a difficult time getting anything done if we didn't divide the responsibilities. Although," he added with a smile, "I wonder at times if we get anything done anyway."

There was a general laugh of appreciation, in which he joined and Hugh didn't. He took the opportunity to go on, because this was important to him. "Still, it seems to me that any subject broad enough to come to the attention of either house of Congress has to overlap numerous committees."

Hugh might present himself as a bumbling fool on occasion, but he wasn't a stupid man. Glancing around, he realized he was losing his audience to Douglas, and he drew himself up. "Why?"

"Well, for one thing, any problem of any magnitude can't be neatly compartmentalized, Senator. Various components have to be considered, and that means that different committees have to be involved. This naturally means there is more input, which I think is a positive approach."

"Name one positive effect," Hugh challenged.

"I can give you several," Douglas said. "One is that jurisdictional overlap enables committee members to develop expertise in several fields. This not only prevents one group from dominating a topic, but gives access to different viewpoints. All of which—"

"Proves my point," Hugh interrupted, with a victorious

glance all around. "From what I can see, all this means is that there are intercommittee battles!"

"Or healthy competition among committees," Douglas countered, and added politely, "Which proves mine."

Then, as they stared at each other, Hugh red-faced and annoyed, Douglas doing his best to disguise his dislike, Lenore came in. "My, my, such harsh words!" she said, with a quick glance at Caleb Young. "You know I don't allow that at my parties! There's plenty of time for such things on the Senate floor!"

Insinuating herself into the group, she shook an admonishing finger in each direction, but made sure they all noticed the proprietary hand she placed on Hugh's arm. "And at my good friend's birthday party, too!" she chided. "Now, what was it all about? I leave the room for five minutes, and an argument breaks out!"

Douglas wasn't fooled by this little act, not from a woman who lived and breathed and slept politics. He was sure she knew exactly the source of the disagreement, and he suspected that she'd stepped in just now to rescue Hugh. Still, it wouldn't gain him anything by being rude, so he said easily, "It wasn't really important, Lenore— just an exchange of views. Please, forgive us for allowing politics to intrude on such a special occasion."

Beside him, Sarah muttered approval, and he saw a flash of anger in Lenore's eyes. It was obvious she'd decided to support Hugh, but why? He was wondering what the Speaker had to say about that when the three-tiered cake was brought in. Under cover of the obligatory ceremony, he took Sarah aside. "You could have joined in at any time, you know."

"And spoil the fun?" she said, tossing her head. "Besides, you were doing just fine without me. I told you Hugh wasn't a worthy opponent. Now do you believe me?"

He gazed at her for a moment, uncertain whether to laugh or be annoyed. Finally he smiled. "You're impossible."

"I know," she said. "Isn't it a good thing I'm in your corner?"

He didn't notice until then that Lenore was standing close by. It was obvious that she'd overheard their conversation, and as he glanced from her to Sarah and saw her satisfied expression, he knew that she had intended Lenore to hear. He shook his head, amused and feeling a little helpless at the same time. It was obvious from the challenge he saw in both the women's faces that whether he wanted it or not, the battle line had just been drawn.

CHAPTER SEVENTEEN

Dawn stood at the window of her tiny office at the *Eye*, staring out at trees bare of leaves. It was the end of October—nearly a year after that humiliating interview with Lenore about the abortion—and her mood matched the gloomy, overcast afternoon. She didn't know why, but she'd started thinking about that party at Deer Hollow Farm last month, and she got pissed off all over again at the way Lenore had raked her over the coals once more.

Turning away from the window, she sat down again and drummed her fingers agitatedly against the top of the desk. What a fool she was at times. Whenever she thought about how much she'd thrown away just because she'd been so shook up about that damn green car following her from that clinic, she could scream. Instead of having a cushy job at the *Post* or the *Daily*, she was stuck here for who knew how long. All her plans dashed, just like that. She'd never be so stupid again.

But in the meantime, she was still in debt to that mad old woman, and that party last month was a perfect example. Even more annoyed, she grabbed the pack on the desk and lit a cigarette. Throwing down the lighter, she expelled a long plume of smoke and tried to calm down. She couldn't calm down. She didn't know what the hell Lenore expected her to do.

"Cultivate the man," she mimicked, muttering to herself. "Get to know him. Let him know you. . . ."

Well, she'd tried at that birthday party for Cal Young. She'd waited for her chance, and when she saw Rhodes slip out to the terrace, she waited a moment before casually joining him. As she'd tried to explain to Lenore, everything had been going just fine until they were interrupted. Was it her fault that Sarah Ambrose had followed them out? If she didn't know better, she'd think the woman was guarding him or something; she'd certainly appeared at just the right moment. Maybe she'd been waiting at the door, just for her cue.

"Damn it all to hell," Dawn muttered, and took another drag of the cigarette. She was still smarting from that dressing-down Lenore had given her, and she vowed that was the *last* party she'd ever attend at Deer Hollow Farm.

She knew she was in trouble when Chester took her aside that night under cover of the cake ceremony to tell her that Lenore wished to speak to her after everyone had gone; the old woman's beady little eyes didn't miss a thing. She was sure Lenore had seen her come in from the terrace after joining Senator Rhodes there, and wanted to know what had happened.

What had happened was exactly nothing, she thought angrily; she hadn't had time to do anything else. But she knew Lenore would never accept that as an excuse, and because, despite everything, she still had a healthy respect for the old hag, she'd spent the rest of the evening in a state of tension, not sure whether she wanted everyone to leave so she could get this little tête-à-tête over with, or if she should ask them all to stay so she could postpone it as long as possible. Inevitably the moment arrived, and she was ushered into one of Lenore's "little" sitting rooms that was as big as Dawn's entire apartment. There the grande dame sat, like a spider in her web, drinking another of those damned cups of tea. That was another thing: she was getting a little tired of this stupid *tea* ceremony they always had to go through.

"You look a little pale, my dear," Lenore said. "Perhaps a cup of comfrey?"

She'd drunk so much champagne in anticipation of this little chat that what she really wanted was a stiff drink. But she had a long drive home, and she'd been so keyed up that she felt exhausted. When she remembered she had to be at work early the next day, she'd said, "What I'd like is a cup of coffee."

Lenore nodded to the waiting Chester, and when the door had whispered closed behind him, she indicated the chair next to hers. Dawn sat, trying to prepare herself. The ax wasn't long in falling. Before she could even defend herself, Lenore said, "I'm disappointed in you, Dawn. I thought you were more ingenious."

She'd been stung at that, and replied sharply, "It wasn't my fault. You saw what happened. I'm surprised Senator Ambrose didn't break her neck hurrying to follow me out there. What was I supposed to do—snatch him out from under her nose?"

To her surprise, Lenore had seemed thoughtful. "Poor Sarah does seem a bit protective of him, doesn't she?"

Picturing Sarah Ambrose, with that titanic assurance and impenetrable dignity, Dawn nearly snorted. *Poor* was not an adjective she would have used to describe the senator—in any sense of the word. "Yes, I'd say so," she said dryly.

"What did she say to you?"

"To me? Nothing exactly. But I very definitely got the idea that she wanted me to get the hell out of there."

Grimacing at the profanity, Lenore said, "Which you did."

"What did you expect me to do?" she flared. "Tell her to buzz off because I had my orders?"

"Don't be absurd," Lenore said, in that tone that raised Dawn's hackles. "But you could have found an excuse to get together with him later in the evening, couldn't you?"

Her eyes met Dawn's over the rim of the cup she held to her lips, and despite herself, Dawn glanced away. She hated it when Lenore looked at her like that; it made her feel so . . .

She didn't want to think how it made her feel . . . except angry. And because she was so annoyed, she got careless. "I didn't have a chance, did I?" she sneered. "After your boy Hugh made his little grandstand play and a fool of himself in the bargain, we all had to sing happy birthday and go through all that business with the cake, remember? You might also recall that the senator and his watchdog left soon after that. So when was there opportunity?"

Lenore's eyes had flashed at the mention of Hugh Redmond falling on his face, and she put the cup down with a little *chink* that showed her displeasure. "I'm not paying you for excuses, Dawn," she said severely.

Thinking that she wasn't paying her much at all, Dawn tried, but couldn't hold that cold blue glance. "So what do you want me to do? Forget it?"

"On the contrary. It's more important than ever for someone to get close to him. I want to know his every thought, his every plan, his every breath. Do I make myself clear?"

Wishing she could just tell the old hag to go to hell, she tried to disguise her impatience. "Yes, but how do you expect me to do that?"

Lenore was still annoyed with her. "You'll think of something, I'm sure—if you want to continue collecting your little bonuses, that is. Otherwise," she added slyly, "your plans for moving to Dupont Circle in the next few months might have to be postponed . . . indefinitely."

212

Dawn couldn't believe Lenore already knew about that. The manager of the apartment house had only called the other day; she had been on the waiting list for months now, and her name had finally come up. "How do you know about that?" she demanded.

Lenore smiled. "I have my ways," she said, and paused a fraction. "But of course, you know that."

How could she forget? Despite the fact that it had been months ago, her heart still jumped whenever she happened to glimpse a green car. Glancing away from those glittering eyes, she muttered, "I'll do my best."

"See that it's good enough," Lenore replied, and waved a hand in dismissal.

That had been a month ago, and she was still seething at that humiliating interview. *Damn* the woman, she thought, and lit another cigarette. She hadn't heard from Lenore since then, but she knew it was only a matter of time. And when Lenore did call, she'd damned well better have something to tell her. She hadn't given up on Dupont Circle, not when she'd already put a deposit down. She couldn't go back to the manager and say she'd changed her mind; she'd waited too long for that apartment, and she wasn't about to let it go to someone else.

I deserve it, she thought fiercely, and wondered how she was ever going to do what Lenore wanted her to do. It seemed an easier task to bed the pope than to get close to Douglas Rhodes. In all the time she'd been here in Washington, she had never heard even a breath of rumor about him; for all she knew, he went home to his Georgetown apartment every night and turned into stone.

Impatiently she shifted position. There had to be something she could use, she thought; a man that good-looking had to have some secrets. No one was so squeaky clean that a little background digging didn't unearth something; Christ, look at what people could find out about her if they tried. The biography she'd concocted was a fairy tale compared to the way she'd really grown up, and since Rhodes seemed to be so damned pure of heart, she'd have to try another approach. The only question was where to start.

"You busy, Dawn?"

She glanced toward the doorway. Her boss, Barnaby Hyde, was standing there, and she stubbed out her cigarette. "No, come on in."

She didn't like or dislike Barnaby; he was a means to an end for her, and even though it was a trial listening to his childish jokes with the inevitable sexual overtones, she could put up with it. As long as he stuck to jokes, she figured he was harmless; it was when they started asking you to take dictation topless or give them a blow job at noon that you really had a problem. Not that she had to worry about that; he was married to an absolute shrew of a woman who breezed in unexpectedly at odd times to check the books or to poke her long nose into things, and since Barnaby was obviously afraid of her, Dawn figured the wife would keep him in line.

Besides, sometimes she almost felt grateful to him. He'd hired her when no other paper in town would give her the time of day, and she figured she owed him. But only as long as she didn't need him anymore; gratitude only went so far these days.

"You look like you've seen better days," he commented, lowering his bulk into the chair opposite hers. "Whatsa matter? Have a rough night?"

She had never liked hairy men, and Barnaby was like an ape. He always worked with his sleeves rolled up, and she glanced away from the thick, matted forearm hair tufting out from the turned-up cuffs. Since she wasn't interested in discussing her private life—or lack of it—she said, "Not particularly. I was just sitting here thinking—"

"Uh-oh," he said with a wink. "You'd better watch that. Don't want to strain yourself, you know."

Dawn debated a remark to that, decided she really didn't want to get into it, and opted to ignore it. An idea had just come to her, and she was much more interested in pursuing that. In fact, she thought excitedly, it seemed the answer to everything. "I mean it," she said. "Don't you want to hear about it?"

Instantly he looked suspicious. "I'm not sure. Do I?"

"Yes, you do," she said, and leaned forward, her eyes alight. "Barnaby, I want to do something different with my column."

"What do you mean?" he said cautiously. "What's the matter with the way you're doing it now?"

She sat back. "It doesn't have enough depth."

He looked alarmed. "We don't do depth here, Dawn—we're a gossip rag."

"But we could be more."

"No! No, we can't!"

"Why not?"

"Because . . . because . . . well, it's just not the way it's done!"

"Then we'll change the way it's done."

"No, I'm telling you we can't do that!" He was really agitated now. "The *Eye* has a certain format; the readers expect that. We're not going to fool around with success."

"Don't you even want to hear my idea?"

"No!" She was surprised he didn't clap his hands over his ears. "I told you—we have a certain way of doing things, and that's that."

Was it? She sat back, studying him. She had never asked, but she'd always been curious about the way her promotion had come about. She knew Lenore had arranged it, but she also knew that the old biddy wouldn't have dreamed of picking up the phone and calling Barnaby herself. She just didn't do things like that; it was too simple. People here had perfected the art of the maneuver; manipulation was the name of the game. Why call and be direct when you could be so subtle about it, mentioning it to someone, who would tell someone else, who would casually comment to yet another, who would finally get in touch with Barnaby? That's how things were done in this town, and she figured that's probably how it had happened in her case. She didn't really care. All this hush-hush, under-the-table, behind-closed-doors business irritated her; it seemed so childish, like kids playing games.

She decided not to play. "I've been thinking of the *Eye*, Barnaby," she said, "and how to improve it."

He seemed to remember he was the publisher. "What's to improve?" he demanded. "We're doing fine with the format we have now!"

"Yes, but we could do better. With a slightly different approach, we could add to our readership, reach different sectors of the population, and—" she gave him a sly glance "—increase our circulation."

Ah, the magic word. She knew she'd hooked him when he shifted in the chair and tugged at his collar. She waited until finally he said reluctantly, "All right, I'm listening—but only that, remember. I'm not sure this is a good idea at all."

"You haven't heard it yet," she pointed out, and wondered why she hadn't thought of this before. She'd been wracking her brain about this all month, and the answer had been right in front of her the whole time. Thinking it out as she went along, she told him, "As I said, I want to do something more in-depth for the paper. No more gossip, or funny stories, or nasty little comments, but some real reporting for once—how's that sound?"

"Real reporting," he repeated cautiously. "What exactly does that mean?"

She was getting too excited about this; if she wasn't careful, she'd scare him off. Trying to calm down, she lit another cigarette and quickly expelled the smoke. She couldn't chance having him say no, not when she was so sure she'd found the answer to her problem—to all her problems. With this idea, she could get close to Douglas Rhodes as Lenore wanted, and she could establish herself as a serious journalist at the same time. Tantalized by the visions that rose in her mind, she tossed the lighter back onto the desk and leaned forward. She had to convince him.

"I mean," she said, "that I want to choose a subject—a prominent person here in the city, someone important . . . like a senator, for instance—and stick to him like glue for a while. I want to follow him through his day, and listen to what he has to say. I want to know what his problems are, what his dreams and aspirations and goals are, what he thinks of himself, and his family and his country. I want to present the man—or the woman," she added hastily, not wanting to be too obvious, "so that our readers will feel he, or she, could be the neighbor next door. What do you say?"

He seemed uncomfortable with the idea. "That sounds more like interviews, Dawn—not subjects for your column."

"Yes, that's right," she said, and looked at him, her eyes widening as a new idea occurred to her. "You know what?" she said excitedly. "I'm going to need more space for this. It's going to be too much material for a column!"

He groaned. "What—"

She hardly heard him. "Yes, I can see it now! This will be separate from the column, Barnaby; it will have to be a feature—two or three pages, at least!"

"At *least*!" He looked at her in horror. "Are you out of your mind? We don't have a extended story format here! Our readers wouldn't understand! They'd never go for it!"

"How do you know?" she demanded. "Have you ever tried it?"

"Well, no, but—"

She was carried away with her own enthusiasm. Puffing furiously at the cigarette, she was too excited to sit, and jumped up to pace behind the desk. "I think it's time we tried, Barnaby. This could be the most thrilling thing to happen to the paper since the beginning. Think of it—there's a wealth of material in this town, and we could plumb it all! There'd be no stopping—"

"Wait a minute," he said, and when she swept on, shouted, *"Wait a minute!"*

She stopped in midstride. "What?"

"We . . . can't. I've told you before, Dawn—we're a gossip rag, not a newspaper or a magazine."

"But we could change that," she said, coming around the desk and perching on the edge right in front of him. "*You* could change that. After all, you're the owner of the paper, aren't you?"

He shifted away from her gaze. "Well, not exactly," he muttered.

She drew back. "What do you mean—not exactly?"

He still couldn't look at her. "Well, actually, Flora is majority owner of the paper."

"Flora!" She sat down again on the edge of the desk in dismay. Flora was his wife, the harridan who flew in occasionally riding her broom.

Now that it was out, Barnaby gave her a pleading look. "And she likes the format of the paper, Dawn," he said. "In fact, *The Eye* was her idea."

Dawn couldn't believe it; all her plans were dashed before they even got off the ground. "I see," she said, suddenly so angry, she could hardly speak. She looked at him contemptuously. "Does that mean you do everything she says?"

"I didn't say that," he muttered.

"Ah. Then you do put your foot down occasionally."

Stung, he glanced at her. "Of course I do. What do you think I am?"

She didn't want to tell him. But with him puffing up like a rooster, she'd found a new tack. "Then you'll discuss this with her?" she asked innocently.

He stood, hooked by the implied threat to his manhood. "I don't have to discuss anything with her," he said indignantly. He drew himself up, sucked in his gut. "Go ahead and do it, Dawn. I'll handle Flora."

"You're a prince, Barnaby," Dawn said, and waited until he'd stomped out before she snickered. Goddamn, she thought as she lit another cigarette: it worked every time.

CHAPTER EIGHTEEN

When Laura slipped into the weekly major cases meeting ten minutes late, Dale raised an eyebrow. Since he'd been appointed head deputy several months ago, he'd instituted this midweek review, and he liked everyone to be on time. She knew that, and usually she was, but she'd gotten up with Peter and another of his nightmares, and hadn't been able to get back to sleep. Then she'd overslept. Clutching a Styrofoam cup of coffee that was going to substitute for breakfast, she sat down in one of the empty chairs around the big conference table and watched Dale ostentatiously check his watch. She rolled her eyes; he winked back. She was one of the few who could get away with this, but since she never took advantage, he cut her the slack.

Which was more than she could say for Jack, she thought, still irritated because he hadn't offered to sit with Peter. They'd both heard him calling in his sleep, but Jack had muttered something about being tired and had rolled over, leaving her to deal with it. She didn't mind for Peter's sake, but she would have said something to Jack if the peace hadn't been so fragile between them. Things hadn't been going too well lately, but she brushed that thought out of her mind and decided to concentrate on Kenny Schofield, who was in the middle of a case presentation. He was new to the staff; this was only his second meeting and he was obviously nervous as he outlined what he'd done so far.

She was familiar with the murder case, this one another gang-related death, the type of which seemed to be on the increase lately. Charlie Salde had been a member of the ghetto gang Death Watch, and the person accused of knifing him to death was a rival gang member, Martin Crade. Charlie was dead; Martin had killed him. Kenny knew it; the crowd of witnesses who had observed the killing knew it; everybody in this room knew it. The only problem was that Kenny couldn't prove it—

not in the eyes of the law, or, more important, to Dale's satisfaction.

"How many witnesses did you say there were?" Dale asked.

"Four or five," Kenny said, looking through his files.

"Which was it—four or five?"

Kenny seemed startled. "Uh . . . it was five—yes, that's right. Definitely five."

"And you deposed all five, right?"

Kenny bent his files again. "Well, ah . . . no. I only did three."

"Three," Dale repeated. "What happened to the other two? Did they die in the meantime? Were they struck dumb, kidnapped, murdered?"

Kenny flushed. "No, but . . . but when I got the same statement from the first three, I thought . . . I thought . . . well, they all agreed, you see. . . ."

Dale said kindly, "Kenny, I'd like to ask you something if I may."

"Uh, you don't have to, Dale," Kenny said quickly. He'd seen his mistake and was trying to rectify it. "I'll go depose the other two right away."

"Good," Dale said. "Because I'd hate to think that your two remaining witnesses might have seen something different than the other three, and that at some point during this trial, some clever defense attorney is going to point that out."

"Yes, sir," Kenny said. His face was bright red, and he looked as though he wanted to race out of the room and depose those other witnesses right now.

"Good," Dale said, and glanced down the table to where Laura sat. "Now that you're here, Ms. Devlin," he said, "what's the status on Merrill?"

Laura gave him a look that told him he might be taking this head deputy business just a little too seriously, but said, "We've got a problem."

"What?"

It was another knife-murder case, this one involving Tommy Merrill, who was accused of the brutal murder of his roommate, Daryl Hardesty. The two had apparently been arguing over rent money when Tommy grabbed a knife, stabbed Daryl twenty times in the chest and belly, and then, as if the victim wasn't already dead or dying by this time, had grabbed a pillow and proceeded to try and smother him with it. When the police had arrived, he'd surrendered politely, and his family had retained a well-known defense attorney.

"The problem is that after reviewing the case," Laura said, "I don't think we can make a murder charge stick. We'll have to accept voluntary manslaughter. There's evidence that the defendant's state of mind might not have been rational at the time, and since this is his first arrest . . ."

She shrugged. They all knew that the chances of getting a murder conviction on this one were slim; it was better to accept the lesser plea than lose completely in trial. But it rankled; Tommy might be a confused young man right now, but even with a manslaughter conviction, the odds were that he'd only serve six or seven years before he was out again.

Telling herself not to dwell on it, she went to court for the morning. If she'd learned one thing here, it was that compromises were inevitable. The system was so overburdened that they all had to be realistic, prosecutor and defense alike. You couldn't worry about one case, not when you had thirty others sitting on your desk; you did what you could and let the rest fade from your mind. If you didn't, you'd go crazy.

"Laura? Hey, Laura!"

She was just coming into the hall on lunch break when she heard someone calling to her; turning, she saw it was a transfer member of the public defender's office, from New York. She'd met him before when she stopped by Maurey's office a couple of weeks ago to see him, and had been introduced. She couldn't remember his name. Larry something. No—Harry. Harry Silverstein. She didn't usually go by first impressions, but she hadn't liked him; she had realized why when Maurey told her later that Silverstein kept bragging that one day he'd be right up there with Melvin Belli. She hadn't thought about him since, and she wondered what he wanted with her now.

Harry rushed up to her, briefcase brimming with papers, all shoved under his arm. He had tightly curled black hair, a long, prominent nose, and small eyes that seemed to meet in the middle. Her first impression intensified when, without any other greeting, he said belligerently, "What's the idea on Branaman? You don't really think you'll get away charging him with second-degree, do you?"

Her first thought was that if she hadn't thought she could "get away with it," she would have filed a different charge; her second was: who the hell was Branaman? Then it came to her. That

221

was one of the cases she'd taken over for a sick colleague, and even though she hadn't had time to familiarize herself thoroughly, she remembered the important details. Because she didn't care for Silverstein's attitude, she said coolly, "I take it you have another suggestion?"

"I certainly do," he shot back. "He'll plead to involuntary manslaughter, but that's all."

"You've got to be kidding. The man was driving drunk and killed three people."

"It was an accident."

Quickly she searched her memory. "He had a blood alcohol of point two three at the time, Mr. Silverstein. That's over twice the legal maximum."

Silverstein flushed, but tried another tack. "Come on," he wheedled. "Don't tell me you've never driven when you've had too much to drink. Can't you give the man a break?"

She couldn't believe this. "The man has had a break," she said. "As I recall, he's been issued at least four DUI citations, and has been warned numerous times. How much of a break should he get?"

Silverstein flushed again, but this time with anger. "Are you so pure?" he sneered.

"That's not the point," she countered. "This man is a menace. He obviously can't control his drinking, and because of that, he's a danger to society. He's not only shown willful and wanton disregard for the safety of others, he has demonstrated it—tragically. And if I have anything to say about it, he's going to pay for it."

Silverstein was furious; she wasn't exactly sure why, unless he had promised his client he could wear her down. "Then we're going to trial," he said.

"Unless he pleads guilty and saves us all the trouble," she replied.

"Well, you'd better be prepared, then, Counselor," he retorted, his expression ugly. "Because when we get to court, I'm going to whip your butt!"

Before she could respond to that, he whirled around and started off. Unfortunately his exit was marred by the fact that he didn't see the person behind him. A man hurrying by tried to step out of the way, but the two collided violently and Silverstein's briefcase flew into the air, raining papers all around as he crashed to the floor. The man he'd run into glared at him and continued on, and as Laura tried not to laugh, someone came up and leaned over the enraged public defender. It was Trudy Mankiller, and she said with immense satisfaction, "Before you worry about whipping Laura's butt in court, Mr. Silverstein, maybe you'd better try getting off yours."

Muttering a curse, the red-faced Silverstein started grabbing his scattered papers. Laura automatically reached down to help, but Trudy grabbed her arm and dragged her away.

"Don't you dare," she muttered. "The little fart deserved it."

Laura looked at her in amusement. "It sounds as if you've run afoul of Silverstein, too."

"Nothing I can't handle. We got into a hassle about a drug bust, and he lodged a formal complaint about me."

Her smile disappeared. "You didn't tell me about that."

The narcotics detective waved her hand. "It wasn't that important. Don't worry about it, because I'm certainly not losing sleep. As far as I'm concerned, he's just a two-bit hustler trying to make a name for himself the easy way."

Laura wasn't so sure, and as they went up to the eighteenth floor together, she told Trudy she'd help in any way she could.

"Thanks," Trudy said with a grin, stopping by the office for a second. "I appreciate that. We'll put this guy in his place and then go celebrate at Spago's with caviar and champagne. How's that sound?"

"It sounds divine," Laura said just as her phone rang.

Trudy glanced at the phone. "I guess duty calls—for both of us. See you later, all right?"

"Okay," Laura said, and waved as Trudy sauntered off down the hall. Reaching for the phone, she said, "Laura Devlin."

"Hi. Is this a bad time to call?"

Wondering if her heart would always give that little leap when she heard his voice, Laura felt herself light up. "Douglas!" she exclaimed in pleasure, and then caught herself. "No, it's perfect timing. I just got back to the office, in fact. Where are you? Are you in town?"

"Yes, I just got in. I had to see Malcolm about the last push for my campaign, and I thought I'd call to say hello. How are you?"

"Oh, I'm . . . fine," she said, resolutely ignoring the stacks of messages, the piles of folders on her desk. "How about you?"

"Busy as always—just like you. Too many demands, not enough time."

She heard something in his voice and had to ask. "You sound a little frazzled. Is something wrong?"

He gave a strained laugh. "No, not really. Why?"

"Well, you sound a little down."

"Just tired, I guess. It's been a long week."

"It's only Wednesday," she reminded him. She really didn't like the way he sounded. It was something more than just being tired, and she said hesitantly, "Do you want to talk about it?"

"It's nothing, really," he denied. "But I could use a little cheering up, I guess. Do you have time for a drink after work tonight?"

I always have time for you, she thought, and said hastily, "Of course. We haven't seen each other for a while; it'll be nice to catch up."

He sighed. "Thanks, Laura."

"There's nothing to thank me for," she said, and because she was in danger of saying something she shouldn't, added instead, "You're doing me a favor, in fact. The way the day is shaping up, I'm going to be ready for a drink by the time cocktail hour rolls around."

"About six, then? Would you like me to pick you up?"

"Oh, I think it would be better if I met you there," she said, wondering why she felt she had to keep this a secret. Was she ashamed of meeting him? Guilty?

Neither, she told herself firmly. It was just that he was a public figure, and she knew from experience how easily things could get twisted around. She'd never forgive herself if she was even inadvertently responsible for any rumors getting started; she knew how important his campaign was to him, and the last thing he needed was to defend himself against a nonexistent liaison.

Liaison? Hanging up, she reached quickly for the files she was going to need after lunch, and at one o'clock was back in court.

"Are you ready, Ms. Devlin?" the judge asked.

"Ready, Your Honor," she said.

"Is the defendant ready?" the judge asked.

The defense attorney rose. "Ready, Your Honor."

"Then let's get started," the judge said, and nodded at Laura.

"Your Honor, may I approach the bench?" Laura asked, and the afternoon had begun.

The case was rescheduled pending a psychiatric evaluation of the defendant, and she was leaving the courtroom when one of the DA's investigators hurried up. His name was Avery Jones, and he looked tired and harassed and in a foul mood. Motioning her to one side so they'd be out of the hallway traffic, he reached in his pocket for a pack of cigarettes before he remembered he'd given up smoking.

"I'm afraid you're going to have to talk to Annabel Simpson," he said, taking out a stick of gum instead. "I just heard she's decided not to testify."

"Oh, no," she said, dismayed and disappointed at the same time. Annabel Simpson was a seventy-year-old woman who had witnessed a fatal beating of her neighbor several months back. The victim had been a frail old man who'd been murdered for his Social Security check, and since Annabel had been the only witness, her testimony was crucial to Laura's case.

"Why did she change her mind?" she asked, and then shook her head. "Never mind. She's probably scared, poor little lady. I can't blame her."

"Neither can I," Avery agreed. "The only problem is that I've been over that neighborhood with the proverbial fine-tooth comb and haven't been able to flush out another witness. As usual, everybody else is blind, deaf, and dumb. I thought maybe you could talk to her."

"I'll try," Laura said, but without much hope. The area where Annabel lived was a bad one, and she figured the neighborhood gangs had gotten to her. "Anything else?"

"Nope, that's enough for today, don't you think?" he said.

"I hope so," she said, but it wasn't. A short while later a judge refused her a warrant because of insufficient evidence, then she had to attend a discovery conference with Harry Silverstein, who made things even more difficult than they should be because he was still embarrassed and angry. Then another investigator came up to her as she was leaving that debacle and told her they still hadn't found the murder weapon on yet another case, and by that time, she was in a bad mood herself.

"Swell," she said. "Keep looking, then."

"We will, but you know the longer we wait, the colder the trail gets."

"I know that," she said between her teeth. "Perhaps you have another suggestion?"

He didn't, and she tried to put it out of her mind as she hurried

225

off to depose the six—*not four or five, but six, Dale,* she thought—witnesses on the shotgun murder of a convenience store owner. No one seemed to agree exactly on what had happened, and by the time she got back to her office, she felt beset on all sides. A glance at the clock revealed that she had just a half hour before she was supposed to meet Douglas, and she reached for the phone before she had a chance to think about it. She had to call home and tell them she'd be late, but as she dialed her number, she was tense, and knew it was because she felt guilty. She didn't know why she'd never told her family that she and Douglas met like this; it wasn't because she felt she had to keep it a secret, exactly; it was more that she didn't think they would understand. And they only saw each other for drinks, she rationalized; it wasn't as though they were doing something wrong.

Her mother answered on the fifth ring. "Hello?"

"Hi, Mom, it's Laura," she said. "I'm sorry it's so late, but I've had a day you wouldn't believe. How're things?"

Estelle was immediately suspicious. "Are you still at work?"

"Yes, I am. But I'm leaving soon—in about an hour or so. I just thought I'd call and find out how Peter is."

"As well as can be expected, after staying up half the night with those nightmares again. Honestly, Laura, when are you going to do something about this? It isn't natural."

"I've taken him to a doctor, Mother. What else can I do?"

"Obviously the man didn't know what he was doing," Estelle retorted. "I really think you should take him to someone else."

Who? Laura wondered—a psychiatrist? But as much as she shrank from that idea, she didn't like these continuing nightmares of Peter's either, and after last night, she wondered if they shouldn't take him to a specialist. If something wasn't wrong organically, maybe they should start thinking of counseling. "I'll talk to Jack about it," she said reluctantly.

"Good," Estelle said, satisfied. "I kept him home today, you know."

Instantly she felt her blood pressure rise. "No, I didn't know that. When I left this morning, he was ready for school. Why did you let him stay home?"

"Because he was up half the night, Laura," her mother said defensively. "He was too tired to go."

"He was fine," she said, trying to hold on to her temper. They'd discussed this before when her mother had elected to keep Peter home after one of these episodes. She sympathized,

226

but she didn't want her son to start thinking this was a way to get out of going to class; he was having enough problems already.

"You say that, but only because you're so afraid of spoiling him a little," Estelle said. "And really, Laura—it's only one day. What can it hurt?"

"It's more than one day, Mother," she said sharply, and then gave up. It was too late to argue about it now. But she couldn't prevent herself from adding, "I hope he enjoyed himself."

"Well, I kept him quiet, of course," Estelle said with a sniff. "And I fed him some of my homemade soup for lunch. You know how he loves my soup."

Laura rubbed her temples. "Yes, I know."

"And of course, he had to take a nap this afternoon."

"Of course," she said.

"Are you being sarcastic?"

"No, of course not."

Estelle sniffed. "And I know this isn't going to make you happy, either, but I promised him he could have hot dogs and french fries for dinner tonight in front of the TV. He and Andrea are going to have a picnic."

"Wonderful," Laura said.

Estelle's voice sharpened. "Are you being sarcastic again?"

"No," she said with a sigh. Her mother was aware how she felt about junk food for dinner, but since that had been yet another of their fruitless discussions, she knew it would be futile to pursue it. Wondering if Estelle did these things on purpose or if it only seemed that way to her, she decided to change the subject. Jack had told her this morning that he wasn't going to the office today but planned to work at home, and she wanted to ask him why he'd allowed Estelle to keep Peter out of school. "Mom, can I talk to Jack?"

"He's not here."

Thinking that he'd gone for a run on the beach or down to the store, she said, "Well, is he coming back soon?"

"I'm sure he is," Estelle said pointedly. "Jack always comes home from work on time."

"But he said he wasn't going in to the office today."

"He apparently changed his mind. He left right after you did this morning. Someone called, and he had to meet them."

"A client?"

"Well, I imagine so, Laura," her mother said impatiently. "He said he was going to the office."

She bit her lip, wondering why she should have expected Jack to call with his change of plan. Their six-month separation, of sorts, hadn't done that much good; Jack was still evasive, refusing to talk about what was obviously bothering him, refusing to admit, even, that there was a problem. She would have confronted him more openly if she hadn't felt so responsible herself. It was ironic, really: the first night she had gone out for drinks with Douglas was the same night Jack had decided to come home from Arizona for good. He'd finished the job but hadn't let her know because he'd wanted to surprise her. Well, he had. She still winced when she remembered that homecoming; it hadn't gone as either of them had planned.

Nothing seemed to have gone right since, either, and after she told her mother when she'd be home, and then said goodbye, she hung up feeling depressed. She didn't know what Jack wanted anymore; she'd believed once that he felt everything would be all right if she gave up public service and went into private practice, but it wasn't that. He didn't seem to care anymore what her work involved. Unhappily she sat back in the chair, staring at the wall. He didn't seem to care anymore, period. If she said she wanted to talk, he told her they didn't have anything to talk about; if she said she thought they had a problem, he denied it. He claimed he was preoccupied with work, and it was true, he seemed to be putting in more time at the office, but she knew that wasn't the answer. Wishing she knew what was, she sighed and started gathering her things. The only good thing to come out of this day, it seemed, was that she was going to see Douglas. Feeling better, she grabbed her coat and switched out the light.

Douglas was already waiting when she got there, sitting in the booth that she was quickly coming to think of as "theirs." They saw each other at the same time, and as he stood and gestured, she felt a warm glow inside and quickly threaded her way through the tables.

"I'm sorry I'm late," she said when she reached him. "It's really been a day."

"You're not late," he said, gazing down into her eyes. "I'm just glad you could come on such short notice."

"So am I," she said, and without realizing it, they stood there

228

just looking at each other until a pert waitress plucked at Douglas's sleeve.

" 'Scuse me, please," she said in a lilting accent that contrasted oddly with the place. "I got ta get ta t'other taible, if I might."

Laura blushed. She hadn't realized they were blocking the way until the girl asked to get by, and when she saw the waitress's knowing wink in her direction, she was even more embarrassed. Douglas was, too. Quickly he gestured, and they both sat down.

"I already ordered your wine," he said. "I hope that's what you wanted."

"It's fine," she said, still trying to get herself together. "Were you waiting long?"

"No, I just got here," he said, still gazing at her. He said again, "I'm glad you could come."

"I am, too," she said, and glanced away in an effort to disguise her sudden emotion. Now that she was here, she realized, as she always did, just how much she enjoyed his company, and how much she missed him at times. At the back of her mind she knew how dangerous this was, but she couldn't seem to help herself. She valued these brief meetings with him, innocent as they were, even if all they did was talk. Maybe because all they *did* was talk. But because she knew no one else would understand—or believe that even if she told them—the only person who knew about her friendship with Douglas was her friend Trudy. She'd told Trudy about it because she had to tell someone, and the narcotics detective was someone she knew instinctively she could trust.

Trudy had been, to say the least, overwhelmed. "You know Douglas *Rhodes*?" she'd squealed that day at lunch.

Quickly Laura had glanced around. "Shhh. Keep your voice down. I don't think the whole coffee shop needs to hear."

Trudy leaned forward. For once their schedules had meshed, and they'd actually been able to go out to lunch. "But Douglas *Rhodes*!" she'd whispered excitedly. "I've seen him on TV. He's so good-looking!"

"You know who he is, then?"

Trudy's eyes had widened behind her glasses. "Are you kidding? Everybody in the entire country knows who he is!" She sat back, awed. "And he comes to L.A. just to see you!"

"Not exactly," she'd said hastily. "He has friends here—Duluth is one. And his campaign manager has an office in—"

"Who *cares*?" Trudy said. "Tell me about him! Is he really as charismatic as he seems? He certainly comes across that way on TV. How on earth did you meet him, anyway?" She looked at Laura jealously. "Some people have all the luck!"

She'd laughed at her friend's expression and briefly explained about their first encounter outside the district attorney's office. But she couldn't help wondering what her reaction would have been if she had guessed then how quickly their friendship would develop, how sometimes she would long to hear from him, how eagerly she would look forward to seeing him, if only for a few minutes. If she had known all that, would she have accepted that first invitation to share a drink?

She didn't have to ask herself that; she knew the answer.

"So tell me," Trudy demanded, her eyes alight, "what's he like?"

She didn't know what to say. Douglas was so many things that she couldn't separate them. He was one of the most compelling men she'd ever met, and while their relationship had been strictly platonic so far—and would continue to be, she told herself hastily—there had been times when she'd felt so strongly drawn to him that she was almost weak. She had never forgotten that night at the Beverly Hills Hotel; she remembered even now the blissful sensation of his arms around her; she'd never forgotten how strongly his heart beat under her cheek, or the scent of his after-shave. She could even recall the scratchy feel of the starch in his shirt.

But the strongest recollection she had carried with her was the aura of command he had. She'd known he would do anything for her—anything that was within his power, and so much was. She had felt that power surround her, and she recalled all too clearly her yearning that night just to surrender for once and let him take charge.

She had never allowed herself the luxury of that emotion again; she didn't dare. She knew where it would lead—where she would want it to lead—and she had to remind herself constantly of her duties and responsibilities and obligations—and of his. She had a spouse and a family to think about . . . and so did he.

And so what, really, could she tell Trudy? She knew that she could never explain her complex relationship with Douglas Rhodes even to such a good friend, and so she had finally smiled and said, "What can I say? He's even more handsome in person than he is on TV, and he's every bit as wonderful as he appears to be."

"Are you in love with him?" Trudy had asked.

She'd barely managed to mask her dismayed surprise at the question. "Isn't everybody?" she said lightly, and glanced away.

And now he was sitting across from her in the quiet little bar, and the pianist had started playing "As Time Goes By." Realizing that it was, flying by all too quickly, she came out of her brown study and apologized. "I'm sorry. I was just . . . thinking."

He smiled. "Problems at work?"

"No more than usual," she said, and didn't want to discuss her work, which seemed increasingly to her to involve the seamier sides of life and people. A new case had come in this afternoon and she'd been assigned. People laughed about murder and mayhem, but today it had been all too real, and she didn't want to spoil this precious time by talking about it. She wanted to talk about him. *I'll deal with it later . . . tomorrow,* she told herself, and said, "You're kind of quiet yourself tonight. Isn't the campaign going well?"

Douglas had told her long ago about Malcolm Tanner. He was such an entertaining storyteller that she always looked forward to his next anecdote because she knew he'd make her laugh. She needed a little laughter tonight, but he didn't seem to have any new amusing tales.

"Yes, it's going fine."

She knew something was wrong, and she placed a hand on his arm. "What is it, Douglas? What's the matter?"

He hesitated, then shook his head. "I didn't come here to talk about my problems, Laura. I want to hear about *your* day."

Laura didn't want to talk about her day. She was still trying to adjust to what she'd learned about the new case. It was an appalling thing, something she couldn't talk about yet even to Dale without feeling nearly overwhelmed with revulsion and outrage and sheer horror.

"No, you don't," she said. "Not when you look like that. Please, tell me what's wrong. Is it the campaign? Has Malcolm done something outrageous again?"

This time he did smile. "No, for once it's not Malcolm."

She thought she understood. He'd told her about his family—about his wife and son and the problems he and Marcella had been having because of Rob; he'd told her about flying home that one weekend and meeting his son's pregnant girlfriend. She knew how he felt about that, and she said hesitantly, "Is it . . . Rob? Do you want to talk about it?"

He toyed with the drink the waitress had brought, then took a swallow. "I told you about that girl Calypso, didn't I?"

"Yes," she said. And then, quietly, "Has something happened to the baby?"

"No—not that I've heard, anyway. But I . . . I hired a private investigator to check her out."

She looked at him in surprise. "You did?"

"I had to," he said, looking even more unhappy. "Rob is my only son, my only child. I had to do something."

"What did you find out?"

"That her name isn't really Calypso, of course, but Harriet Jane Gross, and she's from Denver, where she was known for sleeping around. She hit Phoenix a couple of years ago, and was arrested twice for prostitution before she moved on." He gave her a bleak look. "Nice, huh?"

"Oh, Douglas," she said. "What are you going to do?"

"I already did it," he admitted painfully. "When I found out, I told Rob."

He didn't have to tell her what had happened; the look on his face told the whole story. But she had to ask. "What did Rob do?"

"He left, and took the girl with him, of course. We haven't heard from him since—that was a couple of months ago, and Marcella blames me, of course. She's making herself sick with worry."

She didn't know what to say. "Is there anything I can do?" she asked at last.

"No, I already did that, too. When Marcella insisted that I hire the man to find out where Rob had gone, I didn't have any choice. I asked him to follow through, and he did."

"So you know where Rob is?"

"The investigator traced him to L.A."

"That's a start, anyway," she said encouragingly. "Have you told Marcella?"

He shook his head. "I can't."

She was almost afraid to ask. "Why not?"

"Because the investigator also found out that Rob is . . . that Rob is . . ." He couldn't say it for a moment; his throat seemed

232

to close. Finally he forced the words out. "That Rob's involved in drugs."

"Oh, Douglas!"

Without thinking, she put her hand over his. He was in such pain that he held her tightly. "I don't know what to do, Laura," he said. "I . . . just don't know . . . what to do."

She didn't, either. The look of suffering on his face broke her heart, and she longed to put her arms around him and hold him close. She couldn't let herself; she wasn't sure what would happen if she did. "Douglas, if there's any way I can help—"

He tightened his fingers over hers. "You already have—just by listening."

It wasn't enough. Her problems with Peter, who seemed increasingly withdrawn these days at thirteen, struggling with those nightmares, and with Andrea, who was becoming more spoiled and unmanageable as time went on, seemed minuscule now compared to what Douglas faced with Rob. On sudden inspiration she said, "If you want me to, I can ask a friend of mine to check around, Douglas. Maybe there's been some mistake."

He gave her a grateful look, but shook his head. "There's no mistake. After Rob cleared out the last time, I looked in his room. He's involved in drugs, all right. He left some behind." His mouth twisted. "Maybe he meant for me to find them; I don't know. But they were there."

Although she knew it couldn't possibly help, she tried to comfort him the only way she could. "But that doesn't mean he was dealing, Douglas."

"I don't know what it means," he said. He looked so unhappy that she couldn't think of anything more to say. They parted a few minutes later, and she couldn't prevent herself from giving him a quick hug outside. He held her close for the space of a heartbeat or two, and she was sure she heard him murmur her name. Tears sprang into her eyes, and she wished there were something more she could do. She didn't dare. Emotions were running so high that she knew one careless word, one more gesture, and she would be propelled into something she couldn't stop—wouldn't want to stop. Quickly she got into her car. But as she drove away, she decided shakily that if she couldn't do anything else, she could at least have a quiet word with Trudy. Her friend would be discreet, and maybe she'd be able to help after all.

---◈---

CHAPTER NINETEEN

Laura stopped by Trudy's office the next morning before she went to hers, but when she saw her friend up to her eyebrows in case files, she opted not to interrupt. She was just going by when Trudy looked up.

"Don't go!" she cried in mock panic. "I've been praying for someone to come along and rescue me, and if you leave, I'll have to face all this stuff alone. Join me, please!"

Laura did, grimacing at the litter on her desk. "How many cases do you have, anyway?"

Looking at her from under her brows, Trudy lowered her voice. "How many drug deals are there in the naked city? Thousands? Hundreds of thousands? Take a guess. Take your pick. Take these case files!"

"You're in a good mood today."

Grinning, Trudy sat back. "Hey, I got a conviction yesterday, a little roll in the hay, a good meal at midnight, and the covers on my side of the bed when I woke up. What more can I ask? You caught me at the perfect time. What little favor do you want now?"

"What makes you think I came to ask a favor?"

"Elementary, my dear. You look uncomfortable. That either means you've got something juicy on the gossip side to confide— something you never sink to, I might add—or you came to ask me something."

Laura grinned. "You know, with deductive powers like that, you should have been a prosecuting attorney. Ever think about it?"

Trudy shook her head. "Too little pay, too much work, too many criminals, not enough time off," she said, the description sounding suspiciously like her own work. "Need I say more? Definitely not the life for a gorgeous single creature like myself. Now, what did you want?"

Looking serious, Laura set her briefcase gingerly on the desk, hoping nothing would slide off. "You promise it won't go any farther than here?"

Trudy stopped smiling, too. There was a time to joke around and a time not to, and she'd always known the difference. "Sure," she said. "What's up?"

Hesitating, Laura tried to think of the best way to say it, and finally decided just to be direct. "I'd like you to keep an ear out for anything you hear on someone named Rob Rhodes."

"Rob Rhodes," Trudy repeated, frowning. Then comprehension dawned. "Oh, no. You're kidding."

"I wish I were."

Leaning back again, Trudy threw her pen down on the desk. "Damn. I can see why you want to keep this between us girls."

"Can you do it?"

"Yeah, sure—as long as . . ." Trudy stopped. "Well, you know."

Laura knew. Trudy could only keep so much quiet; if Rob were involved in any big deals, or if a bust depended on taking him down with it, he'd be sacrificed along with the rest. She accepted that. She couldn't ask Trudy to do more than keep an eye out and try to do what she could to protect him. Douglas himself wouldn't want more than that.

"Thanks," she said quietly. "I owe you one."

"No problem," Trudy said, and then shook her head. "But what a shame."

Laura agreed with that, and over the next few weeks managed by an effort of will to put Rob from her mind. She didn't have much choice; in addition to other pending cases, one in particular was making headlines and taking most of her time. Arthur Linneman, a forty-year-old unemployed factory worker, had been arrested for kidnapping, rape, murder, attempted murder, and mayhem, among other charges, after one of the most sensational crime sprees the state had experienced in years. The state's only witness was one of his victims, a fifteen-year-old runaway/junkie named Debbie Watson, who had stumbled out of the desert one night babbling hysterically about a murdered friend buried somewhere in the sand behind her and a madman who had killed the friend and was after her, too. She'd been covered with blood and in such deep shock that doctors feared for a while they might lose her. After three hours of surgery and over four hundred stitches from knife wounds and slashes all over her body, they had managed to save her life but not one of her eyes. She'd lapsed into coma for over a week, but by the time she emerged, her friend's mutilated body had been found and a manhunt had been launched for the killer. Laura was there when she awoke, but it took some time to learn all the facts in the story. Debbie had been so traumatized that she could barely speak.

Needless to say, the case was too bizarre and grotesque to stay out of the papers, and reporters haunted the hospital halls until Debbie awoke. Because Laura had the case, she assigned police protection and absolutely refused to let anyone discuss any details with the press. She didn't want anything to jeopardize a conviction; Debbie's description of her attacker successfully led to the arrest of Arthur Linneman, who was being held without bail, and there would be no mistrials here. But a murder conviction wasn't going to be enough; after what Linneman had done, she filed special circumstances—first-degree murder, with intent. In California, that could mean life, without possibility of parole. Or it could mean death. In Laura's mind, there was no question which she would prefer. She'd come to grips with that long ago, and over the following months prepared for trial as she'd never done before.

"Hi, you busy?" Dale said one morning, poking his head around her office door.

It wasn't even nine o'clock yet, but she'd been here working for close to an hour and she was glad to shove the paperwork away. "Yes, but come in anyway," she said, and watched as he walked toward her desk. He was wearing blue today, and she couldn't help thinking how handsome he was. But then, she'd always thought he was good-looking; she remembered when she'd first started at the PD how dashing she'd thought him, with that shock of blond hair and those intense blue eyes. Even though they'd inevitably been on opposite sides of the table back then, she had always liked and respected him, and as their association had grown and they'd become friends, she'd become even more fond of him. "What's up?"

"Have you read the paper this morning?" he asked, casually taking the other chair and crossing one long leg over the other. "They're really raking us over the coals with this Linneman thing, and trial hasn't even started."

"I don't read the paper anymore," she said with a grimace. "Especially when I know it's only going to get worse."

He grinned at her. "You up to it?"

She looked at him. "What do you think?"

He held up his hands. "Just thought I'd ask."

"Yes, well, now you know. Is that what you came in here for?"

"A little hostile this morning, aren't we?"

"Yeah, I guess I am," she admitted reluctantly, and didn't know whether she felt more antagonistic toward Jack, who was giving her a bad time about this case, or toward Harry Silverstein, who, naturally, had been assigned as Linneman's defense attorney.

"Want to talk about it?"

"No . . . yes . . . I don't know," she said, impatient with herself for having doubts at this late date. "Can I ask you something?"

"Fire away."

"Jack accused me of endangering my family by prosecuting this case. What do you think?"

Dale took his time. "Why'd he say that?"

He'd said it during another of their increasing quarrels just the other night, but she'd been too furious—and too afraid that he might be right—to think about it until now. "Well, because he's heard about prosecutors being threatened by people they've put away, after they get out," she said. "Or DAs living in fear when some criminal they've prosecuted escapes. Have you ever thought about that?"

"Sure, I've thought about it. Who around here hasn't? You'd be a fool not to, but it's not something I dwell on, for the simple reason that I can't worry about something that might not ever happen."

"But what if it does?" she asked. "Suppose somebody you think you've put away for three lifetimes gets out on good behavior or something and threatens you. What then?"

"Then I'd handle it."

"How?"

He gave her a speculative glance. "You're really concerned about this, aren't you?"

"I don't know," she said irritably. "I wasn't, until Jack and I had a fight about it. But ever since then I've been thinking about it, and then I started wondering if I was doing the right thing."

"Whoa," he said. "If you're having doubts like that, you'd

237

better get out right now. Otherwise you won't be any good to us, to the system, or to yourself. You'll be too afraid to do what's right.''

"I didn't say I was having *doubts*," she said, annoyed. "I just asked if you'd ever thought about it—and what you'd do if that happened.''

He seemed relieved. "I'd remember that I wasn't alone here, for one thing," he said. "And that this system we have is a pretty powerful ally. And that I have friends like you." He paused, giving her a keen gaze. "Isn't that what you'd do?''

She looked back at him for a long moment, then suddenly she smiled. "That's what I'd do—exactly.''

He made a display of wiping his brow. "Did I pass?''

She had to laugh. "You get an A for today. Now get out of here. I've got work to do.''

He grinned and saluted her as he went out, but once he'd gone, the smile left her face and she sat back thoughtfully. She was convinced; now could she reassure Jack?

She was still thinking about it when she went home that night. She didn't have a chance to think about it long, for her mother was waiting in the kitchen when she arrived, and the first thing she said was, "I'm leaving for my bridge game now, but you might like to know your daughter is in the living room crying. Maybe you can explain it to her. Heaven knows I've tried.''

"Explain what?" she said, taken aback.

But Estelle just shook her head, and went out. Frowning, Laura set her purse and briefcase on the table and went into the living room. As Estelle had said, Andrea was sitting on the couch, tears running down her face. Wondering what was going on, she went over to her. "What's the matter, honey?''

Andrea looked up with tragic eyes. "Is it true?''

"What? Is what true?" Quickly she sat down and put her arm around her daughter, drawing her close.

"That you're going to murder a poor crazy man for something he didn't do.''

Appalled, she drew back. "What are you talking about?''

"It was in the paper, Mama," Andrea said. "Peter showed it to me. They're calling you . . . calling you—''

"The Death Penalty DA," Peter said, coming down the stairs.

Laura looked over her shoulder. Her son stopped on the bottom stair, one hand on the newel post. His blue eyes, so like

Jack's, were narrowed, and she was dismayed that he looked so angry. Trying to be calm, she said, "What's this all about?"

"You know," he said sullenly. "The paper had a picture of you tonight, and some guy, Harry something or other, is calling you the Death Penalty DA. Andrea saw it on TV, too." His voice hardened. "So did I."

So that was it, Laura thought, and could have strangled Silverstein. She'd known there was going to be trouble when they were both assigned to the Arthur Linneman case, but she'd hoped the problems would stay at the office. Now it seemed that she'd been too optimistic. The thought that he must be desperate to resort to such measures was small comfort right now when her children were looking at her as though she were a monster, and while she'd been able to shrug off the annoying motions and delaying tactics he'd been using to postpone the trial, she couldn't ignore this.

Quietly she said to both her children, "I'd like to explain, if you'll listen. Would one of you bring me the paper?"

Wearing a sulky expression, Peter brought it to her. One glance at the article told her it was worse than she'd thought. She had expected some kind of slur, but when she saw that Silverstein was not only attacking her, but the DA's office as well, she was really annoyed. It was typical that the press was eating it up; the article was front-page news. *Damn him,* she thought, and wondered at the mentality. According to this, she—with the full weight of the district attorney's office behind her—was willfully going to prosecute an innocent, confused man whose only crime was that he'd been in the wrong place at the wrong time. Then she saw another sentence that infuriated her. According to Silverstein, he was merely quoting "highly placed sources." *Hah,* she thought scornfully. These sources of his probably existed in his own tiny little mind. Her lips tight, she read the article.

In one of the more bizarre cases ever filed by the District Attorney's office, the case of Arthur Linneman has to rank right at the top. According to defense attorney Harry Silverstein, the prosecution has only inconclusive forensic reports, circumstantial evidence, a missing murder weapon, and a hysterical witness to buttress their case, yet Deputy District Attorney Laura Devlin stands firm in her resolve to put the defendant, Arthur Linneman, on Death Row for a crime he swears he didn't commit. Highly placed sources reveal that this Death Penalty DA is so eager for a conviction that she is ignoring the very real possibility that Linneman is, indeed, innocent. . . .

There was more, but she didn't read on. Throwing the paper down, she forced herself to think. She had to explain this to her children, in a way they'd understand. She knew what was going on, and why the paper printed such garbage: it was sensationalism, pure and simple. She had a notion to call the paper and demand a retraction—or at least equal time. She could just imagine what Dale would say—what *Duluth* would say—when they saw this, when Peter said, "Mom?"

With an effort, she thrust away her infuriated thoughts and looked at her son. Peter was thirteen now, and soon would be as tall as she was. The nightmares had stopped these past few months, but she was still worried about him. She'd tried to talk to Jack, because he seemed so withdrawn lately, so locked into a world of his own, but Jack insisted it was just his age. According to him, Peter was going through a stage; all the kids went through it; she should take a look at other boys.

But she had, and had reached the unhappy conclusion that other boys Peter's age didn't act like this. They were out playing soccer or softball, giggling over girls, suddenly preoccupied with their looks. Peter was preoccupied with the way he looked, too—but not in the same way. He was so meticulous about the way he dressed, almost . . . prissy. Everything had to be just so, color-coordinated and matched and pressed and clean. He'd even stopped playing ball, and he didn't seem to have many friends. He'd become a loner, always by himself.

Andrea, on the other hand, was always surrounded by friends. At eleven, she was the unchallenged leader of her little group, and Laura didn't know whether to be proud or dismayed that she was growing into such a beauty. She'd always been an attractive child, but now even strangers commented on how pretty she was, and all this attention was having an effect. Andrea was getting spoiled and willful, and Laura knew that if she wasn't careful, her daughter was going to turn into a conceited little prig.

Jack didn't agree with her about Andrea, either. She'd tried to talk to him about this new rebelliousness in their daughter, who seemed lately to challenge everything she said. The slightest request on her part lately had turned into a battle of wills, but

Jack felt that Andrea was only going through a phase, like Peter. He was sure that soon she'd become her former sweet, cooperative self again, and while Laura wanted to believe that, she couldn't help feeling that somewhere along the line she'd lost control.

Doubt rose at the back of her mind again, as it seemed to do so often these days, and she thought of how she felt so torn at times, so pulled in too many directions. She wanted to be a loving wife to her husband, a nurturing mother to her children, a dutiful daughter to her mother, but it seemed that the more she tried, the more she fell behind.

And now so much of her time was being eaten away by this upcoming trial that she felt even more torn. Debbie Watson had been through so much, too—far more than the average person would even dream of—and yet she was willing to testify, to do her part to put Arthur Linneman away so that he'd never hurt anyone else. She couldn't give up on Debbie, who had been so brave, any more than she could turn her back on seeing justice done.

So that meant that she had to find a way to balance things, and when she realized her children were still waiting for her to explain, she said carefully, "You both know that this is a very important case, and that I've been assigned to prosecute this man, don't you?"

"Yeah," Peter said, gesturing toward the paper she'd thrown down. "But it says there that you've got the wrong guy, Mom. How do you explain that?"

Cursing the sensation-seeking reporter who had written the damned article, she said calmly, "The paper doesn't have all the facts, Peter. Do you really think I'd prosecute a man I believed was innocent?"

"Well, no, but—"

"Then why are they saying that, Mama?" Andrea asked.

"Because sometimes reporters . . . exaggerate . . . to make the story more exciting," she said.

"Are you really going to ask for the death penalty, Mama?" Peter asked.

Before she could answer, Andrea said. "What's the death penalty?"

"It's something you don't need to bother your pretty little head with, pumpkin," Jack said just then. Surprised, because they'd all been so intent, they hadn't heard him come in, they turned. He was standing in the living room archway, and when Andrea cried out in pleasure and ran to him, he squatted down and gave her a hug. His eyes met Laura's over their daughter's head, and she knew he was angry. Well, she couldn't help it. She hadn't written the article, and she couldn't ignore their questions about it.

Ruffling Andrea's hair, Jack turned to his son. "Hi, how's it going, Pete?"

"Fine, I guess," Peter muttered.

"Good day in school?"

"It was okay."

"Mine was, too, Daddy," Andrea said, claiming her father's attention again as he seemed about to ask Peter something else. He turned back to her instead, and as he listened to her account of something that had happened in class, Laura glanced in Peter's direction and was startled to see him staring at his father and sister with a wounded expression.

"Peter?" she said softly.

His glance shifted to her. "What?"

"Is . . . something wrong?"

Despite himself, his eyes went to Jack again, then his face closed. "No. I've got some homework to do, okay?"

"Wait—" she said, but she had already started up the stairs. Frowning, she glanced at Jack. He'd been giving Peter a hard time about not participating in sports this year, and she decided to talk to him about it later. Obviously something was going on here, and she wanted to know what it was before she tried to talk to Peter herself.

Andrea was just finishing her story. "And so the teacher put *my* picture up on the board," she said, with a quick glance toward the stairs. "Isn't that neat?"

"That's great, honey," Jack said, giving her a hug. "I'm proud of you."

Watching this little byplay, Laura frowned again. She had seen something in Andrea's face just now when she looked in the direction Peter had gone, and she was surprised to realize that just for a second, her daughter had looked . . . sly. Then she shook her herself. That was ridiculous. Andy might be spoiled, but she wasn't malicious. But because she still felt uneasy, she said, "I'm going to start dinner."

"Can we have hamburgers and french fries?" Andrea asked.

Feeling impatient with her daughter without knowing exactly why, she said curtly, "No, we can't."

"Oh, Mama! Just this once?"

To her annoyance, Jack added his two cents. "Come on, Laura. Andy got an A in school today. I think we should celebrate."

She started to glare at him, then realized she just didn't have the energy to fight it. "All right," she said. "Just this once."

Andrea shrilled in triumph and thundered up the stairs, yelling for her brother. Jack waited until she'd gone before he got to his feet from his squatting position. "I see you've had a good day yourself, Laura," he said. "In all the papers again. How does it feel to be such a celebrity?"

"Not now, Jack, all right?" she said. She knew how he felt about that, and she didn't want to get into a fight. He'd already made it very clear how annoyed he was at all the time this case was taking, and she knew that because of all the publicity, he resented the assignment even more. But she didn't feel like talking about it, and she turned and went into the kitchen to start dinner.

To her annoyance, he wasn't going to let it go. Following her, he said, "Hey, you don't have to act like that. I just thought I'd ask. After all, you're always saying I'm never interested in your work."

Thinking it was going to be one of those nights, she took out a frying pan. But she was still determined not to get into a fight with him, so she said, "Let's talk about your work. How was your day?"

He shrugged. "It was a day."

"That's all?"

He glanced away. "I guess I'm not news like you are."

Her lips tightened and she turned to the freezer for the hamburger. Naturally they didn't have any on hand, and she slammed the freezer door, trying to hold on to her temper. "There's no meat. I'm going to have to go out and get some."

She was just reaching for her purse when he said, "Why don't we take the kids and go out?"

She looked at him in surprise. "What?"

"Am I speaking in a different language or something?" he said with one of those mercurial changes of mood that lately made her feel as though she didn't know him at all. She was still staring at him when he grinned and reached for her. Pulling

243

her toward him, he put his arms around her waist. "I said that maybe we should take the kids out for a treat. We haven't been to a hamburger place in a long time, and we could drop them off at a movie afterwards, or something."

Had she heard right? "But it's a school night!"

"So what?" he said, pulling her even more tightly into him. He kissed the tip of her nose. "If the kids are at the movies, we could have a couple of hours alone. . . ."

What was going on? She couldn't remember the last time he'd suggested something like this, and she was so flustered that she said, "Have you done something I should know about?"

His eyes darkened, just for an instant. But he seemed determined to keep it light, and he made himself laugh. "Just because I want to spend some time alone with you? Why are women so suspicious?"

Now that he'd made an effort, she didn't want to ruin it. Quickly she said, "I'm sorry. It's just that you surprised me."

"Well, what do you say?"

But before she could say anything, the phone rang. She was just reaching for it when he grabbed her hand. "Let it ring."

She was tempted; oh, she was tempted. But she couldn't. "I can't, Jack—"

His eyes narrowed. "Why, because it might be your office? Is that more important than your family?"

"It isn't that—"

The phone rang again, cutting through her feeble excuse. He dropped her hand. "Oh, go ahead," he said angrily. "You know you want to."

"Jack—"

The instrument rang a third time, making her more indecisive. Jack headed toward the refrigerator and jerked open the door. Grabbing a beer, he popped the top and practically drained it in one gulp. "Jack, please," she pleaded. She didn't want him to get drunk again; he'd been doing too much drinking as it was.

The phone rang for a fourth time, scraping her nerves raw. She wanted to scream at it to shut up.

Jack crumpled the beer can in his hand and reached for another. "If you don't answer that," he said, "I'm going to rip it out of the wall."

When it rang a fifth time and Jack started toward it, she had no choice. Snatching up the receiver, she shouted a hello.

244

"Laura?" someone said uncertainly.

She recognized Trudy and was embarrassed. "Yes, it's me. Hi," she said.

"Are you okay? Can you talk?"

She glanced quickly at Jack, who was just finishing another beer. He saw her looking at him, gave her a sarcastic thumbs-up, and drained that beer, too. Wondering if he was going to drink himself into a stupor right here in front of her, she turned slightly away and said, "Yes, I can talk. It's just—never mind. What is it?"

Trudy knew something was up, but she had her own concerns. "I'm sorry to bother you," she said, her voice low. "But I've got a problem."

Jack started to leave the kitchen. Not wanting him to go, she tried to reach for him, but he brushed by. "Trudy," she said, a little desperately, "can't it wait? I've got—"

"I *said*," Trudy repeated, "that I've got a problem."

Something in her tone finally penetrated. Forgetting Jack, Laura slowly straightened. "What kind of problem?"

Trudy hesitated. Her voice even lower, she said, "I'd rather not talk about it over the phone, if you know what I mean."

She felt a stab of alarm. Trudy wasn't one to play games, not like this, and suddenly warning bells were shrilling her mind. "Trudy?"

"Listen, I'm over in Hollywood, near Sunset and Western. Can you come out right away?"

"*Now?* Trudy, I—"

"I think you should, Laura," Trudy said, and gave her the exact address. "It's about that . . . that little matter we discussed a couple of months ago."

She didn't know why, but for some absurd reason, she remembered that it was election night. She'd voted this morning, on the way to work. All over the country, people were voting; this was the night that months of campaigning were either going to fail or bear fruit. She closed her eyes. This couldn't be happening.

"Tell me it isn't true," she whispered.

"Just get over here, okay?"

"I'll leave right now," she said, and hung up. Her hand was shaking, and she didn't realize Jack was standing there until he spoke.

"Going out, dear?" he said. His tone was soft, but the look

in his eyes was ugly—another lightning change of mood that she didn't care to examine at the moment.

"I have to," she said, and was startled when he clamped his fingers over her wrist as she reached for her purse. Surprised, she tried to draw back, but he held her fast. "What are you doing?"

He put his face close to hers. "If you go out now, I'm not going to be here when you get back."

She just looked at him. "What are you talking about?"

"I mean it, Laura," he said. "If you leave now, I'm going, too."

She couldn't believe this. "What are you talking about? Let me go!"

He was still staring into her face, holding her awkwardly over the kitchen table. "Is that what you want, Laurie?" he asked. "Are you more married to your job than you are to me?"

She couldn't take the time to argue with him, not when he was like this. She knew from experience that in this mood he wouldn't believe anything she said anyway, so she jerked her wrist free and said, "We'll talk about this later, Jack. But I'm going out now. I have to."

"We'll talk about it now or we won't talk about it at all."

"Is that a threat?"

His eyes held hers. "If you want it to be."

A sense of urgency had clamped down on her. She had to leave *right now*. Beginning to be frightened at the thought of what she might find when she met Trudy, she reached quickly for her purse again. "I won't be threatened, Jack," she said. "If you have something to say, say it when we can both talk about it. But not now. Not *now*!"

"I mean it, Laura!" he shouted as she ran out the door. "I won't be here when you get back!"

She didn't answer; she was too busy trying to shove the key into the car's ignition. Jack came out to the driveway just as she pulled away, and as she looked into the rearview mirror, she muttered to herself that he wouldn't leave the kids alone. As angry as he might be with her, he wouldn't leave them in the house by themselves; he'd stay at least until Estelle came home from her bridge game. Then she became angry at him. He'd threatened this before, she remembered, and he'd always come home. But why tonight? Why *tonight*?

"Oh, Douglas," she said, and heard the sob in her voice with alarm. Controlling herself with an effort, she accelerated onto the freeway and drove as fast as she could to meet Trudy.

The address Trudy had given her was a decaying apartment tenement in the Hollywood area, dark and grim and reeking of despair. Her heart pounding as she drove through the deserted streets, she tried to tell herself everything was going to be all right. It was a mistake, a ghastly mistake; it had to be.

But then she saw the flashing blue and red lights outside the building, and knew that for someone, things were never going to be right again. Barriers had already been set up outside in the street, and as she parked, a uniformed officer sauntered over.

"I'm sorry, ma'am, you're going to have to move on," he said when she got out of the car.

She didn't have time to argue; flashing her badge at him, she said, "Detective Mankiller called me. Where is she?"

The badge was her ticket. "Sorry," he muttered. "I didn't realize . . . Uh, everyone's on the third floor."

Naturally there was no elevator; she wasn't sure she would have trusted one if there were. An overpowering stench assaulted her when she entered the building, and she grabbed quickly for a tissue to cover her nose, afraid she would gag. Her heart pounding with anxiety and fear, she started toward the stairs. Graffiti covered the walls, and garbage seemed to be piled everywhere. She didn't dare think what she'd find when she reached the third floor; she concentrated on climbing the stairs, trying not to touch anything, caught up in something that had become her worst nightmare.

Trudy was standing just inside the open doorway of an apartment halfway down the hall when she came out onto the third landing, and the instant Laura saw her face, her last hope died. The detective met her, taking her arm. "Thanks for coming," she murmured.

She had to fight with herself not to clutch Trudy in fear and despair. "Thanks for calling me."

"You won't thank me in a few minutes."

"What . . . happened?"

"From the looks of it, a hit that went down wrong," Trudy said, and shook her head. "There's some stuff out on the streets now that's real bad news. One snort and you're dead." She hesitated. "We think that's what happened here."

Laura looked around, her nostrils contracting at the horrible stench. "Here?"

"He must have met a dealer here," Trudy said. "It doesn't look like he was dealing himself."

Laura searched her friend's face. "Are you sure it's him?"

Trudy gazed steadily back. She wasn't wearing the glasses she normally wore for undercover, and her gaze was sympathetic. "We're sure."

Briefly Laura closed her eyes. "I've got to see him."

"I don't think that's a good idea."

"I have to," she said, and steeled herself. One step at a time she made herself approach that open door. Before she could think about it, she went in.

It was worse, far worse, than she'd imagined, and when she saw the body crumpled against one of the walls, she put her hand over her mouth. Quickly Trudy put a hand on her arm and tried to draw her back. "Come on, that's enough."

"Oh, God," Laura whispered, and couldn't take her eyes away. Although she'd only seen pictures of him from Douglas's wallet, she would have recognized Rob anywhere, even in death. He had the same thick, black, wavy hair, the same strong jaw, the same nose. The coroner's office was there, apparently just finishing the preliminary examination, and she gasped when he gestured to two assistants with a body bag. This time she didn't protest when Trudy gently dragged her away.

"Laura, we have to talk about this," she said when they were outside. "I can't keep a lid on it, and you know what's going to happen when the press latches on. You can just see the headlines from here: Senator's drugged-out son dies from deadly overdose—or something equally descriptive."

Laura was taking huge breaths of the night air, trying to calm her roiling stomach. At last she was able to breathe again without feeling as though she was going to faint, but she knew she would have nightmares for a long, long time about that horrible scene upstairs. When she could finally speak, she looked at Trudy. "Can you keep this quiet until I reach him?"

Trudy started to shake her head, but then she saw the pleading in her face and said instead, "I'll try."

Gratefully she grasped Trudy's arm. "Thanks."

"Do you want me to call him?"

She hesitated. She would have given anything not to be the one to relay this devastating news to Douglas, but she knew she had to do it. They were just bringing the shrouded body out now, and she stared at the scene for a long moment before she gave a shaky sigh. The night had turned chill, and she huddled into her coat. There was a hint of rain, and the flashing lights seemed harsh, a strobelike effect that hurt her eyes. Trudy was gazing at her in concern, but she shook her head.

"No, this is something I have to do," she said, and took one last sad look at the deathly still form on the gurney before she turned away to find a phone.

---⊗---

CHAPTER TWENTY

The din was so loud at Douglas's campaign headquarters in Phoenix that he could hardly make himself heard above the noise. It was election night; the polls had closed three hours ago, and a party was in full swing. His opponent hadn't officially conceded the Rhodes victory, and until he did, Douglas knew he wouldn't feel free to join in the hilarity. But it was a foregone conclusion; the landslide everyone had predicted had occurred right on schedule, and as he glanced around, he couldn't help feeling a thrill of pride. After all these months, he'd done it. His eye fell on Malcolm, walking toward him. Together, *they* had done it.

"Well, Senator, how does it feel to win a second term?" Malcolm said. He was holding two glasses and a bottle of champagne, and he held one of the glasses out.

Accepting it, Douglas grinned. "It's a little too early to tell."

Malcolm glanced toward one of the several giant-sized television screens he'd set up around headquarters. Each was tuned to a different station where various network anchors were solemnly giving—or predicting—local and national election results. Every time a station harkened back to the senatorial race in Arizona, the room exploded with a cheer. Before Malcolm could say anything in response, the room erupted again, a hundred straw hats sailing into the air, accompanied by a hoarse cheer. He turned and gave Douglas a significant look.

"I don't know how much affirmation you need, Senator," he said, pouring the champagne for them. "Any more of a landslide and we'll all be swept right out to sea. The Pacific, I mean."

It was past time for false modesty. Even Douglas had to admit he was so far ahead now, a miracle wouldn't make any difference to his opponent, and he clinked his glass against Malcolm's. "I have you to thank."

Tanner returned the toast. "I had the best candidate for the job. We couldn't lose."

Douglas laughed. "You should have told me that before."

"I did," Malcolm said complacently. "You just didn't want to listen."

Remembering the "discussions" they'd had these past months, the differences of opinions, the disagreements about how the campaign should be run, Douglas smiled. Through it all they had gained respect for each other, and had emerged at the end firm friends. When he thought back to his original impression of the man, and how wrong he'd been, he was glad it had turned out this way. He knew Malcolm was, too.

"So when are you going to make your victory speech?" Malcolm asked.

"When we get an official concession," Douglas said. "I think it would look a little too eager before then."

"No, I meant for your next campaign," Malcolm said, sipping.

"What next campaign?"

The consultant winked. "The one for president. We are going to make a run for that one, aren't we? I mean, after all this practice, we should make a pretty good team, don't you think?"

Laughing, Douglas held up his hand. "Aren't we getting a little ahead of ourselves?"

"These things take planning, Douglas. It never hurts to start too soon."

Trying not to smile, Douglas shook his head. "Despite such glorious visions, I think I'll just ride this one out for a while. Otherwise people might get the wrong idea."

"I don't know," Malcolm said, glancing around. "I'm not sure we should wait that long. These people are *ready*."

Douglas followed his glance and had to smile. In celebration of the victory, a long line was forming as his supporters prepared to do a precinct version of the Bunny Hop. Someone had brought out the streamers and confetti, and as the favors exploded in the air and rained down on the giddy participants, the room took on an even more festive quality. A tape deck player appeared, and rock music started to vie with the commentators on the television screens. The noise was deafening, especially since every two seconds someone else started a series of victory yells.

"Then again, they probably wouldn't hear you anyway,"

Malcolm said, and grinned again as he finished his champagne. He put the glass on the nearest desktop. "Well, I'd like to stay around for the final count, but I've got to get back to L.A."

"Another victory?" Douglas said.

Malcolm gave his Cheshire cat–like smile. "There are only so many victories," he said. "The trick is to sift out the people who are going to get them."

"Yes, I remember," Douglas said dryly. "We don't choose you; you choose us."

"It worked out okay in your case, didn't it?" Malcolm said, and then, suddenly serious, held out his hand. "Congratulations, Senator. Go give 'em hell. And I mean it about that next campaign. If you need me, all you have to do is holler."

Douglas knew he meant he'd be available for more than just managing the next campaign, and he was grateful. He shook the proffered hand, hard.

"I will," he said, and waved as Malcolm departed by waiting limousine for the airport. Then he turned back to the room and caught his sister's eye. A vision in red, white, and blue, Deidre was leading the conga line, and she waved gaily and gave an extra little bump to her hip when she saw him looking at her. Shaking his head, he glanced away from the giddy group for Marcella. He'd grown increasingly concerned about her these past months; worried over Rob's departure, she had lost so much weight, she was like a wraith. He hadn't liked the look in her eyes, so blank and withdrawn, either. He'd finally insisted on a doctor, who had diagnosed depression and prescribed some pills, but they didn't seem to make a difference. He doubted anything would, until Rob came home. It had already been so long, he was beginning to fear that wouldn't happen. She hadn't wanted to, but he thought it would be good for her to get out, so when he'd told her how important her appearance was to him tonight, she had agreed to come. Now, as he searched the crowd trying to spot her, he remembered that last quarrel with Rob. It had happened during that long-ago weekend his son had brought Calypso home, but he could remember every word as though it had taken place yesterday. He knew he should have handled it differently, but to this day, he didn't see how.

He'd gone to Rob's room to talk to him—that was all, just talk. Through the bedroom window he could see Calypso lounging by the pool, and he gazed at her for a moment, wondering why his son couldn't see what he saw.

But then Rob hadn't been able to see very much that day, he remembered, experiencing again the same pain and outrage he'd felt then, when he'd seen Rob sprawled out on the bed. He hadn't even been able to focus his eyes.

Even now he couldn't believe that his son, his brilliant boy, the youth with such a bright future ahead of him, could have sunk to such a level. He was unkempt, unshaven, looking for all the world like some skid row bum, and Douglas wasn't even sure he recognized him.

"Whaa . . . ?" Rob muttered.

He'd never been interested in drugs, hadn't even been exposed that much to them. But it was obvious even to him that day that Rob was on something, and he'd become so enraged, he could hardly speak. "What's the matter with you?" he'd said, stifling the urge to shake the boy. "What are you *doing* to yourself?"

"Whaddaya mean?" Rob muttered, and made an effort to sit up. He couldn't seem to find his balance, and after a moment, decided it was too much effort. His eyes glazing, he fell back again.

Douglas had watched with a sense of horror, unable to reconcile this picture with the one he still held in his mind. Was this the child who had made his parents so proud, the boy who had been head of the debating team, the one who had scored the touchdown that clinched the state championship—the one who had been valedictorian of his class? Staring down at him, he'd felt tears come into his eyes. He hardly recognized Rob as his son.

It was that last thought that had spurred him to action. Whatever else he had done, whatever he had become, Rob was still his child. The ties between them had once been so strong that he was sure if he tried, he could reach him. He didn't know what had driven Rob away; he didn't know why he'd turned to drugs to ease whatever pain was in his mind. But he would try to understand; he would do everything in his power to bring him out of this.

And if Rob rejected all his efforts?

The chilling question whispered in his mind, but he thrust it away. He wouldn't let go; he'd never desert him. Rob was his son; he loved him. It was as simple, as painful, as that.

But Rob hadn't wanted his help. When he sat down and tried to help him to a sitting position so they could talk, Rob struck out at his hand. "Leave me alone. . . ." he said, his words slurred. "Go away. . . ."

He was starting to feel afraid. Rob seemed so out of it, so far away. "I'm not going to leave, Rob," he said. "We have to talk. I want to help."

That dark head lolled. "Doan . . . wan yur help," Rob muttered. "Duin jus' fine . . ."

Feeling desperate, Douglas reached for him again. Alarmed by the way Rob's eyes seemed to roll back into his head, he shook him slightly. "Rob, listen to me—"

Again Rob slapped his hand away. "No! Lissened to you too much . . . No more . . ."

Holding himself back with an effort, he said, "Rob, you're sick. You need a doctor—"

"Doan need no doctur! Feel jus' fine!"

Not knowing what else to do, he tried again. "Look at yourself, Rob," he pleaded. "You do need help. Can't you at least tell me what's wrong? What can I do to—"

Rob suddenly focused on him. The hatred in his eyes was so startling that he actually flinched. "You want to help?" Rob said, his lip curling. "You want to help?"

He pulled himself together by remembering that Rob was sick. "You know I do," he said.

"Then leave me the fuck alone!" Rob said. He started trying to get off the bed. "You hear me—just leave me the fuck alone!"

He was so shocked, he didn't know what to say. "Rob!"

Rob finally made it off the bed. He stood beside it, one hand pressed against the wall, balancing himself as he wove back and forth. "Whattsa matter, Dad? No one ever talked to you that way before? Well, maybe they oughta. Then you'd realize you're not such a high-and-mighty fuck after all!"

He couldn't believe his son was saying such things—not the words, nor the meaning behind them. He realized, stunned, that Rob hated him. "Rob!" he said again. It seemed the only thing he could say.

Rob lurched away. Glancing around blearily for something he couldn't seem to find, he muttered, "Aw, just leave me alone. Can't you for once leave me the fuck alone?"

"What are you looking for?" Douglas had asked desperately, because he didn't know what else to do.

Reaching for a filthy duffel bag he'd thrown into a corner, Rob started pulling out the contents of his drawers. "I'm leavin'," he muttered. "Takin' Calypso with me." He looked up suddenly, that awful contempt blazing in his eyes. "You don't like Calypso, do you? Isn't good enough for old Robbie, is she? Well, let me tell you something, Dad—she's better than all the Rhodeses put together. All of us! You hear me?"

He's started to panic. Without questioning it, he knew that if Rob left now, he might not ever see him again. Desperate to make contact, he reached out one last time. "Rob, listen to me—please. I know . . . I know you thought I disapproved of your . . . friend—"

Rob hurled another contemptuous look over his shoulder. "Friend?"

"What do you want me to call her?" Douglas asked, knowing he was making a mess of it, but not knowing how to do it differently. "You said yourself you're not married—"

"No, *you* said that, just 'cause we don't have a fucking piece of paper that says we are. It's your hang-up, not mine."

He tried to get himself under control. Brushing a hand through his hair, he said carefully, "All right. Maybe I made a mistake. Maybe I misjudged you . . . or Calypso. But I want to make it right, Rob. I want to understand—"

Rob's expression was ugly. "Why, because you feel guilty?"

"Guilty! About what?"

"You think about it."

Because he was feeling so scared and frustrated and helpless, he shouted, "There's nothing to think about!"

"Yeah? Well, if there's nothing to think about, why are you freaking out?"

He never should have said it. But nothing else he'd said had gotten through, and he had the feeling that this was his last chance. "You're the one who's freaking out! You're the one who's throwing his life away!"

Zipping up the duffel bag, Rob started toward the door. "It's my life to throw away, old man," he said, "so just butt out."

He couldn't let him go like this. Reaching out, he grabbed Rob's arm and stopped him in the doorway. "Rob, can't we just—"

Rob smacked his hand away. "Fuck off," he said. "I can't make it any plainer than that, can I?"

They stared at each other for a moment, and even he had to admit it was hopeless. Finally he said, very quietly, "No. I guess you can't."

He was still standing there when Rob went out to the deck. He heard him call her through the bedroom window. "Hey, Calypso! We're headin' out!"

She didn't want to go. "Aw, Robbie, I'm still workin' on my tan," she said.

"Now! We're history," Rob said, and started out. She had no choice but to follow, and the sound of the gate swinging shut behind them had been like a gunshot through his heart. That was the last they'd seen of either of them. Two months later, when even Marcella hadn't heard from Rob asking for money, he had hired the detective who'd followed their trail to Los Angeles, only to lose them again. Steeling himself, he'd searched Rob's room one day when Marcella was gone; the detective said he might find some clue. He'd found something, all right, a cache of drugs Rob had left behind: marijuana, some white powder, a few little irregular pieces of something he knew, chillingly, was crack. That was when he knew Rob had meant for him to find them, and he'd sat there for a long time, just holding the paraphernalia in his hand, not even realizing that tears were running down his face until Marcella came home and called to him.

"Well, what do you think, Senator? This is some night to remember, isn't it?"

Jolted from his reverie, he turned at the sound of Irving's voice, and smiled at his side. Even though he'd gone over that scene with Rob a thousand times in his mind, he knew he couldn't change what had happened; the only thing he could do was hope he'd get another chance to make things right. At present, he had to remember this was election night, and he owed it to all his supporters to celebrate victory with them.

"It certainly is," he agreed, and realized then how tired Irving looked. Well, they were all tired; it had been a long haul.

"I just saw Malcolm leave," Irving said. "Is he already on the way back to L.A.?"

"You know Malcolm; always another client on the back burner."

"I hope he does as well for them as he did for us."

Fondly he noted the pronoun, and put his hand on Irving's shoulder. "You deserve a lot of the credit, Irv. I don't know what I would do without you."

"Just doing my job," Irving said. But his eyes brightened, and he looked pleased at the compliment.

Realizing that he'd gotten distracted when he was looking for Marcella, he glanced around for her again. He was so tall, he could see over most of the people in the room, and when his eye fell on Dawn Van Doren, standing off to one side, his expression tightened. Irving, with his sensitive antennae, saw his face and asked anxiously, "Something wrong?"

"No. I was just looking at our personal reporter."

"Oh . . . her."

Neither of them liked Dawn, but there didn't seem much they could do about it. He hadn't been too pleased when she had first approached him all those months ago about doing a story on him, and he'd tried to get out of it. Why him? he'd asked. There were certainly much more important, more influential senators on the Hill. And then, because he could see he wasn't convincing her, he added almost rudely that the paper she worked for wasn't exactly known for its in-depth interviews.

"That's exactly why I'm here," she'd said, unfazed. "I intend to change all that."

And before he could object further, she'd told him that since he was one of the rising bright stars in the Senate, with an election campaign coming up, he was the perfect subject. She wanted to follow him through his days, take notes on behind-the-scene glimpses of how campaigns were run, be on hand election night when he won.

Thinking she was getting a little ahead of herself, he'd agreed to think about it and sent her away, hoping she'd forget the idea. She hadn't. Soon she was calling him nearly every day to ask if he'd come to a decision, and finally he'd gotten so irritated that he'd told her she could come in for a few days. Sarah hadn't been too happy about it when he'd told her, but by then it was too late.

"Well, better the devil you know," she'd said, "than one you don't."

"Don't you think you're giving her more credit than she deserves?" he'd asked, annoyed.

"I don't know, Douglas. I hear that she and Lenore are thick as thieves. You better be careful what you say around her."

"I've got nothing to hide," he'd retorted, and ignored the thought of Laura that flashed through his mind. He *didn't* have anything to hide, he insisted to himself, and resolved just to ignore the reporter.

That proved easier said than done, for Irving took a hearty dislike to her, especially when the original few days around the office extended to visits over a period of months. He would have just terminated the whole arrangement except for one problem: for some reason, Marcella took a liking to Dawn on one of the weekends she visited. Since she rarely took an interest in anything, he had to welcome Dawn's intrusion, and he supposed he should be grateful, in a way. The reporter seemed to be the only one who could draw her out, but remembering Sarah's warning, he stayed aloof himself. Thankful that he wouldn't have to worry about her much longer, now that the election was over and she had all the material she needed, he glanced at Irving. Seeing his expression of distaste as his aide gazed in Dawn's direction, he smiled and said, "Don't worry, she'll soon be out of our hair."

"I can't say I'm sorry."

"I know. I'm not either. But I appreciate your cooperation, Irv. I know you've never liked her."

"I've never trusted anyone I can't get any background on."

Douglas had to admit that had bothered him, too. When Irving had first suggested a background check on Dawn as a routine precaution for anyone wanting to attach herself to the senator's staff, he'd reluctantly agreed. He didn't like such probes, because he felt it invaded personal privacy, but he soon found out that in her case it wasn't going to matter; despite all his efforts, Irving had come up empty-handed. It seemed that Dawn Van Doren had simply sprung into existence at age eighteen. Before that . . . nothing.

This naturally had made Irving more suspicious, and he had to admit it hadn't done much for his own peace of mind. But since there wasn't anything they could do about it, he'd advised Irving just to forget it. It wouldn't be forever, and in the meantime, they'd keep an eye out.

"Irv, have you seen Marcella?" he asked abruptly. He was tired of dwelling on Dawn, whoever she was; he knew he should find his wife.

"Yes, she's—"

But just then one of his supporters came running up, wearing an excited expression and fanning his perspiring face with his straw hat. "You've got a call, Senator!" he said. "Shall I bring the phone?"

Thinking it was his opponent calling to concede, Douglas hesitated. "Maybe I'd better take it in the office."

"Okay, whatever you say," the young man said, and turned to the milling, jubilant crowd. Before Douglas or Irving could stop him, he jumped up on top of the nearest desk and started waving his arms and shouting for attention. "Hey! Quiet everybody! Listen up! The senator has to take an important phone call! Hey, you! Turn off those TVs, all right?"

The instant the television sets were turned off, the noise in the room died down. Realizing that something momentous was about to happen, all eyes turned to Douglas, and when he saw breathless expectation on every face, he glanced wryly at Irving. So much for privacy, he thought, and reached across the desk for the phone. One of the lines was blinking, and he punched the button down. Aware of the ringing silence after all that noise, he said, "Senator Rhodes."

"Douglas?"

He recognized the voice immediately, but couldn't prevent a startled "Laura?"

He thought blankly at first that she had called to congratulate him, but when he realized what she was saying, he stiffened. The people closest to him were the first to notice something was wrong—terribly, irrevocably wrong. When he didn't say anything more, but just listened, his face turning first white, then ashen, and finally gray, an uneasy murmur arose. With Dawn, Marcella appeared beside him.

"Douglas?"

He looked at her blankly, not seeing her. Laura was still talking, and he forced himself to concentrate on the sound of her voice. He felt if he didn't, he'd spin away into horror. Finally she choked to a halt, and it was his turn.

"Are you . . ." His voice was strangled, and he had to try again. "Are you . . . sure?"

When the answer came, he closed his eyes briefly, then reached out and put an arm around his wife. Marcella looked up at him. "Douglas, what is it?"

"Senator . . ." Irving said, and reached out to support him, as though afraid he would fall.

He hardly heard them. Laura was saying something more, about how sorry she was, and asking what she could do, but he couldn't answer. He just wanted her to keep on talking, because once she lapsed into silence, he'd have to face this terrible thing,

259

and he just didn't think he could. But finally even Laura had to ask.

"Douglas, what do you want me to do?"

He had to say something, anything, but his mind was a numb blank. Making a valiant effort to pull himself together, he said, "I'll . . . I'll be there as soon as I can." And then, because he didn't think he could get through this without her, he asked, "Will you meet the plane?"

She didn't hesitate. "Yes," she said quietly. "I'll be waiting, whenever you say."

"Thank you," he rasped through a throat that already burned with unshed tears. He couldn't say much more; he didn't trust himself. Blindly he handed the phone to Irving, who to his eternal credit, seemed to know what to do. Grabbing the receiver, he jerked the long telephone cord away from the desk and turned his back on the room. Hunched over the phone, he found out what he needed to know from Laura and quickly made all the arrangements.

Douglas looked around. People were waiting for him to say something, shifting uneasily, glancing at one another, wondering what was wrong. The silence had ceased being expectant and vibrated with uncertain tension now; no one understood, least of all Marcella, who looked up at him anxiously.

"Douglas," she said, plucking at his sleeve. "What is it? What's wrong?"

He wasn't sure he could answer. Something seemed to have him by the throat, squeezing the breath out of him, squeezing whatever life was left. Without warning, images of Rob flashed through his mind and he saw his son as a toddler, taking his first determined steps, and then later, grinning gap-toothed in triumph the first time they went fishing together. He saw him breaking a young horse, boy and animal challenging each other, and Rob finally astride in victory, raising a fist in elation. The pictures flashed before his eyes so quickly, he could barely see: Rob as a young man, dressed in his first tuxedo; Rob behind the wheel of his sports car, his black hair blowing in the wind, the aviator sunglasses making him look like a movie star. So many pictures, too many to count . . . all lost, gone forever.

"Douglas?" Marcella said again.

He had to look down at her. Trying vainly to control his voice, he choked, "It's . . . Rob."

Tears sprang into Marcella's eyes, and Douglas realized in

260

that terrible instant that some part of her knew right then—a part buried quickly, covered over. Horrified, he watched the door slam shut in his wife's mind, even as a bright smile appeared on her face. "They've found him?" she said.

He tried to draw her aside, away from the crowd. People were backing away, aware that something terrible had happened, something that had to be private. He hardly noticed. He was still caught in the grip of horror.

"Yes," he said, his voice sounding more strangled than ever. "They've found him."

The tears spilled over, but Marcella seemed not to notice. Before his terrified glance, she changed, altered, became like a child, innocent and naive and trusting, unable to understand the terrible things grownups had to face. She hadn't taken a step, but he could see her moving away from him, spinning down into some safe cocoon in her mind, flying fast.

"Are we going to him, Douglas?" she asked, her voice like the trilling of a little bird.

He didn't think he could bear this, knew he had to, somehow. Thrusting his own pain away, to be dealt with at another time, he put his arm around her. Looking down into that blank face with the too bright eyes, he said quietly, "Yes, darling, we're going to him."

He knew he should say something to all the people here, but he just couldn't. Tears filling his eyes, he glanced around and shook his head, grateful when they silently parted to let him and Marcella through. He was almost at the door with his unprotesting wife when someone moved and accidentally hit the play button on one of the TVs. Instantly the shrill voice of a commentator burst forth, shattering the fragile, vibrating silence with a boom.

"Well, it's official, ladies and gentlemen! Senator Douglas M. Rhodes has just been declared the winner in the race for the Senate! His opponent, the businessman from Phoenix, Harold Shawnessey, has conceded what turned into a landslide victory for our incumbent, and I imagine campaign headquarters are in a frenzy. Our mobile team is on the way for interviews, but for now, our congratulations to the senator. This is a great night for Arizona, and I'm sure, a proud and happy night for his family! Yessiree, this is—"

There was a gasp, a flurry, and then the TV was quickly

stilled. Without looking back, Douglas led Marcella from the room.

Laura was standing on the tarmac behind the terminal when the private jet Irving had hastily chartered rolled in. The pilots cut the engines, and as the whine wound down to silence, Douglas looked out at the solitary figure waiting under the lights. Tears filled his eyes. She was here, as she said she'd be; he didn't question how. When the door was opened, he was the first one down the ramp.

"Laura," he said as he reached the place where she was standing. She had never looked so beautiful to him as she did then, the night wind ruffling her hair, the lights picking up the planes of her face, shadowing her eyes. She was wearing a raincoat, belted at the waist, the collar lifted up. Her hands were deep in her pockets, but when he spoke her name, she held them out and he grasped her fingers tightly. Right now he felt that was his only lifeline to sanity.

"Thank you for coming," he said hoarsely. He wanted to say more, but the words wouldn't come; he looked at her in agony.

"You knew I would," she said, and blinked back the tears that filled her own eyes. No one else knew how tightly her hands gripped his, nor how much of a struggle it was not to gather him into her arms. "I'm sorry—" Her voice broke for an instant, but with a great effort, she steadied it. "—so sorry. What can I do?"

The longing to hold her was a physical hurt; he wanted to pull her to him, to bury his face in her hair, to feel her arms around him . . . to give in to uncontrollable weeping.

But he said, "You've done enough just by being here. I'll never be able to thank you—"

She held his glance, willing him to silence. Words were as unnecessary as gratitude. Her eyes went past him, to the little group that stood on the steps of the plane, hesitant, aware that something was transpiring between the two, but reluctant to interrupt. She looked at him again. "I've done what I could, Douglas," she said. "But—"

He knew what she meant, and he shook his head. "It doesn't matter," he said, and to him, then, it didn't. Later, perhaps, but not now. Not now. "Can you . . . can you take me to him?"

She searched his face again. "Yes."

Briefly he closed his eyes. "I don't know how to repay—"

She gripped his hands more tightly. "You already have," she said, and turned to lead the way.

Neither of them noticed Dawn, standing behind Irving on the steps of the jet. She had cadged a seat on the plane, slipping in under the confusion at the last minute, determined to stick close to Douglas if she had to ride on the wing. She'd heard by then what had happened, and she wasn't going to miss the finale. Now she was even more glad she'd come. As she watched the little scene on the tarmac, a surprised look, then a knowing one, flashed into her eyes, and when the woman and Douglas turned toward the waiting car, she smiled to herself. Lenore had ordered her to get something on the senator, and now, after months of searching and finding only Sir Lancelot, she had found the chink in the armor. Right here, all the time, had been Guinevere.

CHAPTER TWENTY-ONE

Dawn knew that she'd never forget the expression on Douglas's face when he saw that woman waiting for him by the hangar at the airport in Los Angeles. He'd kept to himself throughout the seemingly endless and silent plane ride from Phoenix, locked in impenetrable thoughts of his own, ignoring even his chief aide. But the instant he saw *her*, things changed, and Dawn wanted to know why.

By that time she knew what had happened, or as much as the senator wanted anyone to know—which wasn't much. He'd left it to that officious creep Irving to issue a statement, a few terse words that only whetted everyone's appetite. Rob Rhodes was dead; there had been some kind of accident. The second she heard that, she knew she had to catch this plane.

Marcella had been left behind, put under sedation by a hastily summoned doctor who had been as tight-lipped as everyone else. She'd debated an instant or two about that, balancing the scoop of the senator's wife collapsing in shock, under a doctor's care, against what she might find in L.A. But she had learned to go where the action was, and now she blessed such foresight. One glimpse of that tender little scene on the tarmac, and she knew she'd struck gold. She had to find out who that woman was.

Unfortunately there wasn't a lot of time. Douglas gestured to them just then, and before she knew what was happening, he and the mystery lady were heading toward a waiting limousine. Afraid she might be left behind, she started down the stairs, but that shit Irving was in front of her, and he wouldn't let her by. Fuming, she had to take her turn with the rest. The senator's campaign chairman, a stout man named Grady Delany, was beside her, and she nudged him. "Who was that woman with the senator?"

Before he could answer, Irving turned stiffly. "I don't think that's any of your business."

She had never liked Irving; she knew he didn't like her. She had stayed out of his way all this time because she knew how much influence he had with the senator, but her story was almost done now, and she didn't have anything to lose. "Oh, really? Then she's someone he might not want us to know about?"

Irving flushed angrily. "That's not what I meant!"

"What *did* you mean then?" she asked, and was annoyed when someone else pushed by her. She had to grab on to the rail, and when she had her balance again and looked up, Irving was just following Douglas into the limousine. "Wait!" she cried, but the car pulled away, leaving her stranded.

"Irving said we're supposed to take a taxi to the Marriott and wait there," Grady offered helpfully. She glared at him. She didn't want to go to any hotel; she wanted to follow Douglas and the mystery woman.

"Well, you just do that," she said, spying a pay phone outside the hanger and starting toward it. "I've got something else to do."

Grady was alarmed; Irving had left him in charge. Another car was pulling up, and he gestured anxiously to her. "Come on. The taxi's here."

She was already digging in her purse for change. "No, you go ahead."

"But what are you going to do? What shall I tell Irving?"

"Tell him I went to visit a sick friend," she said, and started thumbing through the yellow pages. She called the first cab company she saw and climbed in when it came ten minutes later.

"Where to, lady?"

She'd had plenty of time to decide. "Do you have something like the city morgue?"

He turned around and looked at her. "Say wha'?"

She wasn't in the mood to play games; already too much time had passed, and she wanted to get going. "You heard me," she said, flashing him a twenty. "The morgue. It's where they take dead people."

"Yeah, but—"

She waved the twenty in front of his face. "You want this or not?"

"You're the boss," he said, and shook his head as he turned

around again. "Dames," he muttered. "You just don't know these days."

Dawn ignored him. Her busy mind was already running ahead, planning what she would do when she got there. She'd concoct a story, she thought, something about her brother being killed and having to come down to identify him. If she looked distraught enough, they wouldn't question her that thoroughly, and she might get by. Yes, that might work, she thought, and sat back in a fever of impatience until the cab pulled off at U.S.C. Medical Center.

The cabbie turned around. "Well, we're here."

Dawn glanced out the window at the imposing facade of the building. "This is the morgue?"

"The coroner's office," he corrected, and held out his hand for the fare, plus the twenty. She gave him both. "You want me to wait?"

She didn't know how long she'd be. "No, thanks," she said, getting out of the car. She glanced at the building again. It seemed awfully dark. "You sure this is the right place?"

"It's where they take dead people," he said, and put the car in gear. "You sure you don't want me to wait?"

She waved him away and started inside, trying to drum up some tears. Two seconds later, she found out they weren't necessary. The doors were locked, and no one was at the reception desk inside. Now what? Determined not to leave until she found out what she wanted to know, she started going around the building, and was relieved to see someone standing by a door at the back. Immediately she went into her act.

"Oh, thank goodness someone's here," she said, starting to sob. "When the doors were locked, I thought . . ." She pretended to be overcome, wiping away tears.

As she'd hoped, the officer came forward. He'd been having a cigarette and he flicked it away. "Can I help you?" he asked.

"Oh, I hope so," she wept. "You see, I've just heard that my brother was in an accident, and that they took him . . . took him . . ." She was overcome again, peeping at him from the corner of her tissue to see how she was doing. He seemed uncertain.

"Who told you to come here?"

She hadn't thought of that and had to make it up as she went along. "I don't know," she said tearfully. "They called . . .

at home . . . and said I should come right away. I'm supposed to—'' she shuddered ''—identify the body.''

He scratched his head. ''Well, I don't know. Usually they send someone to escort family members—detectives, or uniforms. Why didn't someone come with you?''

She had no ready answer for that, and tried to think under cover of renewed tears. There was nothing to do but try to brazen it through. ''I don't know,'' she sobbed. ''I just know I was supposed to . . . supposed to . . .'' She dissolved in tears again. ''Can't you help me?''

''Jeez, lady, I don't know,'' he said. He was young, obviously new to the uniform. He glanced at the closed door, then back to her. ''I don't know about this.''

She was determined to get into that building. Grabbing on to his sleeve, she said urgently, ''Let's at least go inside. Maybe there's a list or something.''

He drew back. ''I don't know about that. Maybe you should wait until tomorrow.''

''You want me to wait until *tomorrow* before I identify my father?''

''I thought you said it was your brother.''

She could have killed herself. ''I don't know what I'm saying anymore,'' she said distractedly. ''I'm so upset, and you aren't helping. What am I going to do? What am I going to tell my mother?''

He gave a helpless glance backward again. No one miraculously appeared to rescue him, but she was getting uneasy herself. She didn't want to be here if Douglas came out—or if Irving did. How would she explain that? Quickly she said, ''Can you at least tell me if anyone has been brought in tonight?''

''Well, I don't know. . . .''

''His name is Rob Rhodes,'' she said, and burst into tears. But under cover of applying a new tissue, she watched him carefully, and when she saw his eyes involuntarily widen, she thought, *Bingo!*

''Who did you say?'' the officer asked.

''Rhodes,'' she said, weeping against him. ''Rob Rhodes. They told me he was in an accident.''

''Oh, well, it can't be the same guy then,'' the officer said, trying to hold her away from the front of his uniform. ''The only guy by that name was an OD.''

She wanted to make sure she'd heard right. Tears glistening

on her face, she looked up at him. "An . . . OD?" she asked, as though she'd never heard the term.

He seemed to realize what he'd said, and he backed slightly away. "Yeah," he said, glancing around uneasily. "Does that help?"

She threw off the tears as though they'd never existed. "Yes, it certainly does," she said with a smile.

"Hey!" he called.

But she was already walking away, her heels clicking smartly on the sidewalk. She didn't look back.

It was three A.M. when she checked into the Marriott; she was so pleased with herself that she had stopped along the way for a drink. Then she remembered she hadn't eaten, so she went to an all-night restaurant. Key in hand, she was just passing the newspaper stand when a picture on the front page caught her eye. She knew that woman, she thought, and reached quickly for the paper. After reading the headlines, she laughed aloud. Paying for it, she took the paper with her up to her room, chuckling to herself all the while. Letting herself in, she threw it onto the bed and reached for the phone. This was *one* time Lenore was going to have to answer her call; this news was too good to wait.

Pleased with herself and this evening's work, she leaned back and kicked off her high heels. Grabbing the paper again, she looked at the picture featured so prominently as she waited for Chester or somebody to answer at Deer Hollow Farm. God, what a night, she thought delightedly. After all these months of following Senator Douglas M. Rhodes around and starting to believe herself that he really was a knight in armor, she'd found his weakness in one night. It was too good to be true.

The phone was picked up on the other end. "Deering-Kirk residence, Chester speaking," Chester said.

"Chester, this is Dawn," she said. "And don't give me a bad time. I have to talk to Lenore right now."

She could almost see him stiffen. "You know what time it is?"

"Yeah, I do," she said. "And I know Lenore is up. So let's cut the bullshit. I'm in Los Angeles, and I've got a news flash about Douglas Rhodes that can't wait."

Something in her voice must have convinced him, because he sniffed once and then put down the receiver. As she waited for

Lenore to come onto the line, she reread the article that had caused so much glee.

Deputy District Attorney Laura Devlin presses for the death penalty in the trial of Arthur Linneman, the headlines said, and there, in black and white, was the woman who had met Douglas at the plane tonight. God, it was too good to be true, Dawn thought, and laughed aloud again. She only wished she could be there to see Lenore's face when she told her about this!

It was a few minutes after six when Lenore hung up the phone next to the bed in the huge master bedroom at Deer Hollow Farm. A thoughtful expression on her face, she sat back among the satin-covered pillows. Chester had placed the morning coffee service on the tray over her knees, and she absently poured another cup as she contemplated the call she'd just had from Dawn.

Even though she'd been up until the wee hours because of the inevitable round of election night parties she'd attended, she'd still been awake at five-thirty. This was the time she always answered her correspondence, and just because election results were in was no reason to shirk her duty. Besides, after being at the heart of things so long, she was accustomed to predictability on election night, and last night had been no exception. As she'd confidently forecast, the incumbent had won his four more years; gains had been made. With her help, she liked to think. But she sensed, with a political instinct honed over decades, that the next four years were going to be critical to the party. Already she could sense something in the air, and she was getting too old for this foolishness. She had eight years after the next election to be active; after that, she had other things in mind. Her memoirs were one, and after being such a part of all this, she fully intended to write them. It was what her father, God bless his soul, would have wanted, and she wouldn't disappoint him. Besides, she thought with an evil little smile, it was going to be a pleasure watching certain people squirm when they heard she'd finally put pen to paper. After decades of collecting, it was time to have a little fun. Those who over the years had accused her of meddling, well . . . she'd show them.

But that was in the future, and after meeting with Cal and the others again, she had finally worked it out of them that they were indeed looking with interest toward Hugh Redmond. Cackling to herself, she was pleased. It was coming out just as she'd hoped—a little nudge here, a tiny push there . . . She'd show them who was an interfering old woman!

Smiling again at the delicious thought, she nestled more comfortably in the pillows and glanced at Chester, who was sitting in front of her Queen Anne desk by the opposite wall assisting with her correspondence. This was part of their morning ritual, sacrosanct over the years, and even though he looked out of place and far too bulky for that spindly little chair, she wouldn't have dreamed of changing the seating arrangements, nor would he have thought to ask. It was always the same: He brought her morning coffee, then he went to the desk to sort through the mail. As usual, there were piles of letters to answer, stacks of invitations, requests for charity donations, and all the other detritus of an active social and political life. It was Chester's job to sort through, separating out the most important from those she could ignore, and she never questioned him. After years of service, she trusted his judgment implicitly.

"Well, Chester," she said, sipping at her coffee, "what do you think?"

He knew she was referring to the call from Dawn; when she'd heard what her source had to say, she'd put it on the speaker phone. Even so, he took a moment to answer. Finally he said slowly, "A death in the family is always tragic."

"Indeed," Lenore said. "Especially when it's so unexpected. It seems the boy's mother is quite . . . devastated."

"So it would seem," he agreed.

"Perhaps I should send condolences."

Chester paused. "Personally?"

"That would be best, don't you think? The mails are notoriously careless, and we can't yet be certain of her address."

"Nor that of the woman in Los Angeles," he ventured.

"My thoughts exactly," Lenore said with a laugh. And then, "Who would have guessed our Sir Lancelot is not as pure as he seems?"

"That may be a trifle premature," he pointed out smoothly. "We can't be positive all is not innocent."

She would have been infuriated if anyone else had corrected her like this, but she merely gave him a thoughtful look. "Yes, that's true," she said. "We can't. Perhaps we should find out for ourselves."

"A simple enough task," he said solemnly, and stood. "Will there be anything else?"

"I think that will be sufficient for the moment," Lenore said, and held out her hand for the mail he had finished arranging during their conversation. Smiling after him as he headed purposefully toward the door, she added, "Don't tarry. And do have a good flight."

CHAPTER TWENTY-TWO

"Good morning. May it please this Honorable Court . . ."

It seemed a lifetime to Laura since she'd spoken those opening words in the case against Arthur Linneman; there were times during the following weeks when she felt the trial would never end. There were also moments when she wished it wouldn't. All her energy seemed to be taken up in court; she couldn't dwell too much on Douglas and what he might be doing, or she would call, and she had vowed not to do that. She hadn't seen or talked to him since the night he'd identified Rob, but she knew he was suffering, and what he needed was time.

In the meantime, she had work to do, and she threw herself into it with an almost irrational frenzy. Even at that, there were moments when Douglas's face would flash unexpectedly into her mind, or she would think of something he'd said as she was getting ready for court. At these times she would look even more longingly at the phone. In her weaker moments she would reach for it, but always, she'd pull her hand back. He knew her number, she would tell herself; he would call her when he was ready.

Trudy had stopped by a couple of times, but they'd only spoken about that awful night once. She had tried to thank her friend again for all she'd done, but Trudy shook her head. Autopsy revealed that Rob had died from cocaine overdose, but despite all efforts, the department never had found who had given him the drug. As time went on, opinion seemed to be they never would. The one person who might have helped, the girl, Calypso, seemed to have disappeared, and no one could get a line on her. So when Laura tried to thank Trudy for all she'd done—or tried to do—that night, she wouldn't listen.

"It wasn't enough," she said, and looked very weary for a second. "Sometimes it never is."

There was nothing Laura could say to that; they both knew it was true. They could only keep on doing their jobs, but as busy as she was with her workload and this particular case, she knew she would never forget that night, or the desolation she'd felt as she watched that private jet land. Then—too soon, and not soon enough—Douglas himself was there, gripping her hands, the look on his face enough to break her heart. She would have given anything that night not to be the bearer of such tragic news, but in the end she was glad she had been the one to tell him. Better a . . . a friend than a stranger, she'd thought, and felt a pang when she remembered how grateful he had been. His voice had been a hoarse whisper, but he'd thanked her for being there.

"Nothing would have kept me away," she'd said simply, and held on to his trembling hands with all her strength. She wanted to enfold him in her arms and weep with him over this terrible thing, but she saw the people on the plane and didn't dare.

She hadn't even thought about Jack in that moment—her husband who had threatened not to be there if she answered that call. He hadn't gone, of course; he'd spent the night on some friend's couch and had come home the next day carrying a bouquet of daisies and bearing an apology for flying off the handle.

"I'm such an asshole sometimes, Laura," he'd said abjectly. "I don't know why I acted like that. Can you forgive me?"

And so she did—on the condition that they have a long talk about what was wrong. He was so eager to make amends that he had agreed, and she'd been so hopeful at this sign that they had gone out to dinner and made a stab at it. He'd been his persuasive best, gazing at her over candlelight and champagne, looking very handsome and sincere.

"I'm just so bored with my work," he finally confessed. "It's the same old thing, all the time. I want to . . . I don't know . . . do something different. Do you understand?"

She tried, but she couldn't imagine doing anything other than the work she was doing. Then, in a moment of sudden insight, she thought she understood what was wrong. "I think you're having a midlife crisis," she said.

"That's ridiculous," he said flatly, and then gave her a suspicious look. "Have you been reading those women's magazines again?"

"Who has time?" she said before she thought, and then added quickly, "But I have read about it, and I think I might be right."

"I don't. Men don't have . . . those things; only women do."

"Don't be too sure," she said, warming to the subject. "You're going to be forty this year—a perfect candidate."

He thought about that for a moment. "You really think so?"

She was convinced. "I do."

"If that's true," he said cautiously, "what do I do about it?"

That was a good question; she couldn't remember reading about a solution. "I don't know—ride it out," she said.

He sat back. "Great. Wonderful help. And in the meantime, our marriage goes down the drain—along with my business?"

He looked so forlorn that she had to smile. "You're not thinking of chucking it all and running off to some island, are you?"

"Not yet," he said gloomily.

She reached for his hand, pleased they'd finally had this talk. Now, at least, she had something to work with, something she could try and understand. "Well, before you do something that drastic, maybe you should sit down and think about another career."

He looked shocked. "At my age?"

"Why not?" she said. "As far as I know, there's no law against having two careers in a lifetime. Besides, it might be interesting."

"What if I decide to become a rock star or something?"

She laughed. "As long as you're happy, I don't care. It's this stranger I've been living with that makes me crazy."

He was still doubtful. "Well . . . I'll think about it."

"Just tell me before you make any drastic moves, will you?" she said lightly.

He looked at her. "I will if you will."

Confident that she was where she'd want to stay for a long time, she had laughed and held out her hand. "Deal."

And then, for the first time in months, they had gone home and made love. Jack's sexual problems seemed to have vanished, and in the relief and euphoria she felt afterward, she was sure they were back on the right track at last. Doubts occasionally surfaced, but she did her best to ignore them, even if there were times when she had to wonder if she had seized a little too readily on this midlife crisis business as an explanation, or if she had applied a Band-Aid when more drastic measures were called for. But those were only occasional insecurities; Jack did seem to have changed since that night, and she had to be content with that. And besides, she didn't have much time to worry about it; her work preoccupied her totally as the Linneman trial date loomed. Leaving nothing to chance—she hoped—she was ready and eager to get started when the day arrived.

It seemed later that entire trial was pivotal in her life, and for months afterward she dreamt about it. She could see herself the day of her opening statement, rising from behind the table, outwardly composed, her heart thudding in her chest. It was winter, and she was wearing a dark suit with a simple cream-colored blouse. She knew she looked competent, professional—and determined.

"As the deputy district attorney in charge of presenting the evidence in this case on behalf of the people of the State of California," she'd said, "the law imposes on me the duty of making an opening statement, the purpose of which is to outline what the prosecution expects to prove. You should know there is no corresponding duty for the defense, who may or may not make an opening statement, as they see fit. . . ."

Oh, she'd sounded so calm, so confident, as she'd walked to the jury box. She had even managed a smile, though she was tense. She wasn't frightened, but this case was important to her, and she had worked hard on her presentation because she wanted it to be right.

"Ladies and gentlemen of the jury," she'd gone on, "we intend to prove that this man—" here she had turned to point out the disinterested-looking defendant "—this man, Arthur Henry Linneman, did, during the night of September twenty-third of this year, abduct Debra Mary Watson and Carol Justine Singer, take them to a remote area in the desert, and there, after forcing them to submit to various sexual acts, did mutilate them both and leave them there for dead. . . ."

She'd gone on, explaining that Linneman had been successful only with one victim, fourteen-year-old Carol Singer, whose brutalized body had been found, not by the dozens of law enforcement officers combing the area, but by a naturalist who had gone to the desert to photograph birds. Debbie Watson, his other intended victim, the single witness in the case, had survived, and after a harrowing night wandering around blinded and in deep shock, had finally stumbled onto the highway, where a passing motorist had miraculously stopped to help.

". . . and this young girl, who has bravely fought back against overwhelming odds to survive her ordeal, will appear in the court to testify against the defendant. . . ."

She hadn't allowed Debbie to be there initially; she'd felt that the strain of the opening stages of the trial would be too great for the girl, who was still undergoing therapy and treatment.

Also, she knew how difficult it was going to be for Debbie to face her attacker, and she wanted to postpone the confrontation as long as possible. But finally, after weeks of testimony, the day inevitably arrived.

A hush fell as Debbie came into court. Except in photographs and drawings, this was the first time many of those present had seen the star witness, and none of those had depicted her as she was now. There was a gasp as she slowly made her way down the aisle toward Laura, who smiled encouragingly and whispered, "You okay?"

Debbie nodded without answering. Her pale face was without color, and the eye patch she wore stood out in stark relief, as did the still-angry-looking knife scars. She looked so frail and defenseless and frightened that Laura started to have second thoughts—until she glanced in Arthur Linneman's direction. As he had since the trial started, he was sitting at the defense table looking completely and utterly bored. The only time he'd come to life at all was when Debbie had been called to the stand, but then he'd only straightened and looked around at her. His small, close-set eyes had followed her halting progress down the aisle, and Laura, who had already prepared the bailiffs in case he did something to try and frighten the girl, was glad to see that they were alert, watching his every move. To her relief, he didn't do anything. As soon as Debbie passed, he lounged back again, picking his teeth. She glanced away. His indifferent pose didn't fool her; Debbie was the only witness to what had happened that September night in the desert, and she was here to testify against him. He couldn't be as disinterested as he pretended.

Debbie made an unforgettable witness, huddled as she was on the stand. She looked much younger than she was, and the very precariousness of her emotional state had an effect on the jury. Carefully Laura elicited her testimony of the events of that terrible night, starting with the pickup on Hollywood Boulevard, and ending with her rescue by the freeway. The details were horrifying, gruesome, appalling, and through it all, Debbie kept her gaze on Laura's calm face. Not once did she look in Linneman's direction, and the entire court was absolutely silent as they all tried to assimilate the tale. But finally Laura had to ask.

"And do you see that man in court today, Debbie?" she said quietly, and held her breath. The girl had done well, much better than she had anticipated, but the strain was starting to tell. Her head wobbling, looking as though she were about to faint, Debbie whispered her answer.

"Yes, I see him. . . ."

Up to that point, everything had gone as expected. All Laura had to do was ask her witness to identify Linneman, and she'd made her case. "I know how difficult this is for you, Debbie," she said, "but would you please point him out for the court?"

Slowly Debbie raised a shaking hand and pointed her finger at Arthur Linneman. "That's him. That's the man."

"Let the record show that the witness has identified the defendant, Arthur Henry Linneman," Laura said, and smiled her thanks and her approval at Debbie before reluctantly stepping back to make way for Silverstein. "No further questions at this time."

The defense attorney got to his feet. It was immediately clear to Laura by his patronizing tone that he believed he could discredit Debbie. She tensed, ready to protect her witness.

"Miss Watson," Silverstein said, "I understand what a strain this is for you, and I sympathize with your unfortunate experience. Consequently I have only a few questions. Now, on the night you described, when you and your friend were walking down Hollywood Boulevard looking for a little action—"

Laura shot to her feet. "Objection!"

"Sustained."

Undaunted, Harry tried again. "When you were *walking* down Hollywood Boulevard, and someone pulled up to the curb beside you, it was dark, wasn't it?"

"Yes, it was night."

"And there was no light on inside the car, was there?"

"No."

"And no streetlight in the immediate vicinity."

"No."

"So you really couldn't see the driver very well, could you? Especially when—as you yourself testified—he grabbed you and threw you and your friend into the back of the car."

"I caught a glimpse of him," Debbie said.

"I see. And this *glimpse* you saw of the man's face enabled you to make a positive identification?"

Debbie's voice was a whisper. "Yes."

Even Silverstein's posture indicated his disbelief. He shot a glance at the jury as if to say, *How can this be true? Obviously this witness is confused. I'll help her straighten things out.* At the prosecution table, Laura tensed, and thought: *This guy thinks he's pretty good.* Her expression turned grim. *But not good enough.*

"Well, Miss Watson," Silverstein said. "I have to confess I don't understand how you can be so sure this is the man. You yourself have just testified that it was dark, and that you only saw a glimpse of his face—"

"I saw more of him later," Debbie said.

There was a titter from somewhere at the back of the room, and the judge glanced severely in that direction. Silverstein glared around, and then back at Debbie.

"Please just answer the questions, Miss Watson," he said.

"I'm sorry," Debbie said in a small voice.

"Please continue, Mr. Silverstein," the judge said.

"Yes, Your Honor. Now, where were we?" Silverstein muttered, trying to get himself back into stride after the interruption. He glanced up. "Oh, yes—we were discussing your positive identification, Miss Watson. I confess I'm still having a little trouble with that."

"I know it was him," Debbie said. Her voice was small, but stubborn.

Silverstein leaned toward her. He was as aware as Laura was that the bulk of her case rested on the identification of the defendant by this single witness, and he intended to discredit her if he could. "Yes, so you indicated," he said. "But I'd like to go over it again, if you don't mind. How can you be so *sure* this is the man who attacked you? You've testified it was dark, you've said you only caught a glimpse of him. And from what I can see, Mr. Linneman is just like any other man. There's nothing really to distinguish him from anyone else, is there? No scars, no deformities. There's nothing unusual about him, is there? *So what makes you so sure this is the man?*"

The hectoring tone finally broke her. Just as Laura started to rise to object, Debbie herself leaped up. Clutching the railing in front of the witness box, she screamed. *"You want to know how I can be so sure? Because he had a tattoo, that's why! Because he had a tattoo right above his goddamned dick!"*

Laura was so astounded that only instinct brought her to her feet. Wondering why Debbie hadn't told her, she started forward, but Silverstein was already shouting, "Your Honor! Please instruct the witness to—"

278

"Your Honor," Laura said, "we ask at this time that the defendant be examined for—"

It was too late. Before Laura, or the judge, or even Silverstein could say more, Debbie turned to the ashen-faced Linneman. "Tell them, sucker!" she screamed. "Tell them about the dragon you have tattooed right down to your pecker! You were proud enough of it that night! Show them! Show them just like you showed Carol before you killed her!"

Pandemonium broke out. Shouting like a banshee, Arthur Linneman leaped out of his chair and over the table, knocking everything to the floor. Debbie screamed again, this time a high-pitched sound of pure terror, and deputies appeared from nowhere. There was a pitched battle for a few seconds before the enraged defendant was restrained, yelling all the while that he'd get Debbie like he had her friend. Reporters raced for the phones, and the bailiffs tried to restore order. The judge gaveled until she was blue, but people milled around, thrilled and titillated, refusing to take their seats. In the midst of all the confusion, Laura glanced at Silverstein, who had paled a little himself. It was obvious that this tattoo was just as much news to him as it was to her, and under cover of the noise, she went to Debbie.

"Why didn't you tell me?" she whispered to her panting witness.

Debbie looked confusedly down at her. "You didn't ask."

Wanting to groan, Laura went back to her place as the judge finally succeeded in bringing the court to order. A shaken Silverstein muttered that he had no further questions of this witness, and the judge looked at Laura, who managed to give one of the best performances of her life. Sure she had him, she rose calmly and said, "Your Honor, pending identification of the defendant's tattoo, this concludes our case."

Two hours after the case went to the jury, they returned a verdict. It was the pictures that did it, Polaroids of the incriminating tattoo, taken in an antechamber. For a few moments when Linneman refused to strip for the bailiff so the pictures could be taken, Laura thought she was going to have to get a court order. But finally the defendant cooperated. Once he decided to show off, he was proud of his dragon, and with the silent Silverstein looking on, the pictures were taken. Laura was so sure her case was made that she had to smile when the wincing bailiff whispered that the dragon might be a marvel of tattoo artistry, but all he could think of was what a high pain threshold Linneman must have.

Photos in hand, they all went back to court. When the jury returned a guilty-on-all-counts verdict a few hours after being given the case, Laura held a sobbing Debbie in her arms and thanked whatever kind fate had assigned Silverstein. If he hadn't tried so hard to be a hero, she never would have known the tattoo existed, and things might have turned out differently. Handing Debbie over to her parents, she ran the gauntlet of reporters before finally getting back to her office. She didn't know until she was almost ready to leave that night that she was once again an item on the evening news. The tattoo, naturally, was the sensation of the trial, and Dale was still laughing when he brought in a miniature television set and put it on her desk.

"Want to see yourself in living color?" he said, grinning as he turned on the set.

"Turn that thing off," Laura commanded, and tried to reach past him. He jockeyed her arm out of the way.

"And miss seeing you blush? Don't you want to know what they're calling this case?"

"If it has anything to do with dragons, no."

"Come on, where's your sense of humor?"

Laughing, he pretended to hold a mock microphone up to her face. "Tell me, Counselor, just how *do* you think the defendant got that tattoo? And why? Ah, there's a question—why? Why didn't he have an arrow pointing downward instead? Why not a—"

Laughing herself, she pushed his hand away. "Do you mind? I've had enough jokes about tattoos to last me a lifetime!"

Still smiling, he sat on the edge of the desk. "Well, you have to admit it did add an element of the bizarre to the case."

"Not to mention an element of pain," she said, and looked up innocently at the ceiling, musing aloud. "How do you think he got that thing? Every man I know who's heard about it just cringes when I ask."

"And for good reason," Dale said, wincing himself. "I can't imagine it. I can't even *imagine* imagining it."

They were still laughing when her phone rang. Grabbing the TV, Dale stood. "Congratulations are already starting to pour in, I see. Well, just don't let it go to your head. We need you around here—" he gave her a wicked grin "—in case we get any more identifying marks cases. Now that you're experienced—"

"Out!" she said, pointing. "Out—right now."

"I'm going, I'm going. No need to push."

He winked at her before he left, and she was still smiling as she reached for the phone. "Laura Devlin."

"Hello, Laura."

She caught her breath. "Douglas?"

"I know it's been a long time, but—"

Slowly she sank down into her chair. "You don't have to apologize," she said softly. "How are you?"

"I'm . . . fine," he said. "Most of the time. Well, some of the time. Actually, hardly any of the time," he admitted with a painful little laugh. "But that's not why I called."

She didn't care what his reason was; the fact that he had phoned her at all was the important thing. Feeling tears come into her eyes, she blinked rapidly and said, "I've thought about you a lot these past months, Douglas. I've wanted to call so many times, but I thought . . . I thought it might be better if I didn't."

"I wish you had," he said. "I've thought about you so often, too, since . . . that night."

She could still hear the pain in his voice and knew that nothing she could say would really help. But she had to ask. "Douglas—how are you . . . really?"

He hesitated. "Let's just say that some days are better than others."

"And Marcella?" she said. She had to ask that, too. He'd mentioned in his letter that his wife was under a doctor's care, but that was all. Since then, even though she imagined reporters must have tried, there had been no other word.

"Marcella still isn't well," he said, pained. "Her doctors have decided she needs a long rest and quite a bit of therapy. She's at a private clinic now, and will be for some time."

This, on top of everything else. There didn't seem to be anything she could say beyond a heartfelt "I'm sorry, Douglas."

"I am, too," he said, and made a determined effort to change the subject. "But I'll just have to deal with that the best way I can. In the meantime, I just saw the news, and I wanted to congratulate you."

She didn't want to talk about that, not now. It seemed so insignificant, so paltry an accomplishment in view of all he was going through. "Thank you," she said lightly. "But it's just part of the job."

"Which you seem to do very well, I might add—since you refuse to admit it. False modesty aside, this must be quite a feather in your cap."

"Not really. As I said, it was just—"

"I know—part of the job," he said dryly. And then, "Was that talk show you did part of the job, too?"

She was dismayed. "Where did you hear about that?"

"Oh, word gets around."

"But that was just a local thing," she protested, recalling the television talk show she'd done a couple of months ago. It had been a news feature here, and she'd been invited to participate because of the attention she was getting at the time due to the Linneman case. The panel she'd been on had debated current law and sentencing procedures, and she remembered saying that support for law enforcement had to come from the people, who must make their wishes known on both state and federal levels. She had insisted that good representation was the key, a stand that had led to speculation about her interest in politics. Surprised at the question, she had denied any aspirations in that area, but since then she'd been invited to speak several times about various issues, and she realized she wasn't quite as disinterested as she'd thought at first. She enjoyed these engagements, and after a while had began toying with the idea of running for small local office, something she could do and still keep her job, too.

"So you're still not interested in politics?" Douglas asked.

Uncomfortable because he seemed able to read her thoughts at times, she said, "I didn't say that—exactly."

For the first time he sounded amused. "What exactly are you saying then?"

"I'm saying that I've been too preoccupied with this case to think about anything else, that's what," she said.

He laughed at her defensive tone. "And now that the case is over?"

"You know, you should have been a prosecutor, Douglas," she said in mock exasperation. "You don't let anything go."

"Well, as they say around here, the question stands. Now, don't tell me you haven't thought about it."

She sighed, knowing she couldn't fool him. "All right, I have.

282

I've thought about running for city council, in fact. There, now are you satisfied?''

"Not really. I was thinking of higher office.''

"How much higher?'' she asked suspiciously.

"Oh . . . Washington.''

"Washington! Are you out of your mind?''

He laughed. "One thing you're going to have to learn, Laura, and that's not to mince words. But seriously, why not? You've got all the qualifications—''

"I don't have *any* of the qualifications! I don't know the first thing about politics!''

"That's not true. You engage in politics every day around there.''

"That's not the same thing.''

"Yes, it is. It's just a matter of perspective.''

"And experience,'' she reminded him.

"How are you going to get experience if you don't run?''

Because she didn't have an answer for that one, she said, "This is ridiculous.''

"I don't agree. You're a natural.''

"And you truly *are* a politician, Douglas! Really, I don't—''

"You said you'd think about it, remember? And if you're worried about experience, you'll learn. We all do when we get here. You can't really prepare for office anyway; it's like nothing you've ever done before. So don't worry about it; when you're elected, you'll do fine.''

"*When?* Aren't you getting a little ahead of yourself? I haven't even said I'll run.''

"You haven't said you wouldn't, either,'' he pointed out calmly. "Still, would it make you feel better if I said 'if'?''

"It would make me feel better if we changed the subject,'' she said.

"All right,'' he said agreeably, but she heard his amusement. He was about to say something else when she heard a faint buzzer sound in the background and he said instead, "I'm sorry, I've got to go. We have a late vote on the floor—something you'll find out about yourself one day.''

Deciding to ignore that one, she thrust away the thought of how much she didn't want him to hang up, and said, "Thank you for calling, Douglas. It . . . it was wonderful hearing from you again.''

283

Suddenly serious himself, he said quietly, "It was wonderful talking to you. And I meant it about the congratulations."

"Thank you."

"And about you running for office," he added, and hung up before she could reply.

Smiling to herself, she replaced her own receiver. The phone rang again almost instantly, but this caller was someone whose voice she didn't immediately recognize.

"Ms. Devlin? Oh, I'm so glad I caught you at the office," a woman's voice said. "Would you have a moment to speak? This is Caroline Chandler, of the Women's Political Caucus."

Laura had heard of this woman—who hadn't? Nowadays, with women playing an increasingly larger role in the selection and election of political candidates, the Women's Political Caucus was gaining power, right along with the National Organization for Women, or NOW. Laura knew that Caroline Chandler was a ranking member, as well as chairman or officer of several other women's organizations, and this call on the heels of the conversation with Douglas seemed too coincidental. Wondering if she was getting a little ahead of herself, as she had accused Douglas of doing, she said, "Yes, of course I have time, Ms. Chandler. What can I do for you?"

Caroline Chandler laughed, a tinkling, musical laugh that sounded just like all her pictures in the society sections of the papers looked. Born to wealth and influence, married for thirty years to the president of Chandler Pharmaceutical, a drug company with branch offices in New York and Paris, Caroline still resembled the debutante she'd been in 1945. Tall, slender, and blond, with piercing blue eyes, she was regal on and off the polo field, one of her passions. The other passion was politics—specifically, women in politics—and Laura sat back, trying to maintain her composure.

"I'd like to do something for you, Ms. Devlin," Caroline said. "But first I must ask you a question."

"What is that?"

"Have you ever thought about running for office?"

Despite herself, Laura laughed. "You're the second person in about five minutes to ask me that."

"And what is the answer?"

"My answer is that I haven't really had time to think about it."

"Does that mean you are too satisfied with your present position to consider making a change?"

"No," Laura said, surprising herself. "It really does mean that I haven't had time to think about it."

"Then perhaps you should," Caroline said at once. "In addition to calling to congratulate you on your court victory today, I phoned to ask if you would consider coming to a little meeting I'm having at my home on Saturday. We're a small group, but politically active, and we would be most interested in hearing some of your views."

A small group? Laura knew Caroline Chandler was undoubtedly referring to the WPC, and that this active women's group didn't just meet for coffee. Surprised at the thrill of excitement she felt, she managed to say calmly, "Which views are those, Ms. Chandler?"

"About anything you care to share, Ms. Devlin," Caroline said smoothly. "You know, of course, that Congressman Wendell Sheldon from your district is retiring next year. . . ."

"Yes, I'm aware of that."

"And we were wondering if you would consider standing for election in his place."

Now that it was out in the open, Laura wasn't sure what to say. This was all coming upon her so quickly that she felt flustered, confused. "I'm very flattered that you asked me, Ms. Chandler—"

"Oh, do call me Caroline," the woman said. "And I know how sudden this is. I'm sure you'd like some time to think about it, but in the meantime, I and the members of my little group would be delighted to meet you in person. Would you possibly consider coming to tea Saturday afternoon?"

"Tea?"

Caroline laughed that musical little laugh again. "I know what an old-fashioned request that is, but in these days of frozen TV dinners and microwave ovens, such ceremonies remind us that we were once civilized."

Despite her sudden tension, Laura smiled. Already she liked Caroline Chandler, and she said, "I'd be delighted to accept your invitation . . . Caroline. And please call me Laura."

"I'm so glad you're free, Laura," Caroline said, sounding as if she genuinely was. "I have a feeling that we're going to get to know each other quite well. So then, I'll expect you at three. Shall I give you directions?"

Smiling, because everyone in the city knew where the Chandlers lived, Laura said, "No, that won't be necessary, Caroline. I'm sure I'll find it."

"Then good-bye for now. I'll look forward to Saturday."

"So will I," Laura said, and realized she meant it. Her expression thoughtful, she hung up and sat there staring at the phone for a few minutes before she shook herself. But as she started gathering her things so she could leave, she wondered if these two phone calls had been prophetic. Was it time to make a change? Douglas thought so; Caroline Chandler apparently believed it, too. What did *she* think? Did she want to run for office?

Leaving her desk, she went to the window. The sun had long since set, and the lights of Los Angeles twinkled around her; the freeway was a blur. Staring blankly out at the night, she really didn't see the beauty; she was thinking that as much as she enjoyed her work here, it just wasn't . . . enough. Even this conviction today, as satisfying as it had been, hadn't really changed anything, not in her mind. She had begun to realize long ago that reacting to problems by punishing wasn't the answer—for her, anyway; she needed to do something more. As successful as she'd been as a prosecutor—and she'd been more successful than most, she couldn't deny—she wasn't solving anything by putting people away. The other side, the public defender's office, didn't have the answer, either. She had learned from bitter experience that rehabilitation, or attempts at it, was just as ineffective as incarceration. The majority of criminals went back to crime once they got out of jail, no matter what their sentences were, and she'd seen herself how limited current laws were in helping victims of crime. She hadn't wanted to admit it until now, but no matter what she did, she just wasn't making the difference she'd hoped. Even with her successes here, the most she'd done was act as a tiny drag on the tide, and it just wasn't enough. It would never be, not from here.

Contemplatively she turned from the window and glanced around her tiny office. Without really being aware of the process, it seemed she'd already made her decision, and while she would miss this place—just as she missed, at times, the cramped cubbyhole she had once shared with Maurey—it was time to move on. She had always wanted to be part of the solution instead of identifying the problem, and this was her chance. Before she could change her mind, she reached for the phone and dialed home. To her relief, Jack answered on the third ring.

"I just saw the news," he said. "Congratulations."

"Thanks." She didn't want to talk about that. "Guess who just called me?"

He immediately sounded cautious. "Who?"

She couldn't hide her excitement. "Caroline Chandler!"

Everyone who read the papers knew about Caroline Chandler, and he became even more wary. "What did she want?"

"She wants me to have tea with her on Saturday."

Definitely suspicious now. "Why?"

She took a deep breath. She'd talked about this before, offhandedly, more as a matter of curiosity and speculation than as a plan of action. She wasn't sure he'd remember, or approve if he did, so she said carefully, "Jack, I think she wants me to run for Congressman Sheldon's office after he retires this year."

He was silent for so long that she didn't know what to think. "Jack?"

"Does this mean we'll have to move to Washington?" he asked finally.

"Only if I get elected," she said, beginning to get excited despite herself.

"Does this mean that you're planning to run?" He sounded distant, distracted; she didn't know what his reaction was.

"I don't know," she said. "What do you think?"

"I think we'd better discuss this over dinner," he said.

She knew he needed time to adjust, that they did have to talk about something that would mean such a major upheaval in their lives. But she couldn't help feeling disappointed at his lack of enthusiasm; after all, just the call from someone like Caroline Chandler had been an honor. Trying not to feel resentful because she would have been thrilled if it had happened to him, she said, "Okay, tell the kids—and Mom, too. We'll go out for dinner. My treat."

"Isn't the celebration a little premature?"

"You said we should talk about this, and I agree. I think the whole family should be in on it, that's all."

"Okay," he said reluctantly. "When will you be home?"

She wasn't going to let him ruin this for her. "As soon as possible," she said, and couldn't help adding gaily, "I'm on my way!"

* * *

Her prediction was more prophetic than she knew. Once she'd made the decision, events swept her up and carried her away. She didn't know what she would have done without Caroline's help, for even though she was dismayed to discover that she was running against three people with more political experience, Caroline was confident throughout. In a landslide election, she defeated a city councilman and a district leader in the primary, and in the general election she soundly trounced the extreme left-wing assemblyman who was her opponent. Suddenly, almost without warning, it seemed, she was a member of Congress, en route to Washington. As she had so gaily predicted on the night she made that call to Jack, she was indeed on her way.

CHAPTER TWENTY-THREE

Laura thought the campaign was the most exciting, exhausting, exhilarating, and satisfying experience she'd ever had in her life, and she knew even before she arrived in Washington that it was all worth it. Even though she came in the middle of a blizzard, with the airport closing down five minutes after her plane landed, she had finally found her niche. Stuck in traffic backed up on the beltway—not freeway, she reminded herself—with people looking harried and harassed all around her, she still thought the capital was wonderful. She'd visited once, long ago, and even though she was again awed by glimpses of the famous monuments, this was different. She'd always been intrigued by the concept of power, as it related to the happenings here, and now the thought that she was going to be involved in that process made her feel humbled and excited at the same time. To be part of all this! It didn't seem possible.

Her only regret was that her family wasn't with her. Against her better judgment, she had finally agreed with Jack that it would be better not to uproot the kids in the middle of the school year. They would come for visits, and stay through holidays and school vacations when she had to be here, and of course, she would fly home as often as possible. It wasn't the best solution, especially for her, but all their lives had been uprooted with this campaign and her election, and she didn't think it was fair of her to ask for more. But it wouldn't be the same without them, and that reminded her again how much her life had changed.

But then, nothing was the same. After the tea with Caroline Chandler, where she'd met some of the most powerful and politically oriented women in the state, who joined in persuading her to run, things had been different at the office. It hadn't been difficult to replace her, but it was still hard seeing cases she would have liked going to others, and hardest of all had been the day she had turned in her shield. As she'd handed the badge to Dale, she'd suddenly been assailed with doubt. Was she doing the right thing? It had seemed such an impossible dream then that she wanted to snatch the leather folder back and say she'd made a terrible mistake.

As always, Dale had sensed her confusion. "You're doing the right thing, Laura," he'd said. "Washington is where you belong. You know it, Duluth knows it, and I—" he sighed heavily "—I know it, too."

"I wish I could be as certain as you," she'd said gloomily, and then had to say good-bye to Trudy. She had never seen her friend cry before, but they'd both nearly been in tears.

"Maybe I could come and be your legislative assistant," Trudy had suggested mournfully. They were in the ladies' room, during the going-away party Dale had sprung for her. Trudy had just had another permanent, and her hair stuck out around her head like a Brillo pad. She was trying to do something with it when she suddenly threw down the comb. "Oh, Laura, I don't want you to go!"

And at that moment, she hadn't wanted to leave, either. Now that the time was at hand, it was even more difficult than she had imagined. They had been through so much together, and that night with Rob was never far from either of their minds.

"Maybe I won't be elected," she said.

"Oh, you'll get elected, all right," Trudy replied, sniffling. She glanced at herself in the mirror, made a terrible face, and shoved the comb into her purse. Taking out a pack of cigarettes instead, she lit one and saw Laura's startled glance. "Not a word," she commanded. "I know I gave it up months ago, but I'm under stress."

She'd laughed and then Trudy laughed, too. The emotional moment passed—until they joined the party and Dale popped the cork on the champagne. His fervent toast of congratulations and good wishes made her want to cry again, and she could hear her voice shaking as she thanked them all for their support. Never demonstrative, Trudy threw her arms around her on the way out, and as she fiercely returned the embrace, she could only think how much she was going to miss her friends.

She hated good-byes, but Dale insisted on coming out to the car with her anyway. She was carrying the last of the cardboard boxes she had filled from her office, and when he took it from her and put it in the trunk and then turned to her again, she knew he was going to say something that would destroy her precarious emotional hold. "Don't say it," she said. "I'm feeling shaky enough as it is."

"So am I," he said, "so I won't."

Instead, he gave her a quick, hard hug that said more than words ever could. Driving out of the parking lot, she looked back and he was still there, his hand raised in farewell, that crooked smile of his more endearing than it had ever been.

That day was almost a year in the past now, and so much had happened since then. The traumatic leave-taking at the office behind her, the merry-go-round of campaigning began. Then the election. She didn't know how she would have gotten through it all without Caroline, whose serene presence buoyed and strengthened her from the beginning. She'd found a friend in Caroline Chandler, one she was reluctant to leave behind. She'd been surprised to realize that Jack didn't like her; she thought Caroline would be exactly the kind of woman he admired: beautiful, accomplished, chic, polished, magnetic. But he'd been at odds with her from the first, and she couldn't understand why.

But then, there was a lot about Jack she couldn't understand these days; at a time when they should be finding strength in each other, they were further apart than ever. He hadn't seemed to object to her running for office, but then, he hadn't really supported her, either. He didn't seem to care much one way or the other what she did, and her hope that this disinterest of his was a passing thing—a part of his midlife crisis, if that's what it ever had been—was fading. They didn't have much in common anymore, and yet she was reluctant to take that final irrevocable step. She still loved him, and after so many years of marriage, she was loath just to give up. So she told herself instead that this separation would give them time and a new perspective, and resolutely ignored her doubts as she searched for an apartment they could afford near the Hill.

She finally found one, a tiny old place with a refrigerator that thumped on and off half the night, and a Murphy bed that folded up into the wall. She didn't care; as the days passed and she became more and more immersed in the demands of a new career, she was hardly ever there except to sleep.

Sleep itself seemed to become an increasingly precious commodity over the next months; there was always so much to do, to learn. She found herself studying harder than she ever did in law school, for she felt so ignorant. She also discovered why her West Coast colleagues dreaded the east-west commute; even though she only managed to fly home twice a month, she was exhausted for days after because she tried to pack so much into such a short time. In addition to time she wanted to spend with her family, she felt bound to be available to her constituents. Her storefront headquarters at the beach had turned into a popular place, and she was proud of her accessibility, but it was still a drain on those precious moments she wanted to spend at home.

"Sometimes I think it would help to be a clone," Douglas had said to her a while ago, and she agreed fervently.

Douglas. She couldn't think of him rationally, it seemed. She didn't know what she would have done without him when she first arrived, but sometimes, when he surprised her with a call, or an invitation to lunch—never dinner, unless someone else came with them—she knew her feelings for him went deeper than gratitude for his help. There were times when, sitting by herself in that lonely, empty apartment at night, she wondered if he'd been at the back of her mind that day she'd gone to tea with Caroline Chandler. She couldn't remember now if his face hadn't flashed through her mind when she had excitedly agreed to run, but it must have; she thought of him so often. In other, more rational moments, she told herself she was being absurd. He wasn't the reason she had decided to uproot her life and stand for election; he couldn't be. But she wondered, at night, in the dark, by herself; she wondered.

She had accepted long ago that she was attracted to him; what breathing woman wouldn't be? But she had always assured herself that she could keep that attraction under control; after all, she'd once been attracted to Dale, and nothing had come of that but friendship. It didn't have to be any different with Douglas.

But it was.

To her dismay, even though she had managed to keep her feelings at bay when she was in Los Angeles, something had changed now that she was in Washington. There were times she wondered if it had to do with the fact that his wife was still in that sanitarium, with faint hope, it seemed, of ever leading a normal life again, or if it was because she was so far away from a husband who had been withdrawing from her emotionally for quite some time. Because she couldn't be sure it was either of those things, she refused to let herself think about it. Guiltily she thought how glad she was that job demands kept them from seeing each other too frequently.

Yet she couldn't not see him at all; that would have been equally absurd—or so she told herself.. She couldn't deny she looked forward to being with him on the rare occasions their schedules meshed, for emotional confusion aside, she *was* grateful to Douglas for his help. When she had arrived in the capital all those months ago, she had been so overwhelmed that she hadn't even been sure where to start, and Douglas, in his quiet way, had stepped in and rescued her. He had introduced her to a few people, including Sarah Ambrose, whom she had already grown to love, and he had been instrumental in helping her select her staff. And, although he denied it, she knew he was responsible for some of her committee assignments.

Now it was April, and while she was still learning the ropes, along with her way around, she didn't feel quite the new kid on the block anymore. She'd vowed the night of her election to take an active part in the House, to be an effective member of Congress, to become the best representative she could be for her district and her state, but once she had actually arrived, she found that task wasn't going to be easy. It was so confusing at first; there seemed to be so many nuances she wasn't aware of, so many pitfalls and traps to fall into. Even now in the late eighties, there were so few women in Congress, and she learned to her dismay that those who were there were too often targets for criticism, deserved or not. It seemed so incredible to her: discrimination in the hallowed halls of Congress?

Unfortunately it was true. She hadn't been in office two weeks before it became clear that despite all that she, and all the other women there, had achieved, she was going to have to do more, work harder, and produce more to be judged the same as men. The unpalatable fact was that the double standard continued to exist despite the gains made, and that was symbolized, painfully, by the board game the female members of Congress circulated around to newcomers. One of the squares read: "You're two times more qualified than your opponent; you've worked doubly hard. Now the two of you are even. Move to his square." She hadn't wanted to believe it at first, but now she had to.

She and Douglas had talked about this the last time they met for lunch, one of those rare occasions when they were both able to get together, carefully, in a very public place. He was there before she arrived, and when she joined him, she couldn't help thinking how much he had changed since that awful night in Los Angeles, when she had met his plane. He was still the same

Douglas, but he looked older now, and the laugh lines around his eyes had deepened, along with those on either side of his mouth. Even so, he looked distinguished and handsome—very much the statesman, she had teased. To her relief, a sparkle of humor had finally returned to his sad eyes, and after she'd gone on indignantly about the inequities on the Hill, he'd said, "I admit it's not a pleasant situation. But things *are* changing."

"Evolution moves faster!" she had claimed in exasperation, and proceeded to tell him about an argument she'd become involved in with one of her esteemed colleagues concerning "displaced homemakers"—a clever term someone had coined for women who went back to work after years of child raising. Her hackles still rose when she recalled how this supposedly educated congressman had argued that a married woman shouldn't be earning as much as a man in the same position because her husband supported her.

He was sympathetic when she finished her story, shaking his head as he said, "I'm afraid the logic escapes me."

"That's because there's no logic at all!" she fumed.

As always, even though he was on her side, he was amused at her vehemence. "Well, women are allowed to swim in the congressional swimming pool now. That's a start."

She looked at him balefully. "It's a good thing you're kidding."

"I'm not kidding," he said seriously. "Women do swim in the pool; I've seen them with my own eyes."

As he had planned, she had laughed. They had ordered, and the conversation moved to other things. Thinking about that incident, and so many others, when he always seemed able to reel her back onto an even keel when she was about to capsize with indignation, she wondered what she would do without him, especially when the frantic pace here never seemed to abate. Her campaign and election seemed in some distant past, but as busy as she was, she missed her family terribly. She hated to go back to her silent little apartment, because it only reminded her how lonely it was there. Sometimes she wondered why she even kept it; the only time she came back was to watch the late news and to sleep. Because it seemed so empty and quiet there, she developed the habit of working at the office until ten or so before her chief aide, Ellen McGrath, called to see if she'd gone home.

That was another area where Douglas had helped, she thought fondly; he was the one who had sent Ellen to her, and she blessed him every day for that foresight. She hadn't realized until she got here how important a good staff was, even though when she had first arrived and learned that each House member was entitled to a certain annual clerk hire allowance, she'd thought the sum outrageous. What would she need with all these people?

She'd quickly learned that competent people weren't a luxury but a necessity. There had been so many demands on her time right from the beginning that if she hadn't had a good staff behind her to organize things, she would have drowned in work the first week.

Even now, she remembered those first tense days of trying to get the feel of things, organize her office, and decide what she was going to need. She had talked to a few of her female colleagues by then and had learned to her chagrin that no two staffs were alike. She had almost hoped up to that point that there might be a magic formula to follow so she wouldn't have to do it all herself; at that point, when she had so many other things to learn, selecting a staff seemed a monumental task.

Then Ellen had applied. After taking one look at her impressive qualifications, Laura had hired her on the spot. After that, everything *had* fallen magically into place. Ellen, it seemed, knew how things were done, and how to *get* things done; she'd been in Washington for years, and had the system down pat. She soon had the office humming with efficiency, and Laura depended so fully upon her chief assistant that she had nightmares about Ellen leaving.

Fortunately there seemed little likelihood of that, at least on this particular April day. Ellen was waiting for her when she got back to the office after a harried morning of meetings. As always, she had a pencil stuck in her red hair, and her glasses had slipped down her nose. Like Laura, Ellen McGrath was in her late thirties, but there the resemblance stopped. Where Laura was tall and slender, Ellen was round and comfortable-looking, appearing so much the devoted secretary that she could almost have been born with the clipboard she always carried in her hand. She was brisk, efficient to a fault, and never seemed to forget anything. Her only passion, beyond work, that Laura had discovered, was—chocolate. She loved candy, and always had a container of something on her desk. Today it was chocolate candy kisses, and she scooped up a handful when Laura came in. Unpeeling the foil on one, she offered some to Laura, who shook her head, and said, "Do you want your messages now or later?"

"It depends on which crisis I have to deal with first," Laura said, her mind on other things—chiefly the question of how she could ever have thought she was busy in the DA's office. Compared to here, that seemed like child's play as far as demands on her time. As she went on into her own office, she wondered if she should invest in roller skates.

Ellen followed her inside. As a junior member of the House, Laura had been assigned a cramped suite of three rooms in the Cannon House Office Building, and she had allotted two for staffers and one for herself. Since hers was the biggest, it was usually the place where she called staff meetings, and because one had been scheduled when she got back from the morning's meeting, several people were already scattered around, perching on the edge of the desk, leaning against the wall, even sitting on the two chairs she'd tucked into the corners. Her desk took up most of the room, but she didn't mind. She'd worked in close quarters before.

"I'm glad to see you're all here," she said with a welcoming smile as she plunked down her heavy armload of papers and reports on the desk. She sat down. "I've got that Science and Technology hearing right after lunch, so let's make this quick, all right?" She looked up at Ellen, who, as always, was ready with the clipboard. "What's first on the agenda?"

"Glen," Ellen said, turning to one of Laura's three legislative assistants, Glen Cray, who took over to explain what issues were scheduled on the House floor this week. Among them were a vote on federal funding of abortions for the poor—a very hot issue at the moment—and another about establishing a House Select Committee on Population.

Glancing up from his notes, he asked Laura, "How are you going to vote on the population committee?"

She had already read several reports, but she wanted other opinions. "I haven't decided. What are your feelings about it?"

"I don't think we need another committee," he said, and with that comment immediately provoked a rapid-fire discussion of the pros and cons of the measure from everyone present.

Laura listened intently, thinking that this was the part of the staff meetings she liked best. She'd surrounded herself with bright, articulate people who weren't afraid to speak their minds, and since she'd been assigned—with a word from Douglas, she was sure—to Energy and Commerce, and Public Works and Transportation, as well as Science and Technology, she usually needed as many different perspectives as she could get. She'd been mortified when she'd attended her first Public Works hearing and heard all the male members spouting terms like milliequivalents and specific densities as though they'd been doing it all their lives; she hadn't even known half the time what anyone was talking about, and as soon as she escaped back to her office, she asked Ellen to get the transcripts from the past hearings so she wouldn't feel so embarrassed again.

"But you have to remember," Ellen had pointed out, "that these guys have been sitting through hearings on this same subject for years."

"I don't care," she'd said stubbornly. "I'm not going to go anywhere unprepared again."

And she hadn't. After that discomforting incident, she had instituted these daily sessions with her staff to glean as much information as possible from them. Although she read prodigiously, there were still things she needed to know, and she expected them to contribute. Now, after listening for a few minutes, she raised a hand. She'd heard enough on this subject.

"The committee is scheduled only to exist through the end of the year," she said. "I think we need all the input we can get on this problem, so I'm going to vote for it. What's next?"

Another of her legislative assistants, Tom Denton, spoke up. Like the other two legislative aides, he had his own assigned subject areas, among them energy, water pollution, aviation, transit, and water resource projects. He brought up the current issue of waterway user fees, which had recently foundered in another subcommittee, and gave them all a brief summary of advantages and disadvantages. Then he discussed a new measure to support solar power as a major energy source—again—and then gave the floor to Linda Coleman, the staff's specialist on science and technology. Linda didn't look too happy.

"I'm afraid it's going to be the same old thing at the Science and Technology hearing this afternoon," she said. "The subject is the high cost of advanced drugs, specifically those produced by genetic engineering. I've prepared a fact sheet for you, Laura, but don't count on facts here. The only witness scheduled is Dr. Quinlan Maxwell, the head of GenHelix. That's the pharmaceutical company that's riding so high these days after introducing that genetically produced drug that's supposed to prevent heart attacks. In addition to becoming almost a hero in the media, he's also a good friend of Birch Briton. They went to Harvard together.''

Birch Briton was the head of the Science and Technology Committee, and she'd already run afoul of him several times in other matters. He didn't like the fact that she was concerned about what effect genetic engineering and biotechnology might have on the future, and future generations. Now that the matter of his friendship with the head of GenHelix had come up, she understood why.

Briskly she said, ''Well, I went to USC, and I never did revere the good-ol'-boy network. I think for the time being, we'll all just have to put old school ties aside, won't we?''

There was appreciative applause from her crew, but Ellen said, ''Don't get your hopes up. Maxwell is an old hand at hearings; he's been under the gun before.''

''Not this one,'' Laura said cheerfully, and waved on her way out.

The Science and Technology hearing was scheduled in the Rayburn House Office Building, in a spacious, modernistic, fluorescent-lighted committee room. A handful of congressmen were already there when she arrived, as well as a sparse group surrounding a man whom she knew instantly was the scheduled speaker, Quinlan Maxwell. Glancing covertly at him as she made her way to the head table, she had to admit that he made an impressive witness; in addition to flowing white hair combed straight back from a high forehead, he had deep-set blue eyes, an aura of confidence—and a very determined air. She smiled to herself as she took her place. So did she.

As low-ranking member of the committee, she would be the last to speak, and she settled back, her notes in front of her. The committee chairman, Birch Briton, a man in his late forties with styled hair and a three-piece suit, opened the hearing with a clearing of his throat and a tapping of his Cross pen against his water glass.

''This hearing,'' Briton said, ''is for the purpose of obtaining information on trends in genetic engineering. We have as our first and only witness this afternoon Dr. Quinlan Maxwell, president of GenHelix Corporation, a company specializing in the new biotechnology. Dr. Maxwell, would you care to make an opening statement?''

''I would, Mr. Chairman,'' Maxwell said with a regal nod of

that leonine head. Laura looked beyond his chair to the knot of people who had accompanied him today, and then her glance caught that of the single reporter who had obviously been assigned to cover the hearing, and who seemed already bored. Slouched in his chair, he tapped his fingers against the recorder he held and looked as if he would rather be anywhere but here. Wondering how long he was going to remain bored, she returned her attention to the witness.

"Gentlemen," Maxwell said, and then glanced at her. "And lady. As you're no doubt aware, GenHelix is currently the forerunner in genetic research. One of our newest products, in fact, is the genetically engineered heart medicine Plasminex, which has been getting front-page coverage lately. And for good reason. Plasminex has proved to be one of the most effective medicines we have today in the treatment of heart attacks, and we at GenHelix are sure that this discovery will lead to even greater advances in the understanding and eventual conquering of heart disease."

He paused, but whether it was because he expected applause after his blatant plug for his company or not, Laura wasn't sure. After clearing his throat, he went on. "However, I'm not here to promote one of GenHelix's new products," he said, having just done so. "I'm here to answer questions about genetic engineering, which to my mind, and to a great many other scientists, is certainly the wave of the future. Yes, sir, the wave of the future. So please, gentlemen—fire away."

As chairman of the committee, Birch jumped right in. "Dr. Maxwell," he said formally, as if they didn't know each other, "you've been quite emphatic that genetic engineering is the wave of the future. Would you please amplify that statement?"

"Be glad to, Congressman," Maxwell said with a wink. "You see, we've already made great strides in this new technology; the future will hold many more. We at GenHelix envision such practical advances as prenatal diagnoses for scores of hereditary diseases, as well as the development of supervaccines able to confer multiple immunities. Both these sciences, absolutely unheard—and undreamed—of even a decade or two ago, are only a few short years away. Oh, yes, the possibilities are endless. . . ."

The next ranking member, Willie Stout from Tennessee, clearly enthralled, asked him to continue. Pleased to do so, Maxwell complied with a parable about the genetic engineer acting as a sort of agent, employed to "clean up the messes," by which he meant helping sort out genetic defects to relieve suffering, conquering the mysteries of cancer, eliminating the need for chemotherapy, or even fertilizer.

"Fertilizer?" another committee member asked.

"Indeed, yes," Maxwell replied, and called upon another little homey parable, Jack and the Beanstalk, to illustrate his point. It seemed that genetic engineers would eventually be able to alter the genetic codes of numerous agricultural products so that they would grow twice, thrice, quadruple their original size, all without fertilizer, dirt, or even, Laura had the feeling, air.

There were more questions by the fascinated committee members, all of whom Maxwell seemed to hold in thrall. All except Laura, that was, who couldn't wait for her turn. Finally, it came—after the good doctor concluded a ringing tribute to GenHelix, which he was sure would lead them all to a glorious Eden . . . if only the government would stay off its back. Unfortunately for him, she wasn't impressed.

"That's all very well, Dr. Maxwell," she said, after Birch had reluctantly recognized her because he had no other choice. "And in other circumstances, I would truly be impressed. Unfortunately this hearing was not convened to praise genetic engineering, but to come to grips with the high costs generated by advanced drugs produced because of it. Could we address that issue for a moment?"

In the instant before he answered, she realized that the atmosphere in the room had changed. She hadn't recognized it until then, but she had unconsciously summoned her best prosecuting attorney's tone in addressing him, and he looked momentarily nonplussed. This was the no-nonsense manner that had stood her so well in court, the voice that had intimidated so many witnesses, the sound of a woman who knew what questions to ask, and which answers she wanted to hear.

But Maxwell was an old hand at this, too, and he recovered quickly. Crossing one leg over the other, he plucked at the crease in his trousers and looked up with a benevolent smile. "Why, certainly, little lady," he drawled, and caught Birch's warning glance. "I mean . . . er . . . Congresswoman."

Ignoring the little byplay between the two men, she said evenly, "Splendid. Now, since you mentioned it yourself, perhaps we should start with your newest introduction, Plasminex.

According to my figures, this drug can cost over two thousand dollars *per dose*. Is that correct?''

"Oh, I think that's a little high," he said smoothly.

"So do I," she said, and had the data to prove it. "Now this price, if I'm not mistaken, is at least ten times as much as a competitive product not made with the new technology. Do you have an explanation as to this outrageous cost discrepancy?''

She used the word deliberately, and had the satisfaction of seeing him flush. Well, good. She wanted him to squirm. Maybe then GenHelix would think twice about gouging the public.

"I'm afraid you don't understand, Congresswoman," Maxwell said. "Like any other drug company, GenHelix incurs tremendous expenses in the development of these new advances. Why, our research and development costs alone have increased drastically with the introduction of this new technology. But if prices are high, they're necessary to maintain the flow of innovative products. That's why we take the revenues that come from product sales and funnel them right back in a major way to research.''

"Is that so?" Laura said acidly. "Well, unfortunately, it's difficult to discover just how excessive your development costs are, since drug companies do not release information on research and development budgets.''

"We're not required to do that," he said stiffly.

"A situation that might be subject to change," she said evenly, "unless we get some answers, Dr. Maxwell.''

"We're not the only company charging high prices," he complained.

"That's true," she said. "But we're discussing GenHelix at the moment, aren't we?''

Maxwell glanced imploringly at Birch, who took up the cue. "I'm afraid that's all we have time for today.''

"I only have a few more questions," she said.

Birch started to shake his head, but then he became aware of the single reporter in the audience. The man had abandoned his slouched pose and was leaning forward, his recorder in hand. When he saw the committee chairman looking at him, he grinned. Caught between friendship and bad press, Birch did what any true politician would do. "All right," he muttered. "But quickly, please.''

"Thank you," Laura said, as Maxwell glared at the chairman. She had no need to refer to her notes; she had already glanced over them and knew how to proceed. "Unfortunately for that argument, Dr. Maxwell, critics of the drug industry say research and development expenditures can't possibly account for the entire rise in prices. Would you please answer the charge that other factors are at work here, such as the fact that GenHelix bases its prices on the value of the drug to consumers and not the cost?"

"I . . . I can't answer that," Maxwell said, a sheen of perspiration appearing on his broad forehead. "I don't have the exact figures in front of me."

"Figures aren't required to answer the question, Dr. Maxwell," she said. "But if you require numbers, perhaps these will help. According to the latest biotechnology analysis, the estimate on GenHelix's gross margin—the amount by which the price exceeds the manufacturing cost—on the drug Plasminex alone is ninety-five percent. This is a full ten points higher than the already indecent eighty-five percent for most drugs. In light of your defense about manufacturing costs, how do you explain this?"

The reporter, his recorder balanced on the back of the chair in front of him, was now busily scribbling in a notebook. He glanced up, saw Maxwell's face, grinned again, and bent his head to his notes once more.

"I'm afraid I need time to study that analysis, Congresswoman," Maxwell said stiffly. He glanced at Birch again, who this time knew what he had to do.

"This committee is prepared to give you all the time you need, Dr. Maxwell," Birch said smoothly, and tried not to look dismayed as the reporter gathered his materials and left with a salute in Laura's direction. Jerking his glance away, he said hastily, "I declare this hearing adjourned."

If she hadn't been so annoyed, Laura would have been amused at the rush of various committee members to surround and placate the livid Quinlan Maxwell. Wondering if she'd done anything at all except make a few potent enemies here today, she gathered her things and left. Long ago she'd taught herself not to dwell on things she couldn't change, and she put that frustrating hearing out of her mind as she worked through her busy schedule that afternoon. She forgot about it so completely, in fact, during two other committee meetings, and several late votes on the floor, that she was surprised to see her staff gathered around the portable television set when she finally walked wearily into her office at the end of the day. They were all so intent, they didn't even hear her come in.

"What's going on?" she asked curiously.

Ellen whirled around at the sound of her voice. "You made the six-o'clock news!" she said excitedly. "Wow, that must have been some hearing at Science and Technology today!"

Remembering that reporter rushing out, Laura wanted to groan. "All I can say is, it must have been a slow news day."

"So what?" Ellen said, her eyes alight. "Any media exposure is worth solid gold."

"How did I come off?"

"See for yourself!"

Grinning, her staff stepped aside, and there, in living color, was the handsome news anchor just winding up his story on the drug company hearing that had taken place on the Hill that afternoon.

". . . testifying for GenHelix," he was saying, "Dr. Quinlan Maxwell was severely brought to task by a junior member of the committee, Congresswoman Laura Devlin, who sharply questioned this prestigious drug company's profit margins on new drug advances. Rejecting timeworn excuses about research and development costs, Congresswoman Devlin cited new analyses to buttress her argument that prices are based on the value of the drug to consumers and not on the cost of manufacturing. . . ."

There was more, but Laura didn't want to listen. Making a face, she went into her own office. Ellen, and her press aide, Harvey Reiman, followed her in. He already had a sheaf of papers in his hand, and he said, "We're drafting a statement now. The press is going to be here any minute."

She had just sat down behind the desk. "Why?"

The two aides glanced at each other, then Ellen said with exaggerated patience, "Laura, I don't think you understand what's going on here."

Laura looked at her. "You're right. I don't. It was just a hearing—"

"It was more than that," Ellen said, sounding excited again. "Do you realize you took on the president of one of the biggest drug companies in the country and made him look like a fool? The press is going to eat it up!"

"I was just doing my job."

"Yes, but it's *how* you were doing it that's the point! Obviously you don't realize how seldom this type of thing happens to a junior member! Enjoy it! You're in the news! Tonight, you *are* the news! Isn't it great?''

"Great," Laura said gloomily. She'd been in the news before.

"So this is the statement," Harvey started to say. Just then the phone rang.

"See?" Ellen said, thrilled. She reached for the phone. "It's starting!" Pressing down the blinking light for the line, she said breathlessly, "Congresswoman Devlin's office," listened for a moment, her eyes widening, and then said, "Yes, certainly, Mrs. Deering-Kirk. Of course she's here. Would you hold a moment please?" She punched down the line, her expression ecstatic. "Do you *believe* it?" she whispered. "It's Lenore Deering-Kirk, and she wants to talk to you!"

Laura reached for the phone. "Should I bow down first, or what?" she said dryly.

Ellen was horrified. "Do you know who this woman *is*?"

"I know who she is," Laura said calmly, and punched down the line again. "Hello, Mrs. Deering-Kirk? This is Congresswoman Devlin speaking."

"Hello, my dear," said one of the most famous voices in Washington. "I hope this isn't a bad time."

"Not at all," Laura said, rolling her eyes at Ellen's avid expression. "What can I do for you?"

As Ellen looked ready to faint, Lenore said, "Well, I just saw the news, and I think it's time we met. I'm giving a small party this Saturday, and I would be absolutely delighted if you could be here. I'm sorry it's such short notice, but do you think you might be able to make it?"

Aware of Ellen's transported expression, of the awed faces of the rest of her staff, who were peeking around the door, Laura laughingly shook her head and made a gesture with her hand. "I'd be honored, Mrs. Deering-Kirk," she said, "and delighted to come."

The instant she hung up the phone and her staff found out what the call was about, everyone started to jump around and whistle and cheer—everyone except Laura, that was, who couldn't rid herself of sudden suspicion. The invitation, coming as it had upon the heels of that news item, seemed just a little too coincidental.

"This doesn't *happen*!" Ellen cried, thrilled and excited,

dancing around with Harvey, who looked just as pleased, already planning his next press release.

Laura had to agree. Standing there in the midst of all that hilarity, she couldn't help but wonder why it had.

---⊘---

CHAPTER TWENTY-FOUR

Douglas sometimes thought that if he had to describe his life as a senator in five words or less, he would say it involved a juxtaposition of priorities. Sometimes things got jumbled, as on the days when he arrived at the office to find that he was scheduled for three meetings in the same hour; sometimes things just worked out, as they had with the airlines and the missing cat. He always felt a little sad, but glad, when he thought of that episode, for it had taken place at a time when he was still trying to adjust to Rob's death. He'd needed a shot in the arm like that, and some media attention that didn't focus, as it had for weeks, on his family tragedy.

It had started out, as many things did on the Hill, with a letter from one of his constituents, who had shipped her cat by air and found on arrival that the cat carrier was empty. Her admittedly hysterical reaction had prompted a frantic search by assorted airline personnel, but despite all efforts, the cat hadn't been found. The grieving woman had then written to her senator to complain about airline handling of animal cargo, and one of his secretaries, a cat lover herself, had been so upset that she'd come to him. Since he wasn't sure what he could do beyond sending back a personal letter of condolence, he was dictating when his press secretary, Henry Pierce, walked in. Always alert for news value in anything, Henry had put everything on hold while he called the Federal Aviation Agency, the Department of Agriculture, the Humane Society, the Baggage Handlers Union, and anyone else he could think of, and had discovered that while the airline association would admit to about a dozen similar cases, the Humane Society recorded at least a hundred, with animals either missing or even dead on arrival. Armed with his facts, Henry had decided Douglas should draft a bill.

"I'm not sure—" Douglas had started to say.

His secretary, Cheryl, who had originally fielded the letter,

306

came to him in tears. "Can't you do something, Senator?" she'd pleaded. "Think if it were *your* cat. Or your dog."

So he'd found himself agreeing to draft a bill for the purpose of strengthening the rules and regulations governing transport of animals by air. When he introduced the bill on the floor, the story immediately became front-page news, not only in Arizona, but across the country. As Henry had confidently predicted, *everybody* had a pet, and as the days followed and positive mail poured in, he had to admit that his press secretary seemed to be right. In the face of such public outpouring, the bill became law, and he was so pleased with the result that he saved and framed one of the letters that had made him laugh— the first time he could remember doing so since Rob had died. It had come from a man in Prescott, who had written to say that he had never voted for a member of Douglas's party in his life, but that he loved animals and would vote for Douglas Rhodes in future elections.

He'd needed something like the cat and the airline episode, as he'd come to think of it, for it had restored his perspective. He'd been depressed for months, carrying on his work dutifully, but with no pleasure or enthusiasm, and as Sarah had insisted one night when they met for dinner, he was going to have to pull himself together.

"I know this has been a terrible, trying time for you, Douglas," she'd said in that brisk, no-nonsense tone she took on occasion. She had kept quiet for months, offering only support and sympathy, but she would only offer so much, and that night she'd obviously decided it was time to get back to business. "But you have to put all this behind you and get on with your life as best you can."

He hadn't been in a mood for lectures. His son dead, his wife in a sanitarium, he hadn't really cared about his life—or his career. Whenever he thought about Marcella, he felt so guilty. He knew he still loved her—after all, they'd been together so many years—but guilt seemed to be his overriding emotion these days. He felt so responsible for her condition; he couldn't rid himself of the feeling that he was totally to blame for everything.

"I'm sorry, Sarah," he said. "But can we discuss this another time?"

"No, we can't," she said flatly. "Now, listen to me, Douglas. I'm not going to say I'm doing this for your own good, but the truth is that I wish someone had told me to pull up my boots and get on after my darling Lester died. I would have spent a lot less time feeling sorry for myself and a lot more doing something about it.''

"Sarah, I really don't want to talk about this now.''

"Of course you don't,'' she agreed briskly. "But I'm your friend, and this is what friends are for. Now, I understand how unhappy you are, how devastated you feel, and you've got every right to feel that way. You've been through some terrible things these past few months, and no one can deny that. *But you aren't the only one who's ever lost someone,* Douglas, and you'd better start coming to grips with that.''

Naturally he'd been outraged. How dare she talk to him like this? Didn't she understand what he was going through?

"Now, you're about to tell me that I don't understand,'' she said. "But I do—believe me, I do. How do you think I felt after Lester died? He was my rock, my anchor, my support, and suddenly there I was, alone. But if I learned only one thing from that experience, Douglas, it's that life goes on. I know it sounds trite, but it's true. And you *make* it go on by doing something about what hurts so much. Rob died from a dose of crack; well, then, do something about the drug problem in this country. That's what you're here for, isn't it? To do some good? Well, get out there and do it.''

"But—''

She wouldn't accept excuses, nor did she mince words. "Or failing that,'' she said, gazing hard at him, "sponsor programs for mental health, so that people less fortunate than Marcella can get help. There's all sorts of things you can do if you get up off your duff, stop feeling sorry for yourself, and start going about the business of living again.''

She'd been right, of course; he'd known that all along. Deep inside, he'd realized it even before her pep talk. But it had taken her prodding, her true friendship, to make him see that it was time he took steps to heal. And she'd been right about the therapy of action, as well. He'd felt life returning as he directed his assistants to start researching the scope and depth of the drug trade in this country, and now he had a bill pending about mental health. Sarah had been right, but then, she always was.

And so was Laura, he thought, and stopped. He rarely allowed himself to think about Laura, because his feelings stirred waters best left calm. He tried to tell himself it was because he was so proud of her, and all the things she'd done since she'd come to the Hill, but the truth was that Washington seemed different to him now that she was here, and as he left the capital early one morning for his weekly drive to Potomac, Maryland, he was struck again by life's irony. He'd spent nearly all his senatorial career wishing that Marcella would move to Washington even for part of the year, and now that she was here, he couldn't help wishing that things were the same as they had been, and that he was still exhausting himself on that commute to Scottsdale. The old saying about being wary of the wish came into his mind, and he grimaced.

But I never dreamed . . . he thought, and shook his head. He'd been over this a thousand times since the night Rob had died, and every time he'd thought he'd made peace with the fact that there was nothing he could do about it now—that he was doing everything he could about it now, in fact—guilt rose up to haunt him and he felt that devastating pain all over again.

Taking a shaky breath, he hoped that Sarah was going to be right about this aspect of it, too. She'd said that in time the pain diminished, and he clung to that. The thought that he would feel this way the rest of his life was so defeating that he wondered if he could go on—if he wanted to go on.

At least he had stopped having nightmares about that trip to the coroner's office in Los Angeles. If nothing else, that was a mercy. For weeks after that night, he'd awake in a cold sweat after dreaming that he was standing over Rob's body on a gurney in the morgue. Part of his mind knew that wasn't true, that it hadn't happened that way, that instead of asking him to view the body directly, they had shown him pictures. But the dreams kept coming, and he'd relive that nightmare night after night until he thought he'd go mad. The only thing that kept him sane was remembering that Laura had been there, too . . . Laura, his touchstone, his soul mate, his . . . friend.

"Douglas, we've managed to keep this as quiet as possible," Laura had said quietly to him and Irving in the car. "But you know that's not going to last."

He'd made up his mind right then. There was no point in hiding it. Rob was dead, and for this to have any meaning at all, he couldn't sweep that under the rug and pretend it hadn't happened; he couldn't hide behind some clever statement, purged of significance because he was trying to save his political career. What did his career matter when his son was lying dead from some drug on a slab in the morgue?

"No, we can't hide this," he said. "Rob wouldn't want that, and I . . . I don't either."

He'd been startled then by the thought that he had heard the ghost of an approving laugh from Rob at the back of his mind. As ridiculous as it sounded, he was sure he'd heard his son's voice, and he'd known he was taking the right approach. Agreeing to make a statement, he had drafted it himself, and when the press found out, as inevitably they had, he was ready—or as ready as he could have been. Another troubling question had been the whereabouts of the girl, Calypso. He had asked the detective to stay on, but so far there had been no news. Sometimes he wondered if there ever would be.

But things were better now, even though there were still nights at his Georgetown apartment when he'd sit alone in the study for hours brooding over the same untouched drink. He didn't even know what he was thinking during those long, silent moments, only that somehow it was necessary for him to sit there and not to think at all.

Was it my fault? he had wondered, again and again and again. And he would always answer, *But how was I to know?*

Impatiently he shook his head. He hated such self-pitying introspection; it didn't serve any purpose. Rob was dead, and he had to go on living . . . somehow. Marcella seemed to have found a way beyond this terrible pain, but he couldn't take that path himself, tempting as it was at times.

His thoughts had taken him all the way into Maryland, far out into the lush green countryside. Startled at how far he'd come without realizing it, he saw the big wrought-iron gates of Sacred Heart Sanitarium looming ahead, and despite himself, felt tense. It was always this way; even though he came every week, these visits were always a strain. He never knew whether Marcella would recognize him or not, but despite such discouraging results with her therapy, he never gave up hope. She'd been here for over a year now in the care of the Sisters of Mercy, but for all the progress she had made, she might have been admitted yesterday.

It wasn't the sisters' fault, or the sanitarium's. Sacred Heart was rated one of the best in the country, and he'd been fortunate it was so close. But as devoted and skillful as the nuns were, they couldn't perform miracles. Nor could even the acres of carefully manicured lawns, and the graceful old trees sheltering the meandering brick paths, and the low, mellowed rose-colored brick buildings disguise the fact that this was a sanitarium. Inevitably came a glimpse of a white uniform, or a patient in a wheelchair, or another walking slowly along a path, assisted by a concerned aide. Here and there were scenes of blank-faced men and women sitting on the patios in the sun, or by themselves on a bench; all so still that their very immobility guaranteed they would remain where they were until someone came along and gently led them away to another place. As he got out of the car, the only sound was the occasional murmur of conversation carried his way, or the sighing of the wind, high in the trees. As he stood there for a moment, steeling himself to go inside, he was reminded for some reason of the argument he'd had with Deidre the night he'd told her he intended to transfer Marcella to Maryland.

He and his sister rarely fought, but that day Deidre had been shocked that he'd even considering moving Marcella from her home. Of course, Marcella hadn't been "at home" at the time. She hadn't been for weeks, since election night, when they'd found out about Rob. Falling deeper and deeper into her own private world, she had been registered at the very luxurious Scottsdale Retreat, a hospital of sorts, not far from Phoenix.

"You know Marcella hates Washington!" Deidre had exclaimed when he told her. "How can you possibly think of transferring here there, especially at a time like this?"

The only reason he'd kept his temper with her was that he knew she was grieving over Rob, too. Deidre and his son had always been close, and she agonized because she hadn't been able to reach him, either. They'd gone riding one day not long after the funeral—a pilgrimage of sorts, he thought, into the hills where Rob had learned to ride his own horse, so long ago.

"I just don't understand it," Deidre had said, her voice breaking, as they paused and looked out over a knoll. Far below, the city of Phoenix spread out before them, a patch of green seeming to rise from the sand and scrub surrounding it. "He had so much to live for, so much to do!"

He was silent. He didn't know what to say; he couldn't argue. He had already accepted the painful fact that he would never understand what had happened to Rob, just as he knew he'd probably spend the rest of his life searching for answers to that unanswered question. Why does a bright mind throw itself away? What pain and confusion had lurked below the surface, hidden even from the people who loved him most? Questions were never far from his mind, hiding until the dead of night, when they came forward like specters to haunt him. *What happened?* And *Why didn't I see it?* And *What could I have done to prevent it?*

But the answers were as elusive by day as they were at night, and so he said nothing. The horses shifted their weight and blew, the saddle leather creaked, the sun beat down. All was silent and still on that knoll, and because he suddenly felt overwhelmed by a rush of pain at the memories that assailed him, he spoke before he was ready.

"I'm going to move Marcella to a retreat closer to Washington," he said.

From her position in her own saddle, Deidre turned to look at him. She was wearing jeans and a midnight-blue silk shirt that glistened in the sunlight. But her face under the broad-brimmed hat was pale, her complexion blotched from tears. "What?"

"I said—"

"I heard what you said! Why?"

He glanced away from her face, unseeingly out at the magnificent view. "Because she needs help, Deidre," he'd said quietly. "Because I want her close to me."

"Then move back here!"

He'd winced. "You know I can't do that."

"Yes, you can," she said angrily. "You can . . . resign, or whatever senators do! You don't have to stay there!"

He had no answer for that, either—at least none she would understand in her pain. How could he explain that more than ever now, he needed the challenge of his work? He couldn't come back to Scottsdale, not yet, not when the memories were still so raw.

"I can't do that," he said finally. "And Marcella will be . . . happier at Sacred Heart. I've checked into it thoroughly. It's the best in the country."

"The best what?" Her voice was shrill; she heard it, and clenched her hand on the reins she was holding. "Never mind," she muttered. "But don't you think you're being premature?"

He was silent again. He knew she hadn't approved of Marcella going to a sanitarium in the first place, but then, she hadn't his experience with reporters. Nor had she seen the light die in Marcella's eyes, her swift retreat to a place in her mind he couldn't reach. He had to protect his wife, to keep her safe from too many questions and all those prying eyes.

"I don't know," he said quietly, honestly. "I just know I don't

312

want to leave her here, where I won't be able to visit, to look in on her."

"If you're doing this to keep her safe from reporters, they're sure to find out."

"I know," he said again. "But she'll be protected. And I don't care if they find out."

Suddenly fierce, she turned to him again. "Yes, you do! You're thinking of your career!"

He was shocked that she could say such a thing. "That's not true! I'm thinking of Marcella."

"The hell you are!"

He stared at her; she glared defiantly back. Then, suddenly, she slumped. "I'm sorry," she said, beginning to cry again. "I didn't mean that. Sometimes I don't know *what* I mean anymore. I've been so confused since . . . since . . ."

Abruptly tears filled his eyes. He glanced away, out toward Camelback again, blinking rapidly. "Rob felt that way, too," he said.

She sniffed, used the back of her hand to brush away her tears. "What?"

"That all I could think of was my career. Maybe it's true."

"Rob was proud of you," she said, her voice breaking again.

"That's not what he told me to my face."

"He was confused, Douglas. He didn't know what he was saying."

He gave a bitter laugh. "He knew exactly what he was saying," he said. "Rob wasn't stupid—at least not in that way."

"No, but he always felt he could never measure up to you."

Vehemently he started to deny that, but he had to wonder if it was true. Then he shook his head sharply. No, Rob had been so smart, so talented, in everything he tried! It was never a case of measuring up; he had never demanded that of his son. He wouldn't believe that; he couldn't.

"You don't know what you're talking about," he muttered.

"Don't I?" Deidre's blue eyes flashed in sudden anger. "You forget that I'm your sister, Douglas. I've lived under your shadow for years. No one can measure up to you—no one! We all finally realize that, and after a while, we all stop trying. Maybe Rob did, too."

He couldn't understand how she could say such ridiculous things; he wouldn't let himself believe they might be true.

"That's absurd!" he said sharply. I've never asked anyone to live up to my standards, to do what I've done—least of all Rob!"

"You didn't *have* to ask him, Douglas! All you had to do was set the example, don't you see? Rob loved you; you were Einstein and da Vinci and Salk and Galileo, all rolled up into one. Is it any wonder he wanted you to be proud of him?"

"I *was* proud of him!" he cried, his voice hoarse with pain. He couldn't understand what she was talking about. Was she saying he was responsible for what had happened? But what could he have done that he hadn't tried? *What could he have done?*

"I never demanded more of Rob than he could give," he said. "I *never* forced him to live up to my expectations! I never had any expectations at all!"

"Didn't you?" she said, shocking him with her bitterness. "Didn't you? Then you'd better think about it!"

She wheeled her horse around, intending to spur the animal in the side and run away. He caught her arm as she started by, jerking the reins so that the startled animal skidded to a stop.

"What are you doing?" she cried.

He gripped her arm even harder. "Did Rob tell you these things?" he grated.

Their eyes were nearly on a level, and he saw that she was crying again. He felt like weeping, too, but refused to let the tears come. He hadn't cried; he didn't intend to.

"Yes . . . no . . . not in so many words, Douglas! But I knew. I've felt it, too!" She was sobbing openly now, trying to get away from him. "Douglas, let me go!"

He wanted to demand an explanation, a reason, a rationale, an . . . answer. But his voice was no longer his own. The grief he had held at bay, the emotion he had denied, suddenly swept over him, and without warning, he felt choked with tears. Everything blurred and he knew he had to get away, but he couldn't turn his horse; he couldn't see. A sob escaped him, and then another, a horrible sound ripped from his soul. Dropping the reins, he flung himself out of the saddle and staggered a few steps before his will failed him. He fell to his knees, sobbing as only a man in terrible, gut-wrenching pain can sob.

Deidre uttered a startled cry. Leaping out of the saddle, she ran to him, weeping again herself. "Oh, Douglas!" she cried, and put her arms around him, holding him close.

The gesture was his undoing. Placing his head against her

breast, he clung to her and cried. But soon his grief was so overwhelming that it needed a greater outlet, and he lifted his head and cried to the skies.

"Why?" he shouted, agonized. *"Oh, God—why?"*

There was no answer, except for the echo of his voice reverberating through the hills. It was a sound of such denial and pain and heartache that birds took flight and Deidre came and dragged him away from the edge again.

"Good afternoon, Senator Rhodes . . ."

He blinked. He'd been so lost in his thoughts that he hadn't even heard the sister approach. Still reeling emotionally from the memory of that day in the hills with his sister, he pulled himself together. "Oh . . . Sister Agnes," he said. "I'm sorry, I didn't hear you come."

The nuns here had abandoned their habits and wore more of a nurse's uniform of white, with a short white veil covering their hair. Large crucifixes hung from gold chains around their necks, and at first to Douglas they had all looked the same. Now, after so many months, he saw how foolish and blind he'd been. Sister Agnes was one of his favorites; slightly younger than most of her sisters, she had large, blue, compassionate eyes, a sweet curve to her mouth, and the most gentle, graceful hands he'd ever seen. He remembered her soothing an agitated patient by smoothing back her hair; he'd seen her tell someone a story, making him laugh by creating pictures in the air with those long, slender fingers. He knew Marcella liked her, too, for the only time he'd seen her smile was when Sister Agnes came into the room. Marcella had yet to do the same for him when he came to visit, and when once he'd mentioned this wistfully to the sister, she had patted his arm.

"All in God's good time," she'd murmured, but he had reflected that maybe God had more time than he did. Marcella seemed to retreat further and further away from him every time he came, and although the mother superior assured him that his wife was doing well, he had his doubts. *Well* was relative, and the woman he saw when he visited had long ago ceased being his wife.

"Mrs. Rhodes is waiting for you in her room, Senator," Sister Agnes reminded him.

He blinked, wondering where he'd gone again. "Yes, I know," he murmured, and reached into the car for the flowers he'd brought, and the magazines. Although he suspected Marcella did little more than look at the pictures now, she loved magazines, and the nuns had told him that she would sit and pore over them for hours after he'd gone.

"Would you like me to come with you?" Sister Agnes asked.

Touched by her offer, he still shook his head. She knew how difficult this was for him, and she always asked if he wanted company; he always refused. It had become a ritual with them, but even though it hurt that his own wife didn't respond to him, he still tried. "No, thank you," he said. "I know you have other duties."

She placed a quiet hand briefly on his arm. "If you need me, then, I'll be at the nurses' station."

He nodded, hoping this wouldn't be one of the days when he would have to call her. There had been times in the past when it had been necessary, for without warning, Marcella would become agitated at something he said, and Sister Agnes or one of the others would rush in, and he would have to wait out in the hall until they calmed her again, either with words or with a shot of some kind. At those times he felt more despairing than ever, for he never knew what he'd said to cause the upset. He'd tried to confine his conversation to innocuous events, to tell Marcella stories that might amuse her or miraculously generate a laugh, something—anything—that would break through the wall that seemed to surround her. He'd never been successful. Marcella remained behind her barrier, serene—except for those occasions when something upset her—untouchable, unapproachable.

It wasn't that she was completely silent; sometimes he thought it would be easier if she were. She would answer questions politely if he asked, her head cocked a little, that same emptiness behind her eyes. But at times her answers didn't match the questions he put to her; it was almost as though they were on parallel tracks, going in different directions, heading into nowhere. He had asked the doctors here about it and they'd given him some complicated psychological term that was meaningless to him, reassuring him at the same time that some patients emerged spontaneously from this "other reality" they had created because the one they'd left behind was too painful to endure. They advised patience; they suggested he give her time. And in the meantime, her therapy would be ongoing and her care above reproach. They would notify him immediately of the slightest progress.

But there hadn't been much progress, he thought as he looked at the building where Marcella's suite was located. She was little better than when he'd brought her here, and sometimes he doubted he'd ever have her back completely again. Refusing to think what he'd do if that happened, he took the flowers and the magazines and went inside.

Cool dimness surrounded him the instant he stepped through the doorway, along with the smells of polish and wax and that indefinable human odor that seemed to permeate places like this, no matter how expensive or luxurious. His nose wrinkled at the smell, and he quickly crossed the shining tile foyer and headed down the thickly carpeted hall toward Marcella's door. The nurses' station was set unobtrusively down at the other end of the hallway, an island of light and bustle that reminded him without his wanting it to that this was a place for sick people. Feeling a little sick inside himself at the thought, he paused before the gleaming walnut door with the brass 2S attached to it, and gently knocked.

There was no answer; he hadn't expected there to be. But he waited a moment anyway before he went in—whether from courtesy or from a reluctance to proceed, he was never quite sure. It was probably a mixture of both, since this was always the most difficult part for him. He never knew what to expect when he saw Marcella; as he'd so painfully learned, some days were better than others.

Hesitantly he approached. Marcella was sitting by the shaded window, staring out at the parklike scenery of which so much of Sacred Heart was composed. She even heard him enter, and she turned.

"Hello," she said. "What are you doing here?"

Once this simple question would have caused him a knifelike pain. But he had learned to handle it, and he answered, "I've come to visit, my dear. I've brought you some flowers—and magazines."

He held them out, and she took them. "Why, thank you," she said. "I do love magazines."

But she put them aside without glancing through them, and he took another hold of himself as he sat down opposite her. She was wearing a dress of some flowery material today, and he noticed with a pang that she'd lost weight again. Her hands rested idly in her lap, and he cautiously reached for one, enfolding her bony fingers in his. "How are you today, Marcella?"

She had turned to gaze out again, her eyes seeing little more of the grass beyond the window than she had seen of him. "I really must do something about dinner," she murmured. "Rob will be home soon, and growing boys are always so hungry, aren't they?"

Despite himself, he felt a stab of pain. This was when it hurt the most, her speaking of Rob in the present tense. But as the doctors had told him, to Marcella, her son had never died. They'd also told him it would do no good—that it might actually retard what little progress they'd made—for him to insist that Rob was dead. He hadn't needed a psychiatrist to tell him that; he knew the futility of trying to make her face the truth, and after all, what difference did it make? She was far happier in a world where Rob still lived than he was in the one where his son no longer existed.

"Yes, boys are always hungry," he said, and willed her to say something else, to look at him, to acknowledge that he was here. When she said nothing more, did nothing more, he sat silently for a long time, gazing at her still, empty face, her unmoving hand in his. They sat that way until Sister Agnes peeked in an untold time later.

"It's almost time for lunch," the sister said, her expression sad as she looked from one to the other. "Would you care to join us, Senator?"

He roused himself from thoughts he didn't even know he was thinking. Time had slipped away, and he glanced at his watch before he shook his head. "Thank you, no," he said. "I have a committee meeting this afternoon, and I must start back to Washington."

"I understand," Sister Agnes said. "Shall we expect you next week?"

He glanced down at Marcella, who was still staring out the window, as she had been for hours. Painfully he saw that she hadn't even realized he'd let go of her hand, that he was about to leave. To Marcella, he just wasn't there, and he looked away into the sister's compassionate face.

"Yes," he said. "I'll be here."

CHAPTER TWENTY-FIVE

Laura was at her desk long before nine, when the rest of the staff came in. Even at this hour the day already promised to be a trial, for in addition to the ungodly weather, hot and humid even for this time of year, she already had a conflict on her schedule. She was just trying to decide which meeting was top priority when Ellen walked in with the mail and a fresh cup of coffee. Grimacing at the one, she accepted the other gratefully and took a sip before she put it down and began rummaging through the rubble on her desk for the research report she wanted.

"Have you seen the material on the school systems I need for the Education and Labor Committee meeting this morning?" she asked Ellen in exasperation, giving up the search.

Putting her notebook under her arm, her chief aide reached into the pile on the cluttered desk, extracted a folder, and handed it nonchalantly across. She took out her list again. "I take it this means you're going to attend the Education meeting this morning instead of the Public Works Subcommittee hearing on health legislation?"

Already scanning the school material, Laura looked up. Her top aide on the Public Works Subcommittee, Lesley Aron, was standing in the doorway, and she asked her opinion. "What do you think?"

"I think you can skip PW this morning," Lesley said with a yawn. "Since they're going to be debating the acceptable noise level ceiling for garbage trucks, it should be a riveting discussion. I'll go for you. I wouldn't want to miss it."

Laura laughed and glanced at Ellen again. "What else?"

Her chief aide consulted her notes. "Just the usual. We're getting the newsletter together—the last one before recess next week—but you've already approved all the items in that. And you wanted me to remind you about starting those monthly public forums in your district." She looked up with a grin. "You know, those 'Let the People Speak' events our illustrious press aide, Harvey, thought would be a good idea?"

"It *is* a good idea," she said, and realized that it was time for the meeting she had scheduled with the staff to discuss the urban policy she was also putting together. Gathering her notes, she asked Ellen to have everyone come in.

The urban package was a pet project of hers and involved coordinating transportation, housing, and industry that would encourage businesses to stay in the cities instead of fleeing to rural areas. She hadn't forgotten one of the very real reasons she'd wanted to run for office: the need to do something about crime at the street level. And after hours of researching both the problems and possible solutions, she'd decided this policy was a good approach—a start, anyway. Some of her colleagues didn't agree, and she was going to have to lobby diligently to put it across. She shrugged. Debate was what it was all about, and she knew she was on the right track; she just had to convince everybody else she was. She had until the fall, when Congress convened again, to put together a major speech on the policy, and when she thought that soon they'd be in recess and she'd be on her way home for what was left of the summer, she quickly handed out assignments to her staff.

"I'm going to need all the input I can get on this new package so I can study it these next few months," she reminded them. "So please get me what material you can and have it assembled—"

"Crated, you mean," Ellen said, glancing down at the pages Laura had handed her.

Everybody laughed, including the boss. Laura's habit of reading everything she could get her hands on was well known to her staff, and her quick grasp of detail amazed them, even now. But they knew what an information gatherer she was, and they all promised to complete their assignments on time. Sending them on their way, she was about to get going herself when her phone rang. At the door, Ellen turned back to answer it, but she waved her aide on out.

"I've got it," she said, reaching for the receiver. She answered; it was her mother.

"Laura?" Estelle said. "I'm sorry to bother you at work. I know how you hate to be interrupted."

"No, it's fine, Mother," she said, and wondered instantly if something had happened. Estelle rarely called her at the office, especially from California. "Is . . . is something wrong?"

Immediately sounding annoyed, Estelle said, "Nothing's wrong. Why do you always expect the worst?"

Suppressing a sigh, she sat down again. "I'm sorry," she said. "It's just so unusual for you to call me here that I thought something might have happened."

"Well, nothing has. I called because I wanted to know when you plan to come home."

She tried to hide her irritation. She'd given that information twice to her mother; the last time she was home, she had even written it all out—flight times and schedules, everything she could think of—and put it all on the kitchen bulletin board. Estelle knew it was there; she was sure of it. Thinking that she really didn't have time for this game right now because she had so many other things to do, she glanced at the clock and grimaced. If she didn't hurry, she was going to be late for her first meeting.

"Mother, I left all the details tacked to the bulletin board in the kitchen," she said. "Have you checked there?"

"Why didn't you tell me you put it there?"

"I did—" she started to say, and winced at the sound of the phone being banged down onto the counter. Obviously her mother had gone to look, and while she waited, she wondered why she put up with this. Before she could decide, she heard the phone being picked up against and Estelle came back on the line.

"I'm sorry, Laura, I just don't see it there. Would it be too much trouble if you just *told* me?"

She wanted to sigh in sheer exasperation. She didn't remember the flight number; at this moment, she could hardly remember her own name. "Just a minute. I'll have to find it."

"Well, I'm terribly sorry to bother you, Laura. If it's so much trouble, why don't you just forget it?"

"It's not that—"

"I just wanted to be sure when you were coming so we could go ahead with the welcome-home party we planned."

She had already begun to hunt through her desk drawer for her plane ticket, and she stopped in midsearch. "A party?" she repeated. This was the first she'd heard of it.

"Yes," Estelle said with just a hint of smugness. "Actually,

321

it was the children's idea. They do miss you so, and it's difficult for them to have a mother who's gone so much of the time.''

"I miss them, too," Laura said, and felt that knot tighten in her stomach. *I'm not going to get into it,* she told herself, and proceeded to do just that. "Mother, I know how much you disapprove of our living arrangements, but I thought we all agreed that for the time being, at least, this was best. After all, you and Jack both overruled me about moving the kids before the school year was out. This is just as difficult for me as it is for them."

Estelle waved that aside. "As I recall, it was your decision to run for office, not theirs. You should have known this would be a problem."

Trying again to hold on to her temper, she said carefully, "Yes, but we agreed we'd work it out. Don't you remember that dinner we had where we all discussed it? As *I* recall, there weren't any dissenting votes."

"I think you've been in Washington too long. This is your family we're talking about—not some of your constituents."

Realizing this discussion was fruitless, she said, "Maybe we should talk about this when I get home. I've been wanting to discuss our living arrangements for some time now, and—"

"You're not planning to uproot the children after all, are you?"

She couldn't understand how Estelle could sound so incredulous. It wasn't a question of *uprooting* anymore; it was a matter of having her family together. But now that she had definitely decided to run for a second term, she had intended to discuss the move first with Jack. She knew he'd have to make a decision about his business, but she intended to try and talk him into transferring his office to Washington. She just didn't want this separation to continue; she missed them all too much.

But it was a little more than that. She saw the children so infrequently now that she seemed even more attuned to the slightest change, and lately she didn't like the way either of them were acting. Peter was too quiet, too introspective, too given to sullen silences, while Andrea was just the opposite with her unceasing demands for attention and fits of temper when she didn't get her own way. She knew they were both spoiled, and that her mother was to blame for much of that, but even so, her children were her own responsibility, and she wanted them with her so that she could monitor their behavior. Jack didn't seem to notice anything sinister about the way the kids were behaving, and maybe there wasn't. But now that she could no longer pretend, as her family seemed to expect her to do, that her career change was only temporary, she felt they would all be better off here.

Was that selfish? She had to admit it was, but she couldn't see any other way. She was doing some good here, effecting some changes; given the opportunity, she knew she could do more. She couldn't give that up, and yet commuting had proved so unsatisfactory that they had to think of another solution. Moving them all to Washington seemed to be the obvious choice.

But she obviously couldn't discuss this with her mother over long distance, especially since she hadn't even approached Jack yet, so she said, "I'm sorry, Mother, but I have a meeting in a few minutes. We'll talk about this when I get home, all right?"

"Oh, of course," Estelle said sarcastically. "Please, do attend your meeting. I'm sure your family can wait. They always do."

"That's not—" she started to say indignantly, but her mother had already hung up. Muttering to herself when she heard the dial tone, she replaced her own receiver. She hadn't even had a chance to talk to the kids, she thought, and angrily gathered her things for the meeting she had to attend.

Ten minutes later, after a short, equilibrium-inducing walk down Independence Avenue to the building where her meeting was to take place, she had to apologize to the committee chairman for being late as she slipped into her seat. An undersecretary with the Department of Education was well into a long, seemingly interminable speech, and already she saw eyes glazing at the drone of statistics he was presenting. Relieved to have something to occupy her mind other than problems with her family, she concentrated on what he had to say. She'd been given a copy of the speech, and as he ambled on, she followed along, marking passages she intended to question if there was time. He was halfway through when bells rang, signaling that the House was about to convene for a vote. Looking relieved, the chair ended the meeting so they could all go to the floor, and when she came out, Ellen was waiting in the hallway.

"Here, you forgot this," she said, handing Laura the loose-leaf binder that contained her briefing material on the bills that were going to be considered on the House floor this week.

She took the heavy thing with a resigned expression. Obviously she'd been preoccupied when she left the office, and she said, "What else did I forget?"

"Only to sign these letters," Ellen said, holding them out, her ever-present clipboard acting as a miniature desk so she could write.

"What are these?" she asked, signing.

"Letters to the editor of your home paper about your stand on the abortion issue," Ellen said, and added, "By the way, we've gotten more calls this morning."

Signing away, she nodded. She knew this meant antiabortion calls, because the office had been deluged with mail and phone calls from Right to Lifers every time an abortion question had come to a vote. This time it had to do with federal funding again, and both houses of Congress were to vote. The House had scheduled a vote for later in the week.

"It doesn't change your mind, does it?" Ellen asked.

She shook her head. "No, it doesn't change my mind."

"Good," Ellen said, and looked relieved as she glanced over the signed letters before placing them back in the folder.

"Anything else?"

"Senator Ambrose called and canceled lunch today. She said to tell you she's sorry, but they're running overtime again on the Appropriations hearings, and hopes you understand."

She did understand, but she was still disappointed. Now it seemed that she and Sarah weren't going to be able to get together before Congress recessed after all. They'd been trying to arrange a few minutes for two weeks now, but every time they'd set a tentative date, something else had come up. "All right," she said regretfully. "I'll call her when I get back to the office."

They went their separate ways then, Ellen to return to her desk, she to the Capitol building, laden now with the briefing book in addition to her already heavy portfolio, bulging with notes and reports. She took the "members only" elevator down and rode the House subway to the Capitol, using the brief time to scan her notes about pending legislation. Another elevator ride took her up to the House floor, and after using her vote-identification card to register her presence in a quorum call, she spied a colleague she wanted to see. He was Chuck Seager, a California Democrat who chaired the Subcommittee on Public Buildings. When he saw her coming purposefully toward him, he looked as though he wanted to hide.

"It's not going to do you any good, Chuck," she said. "I

324

want to ask your opinion on that general services proposal in Orange County."

Chuck groaned. They'd been around about this before; since Orange County was an affluent area of Southern California below Los Angeles, it was part of Laura's "territory" too, and he knew she wasn't happy about the proposal to spend eight million dollars on a single building so that a Defense Department agency could move in. Further, she wasn't too pleased about the studies proving it was doubtful that enough homes could be provided for the new agency's employees in the area, and that the available housing might be out of that particular income bracket.

"We've been over this until we're both blue in the face, Laura," he said. "We've got charts proving no housing problem is involved."

"Charts are like statistics," she said. "We both know how they can be slanted."

"Yes, so you've said—many times."

She wasn't going to rise to the sarcasm. "All right, aside from that, shouldn't we consider whether it's wise to be moving agencies from city locations to the suburbs? We're both from California; if anyone does, we both know about urban sprawl."

He glanced around, but no one was close enough to rescue him. "Is there a point to this, Laura? Because I've got to—"

"The point," she said evenly, "is that California isn't the only one with this growing problem; everyone's going to have to face it sooner or later."

"Well, then, bring it up in committee. We are going to meet again before recess, remember? It was nice talking to you, but I've got . . . er . . . someone I have to meet."

He dashed off before she could reply, but she let him go. She could see that it was futile trying to enlist his support, but she was philosophical about it. If not Chuck, then someone else. By the time she was through, everyone would know about her urban policy package, whether they agreed with it or not.

It was six-fifteen by the time she got back to the office again. She'd managed to run in and out a couple of times that afternoon to take care of business—a picture with a Girl Scout troop, one of the little girls reminding her achingly of Andrea; an interview with two members of the Duarte Small Businessman's Association, who were in town on a junket. Then she was summoned to the House floor again for back-to-back votes on bills that had been debated that afternoon, and by the time she trudged wearily back again for what seemed like the thousandth time that day, all was quiet. The rest of the staff had gone home, and wishing she could do the same, she went through the stack of messages Ellen had left her, then sat down to call Sarah. By this time, she knew that the senior senator's work habits coincided with her own, and she phoned the office first. As she had anticipated, Sarah was there.

"Hello, Sarah," she said. "This is Laura. Have you got a minute?"

"I do—now that it's too late," the other woman answered. "I'm sorry about lunch, but my esteemed colleagues on Appropriations were acting like a bunch of asses—pardon the expression—and I thought I should deal with them."

"And did you?" Laura said, smiling. She had seen Sarah Ambrose in action, and knew that despite the feminine suits and the flower in her lapel, there was nothing soft about her legislative or organizational ability. Wondering if she'd ever command that kind of power and authority herself, she decided just to be glad that she and Sarah had become friends.

"I did," Sarah said with satisfaction. Then her voice changed. "But now my schedule is jammed until I take the plane home. I don't think we'll be able to get together after all."

"I understand," Laura said. "I've got problems with my schedule, too."

"Is that all? You sound a little . . . down."

She didn't want to burden Sarah with her problems. "No, just tired, I guess. It's been a long day. I did want to ask you something, though."

"What's that?"

"What do you think about this abortion issue?"

"The same thing I think every other time it's come up," Sarah said briskly. "To me, it's obviously another maneuver by foes to oppose federal funding of all abortions except to save the mother's life, so I'm going to vote against it." She paused. "How about you?"

"Well, those are my feelings, too."

"You don't sound too convinced."

"Oh, I am. It's just that I've been getting all these calls—"

"That happens all the time on this issue. We've talked about this before, and you have to do what's right. You still believe this is a matter best left between the woman and her doctor, don't you?"

"Yes, absolutely." She had no hesitation about that.

"And that government has no business getting into it?"

"You know I believe less government is best."

"Then remember that we're legislators, not doctors. Let *them* debate the medical aspects of this."

Relieved that Sarah had succeeded in convincing her that her original decision was still the right one, Laura laughed. "I knew it would do me good talking to you. I'm still convinced. I hope my constituents feel the same way."

"Don't worry about it," Sarah said with her characteristic brusqueness. "I've been elected five times now, and I've survived this issue every time."

After they'd hung up, Laura sat back with a sigh. She was tired, but she really didn't want to go back to that empty apartment. Glancing at all the different piles of things on her desk, she didn't want to dig into that, either. She was just debating what to do when the phone rang again.

"I thought you'd still be in your office," Douglas said when she had answered. "Don't you ever go home?"

As always, she felt warmed inside just by the sound of his voice. Smiling again, she sat back. "Don't you? Or are you calling from your office?"

"No, I'm home. Getting ready for another command performance at some party."

"You don't sound too enthusiastic," she said, swallowing her disappointment. She had hoped he'd called to ask her to dinner.

"I'm not. This is for one of the Greek attachés. And I hate ouzo."

She laughed at his revulsion. "It should come as a welcome respite after all those closed hearings you've been closeted behind lately."

"You're right. I hadn't thought of it that way."

The hearings were one reason neither she nor Sarah had seen much of him; during the past few weeks, he'd been preoccupied with a closed investigation into a highly sensitive probe of Alpha-Techtronica, a Detroit-based company that had been given a multimillion-dollar business contract under suspicious circumstances. She'd been proud to learn that Douglas had instigated the probe, and not surprised when he had once again become front-page news for his part in exposing what promised to be a major scandal. Because of the private nature of the hearings, he hadn't been able to say much, but during a hurried lunch in the cafeteria one day, he'd told both her and Sarah that this was only the tip of the iceberg. More revelations were yet to come, but the investigation had to proceed very slowly and with extreme care, since it was rumored that highly placed officials in the current administration were involved. Sarah had snorted at that, and Laura herself had reflected that sometimes what went on in this town made everything she'd learned as a public defender and a district attorney pale in comparison.

"So how are things going?" she asked cautiously. She knew he wouldn't be able to tell her much, and she didn't want to put him in an awkward position.

"Not good," he said. "We need more time."

"Are you going to continue through recess?"

"I'd like to, but there's . . . opposition."

She sensed he couldn't say more, and so she said, "I'm sorry. I know how eager you are to put this thing to . . . rest."

"Yes, well, that's the way it goes sometimes," he said. "Actually, it might be a relief. This business has kept me so preoccupied, I haven't had time for much else for weeks."

"I know," she said wryly.

His voice changed. "How are things with you?"

She willed treacherous thoughts away. "Oh, the same—busy."

"I bet you're looking forward to going home for a while."

She had been, until she heard his voice tonight. Now she felt a pang at the thought that she wouldn't see him for two months or longer. Autumn looked suddenly very far away, and the glorious summer she'd planned with her family seemed to fall flat. She wondered who she'd been kidding; this wasn't going to be a wonderful vacation; there were too many problems to face at home, too many things to work out. Suddenly she didn't want to go home at all; she wasn't sure she had the strength to face what awaited her there.

But she couldn't tell him that, so she said, "Oh, yes, I'm looking forward to it very much."

He was silent a moment. Then, very quietly, he said, "I wish—"

He stopped. She told herself not to ask, but she couldn't help it. "What?"

It was another second or two before he answered. "That things were different."

She couldn't respond; she didn't dare. But her heart gave a painful little leap in her chest, and she closed her eyes against a

328

spasm of pain. Sometimes she wished things were different, too, especially when she pictured Marcella living out her days in silent pain in another place of the heart. She rarely allowed herself to think of that, because whenever she did, she was reminded even more forcefully just how futile the situation was, and then she felt so guilty. There was no situation, she'd remind herself, and knew that, given the chance, there could be.

But it didn't matter, did it? Because whatever opportunity they might have had—and she wasn't even sure they'd had one, or wanted it, or would have taken it if they could—it was gone now. Marcella might have gone away, but she had taken a part of Douglas with her—a part that would always, ever, remain hers. Knowingly or not, she had bound him to her forever, and nothing would ever change that.

A man or woman in a position of public trust must be . . . above reproach. . . .

She didn't remember who had told her that; it didn't matter. She'd learned it long ago, and had tried to live her life that way ever since. *Above reproach.* It sounded so noble, didn't it? she thought, her mouth twisting. So noble. If only they knew . . .

As though they both sensed they'd said too much and not enough at all, they hung up soon after that. This time she didn't tarry; suddenly she wanted to be free of the office, free of the phone. Quickly she gathered her things, switched off the light, and went back to her empty apartment. At the end of that grueling week, she finally left for home.

To her surprise, Janette met her at the airport. She was waiting at the rope railing with the other people as Laura came up the ramp, trying to get out of the way of some big fellow who still stepped on her feet trying to get to his girl. Giving him a glare, she gave Laura a hug.

"Boy, am I glad to see you!"

"What are you doing here?" Laura said, laughing. "I thought Jack was going to pick me up."

"He was, but he's busy with the party, so I volunteered," Janette said, and took her carry-on. "Why—disappointed?"

"Are you kidding? It's great to see you," she said, and tried not to think how relieved she was that her sister had met her, and not Jack. Now she could postpone what she knew was going to be an inevitable confrontation with him about her plans to move the family to Washington, and she took Janette's arm and gave her a squeeze. "Do you realize how long it's been since we've talked?"

"Ages," Janette said, and gave her a wicked look. "You haven't changed at all."

"What did you expect—gray hair and a cane?"

Janette grinned again. "No, I expected a swelled head. You're pretty important now, sis—big congresswoman and all that."

"Hardly big," Laura said, rolling her eyes. "As a junior, I'm the lowest of the low."

"The lowest of the low doesn't get in the paper or on TV all the time," Janette retorted, and laughed at her startled look. "Don't look so surprised; we do get the news out here in the West, you know."

Laura's eyes sparkled. "Yes, but I didn't think anyone actually *watched* it."

Laughing together, they left the terminal. Laura was about to say something when she realized that Janette's gold Volvo was parked very conspicuously in a yellow loading zone right outside. "You can't park there!"

"Why not?" Janette said blithely. "When you've got a sister who's a congresswoman, as well as a former member of the DA's office, I figure you can park anywhere you choose!"

Laura reached over the windshield and plucked a parking ticket from under the wiper. Handing it across, she said, "Apparently not everyone agrees with you."

Janette uttered a sound of dismay. Glancing up, she said hopefully, "Do you think you could—"

"Not in a million years," Laura said, and got into the car.

They argued amiably about fixing the ticket while Janette maneuvered through traffic out of the airport. But once on the freeway, she turned serious. "I'm glad you're home for a while, Laurie."

Alerted by something in her tone, Laura glanced across. Janette was looking straight ahead, and she said, "All right. What's wrong?"

Pretending to be suddenly occupied with changing lanes, Janette glanced in both mirrors, switched on her signal lights, and crept over one. "I don't know what you mean."

"Yes, you do. You're too serious all of a sudden. Is something wrong?"

"No, nothing's wrong, honest," Janette said, and looked as though she wanted to say more but didn't know how. Finally she sighed. "Let's just say I'm glad you're home for a while, okay?"

She looked across and their eyes met. Laura wanted to pursue it, but some instinct told her it would be better if she didn't. Sitting back, she glanced out the window, trying to tell herself that maybe Janette wanted to talk to her about Peter and Andrea and wasn't sure how to begin. She had expressed her own concern to her sister some time ago in her letters home, and Janette had agreed that the kids were getting a little spoiled. Hoping that's all it was, she closed her eyes. She was so tired; it would be good to get home.

But once she thought of all the problems she faced now that she was here, her mind wouldn't let her rest. The closer they got to the house, the more tense she became; she couldn't stop thinking of the argument she'd had with Jack the other night when she mentioned her plan of moving the family to Washington. She'd only brought it up because she wanted him to think about it before she came home; she hadn't felt it fair to just . . . spring it on him once she got here. Now she wondered if that had been such a good idea after all.

"What about *my* business?" he'd demanded when she told him what she'd been thinking. "What do you expect *me* to do? Close up shop and follow you? What am I supposed to do when I get there?"

"You're an independent contractor, Jack," she had pointed out, trying to be calm. "You can conduct business in Washington just as easily as you can in California."

"I have no contacts there! All my work is here."

She couldn't help it. "You've done jobs out of state before," she said.

He paused the barest fraction; he hated to be reminded of those six months he'd spent in Arizona. "And I probably will again," he said nastily, and raised his voice again. "But not from there!"

She was still trying to be reasonable at that point. "It's not as if I'm asking you to give up everything just to satisfy a whim of mine, Jack," she said. "And there are plenty of government jobs for engineers here. If you would just consider—"

"Oh, so now you're going to use your influence to get me a job, is that it?" he'd jeered.

She had promised herself she wouldn't lose her temper, but she'd felt it slipping. "I don't have any so-called influence, Jack, and I wouldn't use it if I did. I wouldn't have to, anyway. You're good enough at what you do to be hired on your own merit. Won't you at least think about it?"

At least he'd promised. But as Janette turned the Volvo in to her driveway, she looked at the house and wondered if he had.

"Why the big sigh?" Janette asked.

She didn't want to go into it. "Just glad to be home, I guess."

"I hope you say that once you find out how many people are inside. This turned into some big party."

Now that Janette had mentioned it, she could hear the music coming from the house. Wondering if she was up to this, she asked cautiously. "Who all is here?"

"Oh, both families . . . some people from the campaign—a few of Jack's business associates."

Wondering if she'd just imagined that strange note in Janette's voice, she asked, "Which business associates?"

"I don't know," Janette said hurriedly. They got out of the car. "But Laura—"

She'd started heading toward the door. "What?"

Again, Janette seemed about to say something, but once more she changed her mind and shook her head instead. "Nothing. Forget it, okay? Come on—you've got friends waiting."

But instead of going inside, Janette went around the side of the house toward the front to check on the kids. Laura was about to reach for the screen door when she was hit with the feeling that something was wrong. She didn't know what, or why she felt that way, but she did. The beautiful day seemed suddenly stifling, and she glanced uneasily in the direction her sister had gone. She could hear the screeching, laughing group of kids who were chasing one another out front, and she suddenly wanted to go after them, to find her own kids and let them know she was home.

Trying to ignore this inexplicable feeling of . . . of dread, she looked at the back door again. No, first she had to see Jack, then she'd find the kids. And maybe later, after things had calmed down a little, she and Janette could take a stroll up the beach. They had always been able to talk on those solitary walks, and she could no longer deny it was time for them to confide.

But now wasn't the time. She could hear the adults on the patio in front; by craning her neck, she caught a glimpse of another group playing volleyball on the sand. As she stood there and listened, the music changed on the stereo inside the house, and when an old Righteous Brothers song, about losing that loving feeling, came on, she felt herself smile. That had once been "their" song; she and Jack had spent hours dancing to it, wrapped in each other's arms, swaying to the slow beat. Thinking how much fun it would be to ask him to dance with her again, she quickly reached for the screen door and went inside. She intended to go through the kitchen and surprise him on the deck.

She surprised him, all right, but he wasn't outside. When she came in, he was there wrapped around the glistening, gloriously tanned, and long-legged body of some blonde. They were so involved in a passionate embrace that they didn't even hear her enter, not until the screen door banged, breaking their trance and her frozen, shocked stance.

They both looked up at the noise. When Jack saw her, his face paled under his tan. The girl glanced around and uttered a dismayed sound. Laura said nothing; she didn't dare. The blonde's swimsuit top had slipped; one small breast was peeking out from the fluorescent pink material. She was so stunned to see Laura that she didn't even notice, but Jack did. Glancing down, he blanched and muttered something, but she continued to stare in shock at Laura, who hadn't moved or said a word. It was obvious she knew who Laura was.

Jack decided someone had to fill the appalled silence. "Laurie, it's not what you think," he said, trying to pull the blonde's swimsuit top up again. The material caught on that hard, little nipple, and the girl was no help. She was still staring at Laura. Her eyes were very blue and very frightened.

Laura glanced away from her. "No?" she said to Jack.

"Laurie—"

She refused to talk about this in front of this . . . child. In fact, she wasn't sure she could talk about it at all. Very deliberately she reached out and hooked the tip of her finger under the girl's swimsuit strap. Effortlessly she pulled it into place. "You'd better be careful," she said. "You'll get burned that way."

Then, without another word, she left the kitchen and went upstairs. Behind her, the stereo was still playing. She caught a few of the words and stiffened.

You've lost that loving feeling . . . oooh, that loving feeling . . .

Had she? Had they? Quietly she shut the door. The sound died.

333

CHAPTER TWENTY-SIX

Jack followed her up to the bedroom, and after a terrible argument, finally on to Washington. There was no celebration, only capitulation; it wasn't the way she'd planned it, and the victory was a bitter one. But she was still in a state of shock when she heard him coming up the stairs, and she just stared at him when he burst into the bedroom.

"Laura, I can explain," he said.

She didn't want to hear it. Disgusted even by the sight of him, she asked herself if she should have guessed. When she remembered all those unexplained absences from his office, the six months in Arizona, the fact that he hated to be questioned, she wondered if this had happened before, and felt like a fool.

"I can't talk about it right now," she said.

"We have to talk about it!"

"Why?"

"Because we love each other!"

"Do we?" she asked. She still felt numb. "You can say that after what I just witnessed in the kitchen?"

His face was red, his blond hair disheveled. She hadn't noticed before, but he had new lines in his face; his eyes looked shadowed—and at the moment, frightened. She thought she should feel pleased about that, but at the moment, she felt nothing at all.

"I told you, Laurie. That was a mistake—"

"A mis*take*?" She couldn't believe that even Jack would say something so stupid. Anger started to burn its way through the ice that encased her. "What kind of *mistake* is it when I come home and find my husband groping some blonde in my own kitchen?"

"I can explain."

"So you've said. All right. Try."

Now that she'd told him to go ahead, he couldn't seem to find the words. "I . . . I don't really know what happened, Laurie," he said finally. "All of a sudden I turned around, and she was just . . . there."

She nearly laughed in derision. "What kind of fool do you think I am, Jack? Do you really mean to stand there and tell me that this girl made a play for you, and that you just happened to get caught when I walked in the door? I'm sorry, but that's not good enough."

"You don't understand," he said again, his voice rising. She told herself that if he said that once more, she'd strangle him. "If you weren't gone all the time—"

"Are you trying to blame me for this?" she said incredulously.

He reddened, turned away, muttering, "A man gets lonely, Laura. Can I help it if—"

She wasn't going to stand here and listen to this . . . this drivel. "Are you suggesting that because I'm not here to . . . to satisfy your urges, you have a *right* to make a pass at some girl?"

Stung, he whirled around. "No, I'm not saying that. I'm just saying that you're gone so much, you can't blame me if I get a little lonely."

She couldn't believe this. "I get lonely, too!"

"You, lonely?" He laughed scornfully. "Oh, but you've got your job—your career. You're in Congress now. Isn't that all you need?"

Her eyes narrowed. "Don't try to turn this around, Jack," she said. "I'm not the one who was caught groping some teenager in the kitchen. Let's not forget that."

"No, but you're the one who moved all the way across the country, leaving your family here—"

She'd had enough of this. "That wasn't my choice!" she interrupted furiously. "I wanted us all to go to Washington, but no, *you* didn't want to uproot the family. *You* didn't think the kids should be moved! Now I see why! You wanted to stay here and play games!"

"That's not the way it was!"

"Then *tell* me how it was!"

"Why do you care? So I kissed some blonde, so what? What difference does it make just as long as it doesn't hit the papers and have some negative effect on your damned career?"

She absolutely didn't know what to say to that; she looked at

335

him in total shock. "You . . . you can't mean that," she said finally.

"Well, yeah, I do mean it!" he said, his expression ugly. "You asked why I didn't want to come to Washington; well, that's one of the reasons, Laura! I'm not going to be looking over my shoulder every second, wondering if some reporter isn't following me, ready to make me look like a fool! And I'm not going to listen to one more question about how I like being married to such a beautiful, accomplished, clever, intelligent woman! Sometimes I think that if one more reporter says to me how wonderful you are, I'm going to puke!"

She was so angry, she wanted to strike him. "And sometimes I think that if I hear one more word of whining self-pity from you, *I'm* going to scream!" she shouted, enraged. "You think you're the only one who's lonely and frustrated? What about me?"

"That's the problem, isn't it? It's always about you!"

"I hadn't noticed you being so mistreated!"

"That's not the point!"

"No, the point is that while I admit I was the one who wanted to run for office, I didn't make the decision alone, remember? I asked all of you! And you said you'd support me. Some support! I have to deal with a jealous husband who punishes me by groping some . . . some *teenager* in my own house, and when I demand an explanation for such outrageous behavior, he actually tries to tell me it's my fault! Is *that* the kind of support you meant? Because if it is, you can take it and—"

"Are you through?"

She was so angry, her voice was shaking. "No, Jack, I'm not through—not by a long shot! You told me before that all I think about are facts; well, here are a few for you! Number one is that I'm not going to let you blame me—or my career, or my ambition, or my desire to do something to make a difference—for your behavior. I'm an elected official, and whether you like that or not, I still have responsibilities—to my family, to my job, to the people who elected me—"

"Yeah, and not necessarily in that order, right?"

She wasn't going to let him get away with that. "My family always came first. That was one of the reasons why I let you talk me into this ridiculous situation of me living in one part of the country while you all stay in another. But that's going to change, come fall. When I go back to Washington, I'm taking the kids with me—Mother, too, if she wants to go."

He looked at her, red-faced. It wasn't often that she lost her temper, but when she did, she could be fearsome, and he knew it. "And me?"

She nearly said it. The thought flashed through her mind that now was the moment when she should just tell him to go, to say that she felt they'd drifted so far apart, she didn't think they could ever get back together.

She couldn't say it. Despite everything, she knew that this situation wasn't the fault of one or the other, but both of them. And the truth was that she still loved him. He was her husband, the father of her children. They had built a life together before, they had planned a future. It wasn't his fault or hers that things hadn't worked out quite the way they'd planned when they were first starting out, but that didn't mean that they couldn't plan something else, or look forward to another kind of future.

But did she want to try? Glancing at him, she decided that she did. She didn't want to give up on this marriage—not yet, anyway, not until she'd given it every chance. So she said, "I'd like it if you came, too."

He looked so relieved that she knew she'd made the right decision. But she wasn't quite ready to forgive him yet, and when he tried to put his arms around her, she stiffened.

"That's okay," he said shakily, letting go. "I understand. I've been a real jerk—"

She couldn't help herself. "Yes, you have."

He knew that she had to be alone for a while, so he went to the door, but before he left, he looked back at her. "I'm sorry, Laurie," he said. "Truly I am."

She knew he was; he hated quarrels and direct confrontations; he always had. Unable to speak, she nodded.

He was still trying to make amends. "Do you want me to tell the kids about the move?"

She felt some of the ice start to melt; he really was trying. "No, we'll tell them together—later," she said.

"Okay, whatever you say." He hesitated. "Are you going to come down?"

She didn't remember until then that they had a party going on. Closing her eyes briefly, she wondered how she could pretend to all their friends that nothing had happened. Then she

337

realized she had to; she couldn't just stay up here. Wearily she nodded. "Yes. In a few minutes."

He seemed to want to say something more, but she turned away and went to the window. After a moment she heard the door close softly behind him and knew she was alone. Her shoulders slumped. She felt as though she'd been through a storm. As she listlessly went to change, she wondered how she was going to get through the rest of the day. By some miracle—and sheer strength of will—she managed.

In the end, of course, she was the one who talked to the kids. She didn't want to; by the time everyone left, it was after eight, and all she wanted to do was to fall into bed. The strain of playing hostess had taken its toll; she was exhausted. But at least she had the satisfaction of knowing she had succeeded somewhat; no one else seemed to notice her vivacity was forced except Janette, who pulled her aside before she left.

"Everything all right?"

She couldn't lie. "I'm not sure," she said. "We're going to give it a try."

"That's all you can do, sis," she said. "If you want to talk, give me a call."

"Jan—"

"What?"

"Did you know?"

Janette met her eyes. "No," she said. "I just suspected. That's why I didn't say anything."

"Would you have if—"

Janette gave her a hug. "But it didn't, did it? That's why I'm glad you came home when you did."

She left then, waving good-bye from the back of the Volvo. Laura waved in return, but she couldn't help wondering if Janette was right. Then she thrust the thought away. She wasn't going to start dwelling on things that might or might not have happened; she had to go forward from this point, or suspicion would eat away at her and destroy any chance she and Jack might have.

Then she went into the living room and saw Jack putting on a jacket. "Where are you going?" she asked. She'd thought this would be a good time to tell the kids.

"I'm sorry, Laurie, I need to be by myself for a while. I thought I'd go for a walk. Do you mind?"

She minded like hell. How could he leave? She wanted to get

338

in the car and just drive, too, but she couldn't run away; how could he? She couldn't speak; silently she shook her head, and Jack came over and kissed her forehead.

"We'll talk when I get back, okay?"

She nodded and watched him leave. Then, after surveying the party wreckage, she decided she couldn't just leave it, and started in. Her mother was in the kitchen when she came in carrying a towering pile of paper plates she had collected.

"You don't have to do that," she said. "I can get it."

"There's too much for one."

"No, it's okay, really. I know you're tired and want to get to bed."

Estelle grabbed a dishrag and started scrubbing furiously at an empty space on the counter. "What I *want* is to know why you're going to uproot this family after all."

Her lips tightened. She should have known Jack would say something to Estelle, but she wished he'd waited until morning. She just didn't feel she could cope with her mother and the kids tonight, too.

"Jack told you," she said.

Estelle stopped scrubbing. "He did. Now, Laura, I thought we discussed this!"

Telling herself she wasn't going to lose her temper, she put the paper plates in the trash. "We did. But that was before. Things have changed."

Estelle took out a sack and transferred all the plates she had just put in the garbage into that instead. "What things? How?"

Watching all this activity, she told herself to be calm. Wondering why she was bothering to explain, since her mother probably wouldn't listen to what she said anyway, she tried. "Well, for one thing, I wasn't sure I was going to run again. I didn't know if I'd like it in Washington, or more importantly, if I'd be able to do a good job."

Estelle straightened from the trash bag. "And now?"

"Now I know I can make a difference."

"You can make a difference right here!" Estelle snapped. "Really, Laura, I really don't know what's the matter with you. I don't understand all this *career* business you keep talking about. A woman's career should be her husband and children!"

They'd had this argument so many times before, she didn't even bother to reply; she knew how futile it would be, frustrating for her, maddening for her mother. But as she turned to the dishes piled high in the sink, she couldn't help wishing that Estelle would try to understand her need to do something—to *be* something—beyond wife and mother. She'd wanted to make a difference about things all her life, as long as she could remember, even as a little girl. And now she was in a position to do just that. Finally she was able to make some of her dreams come true. Her urban renewal policy; the victims' rights bill she planned to sponsor. Those were just two. Was she being so selfish for wanting to make it happen? Was she deliberately blinding herself to her family's needs so that she could serve her own? But she'd never ask any of them to give up something that meant so much to them; didn't she have a right to expect the same thing in return?

She didn't know what the answer was; maybe there wasn't one, and never had been. But she was never going to convince her mother, and so she said nothing, but started rinsing plates so she could put them in the dishwasher.

"Well?" Estelle demanded. "Don't you have anything to say?"

Slowly she looked over her shoulder. "What do you want me to say, Mom?" she asked wearily. "That I'm going to resign my office so I can stay home and be here when the kids come home from school? That I'm not going back to Washington because no one else wants to come with me? That I've been overruled by the majority?"

"I might have known you'd try to turn this around and blame everybody but yourself," Estelle said, tight-lipped. "But just listen to me, young lady. If you'd been here, where you were supposed to be, maybe your husband wouldn't have—"

She stopped, abruptly turning away to fiddle with the trash again. Laura stiffened. "Wouldn't have what, Mother?" she asked. *"Wouldn't have what?"*

But Estelle didn't answer. Jars of condiments from the picnic were still open on the counter, and she started putting those away, avoiding her eyes. Laura watched for a moment, then she reached out a hand and grasped Estelle's arm, forcing her to look her in the eye.

"You knew, didn't you?" she said. "You *knew* Jack was fooling around! Why didn't you tell me?"

Estelle looked at her for a long moment, then she moved away. Bowls of pickles and olives were scattered around; she reached for the plastic jars and started putting those away, too.

"Mom, answer me!"

Her voice cracked like a shot across the silent kitchen, and Estelle whirled around. Her mouth tight, she said, "I didn't know anything for sure. I just . . . guessed."

She couldn't believe this was happening. Groping for a chair, she sank into it, her eyes on her mother's face. "But you suspected," she whispered. "Why didn't you say something?"

Estelle turned away, toward the sink again, her back stiff and straight. "Because it wasn't any of my business," she muttered. "I didn't think I should interfere."

"Interfere!" She couldn't believe her ears. "You've made your feelings clear about everything that's ever gone on around here!"

"That was different. I felt this was between Jack and you."

"But . . . but—" She was stammering, feeling dizzy. She wanted to get up, rush from the room. But she couldn't move; she could only stare at her mother in total shock. Estelle saw her disbelieving expression and looked angry.

"If you'd been here, you would have known—or guessed," she said. "It wasn't my place to run to you with tales; it was yours to stay home, where you belonged."

Still stunned, she managed to shake her head. "Oh, no," she said slowly. "You're not going to blame me for this. You're not going to tell me that Jack was *lonely*—" She nearly choked on the word, made herself go on. "Because *I* was lonely, too, in Washington without my family, and I didn't . . . I didn't—"

But you wanted to.

The insidious little voice hissed like a serpent from the back of her mind, and just for a second, she saw Douglas's face behind her eyes, the strong features, so different from Jack's, the dark hair threaded with silver, the imposing presence . . . the aura. She swayed. Was she so different from Jack? Was the committing of the act more reprehensible than the coveting of it? Maybe, unlike Jack, she'd just never had the opportunity.

No! That wasn't true; she knew it. She and Douglas had had many opportunities—chances they'd never taken. And they had wanted to; oh, they had wanted to. There had been times when she had wanted him so badly that she would have done anything, and she knew he felt the same way, too.

Above reproach . . .

And they were, she thought fiercely. Always, always, they had denied the attraction that had leaped like a living thing be-

341

tween them almost from the first moment they'd met; never had they succumbed.

Above reproach . . .

Her mouth twisting, she looked down at her clenched hands. It was a moment before she had the strength to will Douglas's face away and look up at her mother.

"I'm not going to discuss this anymore, Mother," she said tersely. "Jack and I have talked about it, and he's agreed that the best thing for our family is to move to Washington—for the year, at least. We'll rent the house and come home during recess. That's the way it's going to be. I'm sorry if you don't understand."

Her expression bitter, Estelle grabbed her dish towel again. "Oh, I understand," she said. "And don't think I didn't know it would come to this. As soon as you don't need me anymore, you're off without a thought. Well, I suppose Janette can put me up for a while, until I get an apartment of my own."

Still feeling as though she were reeling, Laura tried to get a handle on this new twist. Oh, it was so tempting to say that was fine with her, to agree that it would be better for both of them if they didn't live under the same roof. But then, almost against her will, she thought of all her mother had done for her over the years: being here, helping with the children, baby-sitting, meals—the list was endless. Thinking of that, she felt ashamed. She couldn't repay all that by volunteering to help her mother find an apartment somewhere; she couldn't.

Taking a deep breath, she committed herself. "Don't be silly, Mother," she said, wondering if she knew what she was doing at all. "I'll understand if you don't want to come with us, but we'd love to have you."

Slowly Estelle turned. "Do you mean that?"

This was her last chance. But one look at the almost pitiful relief in her mother's eyes decided her. "Yes, I mean it," she said, and even managed a faint, tense smile. "I'm sure that if we pool all our resources, we'll be able to find a house that's big enough for all of us."

The gratifying moment passed as quickly as it came. Glancing down at the dish towel she held, Estelle said, "Oh, well, I wouldn't want to put you out. I can always sleep on the couch."

Seeking strength, Laura stood. This was her mother at her most exasperating, and she counted to ten before she answered.

342

"I'm sure that won't be necessary," she said, and went to tell the kids.

Her faint hope that they were asleep by now was dashed when she heard the murmur of the TV from behind Peter's bedroom door, and steeling herself, she knocked.

"Who is it?"

Wondering if this was going to be more difficult than she anticipated, she said lightly, "How many people could it be, Peter? This is your mother. May I come in?"

"Yeah, sure—just a minute."

There was the sound of hurried rustling, and it took him a minute to open the door. Intending to tease him, she said, "What were you hiding?"

"Nothing," he said quickly, and flushed to the roots of his hair. She'd thought until then that he was doing something harmless like getting into his pajamas, but when she saw his embarrassment, she wondered if she was mistaken.

"Peter?"

He turned away, striding with long, gangling legs to the bed, where he threw himself down with his back to her. "What did you want, Mom?"

His voice was muffled by the pillow he'd grabbed and pulled under his chin; he was lying on his stomach, away from her, and she couldn't see his face. Resignedly she went to him.

"I wanted to talk to you for a minute."

Still he didn't look at her. "What about?"

Now that the moment was here, she didn't quite know how to begin. She didn't know what his reaction would be to the intended move, and she sat down gingerly on the edge of the bed. He immediately moved away, but she told herself to ignore it. There had been a time when he would snuggle into her arms, but that had been long ago. He was nearly an unbelievable fifteen now; he would soon be a man. Already he was as tall as she was, and his good looks had grown along with his body this year. She'd seen the girls looking at him at the beach today, and felt a pang. Was it that time already? Where had the years gone?

That reminded her of why she was here, and she felt her way carefully. He was entering high school this year, and because she was sure he'd want to stay with his friends, she knew this move would be difficult for him.

"Peter, how would you feel about moving to Washington?" she said, deciding just to plunge in.

"You mean it?"

Surprised, she nodded. "Yes, of course."

"Fine by me," he said, his eyes, so like his father's, beginning to glow. She watched in amazement. "A new school and everything. When can we leave?"

"Well, I—" She hadn't thought it would be this easy, and she said cautiously, "You seem happy about it. I didn't think you would be."

He immediately drew back, the sparkle going out of his eyes, his expression turning a little surly instead. "Why?"

Leave it alone, a little voice whispered, but she couldn't. "Well, you've had the same group of friends for years, and I thought you were looking forward to going to the high school with everybody else."

"That school's a dump, and all the kids are dorks."

She couldn't hide her astonishment. He'd never talked about the new school or his friends like this before, and she felt at a loss. Cautiously she asked, "Why do you say that?"

"Because they are, that's why," he said, turning his back again. "Look, Mom, I don't want to talk about it, okay? Besides, it doesn't matter. I won't be going to that school if we're moving to Washington." He looked over his shoulder. "What school will I be going to there? Do they have acting classes? Or an art department?"

She blinked. Acting classes? Art? When did that start? Just what *had* she been missing here? The last time they'd talked— only last month when she'd come home for the weekend—he'd told her he wanted to be an architect.

"Well, I don't know," she said. "Your father and I just discussed moving today; we haven't really talked about schools yet."

He seemed tense. "What if I wanted to major in theater art? Or drama?" he asked. "What would you say about that?"

She didn't know what to say, but only because she was so surprised. "Well, I . . . I wouldn't say anything," she said. "Your father and I want you to be happy, no matter what you do."

He looked at her intently. "Do you mean that?"

Wondering if more was going on here than she realized, she said, "You know I do."

He seemed to want to say more, but finally he just nodded. She was about to pursue it when he leaned forward suddenly and gave her a quick kiss on the cheek. "Thanks, Mom," he said, and smiled.

Her instincts told her definitely this was the time to leave it alone, so when she wanted to gather him in her arms and protect him from whatever might be wrong, she smoothed his hair back from his forehead and bent to give him a kiss, too.

"Aw, Mom," he said, but she just smiled, too.

"Mother's prerogative," she said, and went to face his sister.

Andrea's bedroom was just next door, and she was raising her hand to knock when she heard her daughter talking to someone. Since it was after eleven, and Andy had no business on the phone at this late hour, she flung the door open instead. Andrea was just slamming the phone down. Glancing up, she burst into tears.

Thinking this definitely was not going to go as well as the talk with Peter, she went and sat on the bed. "What's the matter, honey?" she asked. Now was not the time to take her daughter to task for being on the phone so late.

"Nothing . . . everything!" Andrea wailed. "I hate that Randy. I just hate him!"

Randy was the current boyfriend; she knew that much. She'd seen them together today on the beach. Relieved that it seemed to be nothing more than a boy-girl spat, she looked at her thirteen-year-old daughter. Andrea was sitting cross-legged on the bed, looking as tragic as only teenage girls can do. Unlike her friends, who were always slavishly devoted to the latest teen styles, Andrea made her own. Disdaining the current short-cropped hair, she'd allowed her own dark tresses to grow long, and layered bangs framed huge green eyes. She'd also developed a nice little figure these past few months, and now looked a few years older than she actually was. Remembering how shocked she'd been at the skimpy string bikini Andrea had been wearing on the beach, and her own mental note to talk to her daughter about it, she took another look at that tragic face and decided now wasn't the time for that, either.

"You want to talk about it?" she asked carefully.

"I told you, I *hate* Randy! I'm never speaking to him again! He wants to break up and start seeing Mariane Potts. Mariane *Potts*! Can you imagine anything so gross? All I can say is that they deserve each other!"

And with that, she threw herself down and began sobbing into the pillow.

Hiding a smile at all this drama, Laura reached out a hand and stroked her daughter's hair. She remembered all too well how critical things could be at this age, and she said, "Life's the pits sometimes, isn't it?"

Andrea stopped carrying on long enough to peer up at her. "How do you know?"

This time she did smile. "I might be old to you, but I remember how things like this hurt."

Looking surprised, Andrea sat up. "You do?" She shook her head. "No, not you."

"Oh, yes—me. There was one boy in seventh grade, in fact, I've never forgotten. His name was Tom Benjamin, and when he stopped looking my way and started eyeing Janet Soren, I thought I'd die."

Andrea's eyes were wide. "What did you do?"

"I cried," she said matter-of-factly. "Then I told myself they deserved each other and started noticing Jimmy Arvidson."

"And he was just as good?"

Laura smiled. "Better."

Andrea looked hopeful for a moment, then she slumped. "But that won't happen to me. I know all the guys in my class, and I don't like any of them."

Now was her chance. Carefully she said, "Maybe things would change if you went to a new school."

"Fat chance of that. You and Dad would never let me transfer."

"Oh, I don't know. You might find one you like in Washington."

Andrea's eyes widened. "Washington! Are we going to move there?"

"Well, your father and I are discussing it," Laura said, mentally crossing her fingers. "What do you think?"

"I think it would be great!"

"Are you sure? You'd have to leave all your friends—"

"Yes, but think of the new boys I'll meet. Oh, Mom, this is wonderful! A whole new chance. When are we going?"

Laura escaped, marveling at the resiliency of children. Remembering how concerned she'd been, how reluctant she was to force this move, she thought that if she'd known it would turn out like this, she would have insisted on the move long ago. She wished she had—at least where Peter and Andrea were concerned. She was glad it had worked out so well; she missed them terribly, never more than when she remembered times like this.

And Jack?

Suddenly she felt weary again. She didn't know whether to believe him or not. She'd accused him of sleeping with that blonde—with how many others—but he denied everything. It was a mistake, he'd tearfully insisted; something that would never, ever, happen again. Did she believe him? She wanted to; for all their sakes, she wanted to.

But she couldn't help notice as she climbed into bed that his side was still empty. Refusing to allow herself to wonder where he had gone, and what he was doing, she tried to sleep. But she knew that even if they managed somehow to work things out, it would be a long time—if ever—before she trusted him again.

CHAPTER TWENTY-SEVEN

Lenore looked down the long, shining length of the cherry-wood table in the dining room at Deer Hollow and gestured to one of the maids who was standing against the wall. "Marie," she said irritably, "move that centerpiece. I can't see anything."

The huge, heavy floral centerpiece, one of a half dozen scattered daily about the house, was transferred instantly to the sideboard.

"Ah, that's much better," Lenore said. "More wine, Cal?"

The Speaker shook his head. "You don't have to ply me with wine, Lenore. I know what you want. I'm just not sure I'm going to tell you."

"Don't play games with me, Cal," she snapped back. "We know each other too well for that. If you don't want to tell me what I want to know, say so. I can always get the information elsewhere."

"So you can," he agreed calmly. "But it probably won't be as accurate."

She couldn't argue that. "Well, then?"

They looked at each other for a moment, then, as if struck by some private joke, they laughed. The third person at the table, Hugh Redmond, glanced from one to the other and laughed, too. Since he wasn't quite sure what he was laughing about, he tried not to look as ill at ease as he felt, but sat back, longing for his pipe.

If the Speaker noticed Hugh's unhappy expression, he made no mention. His eyes on Lenore, he shook his head ruefully. It was hard to refuse her anything, and he said, "All right. What do you want to know?"

Dismissing her servants with a wave of her hand, she sat forward. "I want you to tell me everything you know about this junior congresswoman who's causing such a stir," she said.

Cal raised an eyebrow. "Ah, Laura Devlin, you mean."

348

Lenore frowned. "You know damned well who I mean, Cal. She's been in the news for months now, first with those drug company hearings, then with her stand on education, and now with this damned urban renewal policy she started lobbying this fall. Sometimes I think if I read or hear one more word about her, I'm going to scream."

"I don't think the congresswoman is your real problem," Cal said mildly. "Aren't you really worried about Douglas Rhodes?"

She sat back, toying with her champagne. Damn Caleb; she never had been able to fool him. Now that the national convention was on the horizon, she wanted to know what the feeling was about this Douglas Rhodes. She'd been hearing rumors, all right; she knew how popular this Rhodes fellow was getting to be. Now she wondered if he could snatch the nomination and leave Hugh standing there with his mouth open. Caleb had privately agreed with her that it was possible, but he didn't think it would happen. She knew that Hugh was the party choice—at least among the top echelon—and she'd never cared for Rhodes. Unlike Hugh, he didn't seem to fully appreciate just what she could do for him. That was why she'd invited them both here tonight, especially Cal. She'd had an idea some time ago, and she wanted their reaction. She respected Cal's judgment even if she didn't always take his advice, and after all this maneuvering the past six years to get Hugh into place, she wanted to do her part to make sure there weren't any last-minute hitches. In addition, she wanted to find out just how likely a Rhodes-Devlin ticket might be.

Her lips tightened at the thought of that independent duo. She'd been prepared to tolerate Laura—until she discovered that the congresswoman didn't know her place, either. Oh, it wasn't like the old days, when everyone deferred to her; now no one seemed to respect the Deering-Kirk name, and before she retired, she intended to remind them all just how important her family was, and had been. She'd show those two what a power she was; she just had to figure out a way to do it.

"Why the curiosity about Laura Devlin?" Cal asked just then. He smiled. "Are you wondering about her suitability as a candidate—or about her qualifications?"

Annoyed that he could read her so well, she snapped, "One of the things I've always admired about you, Cal, is your grasp. Of course I'm wondering about her. Isn't everybody? Aren't you?"

"I'm not!" Hugh said, looking horrified.

The Speaker ignored him. "She's relatively inexperienced, I grant you. But she certainly has a grasp."

Hugh turned to look in shock at him. "If you're referring to that urban renewal policy of hers—!" he sputtered.

Cal seemed to remember he was there. "I take it you don't agree?"

"Agree to what? Are you seriously thinking about having a woman on the ticket?"

"It's a possibility."

So! Lenore thought: she'd been right. Not sure how she felt about that, she turned to Hugh. She wanted to know what he thought. "Do you have a problem with that?"

Redmond looked appalled. "Yes, as a matter of fact, I do! It won't work; it's been tried before—with disastrous consequences!"

"Yes, but that was a different time, and I might add, a very different candidate."

Hugh persisted. "Times have changed," he said, "but people haven't. I don't think the country is ready to elect a woman."

"Perhaps you're just not ready to accept the idea," Lenore said. She turned to the Speaker. "Are you?"

"I don't know. As I said, it's an intriguing notion."

"It's not that I object to a woman per se," Hugh said hastily. "It's just that I'm not sure how well it would be perceived in other parts of the world—"

"Those parts who had an Indira Gandhi," Cal said innocently, "or a Margaret Thatcher, or a Corazon Aquino, for instance?"

Hugh flushed. "I know where you're heading with that, Mr. Speaker," he said, stubbornly plowing on, "but the fact remains that we as a country have very few women in high office. That's not my doing; it's an electorate decision. And from that, it's clear to me that a woman on the ticket at this time would be a disaster."

Cal looked bored. "Perhaps this discussion is a little premature," he said dismissively.

Lenore wasn't so sure, especially when she saw his thoughtful expression. So she decided after her guests had gone to reopen her investigation of Laura Devlin. There'd been that business in Los Angeles, for instance, she remembered, and recalled that

Dawn had done a creditable job where Douglas Rhodes was concerned. Yes, she'd place a call. It never hurt to be prepared.

When the phone rang, Dawn was sound asleep, sprawled diagonally across the bed, her face buried in the pillows, one leg flung over the edge of the mattress. She'd had a hard night, and the jangling of the phone struck a nerve. Without opening her eyes, she reached for the satin comforter and pulled it over her head. It was dark in the room, the draperies pulled tight.

When the phone rang again, and again, she realized from some depth of unconsciousness that she hadn't turned on her answering machine. She groaned. Now if she didn't answer, it would ring all night. Cursing, she reached out, knocked over the empty highball glass that she'd left on the bedside table after falling into bed, and flailed her hand around, seeking the damned phone. Grabbing the receiver, she pulled it under the covers and mumbled a hello.

"Good morning," a voice she recognized very well said briskly. "I didn't wake you, did I?"

"What do you want, Lenore?" she muttered.

"I want you awake. I've got something important to tell you."

She didn't care what Lenore had to say; now that she'd been interrupted from a drugged sleep, she realized how hung over she was, and she winced. "Then call back," she said. "What the hell time is it, anyway?"

"It's just on six."

"In the *morning*?"

"Yes, in the morning," Lenore said crisply. "Now listen to me, Dawn—are you awake?"

She was now. Holding on to her head, she rolled over and tried to sit up. "This better be good," she muttered. "If it's six o'clock, I just got to bed two hours ago."

"Your life-style is your concern," Lenore replied. "I'm calling because I have something I want you to do."

She forced her eyes open. Mercifully the bedroom was still dark, and she groped toward the other side of the bed. Good. He'd gone, whatever his name was. She didn't remember him leaving, but then, she hardly remembered where she'd picked him up. The only thing she did remember was protecting herself. She'd been drunk, but not so blitzed that she hadn't taken precautions. Even so, no more of that. She had to be careful about that now; the way things were these days, God only knew what you could catch from strangers.

But last night had been a celebration, so she'd had an excuse. It wasn't every day she sold something to a woman's magazine, even if it was a pulp, but someone had finally picked up her story on Douglas Rhodes. About time; it was a good piece of work, and God only knew she deserved something like this for following St. Douglas around for months, hoping to pick up some dirt for Lenore. She'd begun to think that the man was so squeaky clean that no one would want to read about him, but now that he was being talked about as a presidential candidate, all those feminine hearts out there were starting to flutter. So she'd put together a story from the bits and pieces she'd already done for *The Eye* and had sent it off. When she'd got an acceptance, she'd immediately made plans to celebrate.

The only problem was that she didn't have anybody to celebrate with. So she'd gone down to the local watering hole and picked someone. Geoff something; that was it. One of those yuppie lawyers who talked only about themselves, but who was good-looking and well dressed and who didn't mind spending money. All she'd wanted was a warm body anyway, just someone to clink a toast with and pretend for an evening that she wasn't alone.

"Dawn, are you still there?"

"Yeah, I guess," she said, and peered carefully over the side of the bed. She needed a little hair of the dog, but she saw by the empty bourbon bottle rolling around down there that she and Geoff had killed that one, too. She didn't remember switching from champagne to bourbon, but they must have. Thinking she'd sell both body and soul if someone appeared at the bedroom door just now with a Bloody Mary, she sat cautiously back. "What do you want, Lenore?"

"I want you to get to know Laura Devlin."

She sighed. "Are you into torture, Lenore? Not Miss Goody Two-shoes!"

"The same."

"But why?" she complained. "I thought we already decided she wasn't worth the trouble."

"I've changed my mind."

She didn't want to do this; she'd already checked out the Devlin-Rhodes connection and learned to her displeasure that there wasn't one. No one knew *anything* about those two, and she could only speculate so much in print. Barnaby was getting trepidations these days about lawsuits, after the one he'd almost lost against the rock star.

"Mind telling me why?"

"I've got plans."

"You always have plans," she said, spying her cigarettes lying on the bedside table. She reached for one, lit it. It tasted terrible, but she didn't put it out.

"Well?"

Knowing Lenore wasn't going to let this go, she took an exasperated drag off the cigarette. "All right! But do you mind telling me what I'm supposed to be looking for? The fact that she cheated on her multiplication tables in third grade? Or threw sand at someone in kindergarten?"

"You really are tiresome when you're suffering a hangover," Lenore said. "If I wanted to know her good qualities, all I'd have to do is ask. Naturally we're looking for a weak spot."

"I can tell you that right now."

Lenore's voice sharpened. "What?"

"Her husband."

"Where did you get that information?"

"In L.A., when I was snooping around."

"And?"

"And the husband is a real jerk—booze and women, not necessarily in that order."

"Are you sure about this?"

She was annoyed. "I go to a lot of parties, remember?"

There was a short silence; she could almost hear the wheels turning. Then Lenore said, "How trite. But how interesting. This does put a different light on things."

Wondering how it could, Dawn yawned. "It does?"

"I would appreciate it if you would at least *try* to follow the line of thought, dear."

Stung, she snapped, "That might be a little easier for me to do if you would tell me what it is!"

"I thought that would be obvious, especially to you."

She didn't like the sound of that, and she said cautiously, "Maybe you'd better spell it out."

"Must I?" Lenore said with an elaborate sigh. "All right, then, I've seen Mr. Devlin—Jack is his name, isn't it?—and he's a handsome man."

Now she was sure she didn't like the sound of this. "Yeah, so?"

"So . . . how would you like to get to know him better?"

"How *much* better?"

"I have to tell *you*?" Lenore retorted. "Weren't you the one who told me that lovers make the best confidants?"

"No," Dawn said. "I wasn't."

"Well, no matter. I'm willing to bet that you've found that to be true. I'm sure this case will be no exception."

"Oh, no," Dawn said. "If you want me to—"

"I do."

"Now, wait a minute. That wasn't part of the deal!"

Lenore's voice was silky. "You've been so cooperative in the past, my dear."

"But this is different!"

"I'll make it worth your while."

As Lenore had expected, she had to think about that. Fuming, she took one drag after another off the cigarette, considering her options. The sun was coming up now, peeking between the heavy silk curtains, and in the growing light, she looked around the luxurious bedroom and knew she couldn't refuse. Lenore was the goose that kept handing out the golden eggs, and until she'd gotten what she wanted, she couldn't afford to offend the old bitch.

"Since you're pimping for me now," she said finally, her voice as cold as she dared, "you're going to have to pay me a lot more if you expect me to turn tricks."

"But my dear," Lenore said. "Don't you realize you already do?"

Furious, she smashed down the phone. But she called back several weeks later with the information, just as Lenore had known she would. This time, though, as Chester went through the act of seeing if his mistress was at home, she lounged at one end of her couch, examining her fingernails, feeling very pleased with herself. She hadn't been sure just how difficult it would be to get what Lenore had wanted, but Jack Devlin had been a pushover. A drunken confession from him, a call to someone else, and *voilà*! The thing was done. She could hardly wait to hear Lenore's response.

For once, Lenore actually came to the phone. Dawn barely contained her glee. The old witch must really want this information to dispense with the phone games, so obviously it was more valuable than she had suspected. Clearly it was time to up the ante.

"I've got something for you, Lenore," she said. "But this time you're going to pay for it."

"I see," Lenore said, unshakable as ever. "Just what did you have in mind?"

She examined her manicure. "Oh, I thought a job at the *Post*, for starters," she said.

There was a silence. Then, to her delight, Lenore said, "I'll see what I can do—providing, of course, your information is useful."

"Oh, it'll be useful," she said, and laughed. She hadn't expected Lenore to give in this easily, especially when her assignment had been so simple. Jack Devlin had been such a whiner, she thought; listening to him, you'd think he was the only misunderstood husband in the world. Remembering how self-pitying he'd been, she sneered. She should have told him to talk to Bud. Now, *there* was a misunderstood, abused husband.

But she didn't want to think of Bud, whom she had abandoned in another world, another life, and she hastily gathered her thoughts. "Well, how about it, Lenore?" she said. "Is one hand going to rub the other this time, or what?"

"You have such a way of putting things, dear. Are you going to give me the information or not?"

"Are you going to call the *Post*?"

An elaborate sigh. "All right. Consider it done. Now, what did you have to tell me?"

"One name, the Beverly Hills Hotel," Dawn said, and examined the nails on the other hand. "It was about six years ago, at a fund-raiser for Jim Duluth. A lot of shenanigans that night, people falling into the swimming pool, senators and public defenders getting together, that sort of thing. Find the assistant manager who took the call for our Ms. Devlin that night. A conversation with him might be very interesting."

There was a silence. "I see," Lenore said. "Anything else?"

"You don't need anything else, Lenore," Dawn said, and broke the connection.

At Deer Hollow Farm, Lenore hung up the phone with a thoughtful expression. She was so busy exploring possibilities that she almost forgot Dawn had had the audacity to hang up on her. Almost. As always, Chester was standing by waiting for

355

instructions, and she smiled maliciously as she gave them to him.

"Call Billy Hendrix at the *Post*, please. I'd like him to hire a new stringer by the name of Dawn Van Doren."

The normally impassive Chester looked at her in surprise. "Her information was valuable, then?"

Drumming her fingers on the arm of her chair, she looked thoughtful again. "Yes, I think it could be," she mused, and then glanced up, sealing Dawn's future with a few idle words. "Oh, and ask Billy to give Miss Van Doren enough rope to hang herself. By that time, she will have outlived her usefulness and we'll be done with her once and for all."

"I do hope so, Mrs. Deering-Kirk," Chester said. "Miss Van Doren has been . . . difficult."

"Yes," Lenore said with a smile. "But not anymore."

Chester smiled, too. "I see. Will there be anything else?"

"Yes. Book another flight to Los Angeles. You're going to vacation for a few days at the Beverly Hills Hotel. There's a certain man I want you to see."

CHAPTER TWENTY-EIGHT

An invitation to the White House was always a momentous event, and the one Douglas received asking him to attend a dinner honoring the French minister of culture was no exception. The invitation itself was beautiful enough to frame, with the seal of the United States embossed in gold, and the details in engraved script. The stock was thick; it felt official just holding it in his hand. An admit card was enclosed, to be presented to the sentry at the gate, and there was also a small card indicating dress. Tonight it was black tie, and as he escorted Sarah to the limousine he'd hired for the evening, he glanced at his watch. There was no such thing as being "fashionably late" to a White House function; everyone, from State Department and foreign dignitaries to the most junior of Congressmen, arrived practically en masse and departed at some later signal almost in a group. He wanted to be on time.

"Relax, Douglas, we'll be there along with everyone else," Sarah said once they were on their way. "Arriving like lemmings, herded into a reception line and then into the dining room. I hope we're not having chicken tonight. I hate chicken."

He laughed. "Didn't you send a dozen complimentary sides of beef to the chef," he teased, "just to make sure?"

"I would have, if I'd thought of it," she retorted, leaning back wearily against the plush upholstery. She looked tired as they pulled away, and when the passing lights illuminated her face, he was alarmed at how fragile she looked. He wondered if she should have come.

But there was no talking to Sarah—especially about age or the possibility that she might slow down a little because of it. She was outraged at any suggestion she should take it easy, especially with the national convention coming up. He was tired himself; getting through the primaries was more exhausting than he'd dreamed possible. Sometimes he felt it was all one big blur.

But when he thought he might actually get the nomination, due in large part to her untiring support, he reached out and put his hand over hers.

"Long day?" he said softly.

"No more than any other, I guess," she said, smiling at him. "I had a letter from a young bride today who wrote to say that since we're giving men's names to hurricanes now, she wanted the first one of the year named after her husband."

He laughed again. "How did you reply?"

"I very politely gave her the address of the Weather Bureau and asked her to write to them. And how was your day?"

It was one of the few these days that he'd spent in the office. "I had a request from one city government for a submarine. Or, failing that, a battleship—either to be used as memorials in the town square."

"And you said . . . ?"

He grinned. "I told them we didn't have either item in stock, and suggested they might consider something a little less . . . cumbersome."

She shook her head. "What next?"

"God only knows."

They laughed, and then turned quiet again, each occupied with his own thoughts. As the limo glided through streets glistening with an earlier rainfall, he glanced out the window, and thought that Washington had never seemed so alive to him, so humming with power. The idea that he might actually take the nomination at the national convention a few months hence seemed staggering; if he weren't so exhausted from campaigning, he knew he would have been even more awed. It was like a dream.

And it might still be, he told himself firmly. A lot could happen over the next months; he knew how quickly things could change—especially here. He'd been the focus of so much publicity this past year: first with those hearings on bribery and lobby abuse, then because of his family. The scandal about Alpha-Techtronica had catapulted him to national news again, and it seemed after that he couldn't do anything wrong. He didn't know when the whispers had started about his suitability as a candidate; one day he was simply a senator from Arizona; the next, his name was being linked with the presidency. He still couldn't believe it. Sarah seemed convinced he could do it; so were many others. Everywhere he turned these days he received outpourings of support and encouragement, and he supposed it could happen. The question was: did he want it to? He must. Otherwise he'd step aside and leave the field open for Hugh Redmond, who obviously coveted the presidency with every fiber of his being.

He wished he were as sure as Hugh. He'd spent so many anxious hours trying to find the answer to that question; he'd endured all those sleepless nights. Maybe what it came down to was that he just didn't feel he deserved it. If he'd failed his family so badly, was he fit to run the country? At times he was convinced he was; at others, he wasn't so sure. Maybe all candidates had their doubts; he didn't know. He only knew he had them, and that made him even more doubtful.

And then there was Laura. Whispers had been following her for weeks now, about her suitability as a vice-presidential candidate, and while he'd stayed mum on the subject, the thought scared the hell out of him. Not because she wasn't qualified, he thought hastily; it wasn't that. In her two terms here, she'd generated enormous respect—not to mention the same publicity that seemed to follow him. She was always in the news now; if not about her urban policy, which was getting such wide review, then for her stand on victims' rights, and another cause, abuse of the young and the elderly. Crime was also on her agenda—a natural progression from her days as a public defender as well as a deputy district attorney. And she'd championed legislation on the environment, the arms race, the budget—all normally "women's issues" that, because of her powerful personality and quick grasp, she'd made everyone's concern. Her most recent coup had been her appointment to the powerful House Ways and Means Committee, and she had argued successfully for the reinstatement of the National Advisory Council on Women. She was everywhere, it seemed, and it was obvious that politics was her natural milieu. He was so proud of her that sometimes it took his breath away.

And that was the trouble. The more she accomplished, the more in love he was with her. She dazzled him, and there were times he almost didn't trust himself alone with her; he couldn't be sure what he might say—or do. With the exception of Sarah, perhaps, and a few others, he'd never met anyone he admired or respected more.

Unhappily he stared out the window. If that's all there were to it, he wouldn't have a problem. But his feelings for Laura went far deeper than admiration or respect; he had been attracted to her from that first moment they'd met.

If things had been different, he thought, closing his eyes against a familiar stab of pain. *If only things had been different.*

But things weren't different, he told himself fiercely. Even if Laura were free, he couldn't abandon Marcella—not now, or ever. It didn't matter that her doctors had told him again and again that her condition wasn't his fault, that he hadn't been responsible, that nothing he had done or should have done could have prevented it; he knew that wasn't true. Marcella blamed him for Rob, he knew, and on those days when he was at his lowest ebb, when despite his frantic activity, his busyness, his preoccupation with campaigning or work or whatever else he had to do, he thought of Rob and knew Marcella was right to blame him. It had been his fault in a way, and nothing—no amount of wishful thinking, or assurances by doctors, or even Sarah's occasional pep talks—could change that. His wife's condition was his punishment for abandoning his son, and his penance was his never-to-be-fulfilled yearning for Laura.

"You seem deep in thought, Douglas."

At Sarah's quiet observation, he turned from the window. He couldn't lie to her, so he said, "I was thinking about Laura."

Sarah searched his face for a moment before she sat back with a sigh. "Yes," she murmured. "Laura."

They hadn't talked about this new ground-swell movement for Laura yet, and he was glad the chance had come up. He wanted her opinion; maybe it would help him form his own. He couldn't think of Laura calmly or rationally; there were times he wondered if he could ever be objective about her.

But it seemed Sarah wasn't thinking about Laura's suitability as a candidate—or at least not directly. "You're in love with her, aren't you, Douglas?"

He didn't know what to say. Had he been that transparent? Even in the darkness of the car, he felt embarrassed. He wondered who else knew.

Sarah put a hand on his tight arm. "I see I've shocked you," she said softly. "I'm sorry. I make it a practice not to pry—or try. Perhaps I shouldn't have said anything. You're entitled to your privacy, but—" she looked at him "—I think you'd better be prepared for such intrusions."

Painfully he said, "I didn't realize it was so obvious."

"Not to anyone else, I think. But to me . . . yes."

Until now he'd thought he'd dissembled so well. "God, this is terrible," he muttered.

"It's not as bad as you think. You see, I know you very well—or flatter myself that I do. And when the three of us have been together . . . well, there was something in your eyes. . . ."

"I . . . I don't know what to say."

"You don't have to say anything. I can't blame you. I don't think anyone could. Laura Devlin is a beautiful woman."

"Yes," he said, his voice low. "She is."

"And given your situation . . ." She left it at that and went on. "Anyway, she is being considered very seriously as vice-presidential material, Douglas, and we have to know how you feel about that."

"I don't know," he said, sighing heavily. "I just don't know."

"Then maybe you'd better find out."

He nodded and glanced somberly away. The silence stretched on, but he didn't notice; he was too deep in thought. Sarah was right; he had to get this under control. He tried picturing the long months ahead if he did get the nomination and decided to choose Laura as his running mate, but he couldn't do it. Even with both of them campaigning, there would still be long hours together, endless meetings, an exhausting strain. Even if he got through all that, what would happen then? Could he guard every word, every gesture? He would have to be a saint or a superman, and he was neither; he was only a man in love with a woman who wasn't his wife. It was so trite, but oh, so painfully true.

And was she in love with him, too? There were times when he knew she loved him, when he caught a certain look in her eyes, or felt something in the light touch of her hand. The attraction between them couldn't be denied, but he felt she was stronger than he was, and he wondered if his desire to hold her, to be with her, to steal just one moment with her, would be their undoing. If he was nominated, could he in conscience ask her to share the ticket, knowing he wanted her for a lover first, before he needed her as a partner?

And if they won?

But they would; he could feel it; he could sense it. He knew they could win if they ran. But at what cost? Was it worth so much?

Great ambition requires great sacrifice, and those who achieve it must be above reproach.

He couldn't remember where he had heard that, or who might

361

have told him, but he knew it was true. Laura was capable of such sacrifice, but was he? He realized then that Sarah was quietly watching him, and he turned to her.

"I'll think about it," he said.

She stared at him for a long moment, her eyes searching his face. Finally she nodded. "All right, then," she said, and seemed satisfied.

The car stopped just then, and he realized they had arrived. As they left the limousine and joined the line that had already formed, he was glad of the distraction. As they seemed to do lately, his thoughts had led him in circles; it would be a relief to think of something else. As he and Sarah approached a military aide who handed them a table number from a silver bowl he held, she glanced up at him and smiled. She seemed relieved, too.

There wasn't time for more discussion. They followed the crowd to the East Room, where another line had formed. A second aide announced each guest, and as he and Sarah passed through, they joined famous people from the world of the theater and literature and politics in the reception line. The president stood at the head with the French minister and his wife and other dignitaries; he looked resplendent with his silver hair and black tie. Beside him, the first lady looked tiny and very elegant in a long gown of glittering gold.

But it was Laura who caught his glance and made him catch his breath; she was ahead of him in the line, just being greeted by the president. He couldn't take his eyes off her. Every woman in the room paled in comparison; he'd never seen her look so beautiful. She was wearing a long, sheathlike gown of some sparkling green material that had a sequin and beaded floral spray design beaded down one shoulder, and her hair was up for the occasion. Twists of diamonds glinted in her ears. She wore no other ornamentation, but to Douglas, she didn't need it. In his opinion, she was by far the most lovely woman here.

As though she felt his gaze on her, she turned; their glances met. Even from this distance, he saw those beautiful eyes widen, and he had to force himself to give a slight nod. She smiled in return, and then her husband said something to her, and she looked at him. The line moved along, and she was hidden from view. Trying not to feel bereft, he concentrated on playing the perfect guest the rest of the evening, but because he didn't dare go up and talk to her openly, the night was a strain, and he couldn't wait until he and Sarah could leave again.

Finally, dinner over, along with what seemed to be an interminable musical program given in honor of the French minister, they were free to go to the marble foyer to mingle, sip champagne, and listen to the Air Force Strolling Strings. By this time, he was feeling claustrophobic, and wondering how he could slip out and get some air, when he felt a stir. He looked around, and there was the president.

"Mr. President," he said, bowing slightly.

"Nice to see you again, Douglas," the president said. "Do you have a moment?"

Amused, he answered, "I think I can find one or two—for you."

The president laughed. "Let's take a little walk."

Nothing escaped sharp eyes in Washington, and he knew that the instant the president stopped to talk to him, the fact was being noted, catalogued, and analyzed by everyone there. He could almost feel the envy, the curiosity, the irritation, and the jealousy as the president gestured him forward; and as the secret service cadre fell into step around them, he tried to look casual. A difficult feat, he admitted, since it was an honor being singled out for such attention.

"Did you enjoy the dinner?" the president asked as they walked along.

"Oh, yes," he said. "The wife of the Indian ambassador enlightened me on the relative merits of rubies."

"I, on the other hand, had a fascinating discussion with an undersecretary in Transportation who talked about the retrofitting of engines to meet noise standards. I learned more about decibel levels than I'm ever going to need in my entire life."

They laughed together, and by that time were far enough away from the crowd to talk privately. The president stopped; the phalanx stopped with him; Douglas stopped too. It seemed they'd come to the purpose of this stroll.

Without further preamble, the president got right to the point. "I've watched your progress with great interest, Senator," he said. "You've done well in the primaries."

"Thank you, sir. But so has Hugh Redmond."

"Indeed," the president said, and then added something that made his heart race. "I'm not in the position to endorse anyone at this point, Senator—you understand. But if I were . . ."

363

He let the sentence trail, but there was no doubt about his meaning. Before Douglas could think of something appropriate to say, the president held out his hand. "Good luck, Senator," he said, and gestured to his secret service. As Douglas watched, bemused, the group returned to the ballroom.

It took him a few seconds to realize he wasn't alone. Thinking Sarah had come to find him, he turned. Lenore Deering-Kirk was standing there, and it was obvious from her expression that she'd overheard and wasn't too happy.

"Well," she said. "It's no secret now, is it?"

He wasn't about to say anything that could at all be misconstrued, especially since he hadn't had time to digest the implications himself. "I beg your pardon?"

Scornfully she gestured in the direction the president had gone. "A sitting president doesn't casually saunter out of a formal affair with a potential candidate just to chat about the weather," she said, and gave him a keen look. "He endorsed you, didn't he?"

"The president himself said that he's not in the position to endorse anyone."

Her eyes flashed, but she controlled the sharp retort that obviously rose to her lips. "I see," she said instead, and surprised him totally by adding, "Would you be free to come to tea tomorrow, Senator? I have something I wish to discuss privately with you."

The last thing he wanted to do was meet with this woman alone. He didn't like her; he never had. But he knew how imprudent it would be to be rude to her; men more powerful and influential than he had done so—much to their chagrin. A word here, a whisper there, and rumor became conjecture that suddenly solidified into fact. Besides, he was curious about what she had to say.

"I'm not sure about tea," he said, "but perhaps I can stop by Deer Hollow earlier in the afternoon. I will be out visiting . . . someone."

"Ah, yes," she said slyly. "Your poor wife. How is Mrs. Rhodes? Improved, I hope. Sacred Heart is such a restful place, and I've heard that Sister Agnes has quite a way with patients."

He had to fight to keep his expression neutral. How did she know about Sister Agnes? He wasn't surprised that she was aware of Marcella's being at Sacred Heart, but it made him uneasy that she knew which of the sisters took care of her.

Wondering just how much she did know about his private affairs, he said coolly, "Yes, she does."

"Then may I expect you at two-thirty?"

He was still annoyed. "I can probably manage it by then."

"Splendid," she said, her eyes hard on his face for a long moment. Then she turned and glided away on tiny little feet. Although he knew it was absurd, he felt as though an evil wind had just blown through.

"What was all that about?" Sarah asked when he had joined her again. "I saw you leave with Edward—"

Since she was one of the few people in the room who addressed the president by his first name, he shook his head wryly. Nothing like conversation with Sarah to return one to earth, he thought, and said, "I'll tell you in the car."

Fortunately they were able to leave soon after that. Sarah waited until the chauffeur had closed the door before she turned to him avidly. "Well?"

He smiled. "Which do you want to know about—the president, or Lenore?"

"Lenore, of course," she said with a wave of her hand. "I know what Edward had to say."

Why was he surprised? "All right, then—Lenore. She wanted me to come to tea tomorrow. Apparently she has something important she wants to discuss."

"I can imagine," Sarah said, her eyes narrowed. "What did you say?"

"I said I couldn't make it to tea, but that I'd stop by."

"I wonder what she wants."

"I'll find out soon enough. It can't be that important."

"No, but she can make trouble."

"Don't worry," he said confidently. "I can handle Lenore."

He arrived at Deer Hollow Farm the next day ten minutes late. He'd forgotten when he was making this absurd appointment the night before that the mother superior at Sacred Heart always gave him a report at the end of every month, and this had been the day. Marcella had improved enough to be allowed weekends at home with him, and as he drove slowly away from the sanitarium, his thoughts were far away.

"Don't expect too much at first, Douglas," the mother had warned. "She's still very fragile. But we feel that being in a more familylike setting should be a big help."

He hoped that it would be; devoutly he did. But he still felt uneasy at the thought of being alone with Marcella; after all, the nuns at the hospital were professionals; they knew how to handle a problem. Hesitantly he mentioned that to the mother.

"We can recommend a live-in nurse, if you like," she suggested.

Relieved, he agreed that would set his mind at ease. Now he was at Deer Hollow, anxious to get this over with, more abrupt than he intended to be after he was ushered into the sitting room where Lenore perched on a high wing-backed chair. He was prepared to be taken to task for his lateness, but to his surprise, she didn't mention it. Tea things were laid out in front of her, and she asked if he'd like a cup.

He shook his head. What he really wanted was a cup of coffee—or a by-your-leave. He wanted to get out of here; he had so many arrangements to make for Marcella.

"I know you're a busy man, Senator," Lenore said. "So I'll get right to the point. It's no secret that the party is split between you and Hugh for the nomination."

He forced himself to pay attention. "No," he agreed, "it isn't."

"It's no secret, either, that I support Hugh. Would you like to know why?"

He just wanted to be on his way. "Not particularly. This is a democratic society; we're all free to vote for whomever we choose."

Her eyes flashed. "Yes, we are. But voting privileges aside, there are some things to consider here, and one of these is the feeling that the country is in a period of . . . transition at the moment, and that it needs a breathing spell of sorts. Do you agree?"

What was this *feeling* she was talking about? he wondered, and exactly who felt it? Impatient with the fact that she was a meddling old woman he didn't need to impress, he said, "No, I don't agree. The issues we face today as a country, a people, are thorny ones, and must be dealt with. We can't relax."

"You're not on the stump at the moment, Senator," she said tartly, "so do me the favor of saving the campaign rhetoric until you are."

Sharply he replied. "That wasn't rhetoric, Mrs. Deering-Kirk. I meant every word."

Abruptly she changed tactics. "You think the country is in need of strong leadership, then."

He returned her glance evenly. "Yes, I do."

"And you think you could provide that leadership."

"I do."

She relaxed her stiff posture, but only for a second. Surprising him, she said, "I think you could, too." Then her back went ramrod-straight again. "But not now, not at this time."

He was almost amused. "I don't believe that's a matter for you to decide."

"Can you be sure?"

What was this? She had obviously deluded herself into thinking she had more power than she deserved, and he was tired of going along. He had better things to do than sit here and pretend a polite interest.

"Lenore, I don't mean to be rude, but I have appointments. Is there a point to all this?"

Her eyes flashed again; for a moment she truly looked like a formidable opponent. Then he dismissed the thought. She was just an old woman, playing at politics.

"Yes, there is a point," she said.

He barely resisted glancing at his watch. "Would you mind telling me what it is?"

She looked ready to strike him. "Of course. I asked you here today to discuss your withdrawal."

He thought he hadn't heard her right. "I beg your pardon?"

She pretended not to hear him. Her eyes still glittering with fury, she said, "Of course, at this point, I doubt you would step down without incentive."

Now he was sure she was crazy. "I don't intend to *step down* at all!" he said sharply. "And if by 'incentive' you mean some kind of bribe—"

She gave a short hack of a laugh, stopping him in midsentence. "Bribe you! My dear senator, I don't *bribe* people! I merely offer them something they can't refuse!"

He was so incredulous at the turn of the conversation that even though he wanted to leave, a morbid fascination held him in place. He heard himself say, "You have to be out of your mind. There is nothing—I repeat, *nothing*—you could offer me that I—"

"Oh, but I think there is, Senator," she said, and paused. "Laura Devlin."

There was a silence. Finally he said, "What do you mean?"

"I mean," she said, "that we can further Laura's career through a vice-presidential nomination, or we can . . . do otherwise. It's up to you, Senator."

He wanted to tell her this was insane, that she was out of her mind to threaten him—and Laura—like this. But then he looked at her, and saw that she, at least, was utterly convinced that she could do exactly as she'd said. Incredulously, in that moment he actually wondered if she could. "How?"

"Let me ask you something, Senator," she said. "Do you think the country is ready for a female president?"

What was this? Feeling as though he'd somehow stepped into another world, he answered, "No. Not yet. But in four years . . . perhaps."

"Much can happen in that time."

Why was he going on like this? He couldn't seem to stop. "I agree."

"And you are not averse to seeing Laura Devlin in the vice-presidency . . . now."

His throat felt tight. What was going on here? "Of course not."

Her voice was silky. "Even at the expense of your own ambitions?"

His stiffened. "I was not aware the two were mutually exclusive."

"They are—if you persist in running."

This was absurd. She truly was crazy, and he'd had enough. Rising, he said, "I'm sorry to foil your little plans, Lenore. But as I said, I've no intention of stepping down."

She looked up at him, a little beady-eyed predatory bird. "Are you in a hurry?" she asked. "Perhaps you have a previous engagement at the Beverly Hills Hotel."

He'd already started out, but at the mention of that hotel, he stopped. "What did you say?"

She looked disappointed. "You're not really going to make me say it, are you?"

Slowly he turned again to face her. "Say what?"

"Don't tell me you've forgotten a certain night, about six years ago, at a fund-raiser for your friend—what's his name? Oh, you know. He's the district attorney in Los Angeles—"

Comprehension dawned suddenly, but it couldn't be. "What are you talking about?"

She pretended not to hear him. "I remember now, his name is James Duluth. Oh, I see you do recall that particular night, after all. I'm not surprised. My sources tell me there was so much going on—people falling into pools, mysterious telephone calls . . ." She looked slyly at him. "Trysts . . ."

He didn't know why, but the old-fashioned word held more menace than anything he'd ever heard. Instantly his mind flashed back to that scene so long ago. He'd never forgotten the sensation of Laura in his arms; it was the one and only time they had ever embraced, and he had cherished the memory since. Now to have her speak of it as though . . . as though . . .

"Nothing happened that night," he said, his voice shaking despite himself. *"Nothing happened!"*

"I know that, Douglas," she said calmly. "But that doesn't matter, does it? It could have, and that's all that counts."

He had to clench his fists to control himself. But even as he did so, his mind was leaping ahead, assessing the situation, the disaster that would ensue. He might survive something like this, but Laura wouldn't. Rumor and conjecture would follow her, hound her, destroy her. No amount of denial or proof would restore her reputation, and the bright and shining career she'd embarked on would wither and die. So would she. His eyes blazing, he looked down at the evil little woman who—somehow—held the key to Laura's future.

"What are you after?" he asked hoarsely.

She was complacent. "I told you. Your withdrawal."

He had never felt so impotent in his life—or so enraged. His hands clenched again; he wanted to do violence. "Why are you doing this?"

She looked up at him again, a satisfied, arrogant smile twitching her lips. "To prove I can," she said.

He stared at her in amazement. *To prove I can.* She really was out of her mind.

"I see," he said. His voice didn't even sound like his own. "Well, in that case, take your best shot, Lenore. I won't be bullied or threatened or—or bribed—to step down to satisfy a whim. Do what you want. So will I."

On that, he turned and headed for the door. He'd gotten two steps before she clapped her hands. "Bravo, Douglas! I admire a strong man! There's just one thing—"

He whirled around again. "I told you, there's nothing you could offer me to make me step down!"

She gave him that sly look again. "Not even your grandson?"

If she'd taken a bat and slugged him between the eyes, he couldn't have been more stunned. "What . . . what do you mean?"

She smiled. "You didn't think I'd ask you to make such a great sacrifice at this time if I couldn't replace it with something of equal value!" She actually wagged an admonishing finger at him. "And certainly a grandchild—your first and only—would come under that category, don't you think?"

His throat felt closed; he could hardly force words through it. *His grandson?* But even the detective hadn't been able to . . .

"You . . . you don't know what you're talking about. You're bluffing."

"Am I? Are you willing to take that chance?"

He didn't know what he was willing to do. He didn't believe her; how could he? He'd had detectives on Calypso's trail for months after Rob . . . died. How could this raddled, interfering old witch have found out something he hadn't been able to? His eyes aflame, he looked down at Lenore and said, "Yes. I'm willing to take that chance."

"Perhaps you should withhold your decision until tonight."

His eyes burned. "Why?"

"If I can fulfill my part of the bargain, will you stand by yours?"

He hesitated, God damn him; he hesitated. "By bargain, you mean my withdrawal in exchange for my . . . grandson."

"Yes."

"What if I agree now, and then change my mind?"

"You wouldn't do that, Senator. You're an honorable man." She smiled, evilly. "Like me, your word is your bond."

He nearly laughed at that. "We'll see."

She inclined her head again. "Tonight. I'll expect your call."

He didn't believe her; he couldn't . . . he wouldn't. But that night, when the doorbell rang, he realized he'd known it all along. She'd been too confident, too sure of herself. When he opened the door, and saw who was standing there, he knew why.

"I can't take care of him anymore," Calypso said, shoving the little boy forward. "I tried, but I can't." She ran a forearm across her face, wiping her nose. "You sent that detective after me; you must want him real bad. Well, now you can have him.

His name's—'' She faltered for the first time. "His name's Robbie."

Still in shock, he looked down at the child who gazed interestedly up at him. There was no doubt: the same black, wavy hair, the same intense blue eyes. He was so like a young Rob, he felt a knifelike stab through his heart. He tore his eyes away, intending to ask the girl—

She had already gone, running down the street, fleeing from him and what questions he might have. "Wait!" he cried. "Calypso, wait!"

She didn't even look back. He was still staring dazedly after her when he felt a grubby little hand slide into his. He looked down and his heart contracted again. Even if he'd wanted not to believe, he couldn't doubt. Rob's son . . .

"My God," he choked, and realized with pained wonder that the little boy had to be . . . nearly five years old now. Where had the time gone?

Robbie cocked his head, a gesture that reminded him even more poignantly of Rob. "Am I going to stay with you now, mister?" he asked.

Tears in his eyes, he gathered his grandson in his arms. "Yes," he whispered, and buried his face in the little boy's silky hair.

Later, the child still in his arms, he called Deer Hollow Farm. His conversation with Lenore was brief and to the point. Then, not knowing what he really felt, he dialed Laura's home phone.

CHAPTER TWENTY-NINE

Laura was still reeling when she read about Douglas's withdrawal from the presidential race in the paper the next morning. Even though he had called her the night before to relate the news of his grandson's miraculous appearance, and to tell her of his decision not to run because of it, she hadn't really taken it in until she saw the headlines in the paper. He'd made it so clear last night, so logical and obvious; she'd thought she understood. She *did* understand. She was happy for him, delighted. She knew how much Robbie meant to him. But . . .

This morning, of course, the story was front-page news, splattered over the three major papers she had delivered every morning to scan before she went to the office. In all it was the same. Senator Douglas Rhodes had withdrawn his candidacy due to family reasons. There were even pictures with his grandson in his arms—he looked so much like Rob! Laura thought with a pang—as he told reporters that with new responsibilities and an ailing wife, he didn't feel he could attend to them and the demands of running for office at the same time. Staring at the poignant photos, Laura told herself again that she understood his reason for withdrawing—if that's what it was. But she knew Douglas, and so she was aware on some deep inner level that he hadn't told her everything. Troubled, she glanced around the breakfast table at her own family.

They were all here: Jack with his nose in the paper, her mother reading an advice column, Peter toying with his eggs, a sullen Andrea drinking her orange juice. They all seemed oblivious to the news, and even though Douglas had asked her not to say anything until the story broke this morning, now she could speak. She did. "Douglas Rhodes has withdrawn from the presidential race."

"That's nice," Jack said absently, reaching out from under the paper to grab another piece of toast.

"It says here that the proper way to install a roll of toilet paper is so that the tissue comes over the top instead of hanging down underneath," Estelle said, putting down her section of the paper with a frown. "I wonder. Do we do it that way?"

"Mom, can I be excused?" Andrea said. "Grandma won't let me have the fashion section, and there's nothing else worth reading."

Laura looked at each one. Didn't they care? Didn't they realize what had happened? This was something that would affect them, too, and yet they sat here talking about toilet paper, of all things, or boredom, or as in the case of Peter, saying nothing at all. Didn't they understand what they'd just lost?

Involuntarily her glance went to Jack, who was still immersed in his sports. Her mouth tightened, and she looked away again. She and Jack had been getting along much better since that time nearly two years ago when she'd found him clutching that blonde in her kitchen, but their relationship was still fragile; sometimes it seemed to her that they tiptoed around each other, both wary and suspicious. For the kid's sake, she was glad they had tried, but she wondered at times if the strain was worth it. She'd thought that Jack's success with his new office would help, but so far it hadn't. They remained strangers, and she was beginning to doubt they'd ever recapture the closeness they'd once shared.

Her glance fell on those black, bleak headlines again, and she was just deciding whether or not to call Sarah and ask her opinion when Peter shoved away his plate and said, "Mom, Dad, I've got to talk to you."

Distracted, she looked up. She didn't like the way Peter had been behaving this year; he seemed more pale and silent and withdrawn than before. But his grades in school were good, and when she had tried to get him to open up, he insisted nothing was wrong. "What is it?" she asked.

"I've decided to move out," Peter said. "I'm going to get an apartment with a friend from school and we're going to share expenses."

She was so shocked, she didn't know what to say. This was the first she'd heard of the idea, and she looked blankly from him to Jack, who had slowly put down the paper.

"What was that?" Jack said.

"Now, Dad, don't get mad," Peter said quickly. "I've been thinking about this for a long time now, and I've got it all worked out."

Jack flashed a glance in her direction, but she was still trying to absorb the news. When she saw how angry he looked, she said quickly, "This is such a surprise, Peter. Why do you want to move out?"

"I'm eighteen, Mom," he said. "Isn't that reason enough?"

"No, it is not," Jack said, his tone on edge. "Why haven't you mentioned this before?"

"Because I wanted to get all the details ironed out, Dad. I wanted to show you that I could do it."

A muscle twitched in Jack's jaw. Eyes narrowed, he said, "For starters, maybe you'd better tell us how you intend to share expenses if you don't even have a job."

"Now, Jack—" Laura said quietly. She didn't want this to turn into a shouting match, even though it seemed unavoidable. Jack and his son hadn't been getting along very well this past year, in part because Peter had elected theater arts his college major. Jack thought it was sissy stuff and made no bones about it. She had done her best to keep the peace, but she had suspected something like this might happen. She just hadn't expected it so soon.

Peter flushed, but he held his ground. "I have a job. Starting today, I'm going to bag at the market."

Andrea snickered. "Great job," she said. "You'll make tons of money doing *that*!"

"That's enough, Andrea," Laura said.

Andrea immediately went into a pout. "Aw, gee, I can't say *anything*!"

"At the moment, no, you can't," she said. Andrea was sixteen now, increasingly rebellious. She wasn't getting along well with her daughter, who looked older than she was and wanted to date college boys.

"Do you mind if we get back to what *I* wanted to talk about?" Peter said loudly. "Why does everything have to revolve around Andrea? Can't you listen to me for once?"

She turned to her son again. "We are listening, Peter—"

"Can I be excused?" Andrea interrupted sullenly.

"No, you can't!" Laura said sharply. "Now, please, just sit there and be quiet!"

"Well, really, Laura, there's no need to shout at the girl," Estelle said.

The last thing Laura needed at the moment was criticism from

374

her mother. "Mother, can we *please* just listen to what Peter has to say?"

But Peter had said enough. Throwing down his napkin, he pushed his chair back and stood. "Never mind!" he shouted. "Just never mind! Why is it that whenever I try to say something around here, no one wants to listen? Just forget it, all right? Just forget it!"

He started to leave the breakfast nook, but Jack reached out and grabbed his arm. "Now, wait just a minute. You're not going anywhere."

Peter's formerly pale face flushed with anger. "I don't *have* to tell you what's going on, remember? I'm eighteen now; I can do as I damned well please!"

He'd never spoken to either of his parents like this, but as shocked as Laura was, she saw Jack's face darken and got to her feet, too. "Peter," she said, "I think we should talk about this—"

He turned on her. "Talk? You want to talk *now*? Why, Mother? Do you have a few minutes between committee meetings? A moment before you have to rush off to the office? Tell me, do you have *time* for me now, or shall I make an appointment like the rest of the world?"

She couldn't believe he'd said such awful things. "How can you say that to me?" she said. "I've practically *begged* you to talk to me for months now, but you've refused every time. What more—"

"—can you do?" Peter interrupted. "Nothing. Not a damned thing. I'm going to take care of it all myself." He glanced at his father. "And don't worry about money, Dad. If I have to, I'll quit school and work until I can pay for it myself."

Jack was furious. "You're going to quit school to work as a *box boy*? Is that what you want to be for the rest of your life?"

"Your father's right," Estelle said anxiously. She put her hand out to her grandson. "Please, Peter, think before you quit school."

His expression softened for just an instant as he looked at his grandmother. Laura couldn't help it, but she felt a flash of jealousy. Then he glanced at both his parents again, saying, "I'm sorry, Grandma, but they just don't understand."

Laura tried again. "Give us a chance, Peter," she said. "We'd like to understand. I want to know why you feel such a need to leave."

He looked at her, and she was shocked once again at the look of—what was it? Hopelessness? Despair? No, it couldn't be.

375

How could he possibly feel such things? But then, against her will, an image of Rob Rhodes flashed into her mind, and she nearly cringed. Rob had felt hopeless and despairing, and Douglas still didn't know why. Remembering that, she glanced quickly at her own son, and for the first time, felt real fear. Had she missed something, too?

"Peter," she said, trying to keep her voice steady. "Please, I want to listen. I'll give you all the time you need. I do want to understand."

"I know you do, Mom," he said, and looked resigned. "And unlike Dad, you might try." He took a deep breath. "But it's too . . . complicated. Trust me; I know what I'm doing. And we'll all be a lot happier this way."

"What do you mean—happier?" she asked. But he had already brushed by. As he left the kitchen, she looked dazedly at Jack, who seemed just as bewildered as she did. "What did he mean?"

"You don't know?" Andrea said scornfully.

They all looked at her. "Know what?" Laura said.

But Andrea just smiled a secret little smile as she pushed back her chair. "It's Peter's business, but if I were you, I'd find out who he's going to take that apartment with," she said, and sashayed out after her brother.

Jack muttered a curse. "If he thinks he'd going to move in with some girl we've never even met, he's got another thought coming."

Nervously Estelle started to clear away the breakfast dishes. "What are you going to do?"

"We're not going to do anything until we find out more," Laura said with a warning glance in her husband's direction. She looked at her mother. "I've never heard Peter mention a girlfriend, have you?"

Estelle thought about it. Sounding surprised, she said, "No, I can't believe I have."

"Then he must be taking an apartment with some boy he met at school," Laura said, and couldn't help a glance in the direction her son had gone. Was that what it was? She decided to talk to Andrea about this; her daughter seemed to know—or think she knew—more than she was telling.

"Fine," Jack said, still angry. His briefcase was on the counter; he grabbed it. "Then you handle it. I'm late for an appointment."

Laura glanced at the clock. "I've got to get going, too. Don't worry, I'll take Andrea to school. I want to talk to her anyway."

"I hope it's about that kid she's been hanging around with," he said. "I don't like the looks of him. He's too old for her."

Jack always surprised her when he said things like this; until now, she would have bet that he hadn't the faintest idea which boy Andrea had been seeing. But then, Andy had always been his favorite. When he left, she realized her mother was tight-lipped, staring at her.

"What is it, Mom?"

"I hope you're happy."

"What does that mean?"

"You know very well what it means. How can you let Peter move out like this?"

She was wondering that herself. But she had no choice, and so she said, "I don't see how we can stop him, Mother. As he pointed out, he *is* eighteen."

"That's still young."

"I know," she said, her voice breaking despite herself. Abruptly she sat down at the table again. "I know," she repeated, forlornly.

To her surprise, Estelle came and put a hand on her shoulder. "I'm sorry, Laura. I'm being selfish. I don't want Peter to go, either. It's hard when they grow up."

Without warning, tears came to her eyes. Blinking, she looked up. "Is that how you felt?"

Suddenly teary-eyed herself, Estelle squeezed her shoulder. Moving to the sink, she said, "It's how every mother feels."

The unexpected gesture touched her, and she got up to give her mother a quick hug. "Thanks, Mom."

Estelle smiled shakily at her, returning the hug. Then she gave her a little push. "Go on, you've got to take Andrea to school."

Not trusting herself to speak, Laura nodded. Her things were in the hallway, and as she went to call Andrea, she caught a glimpse of herself in the mirror over the telephone table. She had turned forty last year, a milestone, a life mark—a watershed—in anyone's life. Did she look it? This morning she felt twice that age, but apart from a few lines around her eyes and a strand or two of gray in her hair, she saw she looked much the same as she always had. It was only on the inside that she felt different, and she knew that the greatest changes had occurred there. Taking a shaky breath, she called to Andrea and went out to start the car.

They drove in silence for several blocks, her daughter staring sullenly out the window, as she did far too much these days, Laura preoccupied with her own thoughts. The argument at breakfast had briefly driven Douglas from her mind, but now she couldn't help thinking about him and wishing she could call. But he had told her he'd be away for a while, getting to know his grandson, so she had to wait. But something still bothered her about that, and she decided to call Sarah as soon as she got in. In the meantime, she had to deal with Andrea.

"Andy, who was that young man I saw you with yesterday?"

Instantly Andrea looked guarded. "Who do you mean?"

Wondering why the simplest question these days seemed an invitation to battle, she said, "You know who I mean. That boy I saw you standing with on the corner by school."

Andrea flounced around. "Were you spying on me?"

"No, I wasn't spying on you. I happened to go by and saw you standing there. But don't try to change the subject. Who is he?"

"Why do you want to know?"

"Because I like to know who your friends are, that's why," she said, trying to be reasonable. "I like to know who you're seeing, and that boy looked too old for you. Is he still in school or what?"

Andrea slouched down in the seat. "His name is Greg Wilson."

"And?"

Mutinously Andrea looked out the window again. "And . . . and no, he's not in school. He works at A and B body shop as a mechanic."

"I see," Laura said. "And when did he graduate?"

Andrea was silent.

Laura glanced at her again. "Andy?"

"All right! He didn't graduate, okay? He got kicked out of school! But it wasn't his fault. He—"

"When was this?"

"What?"

"When was he kicked out of school?"

Another slouch, this one accompanied by a defiant folding of the arms. "Four years ago."

"What!"

She sat up again. "Honestly, I don't know why you're making such a big deal out of this, Mom! Not everybody can go to college, you know!"

"There's a big difference between not attending college and getting kicked out of high school, Andrea," she said sharply. "And you know how your father and I feel about you seeing someone so much older. We agreed you would only date boys your own age!"

"You and Dad said that, not me!" Andrea said shrilly. "Don't I get to say anything about it?"

"As I recall, we did discuss this. And you agreed you wouldn't date anyone out of school. You were the one who said that—not your father or me."

Andrea sulkily subsided. "Yeah, well, that was before I met Greg."

They had arrived at the school; Laura pulled up next to the curb. But before Andrea could get out of the car, she reached across and took her daughter's arm. "Andy, if you want to defy us, and sneak to see boys we prefer you not to see, there's nothing we can do to stop you—short of escorting you to and from school and locking you in your room at night. But I don't believe in that, so I guess it's up to you. You know how your father and I feel about this, so the choice is yours. I hope we can trust you to do the right thing."

Andrea tightened her lips. "Yeah, right. Anything else?"

Realizing she'd said as much as she could now, Laura shook her head. "Not about that. But I did want to ask you—"

"Mom!" Andrea said, rolling her eyes. "I'm going to be late!"

"This will only take a minute."

"What?"

"What did you mean this morning when you said we should find out who Peter is going to take that apartment with?"

Andrea glanced away. "Nothing."

"You must have meant something. I want to know what it is."

"Look, Mom, I'm going to be late for class, okay? If you want to know anything, maybe you'd better ask Peter."

"I'm asking you."

But just then the bell rang, signaling the start of the first class. "Now I'm going to be late for old Perkins's history class!"

Andrea cried. "And he *hates* for people to be late! He'll give me a tardy and I'll have to stay after!"

"I'll come in and explain."

"Don't you dare!" Scandalized, she reached quickly for the car door and got out. "I'd never live it down!"

She was gone, running across the lawn like a gazelle, her short skirt revealing far too much shapely leg for Laura's taste. *No wonder that boy is interested,* she thought grimly, and waited until Andrea had disappeared inside the school before she started the car. She didn't really intend to do it—or maybe she did—but on the way in to work, she drove slowly by the A and B Garage, where Andrea had said this Greg worked. The place wasn't open yet, and she wasn't sure how she felt about that. Had she planned to stop in and tell him to stay away from her daughter? But that would only have piqued his interest, she realized, and wondered how best to handle this. Deciding that she was too upset to think clearly, she drove on to the office. Here, at last, she felt she was in some control.

The Hill was abuzz with the news about Douglas. It seemed to be the only topic of conversation she heard as she parked the car and went in. Most of her staff was already there when she arrived, all agog as everyone else seemed to be. Ellen, with her ever-present clipboard, followed her inside and shut the door.

"I take it you've heard."

No one needed to know how disquieted she still felt about all this, so she smiled and said, "Yes, isn't it wonderful?"

"*Wonderful?* That he's withdrawn from the race?"

She was still determined. "No, about his grandson."

"Oh, that," said her politically minded aide. "Well, sure. But what about his decision not to run?"

"He has responsibilities, Ellen," she said. She really didn't want to talk about this anymore; she was too disappointed herself.

"But—"

She could feel herself getting more and more uptight. Because of that, she spoke more sharply than she intended. "Ellen, I know this is exciting, but I have several hearings to prepare for. Do you think we might get to work?"

Obviously hurt by this uncharacteristically curt dismissal, Ellen said, "Yes . . . sure." Without another word, she turned and went out, quickly closing the door behind her.

Laura bit her lip. She hadn't meant to be so abrupt, and she

380

got up to apologize, then sank back down again, rubbing her eyes. She'd say something when Ellen came back in, she thought, and wondered if this was the way the entire day was going to go. She was just reaching wearily for her briefcase when her private line rang. When she answered, it was Sarah.

"Laura, are you alone?" she asked.

Startled by the question, she glanced automatically around. "Yes, but what—"

"I don't want to say too much over the phone, but do you think you could come to my office now? The back way. I've got reporters crawling all around, but I have to talk to you."

She straightened. "What's wrong?"

"Just come, will you? Call it a personal favor."

This wasn't like Sarah at all. "I'll leave right now."

"Thanks, Laura. I'll have Clyde waiting for you. He'll let you in the storeroom door."

Clyde Corbin was Sarah's chief administrative aide. As Sarah had promised, he was waiting on the back stairs when she got there. He saw her and put a finger over his lips. "Shhh. The press are camped out by the front door, sure that the senator has more information about Senator Rhodes," he whispered. "They've been here since dawn."

Even though they were still on the stairs, Laura followed suit and started whispering herself. "What do they want to know?"

"Where he's gone, of course. They think Senator Ambrose might be in on it."

"Is she?"

"You'll have to ask her," he said, and held up a key. "We'll go through the storeroom, okay?"

She was anxious to talk to Sarah. "Lead on."

"Follow me."

The storeroom led to an antechamber, then to the outer office, bypassing the waiting reporters locked out in the hall. Sarah was waiting when they got there, pacing back and forth. "Thank God," she said. "I wasn't sure you'd be successful in running the gauntlet."

Relieved that Sarah herself seemed to be all right, Laura gave her a quick embrace as Clyde disappeared. They started toward the inner office. "What's going on?" she asked. "Why all the secrecy?"

"You'll see in a minute."

She had to ask; she couldn't wait any longer. "Sarah, is Douglas all right?"

"Douglas is fine," another voice, a dear, familiar voice, said behind her. She spun around, and there he was. She was so glad to see him that tears sprang to her eyes. He looked so pale, she thought—so tired and drawn. She wanted to embrace him and didn't dare.

"Douglas!" she said, anxiety surfacing again. She was sure now he hadn't told her everything; one look at his face, and she knew.

He reached for her hands. "I'm sorry," he said. "I didn't want you to worry."

"Worry!" Relief made her feel dizzy. She pulled herself together fiercely. "I thought you'd gone!"

"I couldn't go without seeing you."

She realized only then that Sarah had left them alone. "Oh, Douglas!" she said, and couldn't stop looking at him. "What's happening? I know you're happy about your grandson, but to withdraw—!"

His grip on her hands tightened, and she was reminded, searingly, of that night in Los Angeles. "Things will work out."

"Then you might change your mind?"

He hesitated, but only for a mere instant. Then he shook his head. "No. Robbie needs me. So does Marcella. And this time I'm not going to fail them."

She couldn't respond to that; she could only gaze helplessly at him. "Oh, Douglas—"

His dark eyes searched her face, as though memorizing every beloved detail. "Promise me—" he began.

"What? Anything!"

He smiled, but his eyes held such great pain. "Promise me . . . you'll follow your instincts."

What was he talking about? "I don't understand."

He shook his head. "That's all I can tell you now, Laura," he said. "In a short while things will change, and then, you will."

"What things? What are you talking about?"

"I can't tell you now. But when they do, I . . . I want you to remember this—promise me, now. When the time comes, you do what you must."

He seemed fierce about it, willing her to understand. She wanted to, because he asked. But she didn't know what he meant. Do what she must? But she always did. What was he talking about? *What was he talking about?*

"Douglas, I—"

There was a flurry outside in the hall, raised voices, a few catcalls. The reporters were getting restless, determined to get a story. He glanced toward the closed door and gripped her hands again. "I'm sorry, Laura. There isn't much time. I don't want to talk to them again."

That she did understand. But the thought that he was going to leave galvanized her, and now she was the one who gripped him tightly. "Douglas, why do you have to go away? At least tell me where you'll be!"

"I can't," he said, his voice suddenly hoarse with emotion. Time was running out; they both knew it. "I don't know myself. I only know I . . . I have to get away for a while. Try to understand."

"Oh, Douglas, this is so—"

"I know," he said. "I know. Oh, darling, I wish I could—"

Darling, she thought, feeling pain stab through her like a knife. The endearment was nearly her undoing, and she knew that in a few minutes—seconds—he was going to leave her, and she would be left all alone. Why not? she thought, squeezing her eyes shut in agony. *Why not?* What difference would it make? Who would know?

"Douglas, please, can't we talk about this?" she said desperately. The noise from the hall was getting louder, more strident. Someone started pounding on the door, and she jumped at the sound. They'd run out of time. "Please, don't go!"

Again he hesitated, a look of anguish in his eyes. "I wish—" he started to say, and stopped. His voice broke.

She couldn't stand this. The words leaped from her constricted throat before she even knew what she was saying. "I wish it, too!" she cried. "I wish it, too! Every day, every night—"

As though he couldn't bear it anymore, he reached out, and suddenly she was in his arms, holding him tight. "Don't say it!" he whispered. "For God's sake, don't say it!"

"I will! I have to! For once, I will say it!"

But she didn't get the chance. His fingers wound through her hair, pulling her head back. Uttering a hoarse sound, he pulled her to him again and brought his lips down hard on hers. She answered with all the longing and desire she had denied all these years. So fierce was her response that they both swayed. It was the first kiss, the only kiss, the last kiss, they would ever share, and she clung to him as though by sheer force of will they could become one. She never wanted to let him go; he was in her blood, his body throbbed against hers. Desperately she held on to him, but the moment was even now fleeting, flying away, torn from them by the demands of the world they couldn't ignore.

Finally, trembling violently, Douglas broke away from her and raised his head. Dazed, she looked up at him and saw tears in his eyes. Without knowing it, she sobbed.

"My love . . ." he whispered. "Take care . . ."

As though she sensed it was time, Sarah suddenly appeared. Wordless, Laura watched him head toward the storeroom door, glancing away when Sarah briefly touched his arm in a protective, comforting gesture. He didn't look back; she didn't expect him to. What they had shared would have to last a lifetime, and there was nothing more to say. Feeling completely drained, she sank down in the nearest chair.

After closing the storeroom door, Sarah turned briskly to her. "Everything is going to be all right," she said, and handed her a handkerchief.

She didn't realize she had tears on her face until then. Feeling as though nothing would ever be right in her world again, she accepted the handkerchief and dabbed at her eyes. She wanted to say something, but she didn't seem capable. Helplessly she looked at Sarah, who took the chair behind the desk and said, "Now, then. It's time to talk realities."

"Realities?" she repeated. Reality was what had just happened. Dully she realized that the banging on the outside door had stopped and all was quiet. She didn't care.

"Yes," Sarah said. "And you'd better get used to it. From now on, things will happen very quickly indeed."

She had to force her thoughts away from Douglas. Realizing she hadn't even had time to ask him where he intended to go, or how long he'd be gone, she bent her head again, trying not to cry.

"This may seem harsh to you at this moment," Sarah went on while she struggled for composure, "but we have to consider what effect Douglas's withdrawal is going to have."

Wondering if she'd heard right, she lifted her head. She didn't know what Sarah was saying, or why it mattered. "Sarah, do we have to talk about this now?"

"Yes, we do," Sarah said briskly, ignoring the pleading in

Laura's eyes. "Since Hugh Redmond's nomination is better than a fair assumption now, we have to consider who his running mate will be. The Women's Political Caucus feels that that choice should be a woman."

Laura tried to pull herself together. Sarah obviously wasn't going to let her sink into self-pity; this must be some kind of attempt to get her mind off Douglas. Because she respected the older woman so much, she tried. "The WPC can think what they like," she said disinterestedly. "But the chances of Hugh choosing a woman running mate are about even with the tides running backward."

"Don't be too sure."

Just wanting to leave and be by herself, she said, "You obviously know something I don't know."

"Let's just say I'm able to make an educated guess."

That finally penetrated her self-absorption. "Sarah, are you going to—"

"An old war-horse like me? I wouldn't accept the nomination on a bet. You, however, are a different story."

She didn't know why they were going on with this charade. Feeling as though she was going to cry again, she said, "I'm not in the mood to play jokes, Sarah."

"I'm not joking."

There was a silence while she considered it—briefly. Then she shook her head. No. As powerful as Sarah was, even she couldn't change the reality. And the reality was—what? *Was* it time, as the Women's Political Caucus had been saying for months now? *Was* it time, as Caroline Chandler had insisted from Los Angeles the last time they'd met? *Was it time?*

Yes, she thought: definitely. But not with her. "No," she said. "It wouldn't work. I don't have the experience—"

"You have the ability," Sarah said, and looked at her shrewdly. "Do you have the desire?"

"Yes, I do, but—" She was startled at her answer; it had slipped out without volition, without thought. *How could she think of herself at a time like this?* Ashamed, she shook her head quickly and added, "But so do dozens of others—many more qualified than I."

Again that shrewd glance. "But you wouldn't refuse if it was offered to you."

"Well, I—" Without warning, Douglas's words whispered

through her mind. *Things will change. Follow your instincts when they do.* And her instincts said—

"I think we're being premature, Sarah," she said, unable to meet the other woman's eyes. "Let's just wait and see what happens."

It happened one night just as she arrived home from an exhausting day on the Hill. As Sarah had predicted, once Douglas withdrew, Hugh Redmond's nomination loomed increasingly certain at convention's approach, and to the surprise of many, Hugh himself seemed to have changed. He softened his position on several ultraconservative stands; he even adopted some of the policies and platforms upon which Douglas had campaigned. As these changes swung more support his way and he continued to reexamine previously held opinions, Laura found that she could campaign for him in good conscience. She volunteered for two of the steering committees, but that, added to her already heavy workload, consumed more and more of her time. The night that Sarah's other prediction came true, she was just walking in the door when the phone rang. She could see that her family was in the living room with the TV, so she answered.

"Devlin residence," she said, taking off her coat with one hand while she held the receiver with the other.

"Congresswoman Devlin?" said an unfamiliar voice.

"Yes, this is she," Laura said, quickly transferring the phone so she could take her arm out of the other sleeve. "Who is this?"

"My name is Harold Geiger," the voice said. "And I'm Senator Redmond's chief administrative aide. I was wondering if we might make an appointment to discuss a few things."

She straightened, one sleeve still on, her coat forgotten. *This is it,* she thought, and suddenly shivered at the wave of excitement that raced through her. Controlling herself with an effort, she managed to say, "What things?"

"As you are no doubt aware, Senator Redmond seems certain to clinch the party's nomination," Geiger said. "In that regard, we have a few questions for you. I'm sure you're also aware that your name has come up as a possible candidate for the vice-presidency, and so the senator would like to know more about you."

"I see," she said, her heart beginning to do a thrilled little dance. Until now, she hadn't dared to believe it might be true. Realizing she still had her coat half-on, she shrugged out of it,

386

threw it haphazardly over the chair, and glanced through the open doorway into the living room, trying to signal someone. But they were all absorbed in the television, and she drew back disappointedly. "I'd be glad to meet with you—or the senator," she said.

"Good," Geiger said. "If you'll hold a moment, the senator himself wishes to speak with you."

He came on the line before she was quite ready. "Congresswoman Devlin?" he said. "This is Hugh Redmond. My aide tells me you've agreed to meet with him."

Wondering if he had really expected her to say anything else, she said, "Of course. I'll be happy to answer any questions I can."

"I'm glad to hear that, Congresswoman," he said, and laughed. "Might I call you Laura? If this upcoming meeting goes as I hope it will, we will be spending a lot of time campaigning together in the next few months. It would be so much simpler to be on a first-name basis, don't you agree?"

Laura did agree. She also agreed to meet with Mr. Geiger that weekend to answer what he called a few "routine" questions. Knowing they wouldn't be anything of the sort, she hung up and went into the family room. She must have looked as pale as she felt, for when her mother saw her, she said, "What's the matter, Laura?"

She was still feeling dazed. "That was Hugh Redmond on the phone."

"The guy who's running for president?" Jack said, turning to look at her. "What did he want?"

For some reason her throat felt constricted. She realized it was from excitement. "He wanted . . ." She could hardly say it; she had to try again. "He wanted to know if I'd be his running mate."

Andrea looked around. "What?"

Even though she'd said it aloud, she still had trouble believing it. "He wants me to be on the ticket with him as vice-president."

There was a silence. They all stared at her, looking as unbelieving as she felt herself. She wished Peter were here to share this momentous moment, but he was at home in his own place now, with a roommate. She thought of Douglas, who had finally returned from his brief, self-imposed vacation. Marcella was home now; Robbie was enrolled in school. He had hired a housekeeper, a nurse. She didn't want to think of Douglas.

387

Finally Estelle said, "My goodness."

Andrea sat up. "Are you going to do it?"

She looked at her daughter. "Do you think I should?"

"Be the first woman VP?" Andrea said, and thought about it. Then she grinned, for too brief a time the daughter she remembered, not the sullen teenager she seemed to have become. "Are you kidding? Go for it!"

She looked finally at Jack, who hadn't said anything yet. She hardly dared ask, but she had to. "What do you think?"

Jack looked at her, his face expressionless. Even she, who knew him so well, couldn't tell what he was thinking. Finally, looking as though he couldn't believe it either, he shook his head blankly and got up.

"Son of a bitch," he said, and went to fix himself a drink.

CHAPTER THIRTY

As she passed the cheval mirror on the way to the closet, Dawn grinned at her reflection. She was going out on an important date, and she had to get ready, but she paused for a minute to pose seductively. She was wearing a lacy teddy, and she thrust out a hip and balanced on one leg. Pouting, she raised a hand and pushed her hair to the top of her head, turning this way and that. Then, laughing, she abandoned the game and continued to the closet. She didn't have time for this foolishness; she had to decide what to wear.

The walk-in closet was stuffed on three sides, but everything was completely organized and tabulated, down to the last pair of panty hose. Switching on the light, she looked satisfied as she glanced over the racks of clothes, all separated according to style and function, and at the stacks of shelves that held everything from gloves to hats to purses to shoes. One special section held the see-through boxes filled with filmy lingerie, and because she could never resist, she fondly touched the bulky bag in the back that protected her one fur. What to wear. For once, she had plenty to choose from.

A cocktail dress? Perhaps. She was meeting someone in a bar. Something sexy, but not too revealing, about knee length, not a gown. Basic black, maybe? She pulled out a slithery one-shouldered sheath, then put it back. She didn't feel like black tonight; it was going to be a night for celebration. Red, then, but not so fancy. Maybe sophistication would be better, she mused, and went to another section of the closet. A crimson long-sleeved jersey with a wide matching belt caught her eye, and she took that out. Perfect. The dress was fitted, and the belt would show off her small waist. Taking the matching shoes and the other things she needed, she carried everything over to the bed and laid it out. Feeling very pleased with herself, she got dressed. Twenty minutes later, she was in the car, driving to her rendezvous.

How easy it was, she thought. Whoever had said that men were ruled by their gonads knew what she was talking about. A little nooky, and they were ready to spill their guts; a little head, and they were yours forever. Chuckling to herself, she pressed down the accelerator. The car was new, a little sports job she'd coveted for longer than she cared to remember—as she had the apartment in Dupont Circle. Now, thanks to Lenore and her plots, she had them both.

Her smiled cracked a little when she remembered that she was supposed to check in with the old witch tonight after her date, and she was irritated anew at the thought of how that woman had run her life these past six years. Still, it wouldn't be for much longer. She'd done everything Lenore had asked, and more. It was time to get a little for herself.

Good humor restored, she hummed a little song as she drove. It hadn't been so bad, not really; all along, she'd had perks. Getting out of that first crummy apartment had been one; getting this job on the *Post* had been another. She was still just a staff writer now, but the Rhodes story she'd done for Barnaby before she left had certainly led to better things, and if her plans worked out the way she intended, she'd get her own column. She shivered in anticipation. It was hard to believe, but finally, after waiting so long, she was almost there. It had been worth everything, even working with that old witch.

She shook her head. Sometimes you had to wonder at the irony of it all. If she hadn't had this association with Lenore, and if Lenore hadn't told her to get the goods on Jack, this new deal might never have happened. She laughed aloud, picturing the old biddy's surprise when Lenore learned that she'd decided to branch out on her own.

The bar where she was to meet her date was just ahead; glancing at the speedometer, she slowed to the speed limit. The last thing she wanted was to get a ticket out here in the boondocks, where it might be traced; she didn't want anyone to know she'd ever been near here. There was a space at the back of the lot, and she parked the car there, in the dark. Then she went into the bar.

The place was dimly lit and so filled with smoke, it was hard to see. That suited her just fine. She stood in the doorway a moment until her eyes adjusted; then she saw him, at the back, hunched down in a booth. How like him, she thought scornfully; he never had had any balls. She couldn't understand why his wife kept him around so long. The things women did for their men; it was enough to swear you off forever.

Wanting to get on with it, she started walking toward the booth. A whistle or two followed her, but she ignored them. There had been a time when she might have checked it out, but not anymore—and not right now. Tonight she had one goal in mind, and if she was anything, it was single-minded. On that thought, she walked up to the booth and slid into the seat.

"Hi," she said, and smiled.

Jack Devlin looked up. Even in this dim light, his face looked haggard, his eyes bloodshot. She knew instantly that he'd been drinking far more than the two empty highball glasses in front of him showed, but she shrugged. So what if he was drunk? She'd been around drunks before, and after her father, anyone else was an amateur.

"What do you want, Dawn?" he said.

She made a moue. "Why, Jack, is that any way to talk to an old friend?"

"We're not old friends!" he snapped, and then glanced around, as if afraid of being overheard. She nearly laughed again. The anonymity of the bar was exactly why she'd chosen it; no one here gave a goddamn who they were.

"Sure we are, Jack," she said, shrugging out of her coat. "Don't you remember that wonderful night a couple of months ago that we spent together? If we aren't friends after that, who is?"

He looked sick. "It wasn't that wonderful."

"That wasn't what you said at the time," she reminded him, smirking. "As I recall, you were only too eager for more."

"Can we get to the point?" he said harshly, and gave another of those uneasy looks around. "You left me a message to meet you here. I did. Now, why don't you tell me what you want, so we can both get the hell out of here?"

She smiled coyly. "Can't you guess what I want?"

Looking as though he'd like to strangle her, he said, "It's not another roll in the hay, that's for sure."

Genuinely amused, she said, "A roll in the *hay*? Why, how quaint. And here I thought Californians were such free spirits. Wasn't that what you told me that night, Jack? About how free-spirited you were?"

He seemed desperately to want a drink, but didn't want to call attention to himself by calling the barmaid—if there was one. Lighting a cigarette with a shaky hand instead, he said, "Can we cut the crap? I can't be gone that long, you know. It was a bitch as it was, eluding those damned reporters." He exhaled roughly. "Not to mention the fucking Secret Service."

"What do you mean, the Secret Service?" she said sharply. "The last time we talked, you told me you refused protection!"

"Yeah, well, that was a while ago, wasn't it? Things have changed since then."

For the first time, she felt uneasy. The last thing she wanted was to explain to one of those goons why she was meeting like this with the husband of the candidate for vice-president. She gave him a hard look. "Are you saying you think someone might have followed you out here?"

"I know what you think of me, Dawn, but give me some credit, will you?"

She willed herself not to think of it. She had planned too hard and too long for things to go awry at this point, but she decided to stop playing with him and tell him what she wanted. Just in case. "I'll give you all the credit you deserve, Jack—just as long as you do something for me."

His eyes narrowed behind the cigarette smoke. "Yeah, what?"

"A simple exchange of favors."

"Blackmail, you mean," he said flatly.

"That's a little harsh, don't you think?"

"No, I don't. I know about you, Dawn. Since you called me, I've thought a lot about that night at your apartment, and it seems to me you were just a little too eager for information. What did you do with all that bull about that night at the Beverly Hills Hotel that I told you about? Am I going to see it in some rag, or what?"

She looked at him sharply again. "Are you telling me that story was a lie?"

"How should I know? I was plastered to the gills that night in L.A. I hardly remember a thing."

"You remembered enough to tell me about Senator Rhodes and your wife."

Angrily he stubbed out the cigarette and immediately lit another. "I remembered enough to say he was there—the bastard.

But so what? So he was there. Laura said he was friends with the DA; why shouldn't he have been? It was no big deal."

"That's not what you said before."

"I don't know *what* I said before. I was drunk that night at your apartment, too—remember?"

She remembered all too well. If it hadn't been for her expertise and experience, their little liaison would never have taken place. But she'd needed Jack in her bed, and she'd wanted to make sure he vividly recalled the experience.

"I haven't forgotten," she said, forcing herself to speak calmly. "And that's why I'm here. Whether *you* remember or not, we had quite a time for ourselves that night; it's all on videotape. And now it's time to pay the piper."

"Pay the . . ." he said, and looked at her as though he'd just discovered a viper. *"Videotape?"*

"That's right," she said with satisfaction. His next words wiped the smug look off her face.

"You're crazy if you think that will make me cough up any more information on this Rhodes guy. I don't know anything about him, and I don't give a shit."

Realizing uneasily that he hadn't been as shocked about the existence of the video as she'd planned, she said as dismissively as she could, "Oh, I don't need anything more on Douglas Rhodes. He's out of the picture now, anyway."

"Then what?"

She looked at him as though he were a dull-witted idiot. "Come on, Jack, try a little here, will you? Rhodes might be out of it, but since the nominating convention last month, your wife is still very much in it."

"Yeah, so?"

She was beginning to think she hadn't pegged him right, after all. "So Laura Devlin is much more interesting. Got the picture?"

She saw by his ugly expression that he did. Half rising from the seat, he said, "If you think that I'm going to . . . to *spy*—"

"Such a harsh word, Jack," she said with a yawn. " 'Observe' is so much better." She smiled at him. "Show-and-tell is even better."

"You're out of your mind."

She shrugged. "There's still that videotape."

"Fuck the videotape. You think I care about that?"

She was really shaken now, sure she'd made a mistake, determined not to show it. "Don't you?"

"I told you. Show the damn thing on wide-screen for all I care."

She was nothing if not adaptable, and she quickly retrenched. It was time to move to plan B. Leaning forward, she said sincerely, "Look, Jack, I really don't want to threaten you. I just wanted to show you I was . . . serious. You know how much my career means to me, and I thought that if I could get some inside information on your wife's campaign—sort of scoop the competition—I'd get ahead that much quicker. Do you understand?"

"Oh, I understand, all right," he sneered. "But that doesn't have anything to do with me."

At least he was listening. "On the contrary. As I see it, we're both in a position to help each other out."

His lip curled. "You think I want help from you?"

"You would if I could get you a big engineering contract, wouldn't you?"

"You?" he said sarcastically. "Oh, sure."

Encouraged because he hadn't gotten up and left, she leaned forward again. "I've got friends, Jack. Powerful friends—rich friends. And if I could get an exclusive, behind-the-scenes story about our female vice-presidential candidate, I might see my way clear to whispering your name into a few important ears." She paused deliberately. "And then, for a change, people would notice you."

He glanced away, muttering, "I don't want people to notice me."

"Don't you?" She pretended surprise. "Oh, well, I just thought it must be difficult at times seeing your wife get all the publicity. If I were you, I'd be a little . . . jealous."

He jerked his head. "Yeah? Well, I'm not."

"I see. Well, then, my mistake," she said, and held her breath. If he walked out now, she didn't know what she'd do.

He didn't walk out. Slanting a gaze at her, he asked, "You could really get me a big contract?"

She glanced down to hide the triumph that leaped into her eyes. "I said I could, didn't I? But it's up to you."

He hesitated; she could practically see the wheels turning. Finally he wiped his mouth with the back of his hand. "All right," he said. "What do you need?"

The presidential campaign had been in full swing for just a month when the first of the stories written under Dawn's byline appeared. Along with her morning coffee, Chester brought the paper to Lenore in the master bedroom one day, and she hadn't read the first paragraph before she burst into gleeful laughter.

"Madam?" Chester said. He was sitting at the little desk, going through the mail, and he turned curiously at the sound of her hilarity.

Still chuckling, she held out the paper. "Have you seen this?"

He got up to look, his eyes widening as he scanned the first column, then turned to the second. "Interesting," he said as he handed the paper back. "I wonder where she got such personal and private information."

"I wonder," Lenore said, raising an eyebrow. She smoothed the paper on her lap. " 'Woman to Woman, by Dawn Van Doren,' " she read, and laughed again. "It has a certain . . . ring to it, wouldn't you say?"

"It does indeed."

"She definitely has learned a few things in my employ. I couldn't be more proud of her if I'd thought of this myself."

"You didn't instruct her to obtain this information?"

"No, I didn't, Chester. She did this all on her own."

He glanced over the column again, reading about Laura's struggles with her mother, the battle to balance home and career, the rebellious daughter, the son living away from home, and said, "But what if she goes too far?"

Genuinely delighted, Lenore chortled, "She can't go too far, don't you see? Oh, this is too rich. It's just the ticket we needed. Dawn will publish all this dirt about our vice-presidential hopeful, and she'll get all the publicity, and everyone will ignore Hugh. It's perfect!"

"I . . . I'm afraid I don't quite understand."

"You will," she said, cackling. "You will. Just wait and see."

CHAPTER THIRTY-ONE

Laura first read Dawn Van Doren's new "Woman to Woman" feature when she was flying to her next campaign stop. Tired of going over speech notes, she asked for a paper and looked up in surprise as an aide brought it to her with a muttered "I'm not sure you want to read this." She didn't know what he meant until she saw the article, then she groaned. Oh, great. This was just what she needed; Hugh was going to have a fit.

"Charlie," she said, leaning into the aisle from her seat. "Get everyone together, will you?" She gestured with the paper. "We've got to talk about this."

Her traveling staff gathered in seconds, draping themselves over the backs of seats, crouching in the aisle, sitting on chair arms. She hated to accuse anyone, but the information given here was just a little too personal; she figured it had to be one of them, but she wanted to give the guilty party a chance to confess. Pointing to the article, she looked around at them and asked quietly, "Does anyone know about this?"

Uneasy looks back and forth meant that most of them had seen it, but as she glanced into each young face and saw the same indignation she felt, she frowned. She didn't think any of them had said anything. Charlie summed it up, scornfully. "Even if we knew these things, do you think we'd tell anyone? *Especially* her?"

She glanced around again. "Someone had to."

"Well, it wasn't me!"

"Or me!"

"Or *me*!"

As a chorus of denial rose around her, she decided to let it go. Maybe it was a mistake, a good guess, speculation—who knew? As long as it didn't happen again, she wouldn't make a big deal out of it. But as they all filed back to their seats, she glanced uneasily at the article again, trying to convince herself it was a coincidence. After all, it shouldn't be hard to guess that she'd have doubts about running for office, or questions about her performance once she was elected. Deciding these things were commonplace enough, she finally put the paper aside. She had other things to think about, and any candidate for office seemed to be fair game these days, a good target.

Wearily she laid her head back. It was still early; the plane had taken off before dawn, and the sun was just now gilding the clouds below them with gold. As she glanced out the window, she felt as though she'd been flying nonstop for days. She was so tired, she didn't notice at first that Charlie had returned with a cup of coffee for her.

"Here," Charlie said, moving aside all the brochures and files and research reports she'd left on the seat next to her. She sat down. "You look like you could use this."

"Thanks," she said with a grateful smile, and took a sip before she put the cup on the pulldown tray in front of her. The paper was still lying there, and she gave it a disgusted look. Charlie saw, and dropped the paper disdainfully in the aisle.

"You can't worry about these things, Laura," she said. "Especially since it's probably going to get worse."

"I know," she said with a sigh. "But it's just so . . . I don't know. It's like she reached in and read my mind or something."

"These things can't be true."

She smiled at Charlie's loyalty. "But they are. Of course I had doubts; I would have been a fool not to, wouldn't I? But they're gone now. If I'm elected, I know I'll be able to handle the job."

Charlie frowned. "I wonder why she didn't print that."

She looked wry. "Obviously it's not as newsworthy, that's why."

"Yeah, well . . ." Charlie said grumpily. She was a few years younger than Laura's forty-two, tall and blond, with sun-streaked, shoulder-length hair and blue eyes—a woman with a strong sense of politics and a mind of her own. Like her mother, Laura thought fondly. Charlie—Charlotte Chandler—was Caroline Chandler's daughter, and as soon as Laura's name had been confirmed as Hugh Redmond's running mate, Caroline had called her from Los Angeles to offer her congratulations—and her daughter's help. Charlie had managed several state campaigns, and was already known as a wonder. In the two months since they'd started this whirlwind, she had more than justified her reputation. Now Laura didn't know what she'd do without her.

"Yeah, well, let's hope this is the first and last 'Woman to Woman' article," Laura said dryly. "If this continues, the image I'm trying to project as a confident, able candidate is going to tarnish a little. Especially if everybody thinks I'm going to fall apart any minute."

"Nobody thinks that," Charlie said. "Don't let it shake you up. As I said, it's bound to get worse before it gets better."

"Oh, thanks. I could have gone all day without hearing that."

Charlie laughed and got up. "We've got about an hour before we land. Why don't you try to get some rest? We've got a heavy schedule coming up."

"Gee, and here I thought it had been a walk in the park so far."

"Before we're through, you're going to feel like we've been on this plane forever."

"I already do feel that way."

Charlie laughed again. "Get some sleep."

Her campaign manager wandered away, but though she tried, she couldn't rest. Reaching for her cooling coffee, she sipped reflectively and thought that it did seem as if she'd been doing this a lifetime already, and they still had two months to go before the election. Wondering if all candidates felt this way, she put her head back wearily. Everything seemed such a blur; as she looked back on the nominating convention, surely one of the high points of her life, all she could remember was a whirl of events, a changing kaleidoscope of vignettes that moved too quickly from one to the other. She saw her mother's expression as they all stood with Hugh and his wife, Nora, on the platform that final night; she saw the excitement in Jack's eyes, how handsome Peter looked, how beautiful her daughter was. She remembered how proud and thrilled and excited she'd been when Hugh grabbed her hand and held it and they faced the crowd that had nominated them; she thought her heart would burst with the realization that this—this!—was what she'd been meant all her life to accomplish.

And the noise. She would never forget the shouting and stamping and clapping and screaming and whistling that roared at them in one wave of sound after another when the results were announced. The hysteria that erupted had been almost a physical thing, a force that nearly rocked them all off their feet. She'd been so electrified by that sound that she hadn't felt the heat of the lights, or noticed the cameras trained on them, or even heard the increasingly frantic shouting of the announcer as he tried to quiet the crowd. After a while the man had given up, and the roaring accolades had gone on and on. It had been the most enchanting night of her life, and crowning it all had been Douglas.

She closed her eyes again, savoring the memory, because she knew she'd have nothing else. Even now she didn't know how she had endured the time he'd been away and no one knew where he'd gone; after that day in Sarah's office, he'd simply disappeared for two weeks. Even Sarah didn't know where he was.

The press had been frantic, and lurid stories of the reason for his disappearance had been splashed over every paper and tabloid for days afterward. Sarah had assured her that he just needed time, and because she'd seen—and experienced—the pain he felt, she knew that to be true. But the days had never seemed so long, and nothing was truly right in her world until the day he returned and announced that he'd taken his grandson on a pack trip. A pack trip, she thought, and had to smile. He'd taken two horses and started riding, something he hadn't done since Rob, his son, was a child.

The press had a field day with that, too, and suddenly he became a media event all over again, more popular than ever— and just as determined not to run. No one could understand it, but he refused to answer questions, and after a while, they all had to accept it, especially when he threw his support solidly behind the Redmond-Devlin ticket. She'd only had one brief moment to talk to him, but that had been worse than nothing. Now that she was a candidate, they had been surrounded by secret service, uniformed officers, undercover agents, and as many reporters as could crowd around. With so many ears turned their way, they hadn't been able to say what they meant at all, but had been reduced to platitudes: *Congratulations. Thank you. Good Luck. Thank you again.*

They were parted then, carried away by the press of duty as much as the surge of the crowd. But she had seen the look in his eyes, the true congratulations, the pride, and while she told herself to be satisfied with that, she couldn't help wishing things were different. This wasn't right at all, and if giving up her place on the ticket meant he could have assumed his as the nominee, she would have stepped down gladly, eagerly. Any sacrifice would have been worth that, even the one of her own ambitions.

But since that wasn't going to happen, she had to carry on. She did—or she tried. But three weeks into the campaign, she knew there was going to be trouble. She and Hugh had had many meetings and conferences and discussions and briefings to make sure they agreed on the basics of policy, but it was soon obvious that she was going to be the media darling, not he. As much as she hated to admit it, it seemed inevitable; Hugh might be basically an intelligent man with a good grasp of politics, but he came off as dull and uninspiring, while she had always been able to charm the press. She'd had so much practice, after all, from those early times in the public defender's office, to her first days on the Hill. Without even trying, she had always been a magnet for publicity, and she had learned to deal with it.

Hugh, unfortunately, could not. This continual coverage on her was hurting him, personally and politically, and worse, it was starting to affect their relationship. She knew he was jealous, but she didn't know what to do. Now this story by Dawn Van Doren was going to add fuel to the fire. She could just imagine his reaction to that "Woman to Woman" article; the way things were going, he'd probably think she had solicited it.

One hopeful note in all this was that she and Jack seemed to be getting along better. Things seemed to have smoothed out a little between them since her nomination, and she'd been surprised when, for the first time in longer than she could remember, he started asking her questions about what she was doing: how the campaign was going, what she thought about it, or felt—even what interesting things had happened during one of these whirlwind trips. She was so touched at his interest that she'd started to confide in him again. How ironic it was that just when they seemed to have reached a new level of understanding, they were apart so much now. She was away from home more than she was there, and when she did come trailing in, she didn't want to talk about the campaign, but about her family. To her relief, Andy seemed to have settled down a little, even to be proud of her mom, and Peter still seemed happy in his apartment with his roommate, a young man named Cory Wilmot. She liked Cory, even though he seemed a little effete for her taste, and was surprised that Jack, who affected to be so much a man's man, hadn't said anything yet. But Jack seemed just as preoccupied as she did at times these days; they all had a lot on their minds.

Realizing that the plane was beginning its descent, she grabbed her notes and went over them again. Two hours later, she was standing in front of forty thousand people, listening to the cheers and jubilant shouts of supporters who had come, not necessarily to be enlightened politically, but to have an emotional experience. Nodding and smiling and waving, she nearly told Charlie that she felt like a complete idiot, but she realized in time that the mikes were live, so she held her tongue. She'd grown to hate rallies like this; even though she knew they were necessary, she always felt like a glorified fool standing there while everyone shouted her name—or variations of it.

"Laurie . . . *Laurie* . . . *LAURIE* . . . *!*" The chanting of the crowd was electric, hypnotic, and she had long ago given up being annoyed that they used her nickname. Maybe it was better to be familiar; at this point, she didn't know.

They left that rally and went on to Buffalo, where she took a little more heat. This time the setting was a public forum at the university, and the questions were quick and meant to be lethal. But as always, she was prepared as she stood at the podium and fielded questions about her stand on abortion:

"Yes, I'm prochoice, even though—as you have so kindly pointed out—I'm both a woman and a mother." That brought a laugh, and she went quickly on. "But I think a decision like that should be between a woman and her doctor. The government has no business interfering. Heaven knows, we have more than enough to take care of, don't you think?"

That brought another laugh, and a question about education:

"Yes, I believe the quality of education in this country has suffered," she said. "We need, not only more schools, but more incentives. We need teachers who are eager to *teach*, and who are suitably remunerated for it; we need students who are motivated to learn, and who are rewarded intellectually for it. But most of all, we need to remove all the strictures and restraints brought about by special interest groups, and put studies back into perspective. Our kids need to know why the Civil War came about, and what Lincoln did to put an end to it; they need to know the significance of the women's movement, and why that is so important. They must learn mathematics, and science and geography—*especially* geography," she said, getting another

401

laugh, "so at least they'll know New Mexico is a state and not another country."

There were more questions, tough questions, about the environment and defense spending and Star Wars and foreign and domestic policy and crime and inflation and more spending. She answered them all passionately and honestly and with a sincerity no one could doubt. Five minutes into the forum, she had them; by the end, they were eating out of her hand.

"You're amazing," Charlie murmured as they swept out to the car on a tide of applause to rush back to the airport. "Did you ever think of running for office?"

She would have laughed, but she was too tired.

The plane took them to another rally in Cincinnati, then on to New York for another, still another at the University of Iowa, and finally all the way back to Los Angeles. They arrived long after midnight, disheveled, exhausted, ready to fall into bed— only to be greeted by a sea of reporters and a crowd that surged forward despite the ropes that had been hastily erected to hold them back. The television lights were blinding, and she thought fleetingly—and for the first time—that if she couldn't see, her Secret Service escort couldn't see, either. Then she brushed the thought aside. Like all candidates, she'd been offered a bullet-proof vest at the beginning of the campaign, but she'd flatly refused. She couldn't put herself out there wondering if she was going to be attacked or assassinated, and in the final analysis, there was really nothing the Secret Service could do anyway against a determined killer. They'd all learned that, not only in this country, but around the world, and if she agonized over the threats every candidate received regularly, she'd be too paralyzed to appear in public at all.

But still, this crowd was unusually large for so late an arrival, and as she waited for the plane to taxi up to the ramp, she wondered what was going on. She soon found out. The pilot came back himself to say she'd been sent a message.

"I'm sorry to tell you this," he said, looking unhappy, "but we just got word that your daughter has been arrested."

She thought initially that she was too tired to have heard him correctly. Blankly she said, "What?"

"We just got it from the tower," he said. "Apparently she was taken in with some other kids for drunk driving. How the press got hold of it . . ."

With Laura still in shock, he bent over to look out the window.

Even from here the glare of the lights was blinding, and he grimaced. "It looks like news travels fast. I'm sorry. What do you want me to do? We can take off again if you like."

Feeling as though her world were slipping out from under her, she managed a weak smile. "Do you think if I just stay on board, they'll get tired and leave?"

He smiled faintly in return. "We can try. I'll sit out here all night if I have to."

"Thanks, Bob," she said as a worried-looking Charlie appeared by her side. She glanced out the window again and sighed. "But somehow I don't think that's going to help."

"Anything I can do, just say the word."

"Believe me, I will. Thanks again." She waited until he had gone before she looked up at her campaign manager. "You're going to ask me to make some kind of statement, but I can't do that until I find out for certain what's happened."

"I'm sure it's some kind of mistake, Laura."

Wearily she gathered her things. "I hope you're right," she said, and went to run the gauntlet. As soon as she came into the terminal, everyone started shouting.

"What comment do you have about your daughter's arrest, Congresswoman Devlin?"

"Anything to say about your opponent's claim that a good mother would be home with her children?"

"Where is your husband at this time?"

"Is this the first time your daughter's been in trouble?"

"Did you know your daughter was running wild?"

"What about your son? Is he a drinker, too?"

The questions were so fast and furious, she didn't have time to answer. With the lights glaring in her eyes, and the microphones shoved into her face, her exhaustion clearly showed. The noise and shouting were deafening, and she knew from experience that no one was interested in the facts, but in her reactions instead. She was too tired to dissemble, and she didn't intend to tell them anything anyway, at least not until she'd talked to Jack—and Andrea.

Making up her mind, she turned and gestured to one of her hovering Secret Service agents. Faced with a crowd like this, they were hovering even more protectively, hands inside their jackets, eyes never still. One instantly appeared by her side, and she said under her breath, "Is there any way for me to get to a phone?"

"Right away," he murmured, and put the walkie-talkie he carried to his mouth. Instantly, but not soon enough, it seemed to her, a path opened and they grabbed her and sped through. Howls of protest followed, outraged cries that were cut off abruptly when she was whisked into a nearby VIP room. The soft music and dim lights of the place seemed like heaven after the chaos outside, but she wasn't in the mood to enjoy it. Spying a telephone, she dialed home, glancing at the clock. It was a little after two-thirty in the morning, not even six o'clock there.

"Hello . . ."

Jack answered on the third ring, his voice slurred—but with drink or sleep, it was hard to tell. She didn't care. "Jack?"

"Laura?" He sounded disbelieving. "Thank God. Where are you?"

"In L.A. We just got in, and heard the news. Is Andrea all right?"

Angry now. "She's fine. It was all a mistake that the press blew completely out of proportion."

"She wasn't arrested?" Expelling a breath in relief, she sank down onto the nearby couch.

"No, no," he said impatiently. "As I said, it was all a mistake. Andy wasn't drinking; the others were."

Her relief seemed to be premature, and she gripped the phone. "What others?"

Irritated again. "Some boys she met at some service station across from school."

She straightened. "That's impossible. I talked to her about that. I told her we didn't want her to see that young man."

"Yes, well, apparently she decided to do things her way."

Her lips tightened. "I want to talk to her."

"Do you know what time it is?"

"I don't care what time it is! Call her to the phone—now!"

He knew that tone. "All right, just a minute. I'll have to get her."

She waited what seemed an interminable time, refusing the coffee Charlie brought her, trying not to see the worried looks of her staff. She knew they were all assessing the damage this was going to do to the campaign, but at the moment she didn't care too much about that. What was happening at home? What was Andrea thinking of? She'd seemed so much happier lately, her rebellion a thing of the past. Had it all been a pose, an act? Her mouth tightened again. She was going to find out.

Andrea finally picked up the phone. She didn't sound as though she'd been asleep, and she was very subdued. "Hi, Mom."

Until she'd heard her daughter's voice, she had fully intended to give her a tongue-lashing; she didn't care who heard. But there were tears in that tone, and when she thought how hard this had been on her family, too, she reconsidered.

"Hi, Andy," she said. "I'm in Los Angeles, and I just heard. I'm going to take the plane out again and come home so we can talk about what happened, all right? I should be there in—"

Andrea burst into tears. "Oh, Mom, you don't have to come home! I'm sorry you even heard about this. It was all a mistake anyway. I didn't mean for anything like this to happen, honest. Things just . . . just got out of hand!"

"And that's exactly why I intend to come home to talk to you about this. Being picked up by the police is a serious thing, Andy, and—"

"I know, Mom—I know! And it won't happen again, I promise." There was a shudder in her voice, impossible to doubt. "I've learned my lesson, honest. I never want to see the inside of a police station again!"

She didn't doubt that. "I still think I should come home—"

"No, no, please, Mom—I'll feel even worse!" Andrea begged. "Please, I wasn't arrested or anything, so can't we pretend this never happened? I promise, I won't see that guy ever again!"

"Well . . ." She could feel herself weakening. Maybe if she insisted on coming home, that would be worse. "I don't know, Andy. We talked about this boy—"

"I know," Andrea interrupted miserably. "And I told you, I won't see him again. I don't even know why I liked him, or did what I did. I guess . . . I guess I thought it would be fun or something—you know, getting away from these gray suits. . . ." She meant the Secret Service. "So I sneaked out and went over there. But I swear, I didn't know they were going to be drinking. I thought we were just going to go out and cruise."

"And *cruise*? What time was this?"

"I told you it was a stupid thing to do," Andrea sobbed. "And Mom, I'm not trying to get out of it or anything, but it was almost as if someone knew I was going to be there."

"What do you mean?"

"Well, reporters were there when we got back."

"You were surprised? You know they're always in front of the house now."

"No, I mean at the garage. The cops were there, too."

"What?"

"I'm telling you, Mom—it was really like a setup or something. I know you're going to think I'm paranoid—"

"No, just overimaginative. I think it's more probable that you weren't as clever as you thought."

"You're still mad at me, aren't you? Is it because of the campaign?" She started to cry again. "Did I ruin everything?"

"I'm not worried about the campaign, Andrea," she said, dismissing her tight schedule, all the commitments she'd made, the responsibilities she was supposed to fulfill. "I'm more worried about you. I'm coming home."

And she did, despite the objections and pleas of nearly everyone on her campaign staff. Her daughter was more important than any of that, and when Andrea flew into her arms when she arrived, she knew the trip had been worth it.

"I'm so proud of you, Mom," Andy had sobbed after they'd had a long talk. "I promise, I won't be so dumb again. I'll be the perfect daughter from now on, I swear."

Smiling through her own tears, she had gathered Andy up again in her arms. Stroking her hair, she murmured, "Perfect, I don't expect. A little more thought and consideration, yes."

"Oh, Mom, I'll be the best—you'll see! I'll campaign for you and everything! Please, let me?"

And so they had a press conference—a rousing success. Mother and daughter shone, and Laura's popularity escalated again. Everyone, even reporters, seemed touched. Hugh, when they contacted him, wasn't so pleased. They tracked him down in Des Moines, and as soon as he heard her voice, he shouted, "What the hell is going on?"

He was furious; he'd scheduled a big press conference of his own that morning, intending to discuss his foreign policy. They both knew what would be discussed, and she couldn't blame him for being angry.

"I'm sorry, Hugh," she said penitently. "It was all a mistake."

"I'll say!" he replied coldly. "Can't you control your family any better than this?"

She was tired; she could feel herself getting angry. She hadn't wanted this to happen any more than he did, and she spoke sharply. ''I said it was a mistake. I've taken care of it.''

''And now, it appears, so will I. The phone has been ringing off the hook, and reports from the pressroom indicate they intend to grill me. And you know what about!''

''I'm sure you can handle it,'' she said encouragingly, and called Janette for a little sanity.

''Well, excitement seems to follow you wherever you go,'' her sister said. ''How's Andrea, really?''

''She's fine—now.''

''No more midnight runs?''

Grimacing, she shook her head. ''I hope not.''

''Well, you're so far ahead in the polls, it probably won't make much difference.''

Amused, she asked, ''When did you start following the polls?''

''When my sister started running for office,'' Janette said, and wished her luck.

She hung up thinking that she was going to need it. She had never felt time flying by so quickly as it had lately, when she was forced to rush here and there in a never-ending sweep of this immense country. She had never felt the vastness of the country so deeply before either, or the knowledge of how small she was in comparison to it. Each day emphasized that fact. When she wanted to stay home for a while, she had to leave immediately. Her only consolation was Andrea's proud face. She'd been asked by the principal at her school to give a pep rally. Wishing her daughter good luck, she embraced the rest of her family and flew off again in a cloud of dust. A fund-raiser was scheduled that morning, followed by a rally that afternoon. Then it was on to another five-city tour for more personal appearances, more speeches, more debates. The pace was backbreaking; by the time it was over, her staff estimated she would have traveled over fifty-five thousand miles, campaigning in eighty-five cities in eighty-some days.

The people made it worthwhile—the thousands and thousands of people who gathered wherever she stopped. It was something she would never forget: crowds lining the streets, waiting at airports, waving from buildings, standing on cars. . . . It was exciting, a little frightening, always inspiring, unbelievable. She hadn't dreamed that night Harold Geiger came to the house to ask all his questions that it would be like this; she was sure that no one who had never done this before was ever truly prepared. That first interview with Geiger was only the beginning.

She remembered that night so clearly: After he had asked innumerable questions about their private lives, their finances, their health, their medical history, and everything else in between, he'd been replaced by Hugh's top advisor, an even more intense man, who had hammered again and again at her about the stresses and strains of political campaigns, the demands if she was to be the candidate, what she would be expected to do as Redmond's running mate. She'd felt confident and sure of herself until they'd gone, but while Jack slept that night, she'd lain awake. Finally she'd left their bed and crept downstairs to sit in the darkened living room and take stock. Was she capable of this?

The answer had been an unqualified yes. Government was her profession now, and while she knew she was still inexperienced, she was learning. She had never been afraid of work or responsibility, and she would bring to office her already proven ability to work with her colleagues, who had been supporting her in greater and greater numbers on her urban bill, and her stand on education and victims' rights. She wasn't worried about being able to fill the job or the duties that went with it, or even if the worst happened—and every vice-presidential candidate had to consider that—fulfilling that job, too.

Then there had been the *big* question: would she, if she had to?

The answer had been yes again—but this time with a qualifier. She'd already thought about it; she would have been a fool or a complete incompetent not to. So she had looked them straight in the eye and replied, "I would do anything I had to do to defend this country. But I believe there are other alternatives to try first, and with the fate of the human race at stake, I'd be morally obligated to exhaust every avenue before I resorted to destroying us all."

Her brief return home was soon a blur in the past. Off on another whirl, she lost track of time when the countdown started in earnest. She and Hugh pulled out all the stops, flying around the country in what seemed like an endless race from one time zone to another and back through them all again until she hardly knew what day it was, or sometimes even the hour. The only continuity in her life seemed to be the plane, the staff, and the traveling press corps who followed wherever they went. Toward the end of the campaign, they were flying in and out of as many as five states a day, and it almost came to an end one night in Arizona, at another rally.

"It's great to be back in Arizona," she said over the bristle of microphones in front of her, wondering all the while if she'd been here before. She was so tired by that time, she couldn't remember, but she realized by the wild shouting and screaming and thunderous ovation of the crowd that it didn't matter. She went on with her speech, and didn't see Douglas standing to one side until it was over. With that chanting that seemed to follow her wherever she went now, that jubilant "Laurie . . . Laurie . . . LAURIE . . . !" ringing in her ears, she waved for a final time and left the makeshift stage. She saw Douglas at last, and stopped. She was so elated that he was here that at first she didn't notice his expression.

"Douglas!" she whispered, and tried to clear her throat. She was hoarse from all that speechmaking, but how glad she was to see him! It had been so long!

He came forward to take her hands, the proper greeting for old friends from Congress, the United States senator greeting the vice-presidential candidate. "Laura," he said. "I'm afraid I've got some bad news. . . ."

She stiffened, the still-shouting crowd forgotten. It was difficult to breathe; she was suddenly so afraid. "What . . . ?"

"It's Peter," he said, tightening his grip on her hands and pulling her out of the way. Beyond him, she could see the worried faces of her staff, the stricken look in Charlie's eyes. Dear God, she thought, what's happened?

"He's all right," Douglas said quickly, seeing her sudden look of terror. "Physically, I mean. But . . . but . . . Christ, I don't know how to tell you this!"

"Just tell me!"

Looking as though he'd rather be shot, he said, "He was seen coming out of a gay bar in Washington, Laura. With his arms around another man."

She could feel the blood draining from her head and thought for a terrible moment that she would pitch straight forward into his arms. The edges of her vision went black, and she didn't even feel him helping her to a nearby chair. Blankly, uncomprehendingly, she looked around. "No," she said. "It's not possible. There must be some mistake."

He squatted down beside her, still holding her hands. "There's no mistake," he said, knowing she would want to know the truth. "Reporters were there; they have pictures. It's already gone out over the AP wire."

She felt consciousness fleeing again. This couldn't be happening, she thought over and over; it had to be some awful, hideous nightmare. Peter, her son—the boy she had nurtured and loved and raised . . . She couldn't even think the word. Wildly she looked at Douglas. If it wasn't a mistake, there had to be some explanation.

He saw that stricken look in her eyes. "What can I do?" he asked.

She didn't know. "I've got to get home—to see him," she said. All she could think about was that if this was true, she wanted to hear it from Peter's own lips. And if it was . . . she'd deal with it. But oh; God, she thought, agonized. It's so dangerous now, so terribly, terribly dangerous. Blankly she looked at Douglas again. "Can you arrange it?"

"It's already done," he said. "I'll go with you."

She closed her eyes. Oh, she wanted him to; she wanted him there with her. She would have given anything to have him by her side, to feel his strength, to know she could lean on him. But there was Jack to consider—and Peter. Suffering, she shook her head. "No, I have to go alone."

He searched her face, his feelings for her naked in his eyes. She couldn't bear it; she wanted to put her hand up to his mouth before he could say the words. But there were people all around, always so many people. They were both caught in this web, bound by duty, fighting desire, and so she begged him silently to do this one thing for her. She could feel his indecision, and knew the battle he was fighting because she was fighting it, too.

Finally he nodded. "If that's what you want," he said painfully, "I'll have a driver take you to the airport. A plane is waiting. No one will know, or follow you."

She looked up at him, her eyes glittering with unshed tears—for him, for her . . . for Peter. "Thank you, Douglas," she whispered, and left him before she betrayed herself further.

The flight back was a nightmare. As the chartered Lear sped through the night, she sat tensely in her seat, her expression withdrawn and sere, her eyes staring blindly out the darkened window. As exhausted as she was, sleep was impossible, for she kept thinking, inevitably, of Peter, and telling herself over and over and over again that there had to be an explanation.

And if there isn't?

She put her head back exhaustedly against the seat. She had promised herself she'd deal with that, too. Whatever it was, she told herself, she'd deal with it. Somehow.

Douglas was as good as his word. When the private charter landed, another car was waiting for her and she was whisked away into the night without incident. Relieved at that much respite at least, she sent him her silent blessings, but no more. She didn't dare think of Douglas for fear she might weaken and ask him to come to her after all, and she knew there would be a crowd of reporters at home, demanding answers. Douglas's presence would give them more fuel, and things were bad enough. Somehow she held herself together until she got there. The campaign seemed very far away, and the driver interrupted her tense silence only once during that seemingly endless ride to ask if she preferred going home or to Peter's apartment. Stricken, she didn't know. She'd been so preoccupied with just getting here in one piece that she hadn't asked where he'd be.

"I'll take care of it," the man said, and reached for a car phone. He made a call or two, and then said over his shoulder, "It seems the family is with Senator Ambrose."

"Thank God," Laura whispered, and knew that if anyone could help them sort through this mess, it would be Sarah.

Mercifully the press hadn't gotten wind of where Peter might be, and Sarah's town house seemed dark and deserted when they slowly drove by. No reporters lurked that she could see, but the driver stopped partway down the block to make sure. She wouldn't let him get out of the car to open the door for her because she thought it might draw attention, so she leaned over the seat to give him her heartfelt thanks.

"No need to thank me, ma'am," he said, touching his cap. "I was glad to help."

She summoned a ghost of the smile that had entranced so many. "You did—more than you know. I'll never forget."

He gazed at her for a long moment. "You know, I never believed politics was a woman's game, but you had my vote from the beginning. Give 'em hell, Congresswoman—all the way to the White House."

Tears of gratitude in her eyes, she held out her hand, and he took it. His hard shake seemed to give her strength, and seconds

411

later, the car had disappeared and Sarah was letting her into the house.

"Laura," she said, drawing Laura to her in a quick embrace. "We'll get through this, don't worry."

The strain, and Sarah's kindness, finally broke her. Beginning to sob, she said, "No, we won't. I can't, Sarah. I can't do this anymore. Nothing is worth this—nothing!"

Sarah took her aside. "You have to continue. You must."

"I can't!"

"You will!" Sarah said fiercely. "Or what Douglas sacrificed is for naught."

She looked up. "Douglas?"

Sarah glanced away. "I shouldn't have said that."

She took the other woman's arm. "Said what? What do you mean?" She heard her voice rising and couldn't stop it. She gave Sarah's arm a shake. "Tell me!"

And so Sarah did. She had been pale before, but her face was absolutely leached of color by the time Sarah finished telling her what had really happened that day at Deer Hollow. She was so shaken, so stricken, so devastated, at the thought of how far Douglas had gone to protect her that she groped blindly for a chair and nearly fell into it. Sarah looked at her sympathetically.

"Now do you understand why you have to go on?"

She tried to speak, had to try again. Her throat seemed to have closed; she couldn't think. "Why . . . why didn't he tell me?" she said hoarsely. "Why didn't he let me know?"

Sarah leaned close. "He didn't want you to find out; he knew what your reaction would be."

She started to get up from the chair. "And he was right—!"

"No!" Gripping her arm, Sarah bent down again, forcing her back. "I shouldn't have told you," she whispered fiercely. "But I thought that now—especially now—you should know how much others have sacrificed to get you where you are. You can't betray that trust, Laura—you can't!"

She didn't know what to say. Was Sarah right? She didn't know that, either. She couldn't seem to think clearly; she rubbed her forehead. "I don't know . . ."

"I do," Sarah said, and helped her out of the chair, forcing her to stand on her own two feet. "Douglas is sending Malcolm Tanner to help out. He'll know how to handle this. Until then . . ." Her expression softened. "Until then, your son is waiting. He wants to talk to you."

412

"Oh, Sarah, what am I going to say?"

"Say what's in your heart, dear. Just say what's in your heart," Sarah said, and gestured.

She turned, and Peter was standing there in the doorway, tall, pale, uncertain. Without hesitation, she opened her arms, and as he hadn't done since he was a little boy, he ran to her. He was taller than she was now, but even though she had to reach up, her embrace was no less fiercely protective than it had been all those years ago.

"Peter . . ." she whispered.

"Oh, Mom," he said, beginning to cry. "I'm not gay. It's all a big mistake."

Her relief was so great that she almost fainted. Gripping him tightly, she looked him right in the eye. "Don't lie," she said. "I can take anything but that."

He shook his head. "I wouldn't lie about that."

She searched his face for a moment longer, then she nodded. "All right, then," she said with a ghost of a smile. "Then let's see what we can do about this."

As Sarah had prophesied, they did get through it, although at the time, she didn't see how they would. After the emotional scene in the foyer, she went with Peter into the living room, where the rest of the family awaited so they could all hear from him what had happened.

"It was Cory," Peter said, naming his roommate. "I told him he shouldn't go to places like that, but he wouldn't listen. I swear I didn't find out how he was until we took the apartment, but even then, I hoped it wouldn't matter. I—" He glanced quickly at his father, who continued to sit like a stone figure. "I guess I was naive, and stupid. Anyway, when he realized I wasn't like that, he started to go out. He was looking for a new roommate, I guess, and maybe he thought he'd find someone in a bar." His handsome face twisted. "He found someone, all right. He got beat up pretty bad tonight, and when he called me, I had to come and get him." He turned pleadingly to Laura. "You understand, don't you, Mom?"

She didn't even look in Jack's direction. They'd talk about this later; right now, Peter needed all the assurance he could get. "Of course. Go on. What happened?"

"Well, they were waiting for us when we came out of the bar—"

"They?" Laura asked.

"Reporters—you know, the press. I was sure they hadn't followed me, but I guess they had. Anyway, they took some pictures, and I tried to explain to the lady, but—"

"Lady—what lady?"

"That woman from the paper who was there," Peter said. "Her name is Dawn Van Doren—you know, the one who's been writing those articles about you."

Andrea, who had sat huddled and silent and afraid in one of the big easy chairs in Sarah's living room until now, glanced up at the mention of that name. "She was there tonight, too?"

Laura turned to her. "What do you mean, too?"

Andrea looked uneasy. Although she and her mother had come to terms with the incident long ago, she didn't like to be reminded of that night she'd been taken with her so-called friends to jail. "Well, she was there that night—you know, when I got into all that trouble with Greg at the garage?"

That was the first Laura had heard about this. "What do you mean, she was there?"

"I mean, she was *there*! Right there at the garage that night. She had a photographer with her and everything. She was the one who took all the pictures. Didn't I tell you?"

"No, you didn't," Laura said, wondering what was going on here. This Dawn Van Doren seemed to have an uncanny ability to turn up at the most inconvenient moments for her and her family, she thought, and glanced at Jack to get his opinion. Startled by his desperate look, she said, "Jack?"

He had gone completely pale. "I've got to talk to you, Laura—now," he said. "Alone."

She didn't argue; there was something too disturbing about his tone. They went into the foyer, where she turned anxiously to face him. "What—"

He ran a hand through his hair. "Laura, there's something I've got to tell you. . . ." he said, and looked sick.

She'd thought until he told her about his little affair with Dawn that she'd had all the shocks she could bear that night. But when he came to the part about meeting in the bar and the videotape and then the promised contract that had lured him into revealing all these details about his family, she couldn't believe her ears. She was so staggered by the story that she didn't even know what to say. How could this possibly be true?

"I . . . I didn't realize how far she'd go," he finished miserably. "I didn't know she would . . . would set up the kids to get a story. I'm sorry, Laura. Can you forgive me? I know I've been a fool, but I . . . I didn't know what she was capable of."

She hadn't known until that moment what she was capable of, either. "Forgive you?" she choked. "For*give* you?"

She sounded so incredulous that he winced. "I know I don't have the right to ask—"

"You certainly don't! My God, how could you have done such a thing? How could you?"

He looked as though he might cry. "I know what this might do to your campaign—"

"I'm not thinking about the damned *campaign*! I'm thinking about the kids! Do you know what you've done to them?"

"It wasn't my fault!" he repeated. "Please believe me, Laurie, it wasn't my fault!"

She couldn't believe he'd said that; couldn't believe this was happening to her. Staring at him, she suddenly realized that she didn't know him at all. He was a stranger, and in that moment, she was a stranger to herself. In a cold voice she didn't even recognize, "If it wasn't your fault, Jack, whose was it?"

He reached for her; she moved away. "Laurie, please—"

She saw it then, more clearly than she had ever seen anything before. He was right, she thought: he was right. It wasn't his fault; it was theirs—together. She should have seen; she should have known. But no, she'd blinded herself for years; she hadn't wanted to see because then she would have had to deal with it, to make a decision.

One that might hurt her career?

Writhing, she knew she had to admit it. It wasn't the entire reason, but it was partially true; she had to take some responsibility. She had been ambitious; she had wanted this. It was her fault, too.

"I've thought about it, and you're right about one thing, Jack," she said, still in that cold, remote voice. "It was partly my fault. I was a fool, too. I thought we could work it out if we just tried hard enough—or if I forgave enough, or ignored enough. I thought we could hold it together for the kids—"

"We did hold it together," he said desperately. "We can!"

"No. Because I'm through apologizing for what I am, what I do, what I want, what I aspire to. And I'm not going to feel guilty and forgive you everything because I can't be all things to you. You've said often enough over the years that I was involved in my work; well, I was. But that didn't make me a bad wife or mother; it only made me someone who was trying to balance too many things at once. I know you thought I should give up everything I wanted for you, for the kids, for the good of the family, but you know something? The irony of it is that I never asked such a sacrifice of any of you. Why did you feel you could ask it of me?''

"I'm sorry, Laura!'' he said, beginning to cry. ''I won't ever ask it of you again!''

She looked him up and down with scorn. ''You say that as if you still had a right to ask anything. Well, you don't. This time you've gone too far. Do you know what Andrea felt? How Peter suffered? Do you care? And what for? So you could save face, a little pride . . . your hide.'' She shook her head. ''I can't forgive you for this. Maybe your children can, but I can't.''

He tried one last time. ''But I didn't think—''

''That's your problem—you never do. If you had stopped to think, you would have realized that Dawn Van Doren would never have used that tape. Two have to play, and since she was obviously on it, too, she wouldn't have let anyone see it. A paper might hire a journalist who used less than ethical tactics to get a story, but they certainly wouldn't hire one who made her own front-page news.''

He looked stricken at the obviousness of it all, but she didn't look back. Turning on her heel, she left him standing there—as she should have long ago.

The press conference she gave was short, swift, and to the point. As Sarah had promised, Douglas did send Malcolm to save the day, and he arrived via stretch limousine full of schemes and prepared to organize all details. He'd even roughed out a statement for her to make. She glanced over it and handed it back with a tight smile.

''Thanks, Malcolm, but I already know what I'm going to say.''

He was too experienced to look alarmed; too sensible to argue once he'd gazed into those determined, green eyes. He was also astute enough to know what was right, and he smiled and let her have her way. After all, he had contingency plans, and he bowed out and let her face the reporters all alone, which she did with all the equanimity at her considerable command. Without embellishment or excuse, she simply told the facts as Peter had told her: that he'd gone to help a friend who happened to be gay. She left it to the press, and the millions of viewers riveted to their television screens, to decide what they wanted. She'd already had her answer from her son, and she would believe it until he told her otherwise, or until the day she died. For her, it was as simple as that.

Her family was on the dais behind her—Jack included. It was her only concession to Malcolm, who insisted. She felt like a hypocrite, until she rationalized that Jack owed Peter this much. He'd put her son through hell, and Peter deserved his support— he deserved the support of the entire family. And so they posed together, as it should be.

One thing hadn't been planned, and that was the moment that Peter stepped forward when she finished her little speech. She hadn't even known he was behind her until he put his arm around her waist. Then, as she looked up in surprise, he bent, and with infinite tenderness, kissed her on the cheek. There was something so poignant about the gesture that silence reigned for a few seconds, then wild applause erupted. The AP wire carried the photo, and analysts agreed that that picture alone helped turn the tide.

After that, the press—along with everybody else in the country, it seemed—was on her side. Hugh was furious at the flap until the polls showed a sharp increase in support; then he was all smiles. The campaign continued exhaustedly and unabated, and when Charlie wearily told her on election night that they had logged over thirty thousand miles since the beginning of October alone, she collapsed in a tired little heap in the plane seat.

"Just tell me one thing," she begged. "Are we on our way home?"

Charlie grinned. She claimed later that she hadn't put them up to it, but on her signal, everybody stood up and shouted, "No, ma'am, we're on the way to the White House!"

She laughed, gave a weary thumbs-up sign, and then slept all the way to California. It was election night. She'd done what she could; it was up to the voters now.

---❦---

CHAPTER THIRTY-TWO

It was election night, and across the country people were glued to their television screens. All the major networks and their affiliates had been gearing up for weeks to report the results this night; every channel had variations of the same newsroom scene: solemn anchors sitting at planks that passed as desks, busy-looking people with headsets rushing back and forth behind them, pausing occasionally in camera range to place a hand on an ear before rushing on again. Entire walls of electronic maps were positioned behind all this activity, and before the night was over, dictionaries of words would spew forth, detailing everything from what George Washington did with his teeth on election night two hundred and some years ago, to the parties that were going on in the country today. Celebrities would be interviewed for their wise, informed opinions; analysts would be consulted for inexplicable and trenchant data. Mayors and governors and senators and congressmen—and women—would be asked for quotes, and there would be many man-in-the-street impromptus. It was all part of a hysterical, self-important ceremony that was meaningless at the end, when the last vote was counted. That was really what they were all here for, and as the lights went on, and the cameras started to heat up, and anchors stretched their necks and settled in for the marathon, and the maps behind them began to glow, people all over the country waited to see who would lead them for the next four years.

In Los Angeles, the home of one of the candidates, tension ran high in various circles, but the noise level was perhaps loudest at a new bar near the Criminal Courts Building called, appropriately, the Jury Box. Two television screens had been set up behind the bar, and as the votes started coming in, three of the spectators gathered there whooped and raised a glass to an old friend.

"God, this is great!" Trudy Mankiller said jubilantly, grinning at her two companions. "I told you she'd do it. Didn't I tell you?"

"You told us," Maurey Webber agreed. His glasses were steaming in the close atmosphere, and he took them off and wiped them with a cocktail napkin. His eyes looked naked and unprotected without the round lenses, and a little sad. Trudy watched him for a minute before she dismissed him with a grunt and turned to her other companion. Dale Davidson was sitting there looking introspective, and she poked him in the shoulder.

"Can you believe this?" she said. "Our Laura! All I can say is that a woman's place sure is in the house—only this time it's the White House!" And she burst into raucous, jubilant laughter again.

Dale gave her a weak smile. "You're right about that."

Trudy stopped laughing and looked from one to the other, her hands on her hips. "Well, you guys are a barrel of laughs! What's the matter with you, anyway? This is a historic moment, and you both look ready to cry!"

Dale was about to answer, but just then the announcer said something about Laura, and he was diverted. He glanced up at the television set just as her picture came on. It was one of the best photos ever taken of her—her head back, those great green eyes sparkling with wit and intelligence, her lips curved in a delighted smile. She looked as though she had a wonderful story to tell and was about to share it with everyone she met. She had never looked so beautiful, and Dale didn't even hear what the voice-over was saying; his expression transfixed, he couldn't take his eyes off the screen.

Maury saw his glance and followed it. When he saw Laura's picture, his own expression softened, and he sat back, staring up. Trudy, sensing something was happening, looked from one to the other, and craned around to see the TV behind her. When she saw Laura still smiling at them, she grinned from ear to ear.

"God, she's something, isn't she?" she said.

Maurey sighed and grabbed his beer. "Yes, she is. I'm going to miss her. Hell, I already do."

"So do I," she said fervently, and realized that Dale hadn't said anything at all. She glanced his way, saw his expression, and sat back with a marveling one of her own. "You were in love with her, weren't you, Dale?" she said.

419

He didn't take his eyes from the screen. Lifting his glass in a silent toast, he said bleakly, "I still am."

In another part of Los Angeles, not too far from the Jury Box, in Century City, Malcolm Tanner sat by himself in the darkened video room at Tanner, Inc. In front of him was a bank of television screens, each tuned to a different picture, some broadcast, some film, some videotape from his private library. Staring up at the flickering images, he smiled to himself as the first states—designated pink for Laura's party by some wit at a major network, no doubt—began to glow. One by one, New York, then Massachusetts, then West Virginia, then North Carolina, then Delaware, turned fuchsia, and Malcolm grinned.

"And that's just the beginning," he murmured confidently, and grabbed the iced bottle of champagne his secretary had thoughtfully brought to him before he sent her away. He wanted to be alone tonight, to enjoy this victory all by himself. Popping the cork, he poured a glass and raised it in a toast.

"To you, Laura," he cried. "And, thanks to Douglas, to one hell of a profitable partnership!"

Then, draining the glass, he flung it in a magnificent gesture right toward the bank of television screens. Then he sat back and laughed in sheer delight.

In South Pasadena, Caroline and Charlotte Chandler sat in the living room of the vast Chandler estate, surrounded by members of the Women's Political Caucus. A console television had been brought in for the occasion, and no one commented on the incongruous note it struck in the otherwise perfectly proportioned French Provincial room; they were all too busy enjoying the results. Every time another state glowed pink on the screen, mother and daughter led a raucous cheer that was met with equal enthusiasm by the other members of the group. Darien Chandler, Caroline's husband and Charlie's father, had long ago retired to his study. Every time he heard all those well-bred voices shouting in the living room, he shook his head indulgently. But he had a small television set up by his desk as he worked, and he glanced at it in satisfaction from time to time, pleased that the women in his family had played their parts in what was sure to be a historic moment.

"Who in the world is responsible for that ghastly pink?" Caroline asked, back in the living room. "It's so obvious. Why

420

couldn't they just have left it red, white, and blue, like every other election year?''

Charlie, who had been with Laura every step of the way, grinned in pure delight. "Mother, if things go the way we planned tonight, I don't care if they fill in every one of those states with little hearts and flowers, do you?''

As she spoke, Minnesota, Pennsylvania, Illinois, and Iowa began to display that telltale glow, and Caroline grinned back at her daughter. Turning toward the screen again, she led another cheer and they all dissolved in jubilant laughter.

Holed up in a hotel room in Baltimore, where she'd fled after being fired from the paper that morning, Dawn wasn't laughing. The television was on, but because the accommodations weren't the best, jagged lines alternated with snow across the damned pink screen until she threw an empty bourbon bottle right at it in angry frustration. She'd already had too much to drink, and her aim was off; the bottle crashed against the wall instead, and instantly someone on the other side began pounding with his fist.

"Knock it off in there!'' a man shouted. "Don't you know people are trying to sleep?''

"Fuck off!'' Dawn yelled back, and put her aching head in her hands. The exchange had reminded her of how things had once been back home—her drunk of a father yelling; people banging on the walls, screaming for quiet. She wanted to cry. She'd come a long way, hadn't she? How could this have happened?

Still feeling bewildered, and now befuddled by all she'd had to drink, she tried to recall that humiliating scene this morning. She hadn't dreamed she'd be fired when she was called into the publisher's office; she was so sure she'd been promoted that she was already planning the party she intended to give. Then came the words that had clanged like a death sentence—death to all her hopes, her dreams, her ambitions. She hadn't even been given a chance to defend herself.

"You don't *make* the news, Miss Van Doren, you simply report it,'' the publisher had said coldly as she stared at him in uncomprehending dismay. "Now, maybe you 'arranged' things at that gossip rag you came from, but we don't do that here. Pick up your severance pay on the way out.''

She couldn't understand what had happened. Other reporters

took advantage of situations; what had she done that was so wrong? All right, so she had set up Peter Devlin; so what? He *looked* like a fag, didn't he? And he was living with that other pansy from his college. She hadn't intended to *prove* he was gay, just suggest the possibility. After all, what better news?

Barnaby hadn't understood, either. He wouldn't even take her call, and she knew then that she was dead in this town. If she couldn't get a job even at the *Eye*, what was she going to do?

Another sob escaped her, and her glance fell on the phone. Swaying drunkenly, she tried to form a plan, but all she could think of was that that old bitch was responsible for getting her into this, so she could damned well get her out. Half falling over the bed, she grabbed the phone and dialed. It took her three tries, but she finally reached Deer Hollow Farm.

"Chester, this is Dawn," she said, trying fiercely to concentrate. The room swayed, and she had to hold on to the bedside table for balance. "And don't give me any bullshit about seeing if Lenore is home. I know damned well she is, and I want to talk to her. Right now!"

"Certainly, Miss Van Doren," he said, calm and supercilious as ever. "Would you hold a moment please?"

Even in her alcoholic daze, she felt surprise. She knew Lenore never answered the phone just like that, and she clutched the receiver in sudden, desperate hope. It was obvious the old bitch had heard what happened; now she was going to help. A relieved laugh escaped her, turned abruptly into a wrenching sob. She hiccuped and put her hand over her mouth, trying to hold herself together until Lenore came on the line. Groggily she glanced around, wondering for a second or two where she was, and why she'd come to this godforsaken place. Then she shook her head. Never mind. Lenore was coming to the phone; she'd take care of things.

There was a click, and suddenly that voice in her ear. "Miss Van Doren." Coolly. "What a surprise. I hadn't expected you to call."

Her head was reeling; she desperately needed a drink. "Yeah? Why not? Don't tell me you haven't heard. You hear everything in this town—even before it happens."

"I assumed you're referring to your dismissal from the paper," Lenore said calmly. "Yes, I heard."

"Well, what are you going to do about it?"

Lenore laughed that silvery, tinkly little laugh that had always raised the hackles on her neck. "Do?" she repeated. "But, my dear, it's already done!"

The room was spinning again, the bed swaying under her as though she were on a raft at high sea. Somehow she managed to hang on. But even though she'd had all that to drink, she suddenly knew for certain. "You bitch!" she hissed. "You planned this."

That tinkly little laugh came again. "Of course. You didn't imagine anything else, did you?"

She was silent, trying to digest this. Finally she said, "You owe me, Lenore. I've done everything you said!"

"And you were suitably rewarded for it, I remind you."

"You said you'd get me a column at the *Post*!"

"I said I'd get you a job. Was it my fault you couldn't keep it?"

"You told them to fire me!"

"No, my dear," Lenore said pityingly. "You did that all by yourself."

She heard the click in her ear before she could gather her wits enough to reply. "Lenore!" she shouted. "Damn you, Lenore! Don't you hang up on me!"

Only the dial tone answered, and with a cry, she ripped the phone out from the wall and flung it away from her. It landed with a jangle of bells next to the empty bourbon bottle, which started to roll away. Desperately needing a drink, she dropped to the floor. She had to get that bottle; it was the only one she had. But the room was spinning uncontrollably now, and she had to crawl to where it lay. Seizing it with a drunken cry of triumph, she raised it to her lips, but there was only a single drop that trickled slowly down the glass and finally landed with a little sting on her tongue.

"Damn!" she sobbed, and threw it away again. A sudden, awful image of her father doing the same things when she was little came to her, and she cried out. Terrified by the vision, she tried to get up, only to slide down again as the floor tilted under her. Groaning, she fell back, sure she was going to be sick.

It was over, she thought with drunken self-pity; over. All, everything she'd done. All her hopes and plans and dreams, vanished, gone up in smoke. She'd never get a decent job as a writer now; even Barnaby wouldn't hire her. Why hadn't she seen this coming? She knew what a bitch that old woman was; she should have guessed that once she'd outlived her usefulness,

Lenore would make sure she never worked in journalism again. As drunk as she was, she knew that wherever she went, Lenore would have gone before.

Oh, Mama! she thought, longing for the comfort of her mother's arms, as she hadn't done since she was a child. Sitting back against the wall, she pulled up her legs and rested her head hopelessly on her knees. Oh, Mama! she thought. What am I going to do now?

But there was only the drone of the television in the background, and the sound of the bedsprings in the next room. Squeak, squeak, squeak. She fell into a drunken sleep sitting there, listening to the sound of someone else being fucked for a change.

At Deer Hollow Farm, Lenore replaced the phone with a satisfied expression. "Well, I'm glad *that's* over," she said to Chester.

They were both sitting in the cozy study, watching TV. A fire burned cheerily on the hearth, and Chester had just brought her lemon and tea. For this auspicious occasion, he had accepted her invitation to join her, and had even agreed to have a brandy. It was an unusual concession, but this was an unusual night. As Lenore picked up the teacup again and glanced at the screen, another state turned pink, and she smiled.

"We did well, don't you think?" she said, indicating the screen.

"We did indeed, madam," he agreed solemnly, and took an appreciative sip of the forty-year-old brandy. "But one thing still puzzles me—"

She gave him an indulgent look. "What's that?"

He warmed the snifter in his hands, swirling the golden liquid to distribute the bouquet. "I don't understand why you were so pleased at all that negative publicity about Mrs. Devlin during the campaign. It seems to me that you would have wanted to avoid that at all costs."

She laughed and took a sip of her tea. "A presidential campaign is always fraught with negative publicity, Chester. The trick is knowing how to use it. You see, I knew that even though Hugh was the best candidate for this interim period, he was going to have a terrible problem getting elected—even with the circle to back him. He's so dull, you see. He needed a running mate who would not only generate interest and publicity, but

424

one who was accustomed to being in the limelight, and who knew how to handle the press. Someone original, and refreshing—'' she smiled in rememberance, her thoughts far away ''—someone who was already the darling of the media. Who better than Laura Devlin?''

''But all those problems with her family!''

''Yes, that was a masterstroke, wasn't it? But who better to grab the sympathetic vote from all those millions of women out there who are mothers, too? After the gay bar incident, she had them all eating out of her hand. What mother hasn't secretly harbored such fears about her boy? What mother hasn't wondered, looking lovingly over the cradle at her infant son, how he's going to grow, which paths he will take, what relationships he will forge? With Dawn obliging me by writing all those stories about Laura, I knew just how she would emerge. She was every woman, don't you see? Juggling it all, and best of all—doing it with style!''

Chester looked at her in admiration. ''You took a terrible chance. What if you were wrong?''

The predictions on the screen changed at that moment, several more states turning pink as they watched. ''But I wasn't, was I?''

He glanced at the screen, then back to her. ''What happens now?''

''Now we wait,'' she said complacently. ''Douglas Rhodes will only be fifty-four at the time of the next election.'' She smiled into her tea. ''Then we'll see.''

At his home in Georgetown, Douglas settled Marcella in an easy chair before the television and gently smoothed back her hair. She glanced up with that slightly puzzled look that often came to her eyes, but she smiled slightly in return. She had improved. His glance went to his grandson playing quietly by the fire, and a fierce wave of love swept over him. At times like this, he almost felt reborn.

Hearing a sound behind him, he looked over his shoulder at Sarah. She was standing in the doorway, holding a tray of coffee things she'd insisted on getting herself in the kitchen. He was glad they were going to watch the election results together. He'd given the help the night off, but he hadn't wanted to be alone tonight.

''Let me take that,'' he said, taking the tray from her hands.

425

They smiled at each other, then he looked toward the television, which was tuned to one of the networks. A bland news anchor was droning on about predictions and analyses, and in the background, the map of the United States seemed to be a pink blossom. As he watched, the picture changed to the montage of Laura that Malcolm had produced during the final days of the campaign. Even though he had seen it many times before, he still felt transfixed. As always, Malcolm had done his job well, and the screen showed Laura talking to two old people in the park, walking with them, sitting on a bench and holding their hands as she listened intently to their problems. Watching, you knew she wouldn't forget.

Then the picture changed to a shot of her at the ocean, walking along with her hands in the pockets of her windbreaker, her hair blowing in the wind, deep in thought. Another change, and she was arguing her urban policy bill before the House; another, and she was surrounded by teenagers, all eager to talk to her, to ask her opinion, to express their admiration. In every scene, the camera had captured the essence, the charisma she had, the ability to draw the best from people—and from herself.

Sarah murmured a soft sound of approval and he glanced at her with a brief, pained smile, then back to the screen. The montage was just ending, with his favorite shot of Laura laughing, the sun in her hair, a sparkle of wit and humor and intelligence in those glowing green eyes. She looked so vital and alive. He couldn't tear his eyes away until Sarah spoke.

"Was it worth it, Douglas?" she asked softly.

His glance went to Marcella, sitting quietly, her face soft as she watched Robbie. Just for an instant, his expression became unutterably sad, and he shook his head. "If this hadn't happened . . . if things had been different, and Laura were free, maybe—"

He glanced at the television again, with that last glorious shot of Laura still evident. Then his eyes went to his grandson, who looked up at him at that moment, with a smile so like Rob's that his breath caught.

"Yes," he said. "It was worth it."

Peter and Andrea had never stayed in a suite before, but the one at the Marriott in Los Angeles was so luxurious that when Andrea saw it, she squealed and danced around the room, finally throwing herself onto one of the overstuffed couches with a shriek of delight. "God, isn't this fabulous! Call room service, Peter. Let's have a feast!"

Her brother shook his head. "How can you be hungry? Aren't you nervous?"

Looking so much like her mother, Andrea sat up, brushing back her long, dark hair. "Why should I be?"

Peter indicated the television that he'd turned on when they came in. "Oh, a little thing like the election," he said sarcastically. "After all that campaigning, aren't you curious about how it's going to come out?"

Andrea got up again to wander restlessly around the room. The drapes were pulled back from the two adjoining windows in this part of the suite, and the lights of Los Angeles stretched out far below, as far as the eye could see. "I know how it's going to come out," she said. "Mom's going to win, of course." She turned and looked at him. "Don't tell me *you* have doubts."

Peter laughed. Even with the stresses and strains of the campaign, and all the traveling the family had done these past two months, he'd seemed much more relaxed, happier . . . content . . . than he'd ever been. His most treasured possession now was that wire photo of him and his mother at the press conference; he'd had it framed, and carried it with him wherever he went.

"No," he said. "I don't have any doubts."

She looked at him. He was her big brother, just old Peter, but even she could see the change in him these past months, especially in the way he dressed. He didn't look so . . . arty now; he'd started dressing prep. She liked the change, she thought, and giggled. So did her friends. She couldn't understand it herself, but they all seemed to spaz out when he was around.

"Peter . . ." she said, and stopped.

"What?"

"If Mom wins—I mean, *when* she wins—how are you going to feel about it? I mean, really feel?"

"Happy, proud—I don't know. What do you mean?"

She turned away. "I don't know. I've always felt I could never really measure up to her, you know? And now it will be even worse."

"I didn't know you felt like that."

She looked back at him. "Come on, it was obvious. What do you think? I mean, a daughter is supposed to be like her mother, right? And here was mine—so beautiful and so talented, and so

. . . so everything! God, I used to just die every time I saw her name in the paper!''

He perched thoughtfully on the arm of the couch. "So did I," he said. "When I was a kid, I always wanted her to quit her job so she could stay home like some of the other mothers I knew."

"And now?"

He shrugged, older, wiser. "And now I know that even though her job took so much of her time, she always cared about us. That business with you and that garage mechanic brought that home—and mine with that stupid bar scene. We could have really screwed up her campaign, not to mention her career, but the only thing she cared about was us."

Andrea looked down. "I guess we were wrong about her all these years."

"I guess we were."

She sighed. "I still wish she'd been home more."

He nodded slowly. "So do I. But if she had been, she never would have done all the things she did. She wouldn't have gotten this far."

"Yeah, and now look where she is!" Andrea said, her face suddenly alight. "God, I'm so proud of her, aren't you?"

"Yeah," he said with a grin that suddenly faltered. "I wonder if Dad is."

Brother and sister looked at each other for a moment. Then, without saying anything more, they both turned to the TV.

Jack heard the kids talking in the suite next door as he let himself in to the one he'd taken. A wet bar was in the corner, and he went immediately to it and poured himself a stiff one. He'd left the TV on when he went for a walk, and as he added ice, he glanced at the screen. If the announcer was right, in a very short time his wife would have been elected to the second-highest office in the land. The first female vice-president of the United States. Suddenly feeling weary beyond belief, he went to the couch and sank down. With a heavy sigh, he put his head back and closed his eyes.

God, he'd been a jerk for being so jealous of her all these years, but how could he help it? She'd had the Midas touch, while everything he did turned to shit. How could he not have been jealous of her success?

Maybe that was why he'd had all those flings, those brief,

meaningless little affairs with girls whose faces he couldn't even remember now. He didn't know what he'd been trying to prove; no one could match Laura; maybe he thought he could hurt her instead. Even then, he hadn't realized just how great a fool he'd been until that night he'd had to tell her about Dawn. He'd felt so low when he'd seen the contempt in her eyes, especially when he knew he deserved it.

He still couldn't believe she'd let him stay; he'd been sure she'd kick him out on his ear. It was that damned sense of honor she had; she couldn't let him take all the blame, even though it had been his fault. And . . . and he wanted to stay, to at least have the chance of doing something right. He owed her that; even he knew what a separation or divorce would have meant to her campaign, her career. And he'd done so many other things wrong; he'd begged her for a chance to prove he could do this. And who knew? Maybe in time . . .

He shook his head. He was fooling himself again; he knew it was over; he'd seen it in her eyes. That had really hurt—the knowledge that he'd finally killed the one thing he valued the most: her love. Oh, Laurie! he cried silently, and put his head back in real pain. On the television, another state turned that characteristic pink, and the point level jumped. He didn't notice; it was all a foregone conclusion now, and he looked at his drink. Maybe what he should do was just start drinking and keep drinking until the pain went away.

Then he knew he was fooling himself again. This went too deep; the pain would never go; he would carry it with him the rest of his life. His mouth twisting, he looked at the glass, and then, very slowly, put it aside.

In another suite down the hall, Janette was so excited, she couldn't sit still. After she had jumped up from the couch the fifteenth time to adjust the television, her mother, who was sitting there with her, said irritably, "For heaven's sake, Janette. Use the remote!"

Janette started dancing around the room. "I can't, Mother, not when this is the most exciting night of my life! Just think, by the time morning comes, my sister, my very own sister, will have been elected vice-president of the United States! I can't believe it. Tell me it's not all a dream!"

When Estelle was silent, Janette stopped her twirling around and looked over her shoulder at her mother. "What's wrong, Mom? Aren't you excited, too?"

Tears filling her eyes, Estelle turned away. She always carried a handkerchief in her pocket, and she took it out and dabbed at her face. "Of course I'm excited."

Her own elation disappearing, Janette returned to the couch and sat down. She knew she'd probably regret asking, but she had to anyway. "Then why are you crying?"

"Leave me alone, Janette," Estelle muttered. "Just leave me alone."

"But—"

Estelle gave her a fierce look. "Didn't you hear me?"

Janette drew back. "Yes, I heard you," she said, and then decided she'd had enough of this. Her mother wasn't going to ruin Laura's night of triumph, not if she could help it. "And now I want you to tell me what's wrong."

"Nothing's wrong, I tell you! Nothing!" Estelle said, and burst into tears.

This was Janette's cue to put her arms around her mother and comfort her. It had been the pattern for years, one she and Laurie had both fallen into. Well, it wasn't going to work tonight. She sat right where she was and said, "Mother, you're not going to make a scene, do you hear me? You're not going to complain and criticize Laura—not tonight! For heaven's sake, your daughter—your daughter!—is going to be the vice-president of the United States! Doesn't that mean anything to you? I'm so proud I could burst! Why aren't you happy, too?"

" "I am proud!" Estelle cried. "I am happy! But what do you want me to do? Dance around the room like a fool?"

"Yes," Janette said. "That's exactly what I do expect! What's the matter with you, Mom? If I didn't know better, I'd think you were jealous!"

"Jealous!" Estelle was outraged. "Jealous! Of my own daughter? You always have been a fool, Janette—a silly fool!"

But Janette continued to stare at her. "I don't believe it," she said. "All this time . . . all these years . . . you *were* jealous!"

"That's not true—"

"Yes, it is," Janette persisted, marveling at the revelation, seeing it for the first time. "I thought you just didn't approve of what Laura was doing—the law school, the high-pressure jobs, the running for office—but I was wrong. It wasn't the things she did; it was that she could do them, wasn't it? Wasn't it?"

"She should have stayed home, where she belonged!" Estelle cried. "She should have been what she was supposed to be—a good wife and mother!"

Janette blinked, then her expression turned scornful. "Like we did, Mother? Like we did? But what have *we* accomplished, compared to Laura?"

Her mother turned fiercely to her. "We raised families! We cared for our husbands, our children!"

"So did Laura!"

"Laura had me!" The words burst from Estelle like a wound that had been festering for many years and had finally been excised. As Janette stared at her, stunned, Estelle said it again. "Laura had me! How far do you think she would have gotten if I hadn't been there to take care of her family—how far?"

Bewildered by this sudden twist, Janette said, "But you wanted to take care of her family. You could have come to live with me after Dad died, but you wanted to be with Laura!"

It was as though now she'd started, Estelle couldn't stop. "Because Laura was doing all the things I wanted to do and never could," she said bitterly. "I never had the chance."

"That's not true!" Janette said. "You had the chance; you just didn't want to take it!"

"You don't know anything about it! I wanted to accomplish things; I had goals. But Harry wouldn't let me. He thought that every woman should stay home and be a wife and mother, and because I loved him, that's what I did."

"But you didn't have to!"

"It was a different time, Janette; you don't understand."

"But I thought . . . *we* thought that's what you wanted. All these years, that's what you said—"

Estelle gave her another bitter look. "What else was I going to say? I was married; I did what I had to. And by the time Harry died, it was too late for me."

Janette didn't know what to say. She'd never heard her mother talk like this; she hadn't even suspected. "I'm sorry," she said, holding back tears. "I didn't know."

"You weren't supposed to know."

"But Mom—you can't condemn Laura for following a path we both chose not to walk," she said desperately. "Laura thinks you despise her—"

Estelle uttered a choked, disbelieving sound. "*I* despise her?

431

But I love her! I'm so proud of her—'' Her voice broke. "So proud . . ."

Now Janette did start to cry. "Then why don't you tell her, Mom? Why don't you tell her?"

Alone in the darkened room, Laura stood by the window, her thoughts far away. Los Angeles had never looked so beautiful as it did this election night, but she didn't see the myriad lights spread out like sparkling jewels far into the darkness. And the room was quiet; she didn't have the television on. All the endless babble irritated her, and she'd switched it off with the lights. She'd done what she could; it wasn't up to her now. It was time to take a little personal stock.

Resting her forehead against the cold glass, she closed her eyes. She was tired, oh, so tired. But it was a weariness of spirit that nagged her now, and she knew that soon, somehow, she would have to put aside her depression. She wondered how.

Raising her head, she looked out to the place where the twinkling lights stopped abruptly at the beach; the immense blackness beyond was the sea. The ocean had always comforted her, and for just an instant she was tempted to drive out to the beach. She wanted to walk on the sand, to feel the wind in her face, to sense that vastness that always comforted her because she drew from its strength.

But her time wasn't her own, not now, perhaps not anymore. Maybe it never had been. She had always felt the pressure of time, as though it were speeding along, soon to leave her behind because she couldn't run fast enough to keep up with it. She felt so pressured because there were never enough hours in the days, or days in the week, or months in a year, and as she stared out at the night, she wondered if she had chased time so much because to stop meant she had to face what she wanted to leave behind.

Her thoughts went to Jack, and her expression became even more sad. When had she stopped loving him? Was it the day she caught him with that blonde in her kitchen? Was it the night he told her about Dawn? She didn't know anymore; maybe it didn't matter. Sometimes she wasn't sure why she had let him stay on, continuing the fiction that this was a happy marriage. Was it because she needed that fiction to succeed—or because she couldn't quite admit that the superwoman she'd tried to be had failed at something so basic as her marriage? She didn't know about that, either; she only knew that after twenty years, it was hard to let go.

With a heavy sigh, she thought of Douglas. She had only seen him once these past two months—a short time they had stolen together because she had insisted on it. After what Sarah had told her, she needed to hear it from him, his own lips. They hadn't even had to meet secretly, like clandestine lovers; he'd simply come to her office, an old friend wishing her well. But he knew what she wanted, and after she'd taken one look at his face, she knew what her answer was. She still had to ask.

"Is it true, Douglas?"

He didn't lie. "Yes," he said quietly. "It's true."

She couldn't hide her anguish any longer. "But why?" she cried, and then, without knowing how it happened—or perhaps not caring that it had—they were in each other's arms, and she was looking up into that beloved face through her tears. "Why, Douglas?" she asked again. "You gave up so much!"

His arms had tightened around her, and even though tears glinted in his own eyes, he'd said simply, "Because it wasn't my time, Laura. It was yours."

"But—"

He put a finger over her lips. "My day will come," he whispered.

He seemed so sure. She wanted desperately to believe him, but when she thought of the tremendous sacrifice he had made for her, her heart ached. "And if it doesn't?" she whispered.

She could feel him trembling with the same intense emotion that swept through her. If he had said at that instant that he wanted her, she would have thrown everything away to be with him. Her longing threatened to overwhelm her, and she was just reaching for him when he released her and stepped back. He was stronger than she, but she'd always known that.

"Then it was worth it," he said, and was gone.

Remembering that agonizing scene brought tears to her eyes again, and an ache in her heart that would always be with her now. For she had seen the love and regret in his face that day—not for what he had sacrificed for her, but for what they would never have together. And after that, whenever she had longed to quit, to give up, to surrender and go home, she had forced herself to go on. She couldn't cause his sacrifice to be in vain, and tonight she would see the results of what her ambition had wrought.

Because Douglas wasn't the only one who had sacrificed, she thought. She had given up so many things, too. Thinking of Jack, and the children, and all those moments lost forever now, her vision blurred. Looking out over the glittering night, she wondered if all ambition exacted such a toll.

But the night gave no answer, and she was just turning away from the window when she realized she wasn't alone. A familiar figure was standing in the doorway, the light spilling in from the hall.

"Mother?"

Estelle came in and shut the door. "The results are just in."

She tensed. "And?"

Her mother came forward to take her hands, a rare gesture that nearly made her cry. "We only have seconds, my dear," Estelle said, "but I know that if your father were here, he'd be as proud of you as I."

She was so choked with emotion, she could hardly speak. She had dreamed of hearing those words, and her grip tightened on her mother's hands. "Thank you," she whispered. "You don't know how much that means to me."

"And how much this means to me," Estelle said, tears filling her eyes. Her hands trembled, but she held her head high.

Laura didn't realize it, but she was trembling, too. This was a historic moment, and when she thought of all that had gone before to create this, she knew, at last, that it had been worth it.

Great ambition requires great sacrifice, and those who achieve it must be above reproach.

The words whispered through her mind like a sigh, and she saw, for an instant, Douglas's face—that dear, beloved face. *And so we are, my love,* she thought, and banished all regret. There would come a time, she thought . . . a time . . .

Her mother's hands tightened, bringing her back to the present. They could both hear the noise in the hallway, the shouts and jubilant cries, the banging and clanging and joyful cheers. And then, just before the door was flung open and Laura's world changed forever, Estelle looked into her eyes and said, her voice trembling with emotion, "We don't have much time, my dear, but I wanted to be the first to say it. I offer you, with pride and love and joy, my congratulations . . . Madame Vice-President."

434

---⚘---

EPILOGUE

Laura had been in office two months when the call came. A limousine was taking her to a speaking engagement when the car phone rang, and an instant before she answered, she was seized with a terrible, inexplicable dread. Twenty minutes later, she was in a hastily commandeered helicopter on the way to St. John's Hospital in Maryland, where they'd taken Hugh. She was silent during the flight; even with earphones, no one spoke. One look at her face, and they all left her alone.

The helicopter blades created a tremendous downdraft as they settled on the helipad high atop the roof of the hospital, and she fumbled with the unfamiliar door. There hadn't been time to summon Marine One; this commercial vehicle had been pressed into service instead, and she was jerking at the handle when one of her Secret Service men put his hand over it and opened it for her. She gave him a grateful glance, but that was all. Despite minute-by-minute reports on Hugh's condition, she couldn't rid herself of the dread that she was going to be too late. Urgency raced through her like an electric current, and without waiting for the attendants to come running, she clutched her coat about her and got out.

She was immediately enveloped by a swirling haze of debris, and she squinted, trying to see her way clear of the copter to the door. Grains of sand, fine as sandpaper, pelleted her face, and her coat escaped her hands and billowed up and around her, like a cape.

"This way, Madame Vice-President!"

When a hand gripped her elbow and tugged her along, she followed in the wake of a uniformed man she could barely see. In addition to the maelstrom generated by the helicopter rotors, low storm clouds obscured the horizon, and a scent of rain filled the air. The day had turned icy and gray, like her heart. If Hugh died . . .

The thought died almost unborn. This was what it was all about, the possibility, the responsibility. One didn't run for the second-highest office in the land without considering the consequences if the unthinkable happened. The time to face any doubts was then. It was too late now.

The thought brought renewed courage and determination, and with a jerk of her head, she whipped through the hospital doors. A man in a white coat, his face nearly as pale as his jacket, started to say something, but there was no time for formality.

"Where is he?" she asked. Her voice was curt, and he bowed. "This way—"

She turned in the direction he indicated, before he even finished his sentence. Her Secret Service protection closed in, but she was used to them now, and she swept them along with her, her high heels sounding like machine-gun fire in the silence of the hall. As she glanced at faces as tense as hers, she knew they were all wondering what they would find at the end of the corridor.

There was a waiting room at the end of the hall, and when the phalanx parted and she stepped inside, she took in the scene at a glance. Hugh's wife, Nora, was here, huddled on the couch, her hands covering her face, her shoulders heaving. Lenore Deering-Kirk was sitting by her side, and when she came in, the older woman glanced up, her expression unreadable before she bent to Nora again.

She didn't waste time with Lenore. She knew the aging hostess believed she ran the Hill single-handed, but she had a few surprises in store. At the moment her concern was for Hugh, and she glanced around. The room seemed filled with Secret Service and FBI and God only knew who else, and she was searching for someone who might be in charge when she felt a hand on her shoulder. She was so tense, she nearly jumped. Then she recognized Orrin Wilcox, the newly elected Speaker of the House. She gripped his arm.

"Any news?"

Orrin shook his head. "They're still doing tests."

She swallowed a quick breath, expelled in relief, before gesturing the Speaker aside. At least five Secret Service agents moved instantly, and protectively, with them. They both ignored the guards as she spoke urgently, in a low voice resonant with strain.

"All I've heard so far was that it was a heart attack," she said. "Is that true?"

He wasn't surprised at the question—or her need to ask it. He'd been in Washington far longer than she, but they both knew that the maddening Need-to-Know could be carried to extremes—even regarding her.

But because Orrin *had* been on the Hill awhile, he glanced around before answering, automatically looking for any reporters who might have edged their way in and were listening, pencils at the ready, for any snippet of news. She glanced around as well, but all she saw were familiar faces in conservative suits. She jerked her head, and Orrin nodded.

"It's true," he said, in a voice so low, she could barely hear. "I was with him when it happened."

She let out another tense breath as visions of guns and assassins and would-be snipers vanished. One less terror to face, but there were still other horrors.

It seemed that years had passed since she'd entered the room; the strain she felt was evident in everyone else. They were all trying not to think what the future might hold, and she glanced toward the couch. It was time to comfort Hugh's wife.

But just then someone came into the room. The new arrival, gray-haired and solemn with another white coat, was clearly the physician in charge, and the tension increased. No one could tell from his carefully guarded expression what news he brought, but as though they sensed something no one else could know, the Secret Service phalanx moved protectively closer to Laura again, even though she hadn't moved.

The doctor saw her standing there and gave her an acknowledging nod. She nodded back, trying to read his eyes for any information. But like any politician, he had spent years schooling himself to reveal on his face only what he wanted someone else to know. The future was still in doubt as he turned to the First Lady.

Laura struggled for control. So much was at stake here; surely they all had the right to be told. She had an impulse to rush forward and demand he tell them all, but she stifled the urge and stepped to the nearby window instead. Staring blindly out, she summoned her formidable composure. The thought occurred to her again that in a few minutes history might be made, but she ruthlessly thrust the idea away. It was too soon for thoughts like that.

Or was it?

A sob behind her made her turn to look toward the couch.

The doctor had finished his whispered consultation with Nora, and was standing, patting her shoulder. The tension increased again, humming like low voltage through the room. Was this the moment?

No one knew. As the doctor helped the first lady to her feet, she glanced in Laura's direction. Their eyes met, just for an instant, too brief for Laura to be sure, for Lenore stepped between them then, breaking that fleeting eye contact. Along with more Secret Service, the two women followed the doctor from the room.

Deep silence reigned behind. There was the rustle of an over-coat, a muffled cough. They all looked in her direction, as though begging to be told what to do, but she didn't say. She was thinking, wondering . . . marveling . . . at the events that had brought them all here, to this hospital, on this particular day.

Lightning flashed jaggedly across the heavy pewter sky just then, and she turned toward the window to gaze at the swiftly gathering clouds. Behind her she could feel the staring eyes, and she knew she had to say something. She was just gathering her thoughts when the wind came up. The first drops of rain sounded like pebbles thrown against the window, and everyone but Laura jumped at the sound.

The promised storm had finally arrived, but she wasn't afraid. She had seen it coming, and was prepared.

---⊘---

ABOUT THE AUTHOR

Born in Montana and raised in Colorado and California, Janis Flores worked for ten years as a medical technologist before she turned to full-time writing. She lives on a small ranch in Sebastopol, California, with her husband, four horses, and several dogs and cats. She is also the author of LOVING TIES, RUNNING IN PLACE, and DIVIDED LOYAL-TIES.